HFCA Publishing House

Ireland

ISBN 978-1-918152-07-4

www.lexibuchanan.com

Published 2020

REVIEWS

"Revenge, love, self-discovery, and dark secrets that can unravel a whole town. Butterfly Girl will keep you on edge to the end."

Nadine

~

"The buildup is freaking awesome even though it nearly killed me!"

Lynne

~

For my Family

AUTHORS NOTE

Port Michael is a fictional town and is located south of Corpus Christi, Texas.

1

____

PROLOGUE – 3 YEARS AGO

Rafael

MY BODY IS COLD.

My chest aches.

In front of me lay two caskets. My mother and brother.

Taken far too early. Stolen.

Rain soaks through my dark blue blazer and slacks while I try to avoid *really* looking. Instead, I move my bloodshot gaze around the old cemetery and the DeLacroix family plot located north of New Orleans. Black wrought iron gates surround the area with stone angels guarding all who rest here. It gives me an uneasy feeling, as though eyes watch me from the dark shadows. Dark-clad mourners watch us—the grieving family—but the prickle of awareness feels different.

The sound of a motorized hum breaks into the silence and forces my fists to clench tightly at my side. My shoulders tighten and my gaze is drawn back to the walnut caskets holding Mom and Roman.

Mourners cry and sniffle, whispering prayers and speaking in low tones as my mother is slowly lowered into the ground, followed next by Roman.

I stand rigid next to my father trying not to remember Roman as I'd last seen him—eight years old, broken and lifeless.

Dad reaches for my hand and peels my fingers open so he can hold onto me.

He hurts too.

Fistfuls of dirt clatter on the caskets as mourners pay their respects before retreating down the water-logged path to their cars.

Nothing will ever be the same again.

I will never wake up to the sound of Mom singing as she takes a cloth to the mantel, the quiet conversations as we cook dinner together, the throaty laugh when she says something funny.

I will never come home and get mad because

Roman has been in my room and left a mess in his wake. Or experience those quiet moments when he'd sit on the couch, shoulder pressed against mine, and lean his head against me as we played a video game.

I will never get the chance to bitch and moan about family time on a Sunday. Until it was all taken, I didn't realize just how much that time meant to me.

It meant everything.

The home I once felt safe in no longer existed. It had been filled with happiness and love. Mom and Dad had always made sure that Roman and I had that and so much more. Now it was nothing but ashes of memories I was going to forget. In the blink of an eye, it had all been taken away.

Destroyed.

I need to forgive myself because no matter what I could have done, nothing would have saved them. Dad told me. The cops told me. Deep in my heart I know. It still plays over and over in my head, as to what I could have done differently. Every time I close my eyes, I hear Mom and Roman crying for help. Screaming in pain. I hadn't thought to call for help. Instead, I ran toward their distressed shouts and will probably have nightmares for the rest of my life about what followed.

Inhaling deeply, I slowly step away from my father and swipe angrily at my tears. Dad passes me a tissue. I dry my eyes and blow my nose as I turn to stare at the large hole in the ground.

Unconsciously, I lift my hand and trace over the red puckered scar with my cold, numb fingers. It covers half my face—a permanent reminder of what happened. If a neighbor hadn't overheard the cries for help as he walked his dog, then my casket would have also been in the ground.

Angry and frustrated, it has come down to minutes now.

Minutes until I have to enter the house one last time to pick up the items I want to take with me to the new house. There's not much, but I do want the dinosaur model in Roman's room. The kid loved his wooden models. I'd helped him with the T-Rex. Dad gave me my mother's slim gold wedding band earlier. He attached it to the chain she always wore around her neck holding a small golden locket. The locket holds a picture of Roman, Dad, and me. Dad and Mom weren't officially married, but in their hearts, they were.

"Son," my father whispers. His voice is quiet as he places an arm around my shoulders and continues,

"You're going to get sick if you stay out in the rain." My body is already soaked. It's the least of my problems.

I turn my head and meet his sad, green eyes. I dig the necklace out from beneath my shirt and clench a fist around the ring and locket. "They have to pay, Dad," I hiss with barely controlled rage. "Promise me. You will find them, and *we* will make them pay."

My father hesitates before he grasps my shoulders in a tight grip. "I promise you, Rafael DeLacroix, they will pay." He pulls me to him and kisses my forehead. "I promise, son."

The moment his promise leaves his lips, the rain abruptly stops, and sun bursts through the dark clouds. My father and I turn toward the grave and watch as it's shrouded in a halo of bright light...and butterflies. A myriad of different butterflies hover over the muddy soil before they take flight, disappearing within the blink of an eye.

I turn to my father who blinks sharply and swallows hard.

"Let's keep that between us." He glances to where the butterflies had disappeared, a frown on his face. "I'm not sure anyone would believe us anyway."

Wren

Rain bounces on the ground making it difficult to see across the garden to my greenhouse, or as I prefer to call it, my glasshouse.

If I go back into the house, the Reverend will expect me to do some other mundane chore. He's irritated and out of sorts more than usual with the weather keeping him inside. For this reason, we are stuck at the house together, and I hate it. I want to fly free away from Port Michael and everything familiar. One day I will.

The only thing I would miss is everything inside the glasshouse, from the green and flowered shrubs, to the beautiful tiny creatures that entrust me with their care.

A sudden heavy thump sounding from the kitchen makes me jump and causes my heart to miss a beat. The Reverend is annoyed. No way am I staying in the house.

The steps in the back of the house creak slightly as I inch down them. The moment my foot touches the garden, the rain hits me in the face. It's not cool and refreshing, instead, it's the worst kind of rain. Hot and sticky that only adds to the humid weather.

By the time I reach the glasshouse across the waterlogged garden, my feet swim in my tennis shoes. I'm drenched to the skin. At least, I've temporarily escaped the Reverend and his wrath.

I glance back toward the house and swallow hard with nerves. I wish I never have to step foot inside there again. One day that wish *will* come true.

Blowing out a breath of frustrated air, I lean against the workbench and keeping myself steady, I empty the water from each shoe. It's only then that the utter stillness hits me. My eyes frantically search for my butterflies. My eyes strain into every nook and cranny. My heart thuds against my rib cage in panic. Where have they gone? I move forward to the tomato and zucchini plants as I search—nothing. Not one butterfly.

I turn in a circle and lift my face to the roof. Tears fall from my eyes and slip down my cheeks. I hold my arms out and whisper a load of nonsense, begging for them to return. My eyes close tightly, and I force myself to slow my panicked breath.

That's when I feel the hair on my arms prickle. The prickle grows stronger as my eyes snap open, and I watch my butterflies land on my arms, and fill the glasshouse. From what I can see, not one is wet from the rain. They should have been trampled with the heavy downpour, but they haven't been. How is that possible?

They are dry and unharmed.

They are home.

But where have they been?

2

———

WREN

PRESENT DAY

MY GARDEN IS MY PEACE AND TRANQUILITY. HERE I can pretend. Alone with my butterflies. I want to call them mine, but I am theirs. They've chosen me. For three summers, the butterflies have followed me around the garden. My only friends. As silent as I am. Their delicate wings flutter as they rise into flight. So many beautiful colors surrounding me as the sun shines down.

I close my eyes and turn my face up to the sun. It's mere moments before the feeling of the butterflies landing on my hands and outstretched arms begins to lightly tickle my skin. Strands of hair move as more attach themselves to the messy bun pinned to the top of my head. What surprises me and makes my eyes snap open is the feeling of one landing on the tip of my nose. I go cross-eyed from looking at it, but my smile grows into pure delight when I focus on the unusual tiger print on the hindwings.

Tiger Lily has come back!

Tiger Lily arrived a month ago and wouldn't come close to me, until it started to rain. I'd dashed into the glasshouse and the butterflies had followed for shelter. Tiger Lily had been the last to enter. It had taken me a few days to encourage him outside, but after that, we became friends. However, for the past two days, I haven't seen him. Honestly, I thought the Reverend had done something to him. I wouldn't have put it past him. But here he is. His delicate wingspan is larger than most of the other butterflies. I know he flew into our small town, from where, I don't know. And it's not like I can just look things up. The Reverend forbade any use of electronic devices in the house, which meant no computer, and no internet. Of course, he allows himself the luxury of a cellphone.

Sighing, I slowly start to turn in a circle when I see *him*.

The boy watches me from the side of a big black SUV that is parked next door. I haven't noticed it before, so they must be the new neighbors, arriving while I was lost in my own world. I freeze not knowing what to do. Covered in butterflies is strange —I guess—but he doesn't need to stare the way he does. It makes me feel uncomfortable having his shocked gaze on me. No one ever pays me any attention, and, even now, I think maybe he is more focused on the butterflies. People usually are.

The boy is maybe a few years older than my seventeen years. He has tanned skin, unlike my pale alabaster. I wonder if he's Cuban like Mrs. Garcia at the grocery store. His hair is ebony black and cropped short, but it's his arms that really hold my attention. They are covered in tattoos. I lift my gaze back to his face and notice his mouth has slipped into an arrogant line. He thinks I'm checking him out. Maybe I am, but not in the way he's thinking. Curiosity has more to do with me looking than anything else.

Inhaling slowly, I gently turn my back to him and decide not to run away and hide in my glasshouse. With the Reverend, I cannot wait to get away from him, but something about the boy next door calms me. I don't fear him like I do most people.

I continue to feel the heat of his gaze and know he

hasn't moved. I have that effect on people when they see me with the butterflies for the first time. Feeling my cheeks start to heat, I'm relieved he is unable to see my face as I finally move toward my glasshouse.

Once inside, the butterflies take flight and find new spots on one of the many plants I keep in here. It's an oasis of different shades of greens mixed with colors—asters, milkweed, phlox, purple coneflower, wild bergamot, willow, and elm. A collection of host and nectar plants for the butterflies to feed from. I had done my research during computer science at school when Mr. Jenkins spent the whole lesson on his phone.

When I planned the garden, I made sure to have lots of host and nectar plants around the outside of the glasshouse too. I also planted herbs and vegetables, which have taken over one side of the glasshouse. Tomato and zucchini plants grow in deep, long bins toward the back. Basil, parsley, thyme, and tarragon grow in a variety of pots up front. I also have four ornamental hanging baskets. Three of them are overflowing with strawberries, and the other with cherry tomatoes. The zucchini plants are pretty with the yellow and white flowers. I've spotted ladybugs a few times on the flowers. I keep my gardening supplies to one side of the entrance so that I won't misplace them. The scent of the growing vegetables and herbs is an earthy welcome every time I step inside my glasshouse. It's home.

The Reverend has no idea I planned the garden to accommodate my friends rather than him wanting a garden to be proud of. It turned out to be both; a place to show off for him—much to my relief—and a true home for my butterflies.

My mind wanders back to the boy. Why would his family move here? Most people move away from this town where everyone knows everyone else's business. I'm leaving one day. I haven't figured out how, but I'm leaving and never coming back. Going back to the boy, I decide to sneak out back of the glasshouse, and crouch down in the middle of my plants. I can't be seen, but I can see the SUV in the driveway. A man pulls things from the cargo area and shouts to someone out of view. He doesn't seem to have a lot of things in the car, which makes me think a moving truck will follow. He must be the father, but where has the boy gone? Why isn't he helping? Why hasn't he come back out so I can look at him some more? After that one glance, I feel compelled to talk to him. I hardly ever speak to anyone, so wanting to talk to the boy confuses me. The need springs up from some-where and, thinking about him makes my heart pound against my rib cage. I shake my head hoping to get a piece of sanity back.

Stupid girl for dreaming.

When it becomes obvious no one is coming back outside, I slowly stretch and move out from between my plants. Tiger Lily floats around my head, so I hold my hand out and he perches on a finger. He really is pretty. When I bring my hand closer to my face, he turns and looks at me. I'm unsure as to why I have such a connection with them, but it's one that seems to get stronger each summer.

Dragging my feet toward the house, I glance past the corn field to where the white church shines brightly in the distance. The Reverend is there. I can make out the bright flash of red from his car. He won't be there for much longer. He'll be home soon and expecting his supper on the table like clockwork. I tread carefully up the four wooden steps leading onto the back porch because they've needed replacing for a few years now.

I whisper, "Go to bed, Tiger Lily." He turns and flies into the glasshouse while my skin prickles with awareness.

I'm being watched.

There is no movement in the house next door, but my eyes hover over every window. I must have imagined it, until I catch the brief movement of a curtain on the first floor, and then I see a hand and a wrist. It's the boy watching me. If I hadn't been watching the window so closely, I wouldn't have seen anything. The hand is gone in seconds, and now there is nothing.

I turn and go inside to make supper.

3

RAFAEL

Wren Jacobs.

The girl looks alone, her only true friends are the butterflies. I know this to be true from the information my father has gathered. She has been kept isolated in the town of Port Michael. So has the rest of the town. No one ever leaves, and no one new is allowed to purchase or rent property without the say so of the secret town council.

In our case, the Reverend knows exactly who my father is. He had no choice but to allow my father, a former agent with the DEA, from purchasing the house that had stood empty for years. The Reverend wouldn't want the law sniffing around the town. He knows, though. The dictator knows my father is after him, and my father believes in the motto "keep your enemies closer," which is what the Reverend is doing.

As I watch Wren from the window, the photograph my father has of the girl doesn't do her justice. Albeit she'd been fourteen at the time it had been taken, a month after my mother and brother had been buried. Three long years ago, the thought burns in the old wounds left from it. I'm surprised to find such a fragile looking girl.

Beautiful too. Dark, curly hair flows in waves down her back and flutters under the light breeze.

My heart had stopped when I caught my first glimpse of her with the butterflies. My mind went back to the brief unexplained appearance of butterflies on the day we buried my family. I've never seen anything like it since that day, until today.

On the first-floor landing of the old house, I continue to watch. My attention hasn't held because of the butterflies alone. It's the girl who holds my interest. I'm fascinated.

The girl, Wren, speaks to me in a way no one else has. She needs help and we will help her. No way can we let her stay with someone so evil. We just have to bide our time, until my father knows more and comes up with a plan. I have to be careful around her until then.

The stairs creak behind me, so I let the curtain fall back into place, shutting her from sight. Breathing heavily over my shoulder, Dad peers through the tiny gap at the top before he gives me a sidelong look. "You can't be *that* friendly with her, Rafael. You know this?" He continues to stare as she slowly moves up the porch. "You're twenty, pretending to be eighteen. Our past is a carefully created lie. You cannot tell her the truth."

"The Reverend knows who we are," I say while running my fingers through my hair in frustration. "You've seen her." I drop my butt on the stairs leading up to the attic. "She's fragile, Dad."

"She's the Reverend's daughter. You have to remember that. Do not let your guard down around her or anyone."

"We've had this discussion a million times."

"For you are my son and I cannot lose you. You're all I have left. I only allowed you to come here with me because I couldn't trust you not to show up anyway." Dad throws his hands up in the air and I grin.

"I did promise to do that, huh?"

"I have a head full of gray hair because of you." He laughs and meets my gaze. "I'd do anything for you, Rafael." He takes my hand and tugs me to my feet, his arms going around my shoulders. "But I am asking you to not fall for Wren Jacobs."

"I won't," I reply quickly in defense. "She's not only the Reverend's daughter, she's also too young for me." I head toward the stairs. "Trust me. I won't be falling for her pale skin or gorgeous hair."

My father curses behind me and I almost feel sorry that I teased him. I did say almost because we both know I lied—like how I noticed her pale skin and gorgeous hair. I noticed a lot more than that, but that is best kept locked away in my head.

The moment my father is out of view, I close myself in my room. The attic. The moment I saw it, I knew I'd make it mine. The four bedrooms below hadn't caught my eye, but the attic had. It is one large room with a small bathroom. Skyline windows and few scattered around the outer walls allowing daylight in.

Tossing my T-shirt in the small plastic tub I use as a laundry hamper, I drop my tired ass in the chair at the small table I've set up. It's comfortable and both had been in the house when we arrived. Dad helped me get the heavy armchair up here.

What I love about the setup is my view of the house where the butterfly girl lives. I know I shouldn't look, nor should I be drawn to her, but there is something about her I don't think I have the will to resist.

She'd looked almost ethereal. An angel.

4

———

WREN

THE REVEREND'S CAR BACKFIRES AS IT GETS CLOSER TO the house and my heart starts to thump wildly in my chest. I have to force my feet to stay firmly planted in the kitchen because I really want to run and hide in my room. A nervous sweat breaks out along my forehead, and the back of my neck prickles with tension. I wipe the palms of my hands down my dress and quickly glance over the kitchen table: two dinner plates, two knives, two forks, two pudding spoons, two napkins, two tall glasses ready to be filled with fresh water. I haven't forgotten anything today. Yesterday, I'd forgotten napkins and that hadn't gone down too well. Everything has to be in a very specific place, or I wouldn't like the consequences. I've learned that the hard way, and until I'm eighteen, I have to abide by *his* rules.

Who am I kidding? I won't be allowed to leave. No one is, least of all me. I remember happier times when I was little, but that's a blurry memory now. With how the Reverend has become, I'm glad I can't remember those times more clearly. However, on occasion, I try to remember the past, so everything now doesn't seem so bleak.

A loud creak comes from the front porch.

He's home.

A slither of fear shoots down my back.

Another creak, the door rattles in the old frame. That one gets me moving. I take a deep breath to steady myself, and carefully remove the chicken and dumplings, along with the mashed potatoes from the oven. I place them in the center of the table and, standing beside my own place setting, straighten my dress, and then my spine.

The front door shudders when the Reverend slams it closed behind his tall, bulky frame. His hair has begun to thin on top, and it displeases him immensely. He wears neatly pressed navy-blue slacks and a short-sleeved button down. Sweat soaks the shirt at his armpits.

As he shuffles forward, I notice sweat beading across his brow. I swallow around the nervousness that fills my belly when he hovers close.

"Hmm," the Reverend mumbles, glaring down at the table. I know he checked every last detail, but I also know that tonight, I've gotten it right. I even made his favorite meal, so he won't be mean and snarky. He scares me a lot more when he's like that.

His eyes bore into mine. "Do you have something to tell me?"

I fidget and try to think of an answer when he rounds the table and grabs my wrist, holding it with all his strength. Tears spring into my eyes at the pain, but he won't relent. A large bruise will form there.

"I asked you a question?"

"I...I don't know what you mean," I stutter. "I haven't spoken to anyone all day."

His face scrunches up and I sense he's about to hit me, but I find myself free. I stumble slightly, only managing to stay on my feet by sheer will.

"Serve the food, Wren. I'm hungry after the day I've had." The Reverend takes his seat then glances at my wrist before meeting my gaze. "Wren! The food."

"Oh, yes! I'm sorry." I have no strength in my right wrist, so I'm awkward and clumsy as I try to serve supper. The Reverend snatches the serving spoons from me and serves himself before passing them back. I continue to struggle until I finally have some food in front of me.

Before we can eat, the Reverend waits for me to place my hands together in prayer, and then he starts mumbling about blessing the food. The direct gaze coming from his black as midnight eyes tells me not to move - it tells me I'll be punished if I don't have my full attention on *his* words. What the Reverend hasn't figured out is that I have to count to ten in my head for the ending of his prayer. "Bless my daughter with obedience."

I struggle not to grind my teeth together in anger. I refuse to give in to him. He waits for a flicker of emotion to cross my face, but after years of practice, I've learned to meet his gaze head on. He terrifies me, but as long as I don't show weakness, he leaves me alone, for the most part at least. There is a list of ten things to remember that I recite in my head every day. If I remember just these ten things, I won't be punished, or I won't be punished as much. *Do not answer back. Do not burn the food. Do not break anything. Do not talk to boys. Come straight home after school. Do not tell lies. Shower every night. Do laundry every two days. Press every piece of clothing. Lights out at ten every night.*

Finally, after I recite the rules in my head, the Reverend decides it's time to eat. He picks up his knife and fork after inspecting the place setting to make sure they are evenly spaced at the side of his dinner plate—another of his rules. I hold my breath while he takes a bite of the chicken and cuts into a dumpling. He sighs and nods toward my plate. "Eat," he commands.

I don't need telling twice. If the Reverend finishes eating first, it marks the end of the meal and I have to clean everything away. I've learned to eat quickly if I'm hungry. It usually isn't a problem, but tonight my belly feels unsettled. It's because of the boy next door. I'm curious because he's unlike anyone I've seen before. I mean why would his dad move them to Port Michael, population one hundred and eight? Port Michael is south of Corpus Christi and overlooks Padre Island, Texas.

A throat being cleared makes me jump and my cutlery clatters to the plate. I wince, but luckily, the Reverend is too distracted to comment.

It only takes me ten minutes to clean the kitchen and make him a cup of freshly brewed coffee. He ignores me and disappears into his office, locking the door behind him.

My shoulders sag in relief as they always do, and I let out a shaky breath. I glance at the stairs and move toward them. With my foot on the bottom step, I cast a quick glance at the closed office door. He will be in there for hours doing whatever it is he does. It's out of bounds. I have never even peeked inside. The thought alone gives me jitters.

Inhaling deeply, I climb the rest of the way upstairs and make sure I don't make a sound as I close and lock my bedroom door. I won't have to face the Reverend until morning, which relaxes me.

The room is dark and still, the tick of my alarm clock breaking the quiet. The old thing sits on the corner of my small wooden desk. My schoolbooks sit to one side with a small lamp to help me see the books. My small closet holds my shoes neatly lined up on the floor. Hangers hold my dresses, skirts, and T-shirts, while the shelving holds my jeans, under-wear, and pajamas. My robe hangs from the bath-room door.

I have a small bookshelf, which only holds novels the Reverend has approved for me to read. One of those books is *The Hunger Games*. I'm surprised he allowed me to read it, which makes me wonder if he knows what it's about or whether someone at the church had raved about it. It would have had to be someone who never misses a sermon, and whom the Reverend likes for him to have listened. I've read the book over and over again, looking for similarities between me and Katniss, but I'd long since grown bored of that game. We weren't alike. The other books lining the shelf are nonfiction and religious, so I ignore them. I've had religion shoved down my throat for as long as I can remember. Besides, reading about religion is the last thing I want to do. For the sake of appearances, I will pick one to read every once in a while. The lines blur into one and have done so for a while. I'm fairly sure he wants me totally brainwashed into believing his mumbo jumbo. I never will.

Trying to lose the minutes that drag on every evening, I idly read one of my textbooks, but as the evening wears on, I wonder about the boy next door as I'm drawn to the window. If I open my window wide enough, I can climb out onto the roof—I like to lie and watch the stars on a clear night. Now I will be seen from the other house. I don't know the new people and I would be surprised if they're not friends of the Reverend. I can't imagine him allowing strangers so close to the house, which means my spot on the roof will be reported back to him.

Reaching out for the curtain, I slowly pull it to the side and look across the way. The neighbor's house is dark, but just as I'm about to give up, I catch a flicker of light coming from an upstairs window. It's difficult to focus from where I'm hiding, but then a tattoo hand appears under the light, followed by the rest of his body. It's him—the boy. As though he senses me looking, everything in him stills and then his head turns. I feel the heat of his gaze for long moments before I become nervous and quickly close the curtain.

My cheeks burn with embarrassment. I'm not used to being looked at, especially by boys. They all fear the Reverend. Plus, he tells me constantly that no one dares look at me.

5

RAFAEL

WREN LOOKS OVER TO THE HOUSE.

Is it me she looks for?

I feel the heat of her gaze across the distance and wish I hadn't reacted at all. If I'd carried on without acknowledging her, would she still be looking?

My attraction to her had been swift and sudden, and that alone confuses me. I desperately want her to be on our side—my father's and mine.

At the thought of my father, I hear him on the worn stairs leading up to the attic. He'd been on a phone call that lasted forever when I'd looked for him earlier, so I'd kept myself busy.

He knocks softly.

"I'm still awake." I wipe a hand over my tired eyes before I face him. "Who was on the phone?"

"Conference call." Dad sits on the end of the bed. "John, Ken, and Jeremiah."

"Oh," I mumble as Dad mentions his closest friends. John works for the FBI and the other two are still with the DEA.

"Nothing to worry about. At least, not yet." Dad frowns and sighs heavily. "I didn't miss the way you looked at the girl," he adds. "We're going to have to use her to get to *him*, Rafael. You knew this might be a way to get close. He won't like it."

"What if she is innocent in all of this? Everything you've learned says she is." I wave my arms around. "She's a victim too, Dad."

Dad sighs again. "I agree she appears innocent, but we can't take that risk right now." Dad pauses. "None of my contacts have any new information on Wren. It's all years old. No one talks. There was a whisper that social services once received a call about abuse going on at the Reverend's address. No evidence was found when they sent a case worker out to check."

"Has anyone spoken to the case worker?"

"No. She died seven months after the visit to the house. Car accident."

"Accident?"

"According to police records. Yes."

"I find that hard to believe."

"Son"—he sighs and leans forward—"one thing I've learned in this life is that anything is possible. More so if it's a secret you're trying to protect. It was classified an accident. I don't believe it any more than you do."

My head spins as blood swirls around in anger. The Reverend is a first-class asshole and he'll pay for everything in the end, if it's the last thing I ever do.

And Wren?

"Wait." A thought suddenly hits me. "Who made the call to social services?"

My father holds my gaze, and I know.

"Wren." I answer my own question. "She called for help, and the people who were supposed to help her turned their backs."

I pace, unable to keep still as the wrongfulness of the situation makes me angry. My fists clench tightly at my sides.

My father watches me, as I do him, and I realize he's still as determined as ever to bring justice to those who are responsible for the deaths of my mother and brother. I am too.

"I can't let her be harmed in this, Dad. She cried for help once. It's about time she was listened to."

With a weary sigh, Dad stands and places his hands on my shoulders. "A lot could have happened between then and now." He cups my face and kisses my forehead. "Be careful, Rafael." He hesitates. "Make sure to always keep the chain hidden." He steps away. "Good night, son."

"Night, Dad."

Frustrated, I go into the small bathroom and splash cold water on my face before I glance into the mirror for answers. It doesn't give me any, only shows how angry the scar on my face looks—red and puckered. A permanent reminder of the day my life changed.

I rub my chest before moving to sit at the window. Before I can think about the wisdom of what I'm about to do, I start to draw. I have an image in my head of Wren and it won't leave me alone.

The black pencil in my hand takes over and I draw as though possessed. Deep lines, fine lines, shading, it all appears on the paper without much guidance. The hum of the air conditioning unit and the scratch of the pencil on the paper are the only sounds in the room as the digits on my phone creep closer to midnight. It's close to one in the morning when I sit back and stare down at my lap in…astonishment. I have no other words to describe the girl I've brought to life with pencil.

My beautiful butterfly girl.

6

WREN

THE REVEREND IS LOCKED IN HIS OFFICE BEFORE HE leaves for church. He always appears busy, which sometimes baffles me considering how small of a community we are. I never ask because he'll take it as an accusation, and he'll think I'm accusing him of not having time for me. I don't want his time focused on me. At one time I had, but the thought makes me break into a cold sweat now.

Sighing, I step into the early morning sun and feel my heart lift with joy when my eyes immediately focus on my glasshouse. The structure has been there for a very long time, since before I was born. It had needed some care and maintenance. The hard work I had put into it has paid off, and even the Reverend had been impressed. It has become a talking point for him during sermons. It's the only time I pay full attention—not that I let it show.

Tiger Lily appears in front of my face, so I lift a hand and let him perch on my finger. His delicate wings ease to a stop and when the sun catches them, he's dazzling. As I slowly move down the path, more of my butterflies appear through the slightly open doorway. I haven't even gotten inside the glasshouse, and I'm covered in about twenty of my delicate friends.

"How do you do that?"

I whirl around.

The boy stands on his side of the bordering fence. I can see him more clearly now. His black eyes trail over my body as he takes in the butterflies attached to me. He has a scar that goes from the corner of his right eye, over his cheek, and then comes to a stop beneath his jaw. Another one goes from his right eyebrow into his hairline.

What happened to him?

He makes a noise in the back of his throat, and hisses, "It's rude to stare!"

My hackles rise. "So why were you?" I gasp in shock and sharply glance toward the house.

I spoke to a stranger! Even worse, I spoke to a boy!

Said boy ignores my question and tilts his head, watching me. "You're unusual," he says. His eyes focus on Tiger Lily. "She your favorite?"

I nod, and the urge to move away before the Reverend catches me close to this boy has my head dropping. I start to turn away and, to my surprise, the boy snags the back of my T-shirt. "Wait! What's your name?"

"Wren," I whisper and turn back around, his hand falling away. "I shouldn't be talking to you."

He frowns and glances at the house before he continues, "I'm Rafael." He doesn't smile and I sense he wants to ask something. He briefly meets my eyes and looks away. "What's the school like?" That hadn't been the question he'd first thought of—I'm sure of it.

I shrug and, feeling confident, tip my head to the side. It's him who gives me the confidence when I speak with him—this boy who is shrouded in darkness.

Confused at the feelings rushing through me, I state, "You look too old for school."

His jaw clenches tightly, and he grinds out, "I missed a lot of school, so I have to catch up to graduate." I notice a slight slump in his shoulders before he shakes it off.

"School is the same anywhere, I guess." I take a step back. "I need to check on the glasshouse." I take another step backwards while Rafael tracks me with his eyes. I know this because mine never leave his, and my breathing changes in a way I'm not familiar with.

The sound of footsteps approaching from behind Rafael snaps my attention away. It's his father. His movements are swift and confident. I get the feeling nothing would faze this man. He has compelling dark eyes, like his son, with firm features. His short curling hair is gray in places, and black in others. Welcome and warmth shine in his gaze as he moves to stand beside his son.

He gives his son a sidelong glance before holding his hand out, and stills. "You're covered in butterflies," he mumbles. "I've only seen this..." He shakes his head and looks at me in a weird way - as though he's seen a ghost. "Where have my manners gone? I'm Marcel DeLacroix, Rafael's father."

I swallow hard, knowing I'm going to be in trouble for talking to them, but I can't turn tail and run back to the house or my glasshouse to hide. The damage has been done after talking to Rafael. *I like that name.*

I quickly step forward and accept Marcel's handshake. His fingers are cool and slightly calloused as he wraps my much smaller hand up in his. His eyes are wary, but I think seeing me with the butterflies really surprised him.

Retreating slightly, he states, "You two should walk to school together in the morning."

Rafael glares at his father while I stare in horror.

I couldn't! The Reverend would kill me.

"That will not be happening." The Reverend's voice booms across the garden.

I visibly pale as air whooshes out of my mouth. My head spins along with my stomach as I fight the nausea flooding me. The butterflies fly from me in one desperate attempt to get away from the noise. They'll go back into the glasshouse.

Rafael's head snaps to the Reverend, and his jaw clenches tightly as I sense the Reverend move in close.

Marcel hardens his features. "Reverend, I had no idea we lived so close to you," he comments, shoving his hands into the pockets of his jeans.

They both know each other. How?

"I find that hard to believe," the Reverend snaps and grabs hold of my arm tight enough to leave a bruise. "Inside." He drags me across the garden.

"Nice to meet you," Marcel sarcastically shouts.

Through the whole exchange, I felt Rafael's gaze boring into me. It's as though he's angry with me when I haven't done anything.

I cast one quick glance in his direction before I'm dragged inside, the back door slamming behind us. The Reverend pushes me so hard in his anger that I lose my balance. I slam into the steel rod attached to the oven door on my way down to the floor - my hip taking the brunt of the fall. Pain shoots through me as the rod pierces my skin. Clenching my teeth, I try not to cry out even though tears leak from my eyes. My hip screams in pain as I move to a sitting position. I'm shocked at the suddenness of his violence. It was like it was unplanned, and the Reverend never does anything unplanned. When he hurts me, whether with words, or his rules, or the basement, or physically, it's slow and methodical, deliberate. The Reverend was not a man ruled by his emotions.

"You never speak to them!" The Reverend stands over me with his fists clenching at his sides. His face turns bright red as he continues, "You stay away from that *boy* and his father. They are not good people and should have never been allowed that house."

Who left them that house? It has been vacant for as long as I can remember.

The Reverend crouches and gets in my face. "Stay. Away. Wren. You hear me?"

"Yes, sir." I keep my eyes on him because if I cower it will just give him an excuse to put me in the basement.

He pulls back slightly and breathes heavily until he visibly calms, then he moves away. "Get out of my sight." He hesitates, and with one last glance, disappears into his office.

Feeling shaky, I roll to my knees and grab hold of the kitchen counter. My hands slip twice but, eventually, I manage to stand. My hip continues to throb as I go upstairs to my room.

My hands tremble as I pull my dress off over my head and move into the bathroom. The dress will be ruined if I can't get the blood out of the material. I chance a glance at my hip and grimace. The gash is several inches long and deep. Blood oozes from it and is soaking through my panties.

With the sink half filled with cold water, I scrub at the stain on my dress and sigh as it becomes fainter.

I'll leave it to soak during the day. Taking my panties off, I add them to the water and scrub them in the same desperate way. Hopefully the soaking will save my clothing.

I shiver as a cool breeze slips through my partly opened window. Slipping into a fresh pair of panties, I leave them around my lower hip so I can clean up the gash. It has started to bruise around the edges. I retrieve the first aid kit from the drawer of my desk and sit on the end of the bed. The antiseptic wipe causes me to hiss in pain as I dab along the open wound. It will be tricky getting a padded dressing to stay on because of the area. I manage but wince when I think about the tape coming off.

I catch sight of the clock on my desk as I put the first aid kit away—I've taken too long. I have chores to do outside.

With ease, I pull my panties on properly and gently get them situated on my left side, so it won't hurt. I tug on a pair of loose-fitting shorts and a blouse. I slip on a pair of dark blue ballerina pumps. And that's when I see him. Rafael DeLacroix. He leans out of his bedroom window and looks straight at me through my bedroom window.

My breath catches in my throat and I struggle to

turn away. When I do my cheeks have a deep crimson color to them and I feel completely embarrassed. He saw me moving around in my bedroom. I'm not sure how to feel about that. I'm startled, and I should be angry but, I don't think I am. I'm embarrassed and hope he'll never mention seeing me.

Nothing makes sense about how I feel about the boy I've only just met.

[illegible] [illegible] a reader [illegible]
[illegible] complete the course [illegible]
[illegible] read about the life [illegible] I could be
[illegible] think I am an [illegible] reading
[illegible] resources [illegible]
[illegible] makes sense [illegible] how I feel about the
[illegible] a book is only meant [illegible]

7

RAFAEL

THE BUTTERFLY GIRL IS AS BEAUTIFUL UP CLOSE AS SHE is from a distance, if not more so. Her eyes are a mixture of ocean blue and green, so unusual that I struggled to look away when I had been close to her. The way those eyes had run over me had left my body hot and tight. I've never experienced tightness like this before, and that alone should scare me. It doesn't. We have hardly exchanged words and I want more.

I wince when I bend to rest my hands on the sill of my window. I have a perfect view of Wren's house. My thoughts of her father are worse than before. He had reacted in a public way toward Wren and that bothered me. The Reverend is known as someone who keeps his emotions under a tight lock and key.

That hadn't been the case earlier. I'm afraid for Wren, the girl I don't know but feel a connection with.

Movement suddenly catches my eye from Wren's bedroom. She walks past her window and disappears. A few moments later she reappears, and I nearly fall out of my window. She wears only her underwear. I blink a few times to clear the shock, but nothing works. She turns and I watch as she pushes her panties down to her upper thighs. I swallow my tongue when my gaze moves upward. I'm not a voyeur, but I can't move my gaze away. She is beautiful.

She straightens up and turns to face the window, giving me a view I'll never forget. My heart thumps against my breastbone as I force myself to move away from the window.

With my hands on my hips, I pace back and forth in my room trying to get myself under control. Getting close to Wren is going to be easy, but difficult on my conscience. I don't want to use her to get to her father. I want her to be one of the good guys. I need her to be one of the good guys. Maybe she is and has been waiting for someone to come along and rescue her. I want inside her head so I know I can trust her. However, I have to be patient.

"What's taking you so long?" Dad yells from the landing below.

We have to head into the next town over for groceries and so Dad can meet up with a friend of his. After meeting Wren, I don't want to go. I want to sneak around to Wren's spot and watch her. It's magical when she's with her butterflies.

Tomorrow at school, my deception will start, and I hate knowing I'll have to befriend her to get to her father. I want to befriend her for myself.

But it's too late to do anything else. I've made a deal with Dad. It's my own fault really, I'd agreed to pretend to be in high school so I could keep my eyes and ears open at the school. That was the only way I could convince my Dad to let me come with him. He isn't comfortable with me being here, despite my three years of self-defense training and being weapons certified. Dad made sure I'm capable of looking after myself. The training started right after we'd buried Mom and Roman. That time in my life isn't pleasant and it isn't something I ever want to repeat. We are so close but so far away from catching the bastards responsible for such an evil act. I think maybe I want payback more than Dad does. It eats away at me like an ulcer.

Dad continues to mutter downstairs about sons, so I take pity on him and clamber down to the ground floor. I certainly get enough exercise running up and down two flights of stairs a few hundred times a day.

"You have everything?"

"Like what?" I roll my eyes. "Don't need anything since I'm not going." I grin, feeling amused.

Dad raises an eyebrow when he notices me. I walk toward him and my grin widens as he watches me warily. I quickly give him a peck on the cheek and laugh. "Have a nice day, dear," I drawl.

He laughs, and reaches out and grabs my wrist, becoming serious. "Did you think it...strange to see the butterflies? And all over Wren? It freaked me out."

The funeral isn't something I want to think about unless I have to, but the butterflies around Wren have thrown me too. "I noticed them, and I remembered the last time we'd seen something similar." I won't meet his gaze.

"Do you think they're the same ones?"

"I didn't think they lived long," I comment. "Not three years anyway."

"It doesn't sit well with me that we saw...what we did after the funeral, only to find the people responsible for your mother's and brother's deaths, and there are butterflies again. It's too much of a coincidence. Because I know what we saw isn't a general occurrence. It's unheard of. I know that. I'd researched it for days after what we'd seen. It's unnatural."

"I don't think we'll ever get an explanation about something so beautiful. It was gone within a few seconds. If you hadn't seen it too, I'd have thought I'd imagined it. But we both know we didn't." I sigh and move to the front door. "I'll keep my ears open about the butterflies."

Nodding, Dad turns back to the hall table to pick up his keys. I step outside. That's when I spot Wren disappearing into the trees at the back of her house, and my feet follow her.

Moments later, Dad shouts, "Don't get up to trouble," as he climbs into his car. From over my shoulder, I see him glance toward where Wren has disappeared before his eyes land on me. He shakes his head. He knows I'm strong-willed and will do what I want.

I won't do anything to screw up *our* plan.

That is something I won't do.

8

WREN

I SLIP OUT BACK, TREADING CAREFULLY IN A STRAIGHT line to the glasshouse so that the Reverend won't see me from his office. As soon as I reach the entrance, I go right around the back of it toward the forest behind. The moment I step foot into the shaded trees, three butterflies land on my shoulder. I smile and hope Tiger Lily follows too. He won't but I hope. I've discovered that Tiger Lily doesn't like dark areas. The others aren't as fussy.

The Reverend has no understanding of the butterflies and why they react to me in the way they do. I have no clue about their reaction either, but I care about them. The Reverend hates anything he can't explain. He had, at one time, wanted them dead and gone, and it had been the only time I'd stood up to him. He hadn't liked it and he'd only relented and allowed them to stay because his followers had complimented him on the beautiful garden and tiny creatures. There was no other reason. He doesn't care whether or not I'm happy. At the beginning, it had been about his followers and gaining their respect and approval. Now, it's because he's too busy with the church and everything that entails—whatever that might be—to do anything about them. Thank goodness for that.

We're not a rich town, but I've brought color in abundance with my garden. Part of me wonders whether he doesn't want another *real* confrontation with me. At least, that's what I tell myself. In reality, the Reverend can choose to get rid of my oasis with the snap of his fingers and I won't be able to do anything about it.

Closing my eyes, I tilt my head toward the sky and inhale deeply. Slowly, I exhale. Each breath brings an opening within me. I can feel my body easing, the sharp pain in my hip fading to a dull pulse and then to nothing. I take another breath and slowly start to feel better. The Reverend always manages to get my hackles up with his temper. But then he leaves me alone and I'm torn. I don't want his attention, but I'm so alone that I hardly ever need to speak. I, of course, speak to my butterflies and they seem to listen. They have no clue what I say, but I hold their attention. The breathing exercises work, the calm spreading through me as I sense Tiger Lily drawing close. I can't explain the feeling he arises in me with his presence. However, the tingles in my arms are real, along with the tiny movement from the hair on my arm as he slowly flutters toward me.

I don't want to scare him off with my excitement, so I stop myself from turning my head to look at him. In the end, I don't need to because he lands on the tip of my nose. A place that he has recently chosen as his spot. Keeping my breathing even, I slowly open my eyes and smile when I see the beautiful orange color shimmering around him.

"Hello, sweet angel," I whisper, hardly daring to move. "You're becoming brave."

His tiny head tilts from side to side as though he knows I'm talking to him and he's trying to figure out what I'm saying.

"You have a special connection with them?"

My face blazes with heat. Not only is he here, in this place that is mine alone, but he saw me in my bedroom. I freeze to the spot as my heart picks up speed, racing in my chest as quickly as thoughts of confusion whirl in my mind. The boy from next door is a conundrum that I want to explore as much as I want to run from it.

I had felt safe, or rather safer, talking to him in the back garden, but in the dark forest with only slithers of sunlight filtering through the thick branches, I feel uneasy. I'm alone with a boy for the first time in my life and I don't know what to do or say. I feel awkward, but not as much as the picture I make with the butterflies and my stillness.

"I didn't mean to upset you," he continues after a lengthy pause. "I just wanted to make sure you were okay. Your father wasn't happy."

"The Reverend doesn't like me talking to strangers. I can't talk to you."

He steps in front of me, and to my amazement, Tiger Lily and his few friends stay resting on me.

"Please go."

"I'm not going anywhere, Wren." He grins. "No one can see us in here. It's safe." Backing away slowly, Rafael drops his butt onto a fallen tree trunk.

The boy is too nice looking for his own good. He sits there and stares at me in all his black clothing:

jeans, T-shirt, biker boots. The swirling lines of tattoos cover his arms and hold my attention longer than polite. I don't see anything wrong with that considering his eyes stay on me the whole time. He smirks and relaxes as he spreads his legs and leans forward, resting his elbows on his thighs and his chin in his hands.

Tightening my jaw, I snap, "Why are you staring at me?"

"Because you're pretty." He frowns and clears his throat, his back going straight as a board. "I meant to say that I stared because of the unusual connection you have to the butterflies. It's true. However, you really are pretty, Wren."

"You can't say that to me."

"Who says I can't?" He stands and moves closer.

I refuse to back away, so I tip my head back so I can continue to see his face. He's maybe a foot taller than me. Certainly, broader in the shoulders. As I look at him, I realize he's big all over. Not in a bad way, but in a very nice way. The thought of which makes me blush and my gaze drops at the heat in my cheeks.

The annoying boy snickers under his breath. I catch it, though. I also see the way his eyes search my face. I can't understand why I continue to stand here with him. Why haven't I run?

"I'll stop teasing you if you come and sit with me. It's been forever since I talked to someone other than my dad." He winces. "Please." His hand goes to his chest and he tries to give me a lost puppy look, but all it does is make my lips twitch. "I caught that, butterfly girl. Admit it"—he leans closer—"you like me." He immediately backs away and drops to the fallen log. He pats a spot next to him.

I know we won't be seen, unless of course, the Reverend decides to come looking for me. He'll probably just yell from the porch. It usually works.

I desperately want to talk to Rafael and, maybe, have a friend. He'll be my only one. Until school that is. No one speaks to me there, unless of course, they want something. Will Rafael be the same once he gets to know me? Will he prefer the others? I sense the hatred the Reverend has for Rafael's father, so I don't think Marcel will be attending church anytime soon. That, at least, gives me a small slither of hope.

Nerves flutter around in my belly as I take the few steps to bring me in front of the fallen tree *and* Rafael. He's beautiful this close, and his eyes are dark pools of mystery. It's his chuckle that clears my head of all this silly nonsense. Rolling my eyes, I glare and sit beside him making sure there's a large gap between us.

He notices. His eyes go between me and the gap a few times before he sighs heavily. "I don't bite." He slides closer. "I promise, Wren. I just want to talk. I won't hurt you."

"I'm not used to being around anyone." Too embarrassed to look at him, I add, "At school, I'm surrounded by others but I'm still alone. I find it hard to believe you'd want to talk to me when no one else does. I don't mean to be wary of you. It's me with the social problem." I feel slightly better after getting all that out. Probably the most I've spoken to anyone at any given time. My nerves still tickle my belly because I don't want him to go. I like being near him. He smells good, too.

"One thing you should know about me, Wren, is I don't do stuff to fit in. I do what I want. Mostly. So, if others don't see how amazing you are, then they're missing out. I'm not. End of story." He bumps into me and I sigh as Tiger Lily takes flight. "Sorry."

"It's okay. He doesn't usually follow me into the trees anyway." I give him a sidelong look and then a tentative smile when he grins in return.

"My charm is working on you, huh? You smiled at me." He gloats.

"Don't let it go to your head. You won't be getting another."

"I will. I don't give up easily."

"Why didn't you take online classes?" I blurt the question, which takes us both by surprise. "Don't answer that if you don't want to. Or answer it. It's a nosy question. But I'm curious—"

He bursts out laughing, which of course, makes me laugh. His eyes sparkle with amusement. However, he decides against commenting on my second smile in less than two minutes.

"I didn't take online courses because they bored me stupid." He looks off into the distance. "Dad wanted us out of the city, so here we are, and I'm enrolled at the school now. Lucky me, huh?"

"Yeah, lucky you," I mumble.

9

RAFAEL

"I SHOULD HAVE SAID, LUCKY YOU, WREN." SHE IS SO damn cute when she blushes, which she seems to do often around me. I like that I'm not the only one affected by this thing between us. It would be a lot easier if I weren't, but damn, the girl is gorgeous.

I haven't once thought of Wren as a real person until I met her. Now, I can't get her out of my mind. She's driving me crazy. Her petite frame is filled out just fine, which I try not to notice. I'm a guy after all. An older guy. I have to remember that. Three years isn't a huge gap, but when the girl is only seventeen, then yes, I have to remember. No matter how gorgeous she is.

"You decided not to talk to me anymore?" I ask to cover up how quiet I went.

"I'm thinking," she comments. "I think you have the wrong impression about me."

I can't help myself. I grin like the cat that got the cream. "Is that so?"

"Yes. You think I'm an outcast and you want to make friends with me because I'm the only person you've met since moving to town." She folds her arms together tightly under her perky tits, pushing them together—not that she's aware of this.

For a second, I'm tempted to tell her, but think better of it. I want her as a friend, not to go running from me because I can't keep my mind off her body and on our conversation. I've certainly seen more of her than I should have. She knows this too but has chosen not to mention it.

"Ugh!" She stands and barely refrains from stomping her foot. "Stop staring at my chest."

I rapidly blink and curse under my breath as Wren starts heading toward her glasshouse. I reach out and gently grab her wrist. "I'm sorry. I didn't mean to. I was thinking about something else. Didn't realize I was staring." I curse again. "I could stare at you all day, but I wasn't meaning to *then*." Wincing, I start laughing when I notice how difficult Wren tries not to laugh. "Shit." I run my hands through my hair and laugh with her. "It's your fault I sound like an idiot."

"That's right. Blame me. Everyone else does."

Well, that statement slaps the laughter right out of me. It catches me off guard and I want to take the hurt from her eyes. "I was teasing, Wren." I take a chance and touch her chin, lifting her face up to mine. "I really was teasing. Kind of. I've never met anyone like you, so I stared and ended up a buffoon. Forgive me."

"Nothing to forgive. I didn't mean my words to sound accusing. I didn't realize how accurate they were until I said them." She shrugs and I feel like hitting the Reverend. There is no doubt in my mind the asshole is responsible for all the hurt flashing across Wren's face.

In that instance, I want to tell Wren everything. The reason why we are in Port Michael. How we got the house. What we know about the Reverend. My father knows even more than he's told me, which I find annoying. I try to understand. One day I might. But never have I wanted to talk to someone as badly as I do Wren. I want her to know how beautiful she is. How attracted to her I am after that first glimpse of her in the garden. I want her to know I'll protect her from *him*. I hope I can and that, one day when she knows the truth about everything, she'll forgive me for not telling her from the beginning.

"Why are you thinking so hard?" She tentatively reaches out and runs the tips of her fingers across my brow.

I hold my breath wondering what she will do next. I'm not disappointed, but now my breath catches in my throat as her fingers run gently along the large, jagged scar on my face. Nerve endings I thought were fried come to life under her touch and I feel each soft flutter deep inside. It isn't something I can explain. Not even my father has touched my scar. Only the doctor and the nurses in the hospital had. I close my eyes and savor everything about the way she touches me. It isn't the touch of someone curious to feel the jagged lines, it's the touch of someone who is trying to take away my pain - as though she wants to see inside of me. The connection I felt at first seeing Wren is getting stronger. It's growing inside of me to the point that I know I have to end this. I have to act my age and step back so she can no longer touch me. I have to. However, my feet refuse to move. I don't want to move.

Her hand cups my rough cheek and, while my heart beats wildly behind my breastbone, I reach up and wrap my fingers around her wrist. Her eyes jerk up and hold mine, and then she flees.

She runs through the trees, back the way she'd come, disregarding the whack of branches as they get in her way. When she reaches the edge of trees, she stops and looks back over her shoulder, her hair flying around her face. She holds my gaze for a split second then I lose sight of her. The only trace left of her is the soft warmth where her fingers had danced like butterfly wings on my skin.

It's as well I can't decide whether or not to follow the enchanting girl because my feet refuse to move, my legs feel like rocks. I don't think anyone has confused me like this before. Her touch had been different, and it makes my head spin as I try to work out what actually just happened between us. Every nerve ending in my body is alive, especially in my groin.

Inhaling deeply, I shake myself free and tilt my face up toward the sky. Slivers of sunlight shine between the dense foliage, which is all I can see. It's quiet here. Dark and quiet. I can think without any judgement or sneers from my peers. My father knows the real me, so had my mother and brother. I want Wren to know the real me too. The one who sometimes feels as though I'm drowning with no ability to surface.

However, when I'm around Wren, I feel at peace. She makes me feel other things, which is not surprising considering how gorgeous the girl is. The fact that she has no clue how beautiful she is, makes my feelings toward her more intense. Too intense for someone I've just met.

Deep in thought, I quickly turn my head to the right as a twig crunches beneath a booted foot—and another twig. I try to focus and see through the semi-darkness and my heart races wondering who is heading toward me as I move behind the nearest tree. I've learned to slow my breathing and keep it paced so as not to panic.

When I hear, "Rafael?" hissed in a very low voice—a *very* familiar voice, anger hits me. I step from my not-so-good hiding spot and go toe-to-toe with Dad. "What the hell?"

He steps back.

"How long were you there?" I snap. "Were you making sure I didn't tell Wren anything?"

"Rafael, calm down." He shakes his head. "I only came after you when I saw Wren run out."

Frowning, I glare. "I thought you headed into town."

"I did. Drove down the road and remembered I left my wallet on the counter, so I turned around." He knows I'm not impressed as he turns and starts to trudge back the way he'd come.

"Make more noise next time," I grumble, sounding like a surly teenager.

Once I'm out of the trees, my eyes stray across to Wren's house. I can't see her and wonder where she's gone. No sign of her in the glasshouse, but as I'm about to glance away, my eyes catch brief movement at her bedroom window. She's there and I'd bet good money she's watching me. I'd be watching her.

I jump up the porch steps, make sure she sees my head swivel toward her bedroom, then I wave before heading inside.

"You're asking for trouble, Rafael."

I am but I can't help it. I want to know what makes Wren Jacobs tick. I realize I want to know a lot more than that. Best keep that knowledge to myself.

[illegible] I [illegible] know this would [illegible]

[illegible] your hand [illegible]

[illegible] and I [illegible] you [illegible]

[illegible] the Drew [illegible] face [illegible] impressed

[illegible] would be the nature [illegible] depend on the [illegible]

have the impressed once [illegible] and said to

the black the way they were [illegible]

Black [illegible] once part-time [illegible] Despite the smoking

his early tremors

[illegible]

We [illegible] can see his hand with when [illegible]

[illegible] to appear just in the grass had a bottle. One

[illegible] glance away, my eyes [illegible] corner of my mouth

[illegible] that for [illegible] Slick their and I [illegible]

[illegible] if anything [illegible] I'd been [illegible]

[illegible]

had [illegible] put on all [illegible] [illegible]

[illegible]

[illegible]

[illegible] keep it up [illegible] I wouldn't know what

[illegible] would [illegible]

anything that I'd keep that [illegible]

10

WREN

THE TICK OF THE CLOCK IN MY ROOM FINALLY DRAWS my gaze and I panic. Tardiness won't be tolerated. I hate going to school because everyone has been brainwashed during the Reverend's weekly sermons at church. Every resident of Port Michael is a member of the church, and they believe the Reverend's word as gospel. He will make a small dig about me during his sermon, which leaves his followers wondering which way he had actually meant the comment. It scares me how much people of Port Michael look up to him.

Even at school, I can't settle. The Reverend isn't there, but his shadow follows me there. Everyone knows who I am. Everyone knows who my father is.

Everyone is ready to gain favor with the Reverend by sharing anything I have done that tarnishes the church. But I don't do anything. I keep quiet because everything I do or say will be reported back to him, no matter how insignificant it might seem. I've learned that the hard way. For the past five years it has been "regimented." I'd overheard that word in conversation once. In my naivety, I had looked up the word during science…and spent two nights in the basement for it.

Goosebumps rise on my arms and a cold shiver runs down my spine at the memory of the dank basement. He loves to use that room as my punishment because he knows exactly how much it terrifies me. He doesn't care one bit.

The Reverend is worshipped in our small community. I learned a long time ago that no one here was going to help me escape him.

One day though, I will be as free as my butterflies.

Unfortunately, it only takes around ten minutes for me to walk to the small school. It takes seconds for Alice—Miss Goody-Two-Shoes—to approach me as though it's the most natural thing in the world. It's not.

To my surprise, she smiles as though she's happy

to see me, which she really isn't. "Have you met your new neighbor yet? Rafael?" she asks. "What's he like? I've heard he's covered in tattoos. Have you seen any? Did he tell you his mom and little brother were killed during a home invasion three years ago? He was injured during the attack. Did you know that? He keeps getting into trouble so that's why they moved here. My dad says the Reverend isn't happy. Apparently, the father inherited the house, so the Reverend had no choice but to allow them to live here. Is your dad really angry, Wren?" Alice throws her arms around while questions and information fall out of her mouth. More words than she's ever said to me.

No way am I going to admit to having a conversation with the boy. The whole town, including the Reverend, will know within ten minutes. I have no interest in Alice or her gossip. "You know more than I do," I reply, hoping she'll run off.

Turning to my locker, I fiddle with the lock and, once the door finally opens, I shove all my stuff inside except for the few things I need for the first class. With a heavy sigh, I glare at Alice, who stands next to me and doesn't say anything more after her rambling. "Alice, if you really want to know about Rafael, then why don't you ask him yourself? I really don't know anything."

Not quite true, but Alice doesn't need to know that.

"You wouldn't tell me if you did, would you?" she hisses.

Correct!

"What has happened to someone else is none of my business." I pause, and add, "Or yours."

"You're a horrid person, Wren Jacobs," Alice says.

I snap my mouth tightly closed and count to ten before replying calmly, "Maybe I am, but what will the Reverend think when he hears about how you spoke to me, huh?"

The Reverend barely tolerates me, but I know he would demand respect for me from someone my age - an adult could probably spit on me and he wouldn't care.

Her complexion fades at my words and I know I've made my point. She continues to stare, but I've had enough. "Don't you have somewhere else to be?" I raise a brow.

"She probably does, as do I, but I don't think she intended for me to hear her babbling about me."

Hearing his voice, I turn and find Rafael shrouded

in darkness. His lips are pulled tight in anger as he glares at Alice.

The stupid girl squeaks and takes off, mumbling, "I have class."

I dip my gaze hoping he will head for class too. He doesn't move, so I lift my gaze and see his features soften slightly. His dark eyes glitter with amusement. I swallow hard and hide my face once more, too embarrassed to continue staring. I could actually stare at the beautiful boy all day.

"Are you going to run off again?" he asks. "Like you did the other day." I feel his stare on the top of my head.

Surprised at his tone, I blurt, "Get over yourself. I'm not going to run off. *Again.*" I lift my face and stubbornly pout. "But I do have a class to get to." Embarrassment crawls up my neck and onto my face as I remember him watching me through my bedroom window. *Am I ever going to forget that, so I don't get embarrassed every time I'm around this boy?*

I have a feeling he is going to be nothing but trouble.

The Reverend will punish me for the rest of my life if I'm seen talking to Rafael. The teachers report everything to him, and I mean, *everything.*

When I start to move away, Rafael grabs my arm, right on the spot where the Reverend had grabbed me. I hiss at the unexpected pain rippling through me. Rafael curses and immediately releases me. "What's wrong?"

"It's nothing," I mutter and sigh when the bell rings.

Rafael winces and glances above to where the bell rings against the wall. I turn and dash to class, hoping he doesn't follow.

He does.

My desk is at the back of the classroom so I can hide. The teacher, Mr. Dickerson, ignores me during the lesson, which suits me just fine. I do my homework on time and keep my grades up. He doesn't have to put any effort into making sure the Reverend's daughter is excelling. As I take my seat, I glance up and watch Rafael moving further into the room. My heart pounds as he comes closer and our eyes meet. He doesn't let go of my gaze until he takes a seat next to me.

I slump down in my chair and feel heat creeping up my neck with all eyes going between him and me. It makes me very uncomfortable and I pray that Mr. Dickerson arrives soon. I sense Rafael tense beside me and then I nearly jump out of my seat when he slams his fist on his desk, shaking the old wooden thing.

It works.

All eyes move from us to the front of the classroom, then we are saved from further gossip when the teacher walks in. He pauses briefly as his eyes scan over Rafael. I notice the moment he realizes Rafael is sitting next to me because his eyes widen and, he momentarily stills before he clears his throat.

"Rafael DeLacroix has joined us today for the rest of the school term," Mr. Dickerson states. "Rafael." He stares. "If you'd like to move to another desk, then do so now."

Rafael slouches. "Am I in someone else's seat?"

The others snicker.

Rafael glares around the room and Mr. Dickerson clears his throat again. "Rafael, I think you should move."

"I'll stay here." Rafael's fist clenches around the pen he's been playing with until it snaps in half. He drops it to the desk and sits forward with his forearms resting on the wooden surface, his hands linking together. He never once breaks eye contact with Mr. Dickerson.

The teacher backs down first and goes to his desk. Seconds later, he writes our assignments on the whiteboard. He never lectures, just writes on the board what sections we have to read from our class textbook, along with the page numbers for the questions we have to answer.

Silence has never bothered me. Until now. Rafael copies what I'm doing and opens his textbook. When it's time for questions, I offer him a pen. His tattooed hand wraps around the offered item and our eyes momentarily meet. I look away quickly and hunker down over my notebook.

"Why are you always alone?" Rafael whispers from the corner of his mouth as he writes in his notebook.

Not answering will be a problem for Rafael. I know this about him even though I don't actually know him. He doesn't appear to be the type to leave it alone when he wants to know something.

Sighing, I give him a sidelong glance. "The Reverend." I swallow hard and notice his frown. "I can't talk."

"He hurt you the other morning?"

Startled, I turn my face to him unaware of how close he is. I'm so close I can see green mixed in with the brown of his eyes.

The bell rings and breaks the spell he's cast over me. I shake my head. "Please, Rafael." I quickly shove my things away and dart out of the classroom and straight into the girls' bathroom.

I drop my books to the floor and turn the taps on, splashing my face with cold water. Having Rafael's attention on me causes butterflies in my belly. It embarrasses me as well. I have no experience with boys, and having no friends, I have no one to ask about boys. The Reverend will lock me away forever if I ask him. Sadness comes over me when I really think about Rafael and how much I like him, if only I'm allowed. He won't want to talk to me once he really discovers what the Reverend is like, and the hold he has over everyone in town. He won't go anywhere near me.

Hurrying to get to my next class, I hope Rafael doesn't sit next to me again, but luck has never really been on my side. I spend the rest of the school day trying to ignore him.

Walking home, my unlucky streak continues as Rafael catches up to me. He doesn't say anything, just walks beside me. Every now and again, I feel his eyes on me, but I continue walking as I face straight ahead. My mouth is dry, so I grab my water bottle and take a drink. I notice Rafael watching me, so I do the polite thing and offer him some. He smiles, which takes my breath away. He is beautiful, and he has dimples.

He doesn't bother to wipe around the bottle and just takes a few long swallows before he passes it back. "Thanks." He pauses, and asks, "What happened to your arm?"

I frown and glance at him. "My arm?"

"I never meant to hurt you, I only wanted to stop you from running off. You gasped in pain when I grabbed you."

Unconsciously, I rub where a large bruise covers my arm from the Reverend's fingers.

"He did that." Rafael tightens his jaw. "Did he do anything else?"

Again, my hand automatically reaches for my hip.

His eyes flash in anger. "He did," Rafael growls. "Wren, you have to tell someone."

I laugh. "You know who he is, right? He has the whole town brainwashed."

"My father will help you."

"No. I'll be okay."

"Wren—" He cuts off when I shake my head and slowly back away. Just in time too as the sun shines on the Reverend's bright red car moving toward us.

"Please don't say anything," I whisper.

The car comes to a stop spewing dust and gravel up from the ground. The car shudders and the Reverend steps out, anger in every inch of his body.

Behind me, Rafael whispers, "Don't go with him," and he grabs the back of my shirt.

"Get in the car, Wren," the Reverend growls, barely holding his temper, his eyes solely focus on Rafael. "Now!"

Knowing it's a mistake on my part, I do it anyway. I turn and meet Rafael's concerned gaze. "Let me go," I mumble. "You're making it worse."

My words reach some part of his brain because he releases his hold, and whispers, "I'll get my dad."

I shake my head. "No." Moving away from Rafael, I know I will be in big trouble once we get back to the house. It's worth it, even though Rafael will probably never look in my direction again after tonight.

"You stay away from my daughter. She doesn't need the likes of you corrupting her!" The Reverend yells at Rafael, who stands his ground. His bravery will annoy the Reverend even more. He loves the control he has over others, in fact, he relishes it. "Stay away if you know what's good for you." The Reverend slams into the car and takes off down the dusty road.

I tremble with nerves in the passenger seat. The car speeds down the road faster than ever before. The tires spin and the car slides as he takes the corner leading to the house.

My heart pounds and my pulse thuds in my ears at the red-hot anger dripping from the Reverend.

I've never feared him as much as I fear him now.

We slide to a stop beside the house in a cloud of dust. He climbs from the car, every bone in his body rigid with anger. He opens the passenger door, and says between clenched teeth, "Get inside, Wren."

I don't need telling twice and scuttle out of the car and into the kitchen. The moment I enter, he's behind me, removing my backpack. He takes my wrist and pulls me to the closed basement door. My heart is shattered with fear. He's really going to lock me down there again. The basement is dark and scary, and the darkness terrifies me. At one time, there had been windows up high that allowed sunlight into the room. The Reverend had long since boarded them up. It has been my punishment for as long as I can remember.

The door creaks open and I'm faced with the steps down. The Reverend brings his face close to the side of my head, but I refuse to turn and look at him. He snarls, "You will never look or talk to that boy again. Do you hear me, Wren? Never! At school you do not sit next to him. You change seats if he sits with you. I know everything. Remember that."

"Yes, sir."

He wraps my hair in his fist so tightly my eyes water. He tips my head backwards and hovers over me. His gaze makes me want to run or hurl. "You will not become like your mother. You will not consort with the devil." His fist tightens and he tugs, drawing fresh tears from the pain. "I mean it. I will not allow you to become like her."

He slowly untangles his hand and smooths my hair down my back. "You need to learn." His large palm on my back pushes me forward. I stumble, catching myself with a hand on the cold wall. I want to run far away from here. One day, I promise myself. One day.

Clenching my jaw tightly, I slowly move forward. The stone wall is cold and bumpy under my hand but I'm too afraid to let go. The banister fell apart years ago, and the wooden stairs leading into the dark space below are worn.

I stand trembling—partly from nerves and partly from the cold. I desperately want to turn and tell him,

"No!" but then I'll never get out of the basement. If I do run today, I have nowhere to go.

I'm wrong.

Rafael will help me.

Swallowing hard, I shove Rafael from my mind as I stand in the basement. I catch hold of the pull string for the light, but nothing happens when I tug.

The Reverend chuckles. "The bulb's still out." I only have seconds to get my bearings before he slams the door and I hear it lock.

The bulb has been out since I turned nine, around the same time the windows were blocked off. The Reverend stomps around in the kitchen above me, and then, a few minutes later, the pipes gurgle with water. It took time but I eventually worked out that the pipes shudder and splutter when a toilet is flushed.

It's cold down here regardless of the heat outside, and I shiver. There is no fight in me. I've been down here many times in the past and I know I'll be down here many times in the future.

My stomach growls as I move in the general direction of the small, metal bed frame. I've spent enough time down here to know I might as well sit down instead of stand. When there was still light, I had memorized every square inch of the place. Where the bed was, the pipes, the uneven patches on the floor. Once the Reverend took my sight in the basement, I spent days slowly counting out the confines of the space and where I could move safely. Moving to the bed was as automatic now as breathing. I never knew how long I'd be here, and this is no different.

The bed creaks as I put my weight down on it, and my nose twitches. An ozone-like tang from metal and cement reaches me. I haven't smelled it before so I'm not sure where it's coming from. The cold floor is cement, but there is no metal down here apart from the frame of the single bed. I can't even see anything to look around.

The Reverend is good and mad this time.

In the dark, there is nothing for me to do, except be alone with my thoughts and fears. But my mind doesn't drift to the darkest corners of the room. Instead, I think about Rafael and the real concern I'd seen in his gaze when he realized I'd been hurt. A strange emotion had run through me at his look. No one has been concerned for my welfare before, and having Rafael show me that concern gives me a funny feeling in my belly. There is something about the boy that has snared my attention from the first moment

I'd laid eyes on him. I'd seen the girls watching him from beneath their brows today at school. I might like to keep to myself, but I notice everything. Not much gets past me. The things I've observed would upset a few people in town—those who are supposed to be *clean and pure*—little did the Reverend know.

Rafael though, he's different.

Different?

Something had been different when the Reverend had opened the door to the basement. I'd quickly glanced around and saw...a door! I'd seen a door. It was dark wood with a silver lock. Why on earth would there be a door in our basement. That made no sense. There was nothing on that far side but earth. I mean, this is a basement, so it's underground. The rest of the place is surrounded by earth.

If I wasn't so scared of what else might be down here with me, I might risk checking out this new piece of my prison. I'm not sure how long I've been in here, but the only thing that's ever gotten me out of this bed is when it felt like an eternity and I needed to move or go crazy.

I try to focus on that energy, but I can't. My mind has been distracted and I'm not stir crazy enough to test the darkness. I stare blindly in the direction of where I'd seen the door, but I can't hear anything. Just the grumblings of the old house. I push myself to stand up but my legs tremble so hard I don't think I'll be able to walk. What if there's something scary and I am locked in here with it?

Wren! You're scaring yourself.

My fear prevents me from moving forward to explore this new part of my prison, and I collapse back on the bed where I huddle and wait.

11

RAFAEL

"Dad, we need to go next door," I demand the moment I open the kitchen door. I'm hot and sticky after running home knowing something bad is about to happen to Wren.

Dad frowns and passes me a bottle of water he quickly grabs from the fridge. "What the hell happened?"

"I was walking home with Wren when the Reverend pulled up beside us. He dragged her into the car." I drop my stuff to the floor and go to exit the house, but Dad stops me.

"Not so fast."

"We don't have time to talk!"

"Sit." He shoves me into a chair at the kitchen table. "You can't be acting like a hothead, Rafael."

"You didn't see him, Dad." I gulp the last of the water down. "He's really pissed she was walking with me." I stand and lean forward over the table. "He hurt her after we spoke to her in the garden. She had bruising on her arm, and I noticed her limp now and again, so I think he hurt her hip somehow." I refuse to look at him because he'll see the truth in my eyes. The truth that I watched her—had seen her beautiful body.

"Hmm." Dad sits at the table and holds my gaze. "Something else you want to tell me?"

I open my mouth to snap a reply, then think better of it at the last minute. "No." I turn and pace to the window that looks out over Wren's back garden. Everything is still and quiet until it's broken by the slamming of a door. I swivel my head and watch the Reverend settle in the rocker on the porch, his gaze directly on me.

"That bastard," I mutter.

"Rafael, you know I don't like bad language coming out of your mouth."

"He's gloating, Dad." I pass a glance to him and then back out of the window. "He's gloating because he knows I'm worried about Wren. It's as though he's taunting me."

"Then move away from the window and let him think he isn't getting to you." Dad sighs. "You're feeding into his sickness by allowing him into your head."

Growling in frustration, I force myself to sit back down. "If he's outside he can't be hurting Wren, right?" I raise my eyes to his.

"That's my take on the situation." Dad moves to stand beside the fridge so he can't be seen from the outside, but he has a clear view over to Wren's house. "Right now, the smug bastard *is* taunting you. He's daring you to go over and check on Wren."

"I need to know she's okay. I can't just stay here when she could be hurting."

After a few minutes of searching for something in my gaze, Dad says, "This girl really has gotten to you, hasn't she?"

"I can't explain the connection I feel with her. It happened when I first saw her, the day we moved in. I think she felt it too."

"I don't think he's stupid enough to hurt Wren. He already knows you like his daughter, so I think we can assume he thinks we'll help her at the first sign of trouble. He'll leave her alone."

"Then where is she?"

"Probably locked in her room," Dad says so casually I can almost believe him. "You'll see her at school tomorrow, ask her what happened. Until then, you have to stay here."

I drop my face into my hands and breathe heavily. "Why now, Dad? Why do I suddenly need to care for someone when it could cause so many problems for what we are here to do?"

Dad laughs. "I asked that when I met your mom. I never got an answer." He tries to lighten the conversation but there is worry behind it. His eyes swirl with emotion. "Mom would be so proud of you, Rafael." He winces. "Not just because of the man you've become, but because of how you want to care for someone who could destroy everything. I know she wasn't your birth mother, but in every way, you're just like her."

Words escape me as I swallow back emotion and clear my throat a few times. Sarah may not have given birth to me, but I'd considered her my real mom from the day she ignored my sully mood and wrapped her arms around me. She'd told me I couldn't hold out on her forever, and that she loved me anyway. She'd made me happy, as did Roman. We had our usual sibling arguments, but we did get on together well, and I miss him—both of them.

"Wherever you've just gone, come back to me, Rafael. They will pay. We need to keep our heads on straight." He glances toward the window. "He's still out there." He pauses. "Tell me how school was?"

I groan. "I hated it the first time around," I sarcastically drawl. "This time though, I think I'm going to enjoy it." I give him a large grin. "The scenery is beautiful."

He clears his throat, but I detect a laugh.

Closing my eyes, I settle down and admit, "I don't think she knows anything. No one at the school has time for her. They treat her like an outcast." I open my eyes and look straight into my dad's black eyes. "They treated me, the new guy, better than Wren." I rub at my brow. "It doesn't make sense when the Reverend is her father. Something isn't right with that."

"I'd have to agree. Based on the information we've received, I'd say she should be the most popular girl in school." He frowns. "Are you sure no one talks to her? What do they say about her? Are there whispers?"

"I caught a few, mainly that she's the weird girl who hangs around with butterflies." I sigh. "I asked about her father. It was whispered not to mention him, like it was a mortal sin or something." I shrug. "School gave me a bad feeling in the pit of my stomach.

"Something else I noticed, they have a sports field, but no sports teams. It isn't even mentioned. What school doesn't have a football team?" I shake my head and move to grab an apple from the sideboard. "I asked what they used it for and was told not to ask." With a mouthful of apple, I add while I chew, "The teachers seemed to *watch* me. I felt their eyes on me most of the day. It was weird." I munch on the rest of the apple. "One of them had to have told the Reverend about me chatting to Wren. Someone also had to have told him I walked home with her. She'd been startled and then panicked when she noticed his car heading toward us."

"You knew to be careful," Dad comments. "You also don't know if it was staff or a student who spied for *him*. Don't trust anyone, Rafael. Not even Wren."

"It wasn't Wren who told her father. I'm sure of

that. Her surprise and panic at seeing him couldn't have been for my benefit. You didn't see her face." I toss the apple core into the trash and sigh at the frown on Dad's face. To appease him, I add, "I won't trust anyone."

His eyes follow me out of the room. He knows my thoughts and knows I want to trust Wren more than anything.

I want to save her.

12

WREN

After spending the night in the basement, I haven't been able to get warm. The cold has seeped into my bones and I've been wearing a sweater all day. I've gotten more attention because of it, and I try not to care, but the truth is, I do care. I want friends. Maybe then I wouldn't feel so alone. In this town, I wouldn't trust anyone because they are all under the influence of the Reverend. Not Rafael. The Reverend had been worked up good and proper over Rafael and his father, and that made me curious. Other than the inheritance, has Marcel DeLacroix said or done something to the Reverend? On the odd occasion, curiosity would get the better of me, but after the nights I've spent in the basement over the years, I've finally learned to let it go. Unfortunately, I'm curious by nature, so it's been difficult.

Not only have I spent the day freezing cold, but Rafael has ignored me. He hasn't even glanced once in my direction. It hurts because I thought I'd finally have a friend to talk to who I could trust not to run and tell the Reverend everything I say. It didn't hurt that he's cute too. And now, he's passing time with the guys in the school yard.

An ache of sadness settles in my belly as I drop my head. My feet eat up the distance down the school driveway. It has been a long day after the lack of sleep the night before. A couple of times I caught myself drifting off to sleep during class and I know the Reverend will know about my unsightly behavior. It's a vicious cycle I'm unable to escape.

Unfortunately, my feet don't move fast enough because Emily, Lucy, and Alice catch up to me. They are the girls who I expect to eventually have their parents bring them inline. The Reverend won't stand *flirty* girls. They unknowingly go against his beliefs, and their parents will also pay the price.

Emily giggles, and asks, "What are you daydreaming about?" while her two friends snicker.

"She's probably wondering why that gorgeous boy

hasn't paid her any attention today," Alice says. "His eyes traveled over me often."

"I saw him looking at you, too." Lucy gushes. "Will your dad let you go out with him?"

"He wouldn't have to know. No one would." Alice turns a death glare to her friends, then openly stares across the yard to where Rafael stands.

His head swivels in our direction and when Alice waves, he hesitates and then waves back. I'm pretty sure his eyes had been on me. I ignore him and continue to walk, hurrying past the three girls. They rarely speak to me. No one does. So, it takes Alice saying, "We'll come over after we've done our home-work and hang out with you," for me to figure out what is going on.

No way are they coming over to my house. I don't even like them much. "I'm busy. Unless you want to hang out with the Reverend, then I suggest you stay away." I glance over my shoulder and notice how they've all paled at my suggestion. They remember who my father is. I turn back the way I'm going and smile to myself. Being the Reverend's daughter has its advantages.

The house is quiet when I step inside, which is to be expected with the Reverend still at his church. I have no idea what he does there all day, every day, but it seems to keep him busy. I head into the kitchen and pour myself a glass of milk, and then take a chunk of cheese and an apple upstairs to my bedroom. I have the same afternoon snack daily and I love it.

I open my bedroom window and can't keep my gaze from wandering over to the house next door. Marcel is on the back porch and there is no sign of Rafael. He's probably stayed behind at school to hang out with his *new* friends. Turning away, I retrieve my homework and sit at my small desk. As the story goes, the desk had once belonged to my mother from when she was a little girl. It certainly looks old enough, but I've learned over time that not everything the Reverend tells me about my mother is accurate. He will twist the truth to his liking. He does it with most things and his followers are none the wiser.

My homework takes no time at all to complete, then I'm downstairs with a salad prepared to go with the steak I've just grilled. After last night I want to be in his good graces, so I cooked another favorite meal of his. As I pull the steak from the grill, I hear his car shudder to a stop outside of the house. Everything is ready and in place as I put the food on the table. I glance toward the doorway and the Reverend stands with a smile on his face. It surprises me, which I hide behind my hand in a fake cough.

"You've made steak?" He shakes his head and cleans up at the sink. He grabs a towel and dries his hands before taking his seat at the head of the table. "All my discipline is paying off, Wren. You're becoming the perfect daughter. One day, you'll make someone the perfect wife."

My stomach rolls at the way he says wife. It isn't just the tone of voice, it's the way he looks at me when he says it. As though, maybe, he already has a plan. Someone in mind. I frown down into my plate while my belly flutters with unease.

Reverend laughs. "Don't worry that pretty little head of yours. I'll find you a strong man who will know how to handle your willful ways." He chuckles. "Eat."

Every bite tastes like cardboard and I try not to choke as I swallow. He knows exactly what he's doing. His actions are always calculated and measured for his entertainment. He loves being the one in control. He relishes it.

All through dinner he watches me, and his eyes stay on me while I clean up in the kitchen. By the time he tells me he's leaving for a while, I'm ready to have a meltdown. My nerves are dancing just under my skin and ready to shatter. I don't know if I'm about to start screaming or curl up in a ball. I glance one more time around the kitchen and then run upstairs to my room. I need a distraction so that my mind stops working overtime. Nothing I can come up with will be what the Reverend is actually planning. No one has a warped mind like him.

It will be warm in the glasshouse, so I slip into my PJ shorts and top. I'll be going to bed soon anyway. I shove my feet into sneakers and move toward my glasshouse. My heart quickens as I approach and everything in me settles as I walk inside. My butter-flies sleep, but a few flutter and perk up when they feel my presence.

A sudden tap on the glass at the back of the glasshouse makes me jump and my heart races into my throat at the thought of the Reverend coming back early. But no, that won't be him. He would never be in the back, and he would certainly never tap on the glass. I try to focus through the dark while I follow the shadow around to the door. It's him. Rafael. He stands in the open doorway, dressed as black as the night, his eyes fixed on me. Tiger Lily has settled on my shoulder and he watches, his movement frozen in time.

"This is your place?" he asks, moving closer.

I notice the moment he spots the bruising on my arm. It's obvious how it happened because there are finger marks imprinted on my skin. He steps close and, reaching out, he gently brushes over the dark marks with the tip of his fingers. A shiver of goosebumps quickly rises on my flesh and I catch my breath. His touch, albeit brief, had felt nice - more than nice if I'm honest. My eyes flicker to his and I find his are already focused on my face.

His fingers brush over the markings once more, and they linger this time. "I knew he wasn't happy to find you with me. I'm sorry..." He trails off.

I'm not sure he knows what he's doing because his hand is loosely wrapped around my elbow as he stares at me. His breathing accelerates, as does mine. His eyes drop to my chest. I don't have to look down to know that the heaviness I'm feeling is showing through my thin T-shirt. My body shudders at this new sensation.

The spell is suddenly broken when Rafael clears his throat and steps away. He turns in a circle looking around my glasshouse, and I can't help but feel proud of what he's seeing. My butterflies hover close but out of his reach as they watch him. He makes me feel weird and my body wants to press close to his.

The silence feels right, but after the way my body reacted to him, I'm nervous. When I'm nervous, I babble, and now is no different. "Tiger Lily is a monarch butterfly. I don't know why I call him Tiger Lily when he's a male. The name just stuck once I saw him. Before I'd had a chance to look him up on the Internet. A female monarch is yellow, while a male has the orange. That one over there hovering close to your face is a Phoebus Apollo. A female. You can tell because the female has more of the black coloring on her delicate wings." I need to shut up, but of course, I don't. "The American copper is pretty too with the upper side forewings a bright orange and the darker outside border and eight or nine spots." I inhale to continue when Rafael puts his hands up.

"I won't remember all that. They just look pretty, I guess." He winces, shrugging his shoulders.

"I think you should go." The words fall out of my mouth and I wish I could take them back. I really don't want him to go, but I'll be in trouble if the Reverend finds him here, or even discovers he's been here.

"Your father, huh?" he comments, his lips twitching into a teasing smirk. "I'll go, if you can get a butterfly to sit on my hand."

"You don't think I can do it?" I counter. "Be prepared to be surprised." I snicker.

Tiger Lily steps on my fingers when I reach for him and I bring him closer to my face. "Be good, Tiger Lily," I whisper.

Rafael watches me closely and when I move into his space, he stands his ground, his eyes narrowing. "Hold your arm outwards," I instruct. Swallowing hard in my nervousness of being so close to a boy, I reach out with Tiger Lily and rest my hand on top of Rafael's. Our eyes meet and hold while feelings I don't know what to do with run through my body. I feel the light blush on my face as heat rises. Rafael's soft gaze caresses my face and focuses on my lips for a few moments before his eyes return to mine.

It's then that I totally feel our connection. Tiger Lily rises from my hand and as I give our hands a sidelong look, I watch my beautiful friend land on Rafael's fingers. He catches his breath and watches in awe as some of the other butterflies follow and land along his arm and mine. I hold my breath at the beauty unfolding in front of my own eyes. The butterflies find places along our arms to settle until we can no longer see our skin. Rafael moves his hand slightly and tilts mine so that he can intertwine our fingers together. I struggle for breath at the feelings pushing for a way out. The intensity scares me. However, I can't move. I need his warmth and I enjoy the connection we've made through my butterflies.

Exhaustion sweeps through me so quickly, and without one thought, I lay my head on his shoulder. His heart races, as does mine, and then I tip my face up so I can watch him. I don't want to miss anything of this experience with him. His face is mesmerizing, then I catch a brief twitching of his lips before a laugh escapes him. I feel it in his whole body as we press together.

It ends as suddenly as it began.

Rafael catches his breath and abruptly steps away from me as though he's been burned. The butterflies fly from us and find plants and flowers to land on. Rafael gives me one long hard look before he leaves without a word.

My heart sinks. What happened? Why did he leave so suddenly? I know he reacts to me as I do him. The Reverend can never know. But I want to continue to be with Rafael. I want to continue to feel my body come alive when he looks at me in that special way he has about him - the way only Rafael looks at me. He might look dark and mysterious, and a bad boy to boot, but I don't think he is. I saw the real him tonight and I want to see it again. He needs me to show him the light, just like I need him to show me how to live and feel like a young girl should.

As I come to that conclusion, headlights wash over the glasshouse and then stay dazzling through the glass. I hear a car engine idle in the driveway and wonder who would be here with the Reverend so late at night. The Reverend is strict about his personal time.

"Wren," the Reverend hollers into the night, followed by the noise of his car locking. "We have a guest. Come into the house."

Panicked, I glance down at myself. I can't meet one of his guests dressed as I am. The Reverend will go crazy once his visitor leaves.

What should I do?

While I freak out, the Reverend appears in the doorway. "I told you to come inside. I meant immediately, Wren." His eyes glance over me and his lips twitch up in a smile. "I see why you would think your choice of clothing would be a problem." He pauses. "Tonight, it isn't." He indicates for me to lead the way.

I hesitate because I don't trust him not to do something in punishment for being outside in my sleepwear.

Stepping outside the glasshouse, I sense Rafael is close. That can't be, because he left in a hurry. Had he been on his way back when the Reverend arrived home? I'm not sure where he is hidden, but I somehow know he's out there watching. I swallow hard around the lump in my throat, hoping he won't interfere in whatever the Reverend wants.

Without missing a step, I glance around and can't see him. Doesn't mean he's left though.

The Reverend huffs out an impatient breath behind me, so I quickly make it to the doorway. Inside the kitchen, I stand frozen in place when I see who the guest is. Peter Wild always *looks* at me and I find him threatening. It isn't just that he looks at me, it's the *way* he looks at me. As though he pictures me without clothing, and it gives me cold chills.

"What did I tell you?" The Reverend breaks the silence. "She's all grown up."

"Hmm, she is." Peter Wild rubs his jaw and licks his lips as he stares at my body.

Uncomfortable is an understatement. I feel dirty and want to hide so the wicked man can never look at me again.

"You can go." The Reverend gives me a push toward the stairs.

There is no hesitation in my step as I shoot upstairs and into my bedroom, locking the door securely behind me.

I lean against it and will my racing heart to slow so that I can hear if there is any movement downstairs, or, God forbid, on the stairs.

13

RAFAEL

Leaving Wren's oasis, my feet stop abruptly. I'm running scared because of how she makes me feel, but there is something—the connection between us—holding me hidden in her back garden.

Instead of staying in the open, I slip behind a tree. It's not big, but it's dark enough that I should stay concealed.

My body feels tight after being so close to her. The butterflies have allowed me to share in the pleasure of their trust. I'm convinced the butterflies from the funeral had belonged to Wren. They had to be because why else would they trust me?

I can't see much inside of the house made of glass, but I sense movement and hear two cars approaching.

I listen wanting them to go past, but no such luck. Then I hear the Reverend shout for Wren and the hair on the back of my neck stands on end. The bastard has physically hurt Wren and it makes me want to hurt him far more than before.

Over the last three years, the level of my anger and need for vengeance have slowly moved to a dull ache, instead of the almost uncontainable rage it had been. I should be focused on that revenge…it's so close now that I could reach out and touch it. Except Wren is in the middle and all I can think about is protecting her. I feel her strength, but against the Reverend, she has none.

Movement catches my eye by the side of her house and the shape of a large man hovers close to the Reverend. Something is going on and I need to get closer to find out what. I move quietly under the cover of darkness and crouch beside the kitchen window. The porch comes to a stop under the window, so I get lucky. Voices are muffled, even when Wren joins them, it's difficult to hear anything.

It isn't long before I hear the sound of footsteps on the stairs and realize Wren has gone. Seconds tick by before I know what I'm going to do.

Keeping low and using shrubs, I climb the fence

between our two properties and sneak into my own house through the back door. I'm not so lucky.

Dad sits at the kitchen table with a mug of coffee in his hand. "Discover anything interesting?" His eyes move next door before they focus on mine.

"No, but I'm about to go and find out."

Dad doesn't get a chance to respond before I'm running upstairs to my room. I know exactly what I want and when it's in hand, I quickly run downstairs. "I'm going to talk to Wren."

I have no time to listen to Dad as he mumbles something about stupid idiots. Instead, I find a way onto Wren's roof.

14

WREN

I'M NOT SURE HOW LONG I SIT BEHIND MY LOCKED bedroom door, but a car moving away from the house indicates that Peter Wild has left. A few minutes later, I hear the Reverend come upstairs and go into his bedroom. He won't be out until morning.

My hands tremble as I get to my feet and move toward the window. I stare outside and look up into the clear night. Tonight there are no clouds and the stars are bright.

Careful to not disturb the peace, I open the window and gently climb onto the roof. I reach back inside for the blanket I keep close for these nightly stargazing activities. This is one of my favorite things to do when I'm not in the garden or puttering around inside the glasshouse. I spread out the blanket—careful I don't fall from the roof—and then settle down on my back. I sigh in relief and finally begin to relax as my eyes dance over the bright stars. I often wonder if there is life on a star or distant planet. I like to think there is.

Over my shoulder, a hissing sound makes me jump in the quiet night. I turn my head and hold my breath when a dark shadow appears—Rafael. He seems to like showing up around me at the most unexpected of times.

Looming over me, he places his hands on his hips and grins. "You look cute."

A blush starts to coat my cheekbones when I realize where we are. "You can't be here," I whisper. "The Reverend will kill us both if he finds you here with me."

Rafael shakes his head and gets comfortable on the blanket with me. There are a few inches separating us, but we can't be like this—at least, not here. My mind races until Rafael says, "I climbed up the opposite side of the house from where he sleeps. I won't let him hurt you, Wren. I promise."

Tears sting my eyes. "You can't promise me that. No one can."

He turns onto his side and his eyes look deeply into mine. "I won't let him hurt you." As his eyes move to my lips, he settles down on his back, his gaze no longer on me. "I'm sorry I left before. I haven't felt...*anything* in a long time, and you made me feel." He pauses. "I've never seen anything as beautiful as you with your butterflies, and to experience a small portion of what you must every time they're with you, it made me happy. For those few seconds with you, I felt really happy, Wren, and then I remembered why I don't deserve to be happy, and I left."

"Why don't you deserve to be happy?" I pause. "And you didn't leave." I keep my gaze on the stars because I think it would be easier for him to answer, plus I don't want to see his face if he lies to me about staying.

"I don't want to talk about it now. Maybe one day I will," he finally answers and sighs. "I was leaving but something compelled me to stay." I feel his gaze as he asks, "How did you know?"

I shrug. "I felt you close, which makes no sense."

He offers a kind of grunt in response before

changing the subject. "Has your father always been such an asshole?"

I wince at his bluntness, but I don't contradict him because that's what I often call the Reverend in my head. "I don't think so. I remember he used to take me for ice cream in town when I was a little girl. He'd take me to the hair salon, and to the diner for supper. I don't know exactly when things really started to change. It was like my father had died and the Reverend took his place. The change was sudden and drastic. Like he'd gone to sleep one night and woken up as the man he is now. I was too young to understand what happened back then, plus, if I'm honest, I never really paid attention."

"Power went to his head." Rafael's fingers gently brush my hand and I realize he's giving me time to get used to his touch before he intertwines our fingers together. "I like holding your hand," he admits. "I wanted to do this today in school so you wouldn't feel alone." He squeezes my fingers. "I didn't want to be in the yard with those idiots. I wanted to be walking home with you. After yesterday, I figured you'd be in more trouble if word got back to the Reverend. So, I stayed away from you. I don't want you to be in trouble because of me."

Silence follows his words and I'm happy to just lie here beside him while he holds my hand. The stars above us twinkle down and I feel brave. As though being here with him gives me the courage to speak my mind. For the first time since I can remember, I know he is someone who will listen and not repeat what I say.

"It hurt that you ignored me today, but now that I know why I'm okay with that. I've never had a friend before." I hesitate. "Are we friends?" We stare at each other in the moonlight.

"You're my only friend, Wren."

I smile and turn back to the stars. "I'm glad."

"I don't really know how to talk to girls anymore. My social skills deserted me a while ago."

Thanks to Alice, I know a brief history of what happened to Rafael and his family, so I stay clear of that for now. I'm sure that's in the "I'll tell you later part."

"Pretend I'm a boy, then."

He chokes on a laugh. "Trust me, you look like no boy I've ever seen."

Smiling, I untangle our hands and roll onto my side so I can look at him. "The Reverend had a visitor tonight." I pause. "Peter Wild. The Reverend likes him, but he gives me a creepy feeling. I feel dirty after the way the man looks at me."

"What do you mean?" Rafael asks, menace in his voice. "Did he touch you, Wren?"

"He kept moving his eyes over my body and it gave me a bad feeling. I got out of there." I chew my lip. "He didn't touch me."

Rafael goes into his own head while I look over his face. He really is beautiful to look at but it's his lips my eyes keep focusing on.

"I don't feel dirty when you look at me…or how you *looked* at me that day."

Rafael blinks and I know he's thinking about that day in the window. He swallows hard, his voice uneven as he asks, "How do you feel?"

I feel a deep blush run across my cheeks, but I'm not going to back down with this boy whom I really like. "I feel hot and flushed." I lick my lips. "Swollen."

"Wren," Rafael hisses. "Stop talking, and please stop looking at me like that."

My eyes snap to his. "Like what?"

He groans and closes his eyes. "Like you want to kiss me."

Of course, my eyes stray back to his lips and I lick mine. "I don't know what it's like to kiss a boy," I admit.

Rafael stares into my eyes and abruptly sits up, grabbing me so I don't fall backwards from the roof. He turns me so I'm safe and leans over me. "I like you, Wren, and I'm not sure what to do about it." He glances away. "Let's try being friends, okay?"

Disappointment flutters through me even as I agree. "Friends."

He nods and withdraws a piece of paper from his back pocket. "I drew this for you." Hesitantly, he hands it over.

I open the paper and find myself shocked speechless at the sketch of my butterflies and me. He's drawn it from memory of the day we first laid eyes on each other. I'm in the garden with my arms outstretched and the butterflies covering my arms and shoulders. He even captured Tiger Lily on the tip of my nose.

"Say something," he begs, embarrassment in his tone.

"It's amazing." Tears clog my throat as I look from the sketch to him. "It's the nicest thing anyone has ever given me." A tear escapes and slips down my cheek. "You have a talent with pencils."

"My therapist suggested drawing might help me to relax. I just didn't know I could draw as well as I do."

"Well! Thank you." I smile through my happy tears.

"I'm glad you like it." His lips twitch up in a half smile.

"I love it."

Silence follows and when I find myself going to sleep, I whisper, "My mother left when I was young. The butterflies are my only friends, well, until you moved in next door." I sigh. "In my own stupid babbling way, I'm trying to tell you that if you need to talk, about anything, you can find me in the glasshouse or here on the roof."

Rafael studies me for a while, and says, "I'll remember that, and when I'm ready to tell you what happened in New Orleans, I'll find you." Then, to my surprise, he hesitates before leaning forward to press a kiss on my forehead. "Go and get some sleep and I'll see you tomorrow."

I'm sad when he moves away after one more glance at me because with Rafael, I've let my guard down and have felt more relaxed than I have in a long time. I want to beg him to stay with me, to crawl into my bed and just hold me while I sleep. I know without asking he would do it. All I need to do is ask.

The only thing that stops me from saying the words is the man sleeping in the room next to mine.

The Reverend can never know of my growing friendship with the boy next door.

15

RAFAEL

Dad meets me at the back door as though he too had been outside. I pause and then enter in front of him. We keep the lights off and move into the darkness of the old house.

"I wasn't spying on you," Dad whispers. "I wanted to make sure you were okay." He runs his hands through his hair. "You don't seem to be thinking straight is all, and I'm worried you're not focused."

"Dad." I grit my teeth. "I'm twenty. I'm also older and wiser after the last three years. I know Wren is under my skin, but there is nothing I can do about that...the butterflies connect us in some way."

He gives me a bemused smirk and raises a brow. "Butterflies? Rafael, that is not very original."

"I'm going to bed." I head upstairs and hear Dad's footfalls behind me.

"Rafael, I'm trying to understand what's going on in that head of yours," he says frustrated. "You're my son, and all I have left."

"Dad." I turn. "You saw the butterflies that day. I think they belonged to Wren. The way they respond to her is unusual. There is something…" I trail off because I don't understand how or why. I'm not even sure I'll ever be able to explain it.

"Who was there?"

Dad switches gears and I take a minute to run my hands through my hair. I tug on the long strands. "Peter Wild."

I'm about to ask him if he can find out about the man when I notice the look of hatred on Dad's face. He knows him.

"Tell me." I wait.

"He was with Lucas Jacobs in Amarillo. You, of course, only know Lucas as the Reverend," he says through barely controlled rage. "We didn't have anything to hold Wild or Jacobs on back then. A couple of times over the years, your mom thought she saw Wild watching her. Each time I would look into it but could never find any trace of him. Frustrating as hell." He holds my gaze. "And now you're saying you've seen him here? This isn't good at all."

"Do you think he's been here all along with the Reverend?"

"I never believed they'd gone their separate ways. They both slowly disappeared off the face of the earth."

Dad looks gray as I slowly approach him and rest a hand on his arm. "Dad?"

He looks haunted when he tilts his face to meet my gaze. "I'm thinking Wild must have been the one to go after your mom." He sits heavily on the stairs and drops his face into his hands. "On the day we raided, I went straight for Sarah, needing to protect her. The sneer on Wild's face that day was something I won't ever forget."

Not knowing how to help, I stay silent and watch him.

"Wild had a temper, and everything we were told back then was hearsay. No one had actually seen anything. The case in North Texas had been solid enough to get a warrant for the raid. Various members—Jacob and Wild—had hidden their involvement well. There was also no evidence that either man had taken part in an underaged wedding, nor had there been any drugs found. I suspected Wild had disposed of his bride when he'd finished with her. Again, no evidence. I felt helpless not being able to get anything solid enough to hold them longer than we did. Perhaps if I'd pushed and pushed, then your mom and Roman would still be alive." His voice breaks and I find myself swallowing back my own tears.

"We'll get them, Dad. We're here and they can't do anything about it because of the house. They'd be stupid to do anything to you or me because they know you're former DEA." I grab his shoulder and squeeze. "I hope you know that I have to protect Wren. I can't leave her to them."

"I know, son. I had no intention of leaving her, I just wanted you to keep your friendship with her as *just* that."

I offer a wry smile. "We are friends, Dad."

"You like her though."

"Yeah, I do. A lot more than I should."

Shaking himself free of the demons that have surrounded him for all these years, Dad sighs. "Let's sleep on it." Dad turns and goes into his room, troubled.

I move up the spiral staircase to my room and sag against the closed door. My head feels like it's about to explode.

They made a mistake when they came after Mom and Roman. A big mistake.

Knowledge is a powerful weapon that the Reverend has used to his advantage for years. No more.

We are going to stop him and we're going to rescue Wren in the process.

WREN

COLD SHIVERS SLIP DOWN MY SPINE FROM THE MOMENT I step foot on school grounds. Unable to put my finger on what is off, I glance at the few students milling around outside of the building. Their conversation stops. Something is *really* off.

The Reverend had been acting strangely at breakfast, and he'd had a mysterious grin on his face. That bothered me too. There is a golf ball sized lump in my stomach, and it won't go anywhere.

I nervously swallow and walk into the building. The hallway is quiet even though students loiter around. I keep my head down and move to my locker. The turmoil continues to grow inside of me as I enter the classroom.

A new teacher is writing on the whiteboard: Mr. Bradshaw.

My eyes focus on Rafael at the back of the room. His gaze moves back and forth between me and the empty seat beside him.

Hiding a smile, I sit in the seat two away from him, desperately wishing I was free to sit beside him. Rafael keeps giving me sidelong glances. I know this because I find myself doing the same until the classroom fills up.

Mr. Bradshaw shows his disinterest in the class. His eyes are drawn to the hands on the clock more times than anything or anyone in class.

In front of me, Alice twitches, and her head tilts to the side. I get the impression she wants to tell me something, which is odd for her. She babbled the other day, but I put that down to excitement. Today, not so much. No one else appears to notice, and Mr. Bradshaw, once again, glances at the clock. A frown mars his brow.

I'm not curious by nature, however, over the past few years, I've watched and listened without drawing attention to the fact. In the future, the knowledge I have could mean my freedom. The something known as "the Reverend" hasn't been right in this town for a long time. His sermon demands worship and for a reason I haven't fathomed yet, they allow it.

As I begin to raise my hand to ask a question, the classroom door opens and a teacher struggles inside carrying a shipping box. Without a word being exchanged between him and Mr. Bradshaw, the man leaves after setting the box down. Mr. Bradshaw smiles and opens it with a flare that surprises me considering how unemotional the man has been since the beginning of the class period.

"This is what I've been waiting for." He digs into the box and retrieves a book. It looks like some sort of journal, which baffles me, and he continues, "All students are receiving one of these today. You are expected to keep a journal from now on. Write down everything you do to help your parents, and the Reverend. Everything has to be written down in this book. The Reverend will choose ten journals a week to read. No exception." He looks so pleased with himself, and all I can do is stare in shock.

I want to vomit.

I glance around the classroom and notice the look of pleasure on some faces, and utter fury on Rafael's. His fists are clenched so tightly on the desk that I'm surprised he doesn't slam them down into the old desk and snap it in half. I don't understand any of this. Has the Reverend finally lost his mind? Is this why everyone has been acting weird? I don't know what to think anymore, but this is too much. Apart from Rafael, it doesn't appear that it's too much for the others. Had they known?

Mr. Bradshaw slowly passes the journals out, and repeats, "Remember, everything you do to help your parents, and the Reverend, must be written in this book. If you misbehave or get in trouble with anyone, it has to be written down. Any test scores from school have to be written down." He smiles. "Because of your gift, I will allow you to leave the classroom five minutes early."

Sitting in shock, I watch as though in slow motion the other students smiling and clutching their new journals. As if they've received a special gift - something they've always wanted but never had, until now. I briefly turn it over in my hand, it's flimsy to the touch. The covering is dark brown, and ruled lines are on the pages. I don't want to see anymore so I don't bother reading the headings.

Rafael bumps into my desk and I move my shocked gaze to his. "Meet me around back," he whispers while moving out of the classroom.

Mr. Bradshaw watches closely before he turns his attention to Rafael and his eyes follow him as he leaves.

Not wanting to be left alone in the classroom, I grab my things and dash to the door, where he stops me. "Wren Jacobs, correct?"

My hackles rise as I slowly turn.

"I was told by the Reverend to say hello to you. Your father, um, the Reverend is a good man. I hope you know how lucky you are to have him as your"—he coughs—"Reverend." His smile is friendly and open, it's obvious by the color high on his cheeks that he's embarrassed.

His demeanor is meant for me to drop my guard and maybe do or say something to him. Maybe trust him. However, I have no plans to completely let my guard down around him. After all, this man obviously worships the Reverend.

"I'll make sure he knows you followed his *instruction*." I reach for the doorknob. "Is it okay to go now? We only get twenty minutes for break?"

"Yes, of course."

My feet can't carry me away from the classroom and Mr. Bradshaw quickly enough. It's such a relief to get outside and into the warm sun that I lift my face and close my eyes unaware of the eyes on me. A hiss from over my shoulder distracts me and my eyes snap open. That's when I see them—Alice and her posse, and the guys they hang out with. They stand around the yard whispering while they stare at me. Nervousness washes through me as another hiss, this time louder, comes from over my shoulder.

"Wren! Over here."

Glaring at the others, I hold my head up high and dash to the corner where I heard Rafael's voice. The moment I'm out of sight, Rafael takes my hand and quickly pulls me around the building to the tool shed. The wooden building smells of oil and mulched grass from the lawn mower that has been used recently. Two lawn chairs are open at one end and it looks like someone has already taken advantage of the secluded spot. "I wonder if this is what's called a man shed," I muse.

"Yes, well, I'm not sure the *Reverend* would be happy to discover this little set up." Rafael waggles his brows and lifts up a batch of magazines. My eyes pop wide at the sight of the naked woman on the cover. Rafael laughs. "And I think a 'man shed' is a term for that." He snickers and waves his arms around before he shoves the magazines back under one of the chairs. "The other—"

"Don't you dare say it out loud!" I gingerly sit in one of the chairs, and when I make sure it can take my weight, I lean back and place my backpack on my lap.

A soft smile teases his lips as he sits in the other chair—the one with the naughty magazines beneath. Rafael reaches into his bag and pulls out a sandwich bag. "I'm hungry. Dad makes my lunch because he knows I wouldn't eat until I get home otherwise."

I frown. "Why?"

"Because it takes forever for me to get up in the morning. I don't even have time for breakfast. I struggle to get to sleep early, so I stay up drawing. I like to read, too. It settles the turmoil inside of me." Rafael eats in silence and refuses to meet my curious gaze.

17

RAFAEL

"WHAT DO YOU READ?" SHE ASKS, GIVING ME A sidelong glance.

"Books," I mumble around a bite of my sandwich.

"Funny boy! What type of books?"

I slowly chew and see her growing impatience, so I reply, "Paranormal." I swallow my bite down with some water. "I like the *Hunger Games* series." Sadness suddenly hits me. "They were the last books my mom bought me." I become *too* interested in my sandwich while I try to hide the emotion my memory brought with it.

"I think that is really nice. You have something your mom bought you because she knew you liked the stories. They were bought with love. I don't have anything of my mom's, other than the old wooden desk in my bedroom." She shrugs. "The Reverend said it came from Mom's side of the family, but I'm not really sure about anything anymore." She stares off, and adds, "I've read *The Hunger Games*, well, the first book that is. The Reverend gave it to me. I don't think he realizes just what the book is about, otherwise, he'd have burned it."

"You have spirit, Wren," I say quietly. "Don't let the Reverend take it away from you."

"I won't," she sadly agrees, not looking as though she'll be able to keep that promise.

It's nice just sitting with her. She doesn't fill the void with senseless chatter. I know she is beside me and that is good enough. Every now and again a slight blush creeps onto her face. I know she's attracted to me and I don't think she knows what to do about it. It's obvious she has no experience with boys, and the way she looks at me makes my body hot and achy. I feel a deep throb behind my zipper. She's so innocent and that scares me. Even now, a deep red blush covers her cheeks while she keeps her face averted. It isn't the only thing my eyes notice as I watch her, and maybe I shouldn't have stared for as long as I have.

I briefly close my eyes from the sight of her, but I have to look again.

She is beautiful.

Her breathing has gotten heavy and I don't know what to do.

That's a first.

She meets my eyes before quickly looking away. I want to capture her face in my hands and turn her toward me so I can taste her sweet lips. Instead, I offer her a piece of apple, which Dad cuts for me each day.

I grin at the surprise on her face. "Enjoy."

She turns and hooks my gaze with hers. I caress her face with my dark gaze and swallow hard as though a piece of apple has gotten stuck in my throat. I'm happy at her reaction—confused and frustrated too. No matter what is happening between us, I have to make sure the Reverend never finds out. He won't like it and if he can't get to me, he'll get to Wren. That isn't acceptable.

Wren suddenly starts coughing and patting her chest. I rub her back as I sit forward, and then pass her my water. "Drink."

She takes a deep pull and only slightly coughs. "I forgot to not breathe too deeply in here. I got a strong smell of oil." She coughs again. "Gross." She screws up her pert nose. "It really doesn't smell good in here."

"No, it doesn't. It's the only place I could think of where we wouldn't be watched." I shrug. "Didn't mean to nearly kill you."

"I'm fine now." She becomes solemn and looks at me, so I raise a brow in question. "What do you think about the journal?" she asks.

My jaw clenches. "I think it's a load of crap."

"Me too," she whispers. "I sensed something was off this morning." She pauses. "What do you think is going on?"

"I don't know, but have you looked inside the book?" I reach for my copy and flip it open. "There is some crap about obedience and punishment on the first page. We have to sign our names under it saying we agree. The rest of the book has printed lines, with sections for good behavior and bad behavior. There is also a space for parents to sign after each entry." I toss the book, satisfied when I hear it clunk on the lawnmower before tumbling to the floor. "This is bullshit."

Full of frustration in more ways than one, I start pacing in front of Wren. I feel like a caged lion, but it's not because the journal affects me. I'll write whatever shit the Reverend wants to see, with Dad's help, but what about everyone else in the school?

The journals, and what are expected from us is far too much. From what Dad has been told, the Reverend demands obedience, from the girls especially. He'd been responsible for the marriages of underage girls in Amarillo, despite what little evidence they could find to prove it. Dad is positive he has the same plans in Port Michael. One of my worries after Peter Wild had visited the Reverend's house and looked at Wren, is that the Reverend is using Wren to demand loyalty from Wild. Will the man let Wren be taken by Wild, though? That is a burning question. I hope not, but from what I've heard about the Reverend, I wouldn't put it past him. Wild, although, a friend of the Reverend's, likes to do what he wants, when he wants. Dad thinks Wild has his own agenda. I certainly believe the Reverend does too.

Wondering about the Reverend brings my gaze back to Wren, and her beautiful eyes swim with unshed tears. The moment I spot them, she blinks them away. I drop into a crouch in front of her and rest my hands on her knees. "Something bigger is going on, Wren. You have to see that."

"I know. This feeling in the pit of my stomach won't go away. It's as though some unconscious part of me is aware of what is about to happen, and it won't let me settle down." She grips my hands with hers, and asks, "Does your father know? Is that why the Reverend doesn't like him?"

I desperately want to tell Wren everything, but, at the moment, I know I can't tell her. Not only have I promised my father, but I'm not sure Wren would be able to carry on as normal if she knew what her father was capable of. She has a good idea on a personal level. However, she has no clue about his past. It would be written all over her expressive face.

"My father is glad to be out of the city." It isn't a lie. "I got in a lot of trouble in the city, Wren. I was mixed up with the wrong crowd and kept getting arrested," I admit, and lean against the door, my head back so I have a clear view of the cobwebs on the ceiling. "I'm not proud of it. For months I wasn't in a good place. I eventually started getting better, but then they tried to pull me back into the group. So, we moved out here." I shrug. "My father will laugh his ass off when I show him the journal." I smile. "It wouldn't surprise me if he didn't make me sit with him while we made up shit to go in it."

"I wish I could do that," Wren says. "The journal will have been one-hundred-percent *his* decision, which means he'll expect me to have it filled before he gets home each evening."

We hold eye contact until the bell rings for the next period. Wren takes a step toward the door, but I don't move out of the way. I reach up and brush a lock of hair over her shoulder and then caress her cheek.

Her skin turns a beautiful rosy shade at my touch and there's a slight tremble in her hands. I caress her delicate neck with a finger and watch as she nervously licks her lips. I cup her jaw and tilt her face up to mine. I whisper softly, "I'm always here for you, Wren. If you ever need sanctuary, come to me." I kiss her forehead and step into her body. She sighs at the full body contact, and the groan that releases from my mouth surprises us both. My hands reach for her hips and I pull her close. "We have to get to class."

"Oh!" She blinks hard and I chuckle, letting her go. She scrambles and collects her bag before she dashes past me into the bright sunlight.

"Wren?" I call.

She glances over her shoulder.

"We have a date on your roof later," I whisper, and dash off in front of her.

18

WREN

ON MY WAY AROUND THE FRONT OF THE SCHOOL, THE
sound of an engine draws my attention along the
driveway. A brown UPS truck moves slowly toward
the school building. I frown. I don't remember ever
seeing a delivery truck in town.

In fact, as far back as I remember, no delivery
truck has been allowed in town. I've seen plenty of
UPS trucks at the church where deliveries usually
take place. The packages will then get delivered to the
relevant person.

"Don't you"—Mr. Bradshaw's angry words startle
me, and I drop my book bag—"have a class to go to?"

Collecting my bag from the ground, I turn as Mr.
Bradshaw, followed by four teachers, make their way

to the truck. Mr. Bradshaw pauses and looks from me to the truck and back again. "You better go inside, Wren. You don't want the Reverend to know you were late for class."

I sigh heavily at the same old line. The Reverend has always been used against me. Giving one last glance to the UPS truck, I enter the school building.

The Reverend uses me to set an example to others. *Oh, look at my obedient daughter*. What utter nonsense. The words "disobey" and "obey" grate on my last nerve.

Annoyed and feeling unsettled, I stride into the classroom with confidence, and everyone stares. I'm tired of everything—the stares, the whispers—but most of all, I'm tired of my life in Port Michael.

It isn't legal the way I'm treated and punished. The call I'd once made to child services had cost me three nights in the basement. Because when *he* wanted to and put in a real effort with his appearance, the Reverend could be charming and have the ladies falling at his feet. A long time ago, I thought he was my handsome daddy, with his sandy blond hair and strong arms to carry me in. I soon changed my mind about that. He'd certainly charmed the pants off the stuck-up woman who had been given my call to investigate. She'd been all smiles and flirty with the Reverend, who had sweet-talked his way into a good report.

One of these days I'll get my own back.

Mr. Bradshaw walks inside the classroom with two large boxes on a wheeled carrier. Guess he replaced our second period teacher too as he's not in here. I'd be lying if I said my curiosity hadn't been piqued, along with the rest of our class. We all look expectantly at the front, and as Mr. Bradshaw stands and looks over us, I get *that* funny feeling in my belly again. Not moving, I stay frozen in my chair as the boxes are placed on the floor and opened.

"To make the school look good, the church has decided to provide uniforms for the pupils."

My heart sinks to my toes, and I'm fairly sure my blood cells follow as the color drains from my face. Others glance around the room and I try not to notice the eyes lingering on me. It's their way of saying they blame me for all this. It worries me that all this change is happening, and on the same day.

I notice Mr. Bradshaw staring in Rafael's direction, so I cast my eyes over to him and notice he's shot his hand up in the air for attention. His slouched position and the ruffled look make me want to smile.

My heart certainly turns over at the sight of him. The moment his words leave his mouth, I cringe. "Are our parents aware of what is happening today?"

"Yes, except your father is not. He isn't a member of the church, so he wouldn't have been informed."

"Does that mean I don't have to wear one? Because, as you can see, I have my own."

"Biker uniform is not a school uniform, so as such, we have a uniform with your name on it, Mr. DeLacroix." At that, Mr. Bradshaw tosses Rafael a package, which he catches on reflex. The items inside look navy blue and red.

Rafael scowls and places the package to one side of his desk. He has no interest and is angry. I feel sick as I watch Mr. Bradshaw sort out the uniforms into neat piles on the desks at the front of the room. When he's ready, he indicates for the students at those desks to pass the packages back. I take the one offered to me with trembling hands. Whatever it is for the girls, ours are a deep red in color. I stare blindly at it and want this day to be over with. Nothing is right about today. Every…single…thing is wrong. First the journals, and now the uniforms. I can't help but feel like there is a message in it all for me. That the Reverend is telling me something. I'm just not sure what it is.

A school uniform isn't the end of the world, I try to reason silently. Tons of schools have them and they can actually look nice. If only there wasn't a rock in my belly telling me this is all wrong. The uniforms haven't been intended to smarten us all up, it's more to keep us under their thumb in some way.

I tune out Mr. Bradshaw's lecture and hope he isn't telling us anything important. My mind won't let me listen when it's so full of panic. I know what is happening isn't right, but, at seventeen, how can I do anything to stop it? Who will I go to for help?

Throughout the rest of the school day, I keep feeling Rafael's gaze on me, but I don't glance over at him. I feel ashamed that today's changes are somehow all connected to me. The Reverend is my father, and it makes me sick to know that he is responsible for the new...regime. I don't know what else to call it. Regime sounds more right than wrong, and when I'm leaving school, the last straw for me today is watching the computers being removed from the building. They pile them up inside a black van while the Reverend stands and watches.

His eyes narrow when he spots me, but they noticeably darken when Rafael appears next to me. The Reverend's body tightens, and as he turns toward me, Rafael runs down the steps at the front of the school. I hold my breath wondering what the Reverend will do. As luck would have it, he does nothing, but indicates with his head that he wants to go home.

Tears run down my face and my breathing becomes heavy as a darkness settles inside of me. I can't understand what has happened to suddenly warrant the changes that have been made. It's as though a plan had been formed and suddenly implemented.

Going home across the back fields from school, I feel totally let down with everything and everyone who is supposed to be important in my life. Then I remember Rafael and the heat between us during break. He's becoming important to me, and he certainly hasn't let me down—not yet anyway. However, I feel that in my upside-down world, he is the only one I can trust and that he will always come for me when I need him.

THE REVEREND ASKS ME TO TRY MY UNIFORM ON FOR him after dinner. The material of the dress is thin and made of soft cotton. The hem brushes mid-calf, and as I turn in a circle in front of the mirror in the bathroom, I realize with horror that I'm too exposed. My cleavage shows, and when I stand a certain way, you can see my white panties. I frown at myself wondering why we're expected to wear revealing clothing. This can't be real. This has to be a mistake. There is no way the Reverend will let me wear anything like this in public. I can't go downstairs looking like this.

I dash back into my bedroom and toss off the dress, then I quickly change into dark-colored tights and a stretchy tank top in the same dark blue color. I tug the dress back over my head and dart back into the bathroom, checking I look presentable and nothing private shows. To my relief, my body will remain a secret.

"Wren," The Reverend shouts. "I haven't got all night."

Grinding my teeth together, I walk downstairs. He waits in the kitchen with his arms folded tightly in front of him, and his chin tucked into his chest. His eyes lift first as he looks at me, and then his whole body seems to relax, and he smiles.

It's the smile that stops me. It isn't quite a happy

pleasant smile, more like a sinister, I know something you don't smile. My heart thumps against my breastbone as he walks toward me and indicates for me to slowly turn. "What do you think?"

"It's different than I expected when they were given to us today. The material is thin, and I hope will help to keep me cool in the heat outside. I think we'll all look nice in a uniform." I want to escape so I can meet Rafael on the roof. There is only one way that will happen quickly, and that is if I show support for what he's given me and the other students.

"I thought so too." He rubs his chin. "And the other thing you were given today. Do you have thoughts on that?"

I swallow and think it best to keep my mouth fully closed on my opinions about the journal. "No, sir. The journal is different." I shrug. "You know I like journals." I like the flowery journals I can write about the butterflies in. I've never kept a personal one before.

"Something tells me you're not happy." He stays relaxed and perches his hip on the cabinet next to me so that he can watch me closely. "I want the truth, Wren, please. How do you feel about the changes that took place today?" He sighs. "If you are honest with me, I promise not to punish you for speaking your mind. Tonight, can be a night off if you like. But I really want to know your thoughts."

It's strange of him to talk to me in this way. He's never offered a "night off," as he put it. Knowing Rafael is close helps with my confidence for the first time in a long time.

"I don't like the idea of others reading a journal I've written my thoughts in, or that I'd want them to know what I've done to please you or done to warrant a punishment. I think it should be kept private between parent and child." His smile tightens and anger flashes in his eyes. He isn't happy and I doubt it's really a night off. But I keep going, almost as though I'm unable to stop. "I like the uniform, even though I thought it was weird at first. I think having all the girls wearing these, and the boys match us in their blue pants and red shirts will be nice to see around the school. I don't understand why the computers have been removed, though."

Wren, shut up!

I snap my mouth closed, knowing I've gone too far with my thoughts as the Reverend stares at me with a thoughtful look on his face. "You look pretty in the dress." He moves from the kitchen, and shouts behind him, "I have work to do. I'll see you in the morning." The door to his office closes.

Confusion wells inside of me.

I don't know what to make of the Reverend. He never gives me a compliment without an ulterior motive. And I'm certainly not used to him asking my opinion on anything. Nothing will change because of my comments. He doesn't work like that. The only advice he takes is his own.

Standing in the kitchen like a home accessory won't get me anywhere, so I turn and flee upstairs to my room, hoping Rafael really does wait on the roof for me.

I QUICKLY REMOVE THE DRESS AND SLIP INTO A PAIR OF sleep shorts before climbing onto the roof to find Rafael waiting. Watching my step so I don't fly off the roof like a butterfly and land with a cry, I take Rafael's offered hand and settle beside him. I don't miss the quick once-over he gives me before he lies back and stares up at the sky.

"It's cloudy tonight," I comment, disappointed the stars aren't out for us. I turn and stare at Rafael instead. He's more gorgeous than the night sky—at least, I think so. His face is cast in shadow and the deep scar on his cheek stands out like a pulsing vein. His lips are firm and sensual, and it does things to my body when my eyes are drawn to them. The set of his chin suggests a stubborn streak, which I know he has. He wears his black and silky straight hair shaggy, and I like it best when it sticks up because it gives him a lazy look.

Pleasure suddenly softens his face and he holds my gaze. "You like what you see, huh?" His lips twitch. "Because I do." His body follows his gaze as he turns onto his side to face me. His hand lifts and brushes a tendril of hair from my face.

He leaves me breathless and I feel heat rising in my body. It feels strange and new, but good. "I do." My voice is barely a whisper. He hears me. His eyes drift toward my lips and narrow, until he suddenly pulls away and lies back down.

"That's good," he mutters, and coughs. "So, did the Reverend say anything about what happened at school today?"

Because I need time to think about my reaction to him and what I should do about it, I let him change the subject. "He asked my opinion and told me I wouldn't be punished for speaking my mind." I shrug and stare up at the small clearing of clouds, enjoying the hint of stars. "He told me I looked nice in the dress."

I feel Rafael's stare and refuse to acknowledge it. My body still feels warm and different. It's a nice feeling and I'm happy to note I've only ever felt like this with Rafael. Does it mean I want him to kiss me? Do I want to do other things too? Perhaps I do. He settles down again and his hand reaches for mine. I hesitate and then intertwine my fingers with his. It feels really good to hold his hand. I feel safe and warm when we are like this.

"How do you feel in the dress?"

"The dress is thin and will keep me cool."

"I sense a but…"

"It's too revealing. I'll have to wear dark, um, things underneath."

He frowns and after a quick glance over me, averts his gaze. "That bad, huh?"

"It is. It shows everything…and I mean *everything*. Leaves nothing to the imagination." Embarrassed, I admit, "I don't have any bras that fit, so I need to make sure I wear a dark stretchy tank top underneath." My cheeks burn in the darkness.

Rafael groans. "I wish I didn't know that." He chuckles. "I look like a dork in the pants and shirt," he offers.

"I can't imagine you in any other color but black."

"I've worn black for a long time." He shrugs. "Since I turned fifteen. The girls thought I was hot." The corners of his mouth turn up in a smirk.

I roll my eyes. "It's all in your head." I tease.

He pokes me in the side. "You think I'm hot." He pokes me again.

Giggling, I grab his hand. "I'm not admitting anything because I think you have a big enough head as it is."

His eyes gleam with laughter and...something more. I feel myself go completely still as he comes closer and leans over me. He stares down at me before placing a kiss to the tip of my nose. "You have had my attention since I saw you in the garden covered with butterflies. I should have realized then you'd be a pain in my ass."

"What?" I gasp. "You pay me a compliment and then you take it away in your next breath."

"I'm joking." He tugs me against his side, and I rest my head on his shoulder. "I'm worried, Wren." He becomes serious. "My dad said the Reverend is the instigator of whatever goes on around here." He gives me a squeeze and sits up. I follow. "And that means you're in the middle because he's your dad."

"He's changed, or maybe, he's always been the way he is, and I've just grown up enough now to notice." I slip my fingers into his hand and he holds on tight, caressing my thumb with his. "I don't think he'd hurt me intentionally." I stop as the lie leaves my lips. He has hurt me. Intentionally and unintentionally. But he's my dad for all his flaws. Don't I owe him some loyalty, even a small lie because of how he used to be? I sigh. "But then, I never thought he'd be as controlling as he's become." That, at least, is the truth.

Rafael gives me a sidelong glance and refuses to look elsewhere until I finally turn and meet his eyes. "Why are you looking at me like that?"

"I'm debating whether to ask you something." He turns away and whispers, "Do you know anything about religious cults?"

I blink a few times in surprise and shake my head. "I read something online in the library at school once. It was about a compound somewhere in Texas that had been raided or something. A long time ago I think." Then it hits me why he's asking. "You think that is going on here?"

"Not as bad as what you're thinking, but it seems like everyone in town follows the Reverend's words. Dad said everyone is very much into what gets preached at the church." Rafael puts his face so close to mine I feel his breath against my mouth. He swallows hard, and whispers, "If you think about it. Everyone in Port Michael attends the church on Sundays. My dad and I are the outsiders, and the only family in Port Michael who doesn't attend. I know my dad worries."

My heart pounds as I caress his face with my gaze. I want to touch his face but can't close that distance between us. I search his face for the truth behind his words. I find it and wish I hadn't. I have to pray that because of who I am I will be okay in the midst of all the coming chaos. Will Marcel and Rafael be, though? They have to be.

"You have to tell your dad to leave."

Rafael shakes his head. "I can't leave you. Not now. And what about Peter Wild? I don't like him or the way he looks at you."

"That man gives me the cold shivers. I can't deny that. The Reverend hasn't mentioned him since he was here." I pause, not wanting to think about what the Reverend and that man have planned for me.

Instead, I beg, "Rafael, you *have* to leave before you can't, because if what you think is true, and I believe it is, then there is going to be trouble."

His large hand cups the back of my head and draws me close. His dark eyes search mine, and I hold his gaze and watch him dip and softly brush a kiss across my lips. He pulls away licking his lips. "Sleep well," he whispers, and before I can get my mouth to work, he's moving to the side of the roof.

He climbs down the side of the house so quickly it amazes me how he manages it. Now that he's gone, I'm left with my mind churning with everything he said…and a whole new emotion I'm not even sure what to call it. Horror? Disbelief? It's there, like a rock tumbling in the waves, rubbing at each thought as I try to piece it all together. Is the Reverend trying to create some sort of cult or group through his religious beliefs and his greed for power and control? I shudder at the thought, but it gives me pause. I believe he would do anything to have everyone do his bidding - I see that clearly.

19

RAFAEL

WREN IS GOING TO BE THE DEATH OF ME IN MORE WAYS than one, I decide as I catch my breath. I have to remember that I'm twenty and she's only seventeen.

What are you doing, Rafael?

I push away from the side of the house, but the low rumble of a van keeps me hidden in the shadows. When I look, the van doesn't have headlights on.

Where is it going?

I move down the side of the house and try to follow it with my eyes. The night is silent but for the van and the creak from Wren's house. The van turns into the church parking lot and light glows from within the building as a door is opened. I can't make anyone out from this distance, but the Reverend is home. I heard him moving around once or twice while I'd been talking to Wren.

Above me, a creak and slide of a window draws my gaze upward just as the Reverend shoves his head out. My heart beats rapidly as my body stills hoping he won't catch me spying. A slight breeze picks up and rustles the shrubs and trees, so I use that to my advantage as I move away from the house and his line of sight. At this point I'm not afraid of the Reverend, not when my father is so close. However, I do fear for Wren. I can't protect her if I'm not with her.

In the distance there are car doors slamming, and the sound of someone shouting, but I can't make out the actual words. Something is going on and I bet the Reverend knows exactly what. Why is he home instead of joining his men? He knows my father is former DEA and one of the investigators of the Amarillo raid. Is he trying not to be seen as involved in anything around the town?

My thoughts are swirling around in my head and they don't make any sense. Surely, if he wanted to appear the good law-abiding citizen, then why would he initiate all this change, especially while we're in town? The journals, the uniforms, and the removal of the computers. All on the same day. Only the

Reverend knows his reasoning, but I'm angry he's willing to throw his devoted followers into law enforcement hands. I wonder if they know who my father is.

Peter Wild does.

I glance through the dark and see the Reverend still at his bedroom window. He'll catch me if I head home. I glance up to Wren's bedroom and see the light is off, so at least she's asleep and won't be aware of anything happening. I can't stay where I am until the Reverend moves away. Instead, I sneak around the back of the Reverend's property and into the trees.

The wind rapidly grows stronger as I step further into the darkness, my eyes taking a few moments to adjust. With the noise of the wind blowing through the trees, I'll be lucky if a branch doesn't snap off and drop on me. Hopefully one of the old trees won't choose this moment to go down either. I shudder at the thought as I glance around worriedly. Perhaps I should have taken time to tell Dad where I was going. He'll be awake waiting for me, and he'll have either warned me against this fool hardy plan of mine or come with me.

I stumble over tree roots on the uneven track just

as a blowing branch catches me in the face. I touch my injured cheek and my fingers come away sticky with blood. My feet keep moving as I tug at the hem of my T-shirt and lift it up to wipe at the scratch. It stings slightly, but that's nothing compared to the antiseptic stuff Dad will use once I'm home and he gets a look at me. I wince at the thought.

There is a small green area behind the church before you get to the trees and the wooded area. Both Dad and I had explored it the night before we moved in. As far as we knew, no one had seen us. A lot of places for people to hide and stay hidden. We hadn't found any cameras but that didn't necessarily mean there weren't any.

My heart thumps hard as I crouch and watch the comings and goings behind the church. It's the same van that had taken the school computers today, only now it's being unloaded. Three men I don't recognize move back and forth a few times carrying the old hardware. There will be a reason why they've decided to store the computers at the church, and I want to know what that is. It won't be to prevent students from using them, the reasoning will be more than that. The Reverend never does anything without having a plan in place. He also never does the expected either, otherwise, my father would have caught him years ago.

"What are you doing?" The question reaches my ears and I freeze momentarily thinking I've been caught watching. It turns out to be Wild addressing a man standing in front of the van. The man is as tall as Wild, around six foot, and broader in the shoulders than Wild. I wouldn't like to come across them in a dark alley.

"How do you know there isn't anyone in the forest watching us?" The man looks toward the tree line where I'm hiding.

"Cameras," replies Wild. "The boss has everything covered. You're needed inside, Thomas."

I need to remember his name.

Thomas shakes his head and disappears inside, while Wild continues to look out toward my hiding spot. If there are cameras, then Dad and I have already been seen. However, I don't think there are. At least, not in the trees—around the perimeter, maybe.

Slowly stepping backwards, my nose twitches when I get a whiff of cigarette smoke. Not a subtle scent, but really strong. I still and slowly turn my head, and squint to try and focus through the darkness. Not five feet away from my position sits a man. He's about forties or fifties, dark hair kept tidy in a short cut. He's slim and well dressed.

How long has he been standing there?

"You need to leave before Wild comes looking for me," the man whispers giving me a sidelong stare. "Go now, Rafael." The man stands and without looking my way, moves out toward the church just as the door opens once more.

Wild stands in the doorway.

"All clear out here," the man says, crunching the cigarette under his booted foot on the stone path. He then bends and reaches for the crushed stub. As he slowly rises, he tilts his face toward me and smirks before he follows Wild inside.

Deliberate.

No chance of grabbing it so Dad can send it off for a DNA match.

I keep my wits about me while I head toward the house. My night vision has kicked in and I can step carefully through the undergrowth. The Reverend's bedroom light is off and their house is in total darkness. Mine is too, except I spot the shape of Dad waiting for me on the back porch. He's in shadow, but I know he waits. His eyes follow every step I make once I'm clear of the bordering trees. I don't make a sound and keep watch at the house next door, but all is quiet.

I feel Dad's temper before I even reach the top step. I cast him a glance and head straight inside. He follows.

"You're mad because I went to the church?"

"I'm mad because you are playing with fire lying on that man's roof with his daughter." Dad fumes. "I want to help Wren too, okay? I won't leave her with him in the end, but you are going to blow everything up in the air if you continue dallying with that girl. The man will crack if he catches you both." He walks past me and I know he'd shake me if he thought it would do any good. He places a foot on the stairs before he stops and asks, "Why did it take you so long to come back here?"

He knows exactly where I've been. He gives me a knowing look, and then I get the full effect. He's furious.

"I stayed hidden and watched them take the computers from school inside the back of the church. They went downstairs to the basement. They didn't see me, but we do need to go back and try and find out whether they've stored them or if they're using them for something. Not now. There are too many men around. No women. Not that I saw anyway. I overheard Wild say there were cameras around the perimeter, so I assume he referred to the church grounds and not in the woods."

Dad sighs. "I'm not angry with you, Rafael. I'm scared something will happen to you and I won't be there to help you."

All the energy drains out of me and I slump against the wall next to Dad. "Both Reverend and Wild are well aware of who you are. They won't risk being exposed here to do anything to me. You know that. They'd be really stupid if they did. And they're not stupid."

Dad reaches out and tugs me into his arms. "I worry." The pause is thick with emotion he's never shared. "And I hope you're right."

"I always am." I chuckle and try to hide a yawn behind my hand. "I'm also going to bed."

"Will you slow down with Wren? Please?"

My fists tighten at the thought of staying away from her and a pain ripples through my belly. "I'm not sure I can promise that."

Nothing else is said as I make my way up two flights of stairs to my attic room.

20

WREN

The plain, dark blue dress hangs on my slim body, and when I turn a certain way, the light from the window shines through the gap between my legs. The shape of my body will be seen through the dress when I'm outside, even with tights covering my naked skin. Goosebumps run up and down my arms at the thought. It makes me wonder whether the dresses have purposely been designed to show off our young bodies, or whether it's an error that the Reverend will be angry about. Either way it's not my fault, so I have nothing to worry about as I clump downstairs.

The Reverend has just finished his breakfast when I arrive, and he smiles when he sees me. I pull up short in surprise and wonder what is going on with him. He never smiles. "Morning, Wren. You look pretty in your new dress." His eyes roam over my body and I get a weird sensation in the pit of my belly, which drops to my toes when he stares too long at my chest. I don't feel like that when Rafael stares. Another smile lights the Reverend's face. "Don't look so horrified. I'm trying to see why Peter is impatient for you to turn eighteen, and I understand now. You are a beautiful, delicate creature that needs nurturing by a man who has the means to do so."

The Reverend straightens his spine at the look of horror on my face and take a threatening step toward me. "Do you have anything to say, daughter?"

"What does me turning eighteen have to do with him?" The words are out before I can sensor myself. The room goes so quiet that I can hear the faucet dripping in the bathroom upstairs.

"You're intelligent. I'm sure you can work it out." He continues to watch my reaction with his beady eyes as he slips his long arms into a dark blazer. "I won't be home until late, so make sure you're in bed by the usual time. I'll see you in the morning." He moves to the front door and turns back. "The journal entries start today. Leave it on the kitchen table when you go to bed." He steps outside and quietly pulls the door closed behind him.

The sudden onslaught of air that fills my lungs makes me sag against the refrigerator. Relief settles over me that I don't have to see or speak to him again until tomorrow morning. The journal, I want to toss into the trash where it belongs.

Idiot!

I'm stupid and should have kept my mouth shut. He'd been extremely specific with the words he'd spoken. My naivety isn't as bad he thinks. I know what Peter Wild wants with me. He wants me for sex, and if he's like the Reverend, which I think he is, then he'll want me to be the good little obedient girl. My plan to leave as soon as I turn eighteen must happen.

I've always known something would happen when I reached adulthood. I've seen other young girls who've been at school with me suddenly get married and then disappear. Their husbands are still around. With what the Reverend said, and with the changes being made around town, I'm starting to wonder about those girls. Have they been forced to be with their husbands? I don't know. And to be honest, I never questioned it before. But one thing I do know for sure, I will not allow myself to end up like they have.

At least with the Reverend, I'm an unpaid house-keeper, one who gets punished with a night or two in the basement every now and again. I haven't been forced to have sex with anyone. I would rather die fighting if that were ever the case.

I need to pull myself together and head to school. The last thing I want on the first day of journal writing is to be late. I grab the largest banana out of the fruit bowl and quickly peel it, then drop the skin into the compost bag. My backpack feels heavier on my shoulders today and it seems to press differently against my lower back. Another complaint to add to the list of complaints I have from the day before.

Part of me is excited as I walk down the lane to school. I'll see Rafael again. He'll be in his uniform, and I look forward to seeing him in something other than black. My fingers reach and press against my lips, remembering the soft kiss he'd brushed against them, and that's when Tiger Lily lands on my hand. He looks at me as though he has a question to ask. Ridiculous really.

"Morning, my little butterfly." I blow him a small kiss. "I'm sorry I haven't been around much. I will be tomorrow morning." I would have told anyone that he smiles at me. I know he doesn't. It's all in my imagination, but it looks so real. "Go on home and I'll see you in a little while."

I watch as his beautiful wings open wide before he takes flight and hovers. Mere seconds later, he is fluttering back toward the house and that's when I notice he hasn't sought me out alone. Other butterflies take flight from the plants at the side of the lane as Tiger Lily reaches them. The sight of them grouped together in flight looks like a moving rainbow with the colors they display as one. It's a beautiful sight and makes my heart flutter behind my breastbone.

I certainly feel lighter as I continue the boring walk to school. It's a pretty walk with all the plants and colorful weeds along the lane, but it's hot and humid even though it's only early. I have walked this lane so many times that I can't even put a name on it, so after all these years, it's a boring walk. The other students start to appear in my vision as I go around the corner. I misstep but quickly right myself.

We all match in our uniforms and I reluctantly admit that we all look nice. There is something about seeing everyone in a uniform. We look clean and part of something. I frown. I'm not sure I want to be part of whatever the Reverend is planning. I shake those thoughts from my head. The boys look neat in their uniform and neatly combed hair. I glance around and notice the girls have the same problem as I do. You can see straight through their dresses as they walk.

Entering the school grounds, I walk closer to the school building and stop. Others stare, making me self-conscious. I quickly glance down at myself and nothing sticks out. I slowly turn and realize everyone is now looking at me. Is it because of who I am to the Reverend? Maybe they don't like what he's forced us all to do. Except the more I watch the others, the more I know I'm wrong. They like what they're wearing. They don't like me any more than before, actually, I get a sense of hate coming from them.

I swallow around the lump in my throat and continue staring at my fellow students—just trying to find that one other person who shows a friendly face. There is no one. I don't understand what's going on.

"Wren?"

I turn and there stands Rafael. He stands so close that I can see the tick of annoyance in his jaw. My eyes roam over him in his dark navy-blue pants that cling to his thighs and cup him nicely. I quickly snap my eyes up and enjoy the fit of the deep red shirt he wears. It's short-sleeved like the black T-shirts he usually wears, but, for some reason, his tattoos seem to stand out more. As I lift my eyes, his jaw is pulled tight and his eyes light with fire.

"You have to stop looking at me like that," he hisses, and takes a heavy breath. "You're too beautiful for your own good."

"I can't help how I look at you." I smile and tease. "You already know I like what I see." I like that Rafael brings this out in me. I've spent too many years keeping my thoughts to myself. Becoming serious, I glance over my shoulder before I meet Rafael's gaze. "Have you noticed they're all staring at me with hatred." I frown and chew on my lip.

His brows draw together, and his eyes look around the school grounds, left to right, before his brows deepen into a heavy frown of confusion. "I don't know what's going on."

"I've lived here all my life and have only had the Reverend look at me like that."

"Follow me." He turns and leads me away from prying eyes into a small alcove at the back of the building. "I think it's the uniform. Everyone is wearing the same thing, so features stand out more."

"I don't like being a novelty. I'm weird because I keep to myself and have butterflies as friends."

Rafael grins. "You're not weird, you're my butterfly girl." He holds my gaze and lightly traces along my forehead with a finger. "Skin so soft." He trails down and along my cheek. "Pale with a hint of sun." My mouth slips open as his finger hesitates before pressing against my lips. "So red and swollen here."

A groan gurgles up from my throat and Rafael's eyes darken and swirl with emotion. Just when I think he's going to kiss me, he drops his face into my neck and breathes deeply. I go with instinct and reach up, wrapping my arms around his shoulders. I slip a hand to the nape of his neck and tangle my fingers in the overlong hair there. He sighs and shudders in my hold.

"Rafael," I mumble against his ear, "what's happening to me? My body feels *tight*."

He grabs hold of my hips and pushes me away from him, his eyes heavy-lidded as he stares. "I shouldn't have done that." He runs his hands through his hair and tugs, his fists tight. His whole body is tight if I think about it, which I do. I can't help it when he's so handsome standing in front of me.

The bell for morning class rings heavily in the air but neither one of us moves. My feet stay planted firmly on the ground, as do Rafael's. Before my brain starts working, I blurt into the silence, "I want to feel like that again."

He swallows hard and takes another step away. He shakes his head. "We have to get to class. The Reverend can't know anything about us being together."

"I know," I admit sadly. "He's home really late tonight. Said he'll see me at breakfast tomorrow." I shrug. "Do you want to come over?"

He wants to. I see him fighting with himself. All his objections to come or not to come flash across his face. "I can't. We're flying up to visit Mom and Roman. I'll be back in a few days. I promise, Wren." He turns and I follow him to class, feeling my heart hurting for him.

21

RAFAEL

THE OLD CEMETERY IS THE SAME AS IT HAD BEEN THE day of the funeral. There haven't been any recent burials, which I'm relieved about. The thought of having to witness fresh earth on a grave makes me shiver. It's difficult enough being back here without having to see that. My eyes dance everywhere but where my family is buried.

I haven't been here since the headstone had been commissioned. The large piece of black granite stands tall on the small rise, beneath a tree. I swallow around the lump in my throat and try to blink my tears away as I trace their names with my eyes. Sarah DeLacroix. Roman DeLacroix. I doubt I'll ever get over their loss.

Throwing my head back, I stare at the darkening gray clouds swirling in the sky above. I welcome the rain because it keeps most people indoors. It also helps me breathe while I'm surrounded by death.

Clearing my throat, I smile as Mom's face swims before my vision. She smiles like I remembered when she was happy, singing and dancing in the kitchen. Her happy place, she would say. Her smiles weren't often, but when she was in such a good mood, Roman and I were too.

Dropping to my knees in the soft earth, I place the flowers I bought on the ground beside me for now and run my hands up and down my thighs trying to think of the words I want to say to her. My body is chilled, even though it's close to ninety degrees. I slow my breathing and force myself to focus on the headstone once again. It had been slightly easier before the stonemason had erected the memorial because then I could pretend it wasn't my mom and brother buried in the ground. I can't do that any longer.

My lungs feel like they will burst as I struggle to take a proper breath and my vision blurs. Seconds tick by. Then a butterfly appears.

I blink a few times to bring my vision into focus,

and I know I'm not mistaken. A large, blue butterfly has landed on the top of the headstone. It's as still as I am. As I stare in awe, the tiny creature flutters its wings, hovers, and then takes flight.

Sitting back on my heels, I realize I'm breathing just fine and the tension, which has had a hold of my body, has dissipated. I'm calm. Whatever just happened has settled my soul.

The granite headstone gleams in the sun seeping through the dark clouds. My eyes trace along the golden edges of my mother's name again.

I'm here to tell her about Wren.

My beautiful butterfly girl.

"Mom," I whisper, "Dad said you'll always hear me talk. I'm not sure I believe him, but I need to tell you about a girl." I smile, imagining the look on Mom's face had she been standing in front of me. "I'd give anything for you to be here to tease me about her. For Roman to be running around the house chanting her name." I catch myself as my voice breaks, and I quickly swallow back my tears.

"Her name is Wren…"

Telling Mom everything I know about Wren feels good to finally be able to get it all out. Dad is good at listening, but I can't tell him some of the stuff I tell Mom. I wouldn't have told her half of it if she'd really been in front of me, though. If she is looking down on me, she's laughing, knowing that too.

I frown when I notice the fresh flowers on the grave. Why hadn't I noticed them to begin with? I shake off my sorrow and really look at them. They have been arranged by the same florist from where I purchased mine. Dad's too, but he'll leave his when he comes to pick me up.

Shrugging off the weight from my shoulders, I stand and move closer to the bouquet of lilies. As I hover over them, I spot a card inside the cellophane. Without touching the flowers, I wrinkle the clear covering as I slip my hand inside. Between my two fingers, I withdraw the card and bring it closer to my face.

Revenge is mine.
S. M.

Who is S. M., and what revenge? Their deaths?

"What's wrong?" Dad asks, coming up beside me.

He takes the card from my hand and I watch as all the color leaves his face as he stares at the words.

"Dad? What's going on? You know who this is from?"

"Sarah's brother," he whispers. "But that's impossible."

"I didn't know Mom had family other than us."

"We thought he was dead." Dad's hand trembles as he puts the card back where I retrieved it from. "He loved Sarah. He had no clue what had happened to her before I met her. I don't think anyone knew he had once existed other than me. And now you."

"How can that be?"

"He was ten years older than your mom. Enlisted in the military on his eighteenth birthday. Sarah believed he would have come for her if he'd known the situation that she'd been in. He was killed in action, or so we were told."

"What's his name?"

He inhales and holds my gaze. "Silas Mathis."

I wonder aloud. "You don't think he's managed to get close to Peter Wild or the others, do you?"

Dad frowns and turns sharply. "Explain?"

I run my hands through my hair and wince, not wanting to admit being caught snooping the other night. "There was a man in the trees close to where I hid behind the church. He was tall with close-cropped hair and a goatee. He smokes, too. Quiet. The kind of man who doesn't miss anything."

"Goddammit, Rafael!" The moment Dad curses, he prays for forgiveness for cursing in a cemetery.

"He made sure I saw him and told me to 'go' before Wild found me. He knew my name and didn't give me away. Could it be Mom's brother?"

"I'll ask John to double-check Silas's military record. I don't see how he could be here if he's supposed to be dead."

"Whoever he is, he must be on our side, otherwise, he'd have told Wild."

"Hmm."

Dad stays silent all the way home, frowning now and again—both of us are clearly lost in our own thoughts.

22

WREN

Puttering in the glasshouse, I collect some tomatoes and small zucchini in a bowl on the work-bench. I'll grill vegetables with chicken for dinner, and I know how much the Reverend enjoys the fresh food. I always make a point of using the homegrown vegetables as often as possible so that he knows I'm at least doing some good in the glasshouse. It keeps him happy and me in his good graces.

A few butterflies hover around as I work, but the majority are out in the garden feeding on the plants. I take the clippers to the strawberry plant and wonder if Rafael likes the fruit. I've missed talking to him and feeling him close since he'd been in New Orleans, but now he is home. I've especially missed his warmth, which had clung to me for hours after we'd laid side by side on the roof. He'd made me feel lighter for having searched me out. My heart and body had felt different, and I want to feel like that again. It's dangerous for me to be anywhere near Rafael because of the Reverend. It terrifies me what he'd do if he were ever to discover that my feelings have started to go beyond friendship for the boy. He'll be angry if he knows we're friends. I'm terrified of his rage if he knew we were anything more. I fear for Rafael more than myself.

"Daydreaming."

Startled, I drop the pruning shears and spin around to face the Reverend standing in the doorway. My heart gives a lurch but then settles when I see he's in a good mood.

"I'm collecting some vegetables and fruit for dinner." I glance around the floor and realize the shears have slipped under the workbench. "Is everything okay?" I ask, crouching down and feeling with my hand until my fingers bump into the metal shears.

I get back to my feet and the Reverend still hasn't said anything. He just continues to stare. He's been looking at me in a funny way recently and I don't know what to make of it. I stand silently and wait for a response, which I don't get until I start to sweat.

"Peter Wild will be joining us this evening for supper," he states. "Make sure you set an extra plate. Everything else as usual."

"Yes, sir." I ignore the urge to stick my tongue out. I'd done that once—a long time ago. It hadn't ended well for me because he'd seen my reflection through the window. Ever since then, I learned to be more careful.

The Reverend continues to stare before he abruptly snaps, "It's time to make dinner," and stomps up the garden path to the house.

I'm not sure what I'm supposed to do. It's early to start dinner, but he'd been adamant. I chew on my bottom lip and look toward the house. My view isn't clear because of the abundance of plants filling the space and the steam on the windows from the humidity in here. I don't mind, if I can't see out properly then I'm assured no one can see in either.

The Reverend, or rather his shape, crosses the yard and leans against the wooden porch. He's waiting for me and how quickly I listen will determine his mood at dinner. I'll have to go inside, which I really don't want to do with the way he's been looking at me. Resigned, I grab the bowl with the vegetables and strawberries and step outside. That's when I realize the Reverend is watching the house next door. I glance over and see Marcel on the front porch, but the back holds my entire focus. Rafael leans against the corner support and stares directly at me. Even with the distance between us, I can feel the heat of his gaze. It burns into my body and I blush from the heat running through me.

I chance a glance at the Reverend, but he's unmoving in the middle of a staring match with Rafael's dad. Rafael looks too before his gaze moves back to mine, and he gently nods his head in the direction of the roof. I let a small smile slip over my lips as happiness runs through me. He wants to talk to me again.

The fact we are doing this in secret thrills me more than it should. I know he doesn't have a problem with being seen with me in public, so I only have to worry about the Reverend finding out. The consequences would be terrible, and although I don't think he'd hurt Rafael, I'm not sure. Not anymore.

BOTH THE REVEREND AND PETER WILD GLANCE IN MY direction every few minutes. If I was brave, I would ask what's wrong with me. I'm not brave, though, so I try to ignore them. Wild has a look in his eyes that tells me he's seeing me without any clothing, and I want to be sick. The Reverend seems aware of the looks, but he is not doing or saying anything to dissuade the man. For some reason, that bothers me more than anything has. Ordinarily, he's possessive of me, and with only one glance, the Reverend usually shoots down anyone who dares to look in my direction.

My head immediately goes to his recent talk to me about marriage, and that he'd find me a man. I haven't really listened to what he talks about, or at least I haven't paid too much heed to what he says. I wish I had now.

The men talk around me and I'm sure some of their chatter is about me, except they make sure to be non-specific. It's a wonder I haven't gone up in flames with the stare from Peter Wild. I take a chance and glance up, freezing at the look on his face. It scares me. He looks ready to pounce.

The knife and fork drop back to my plate with a noisy clink. I gasp and lift my eyes to the Reverend.

I swallow back fear, and ask, "Please may I be excused?"

The Reverend quickly gives me a nod of acceptance. "Clean the kitchen up in the morning."

"Yes, sir."

He smiles and shares a look I don't understand with the creepy man.

Standing, I pause, and say, "Goodnight, Reverend. Goodnight, Mr. Wild." I then turn and run upstairs. I can't get to my bedroom fast enough, and nearly fall into the room when my foot catches on the landing carpet. Flipping the lock is the first thing I do the moment the door closes. A heavy shudder of unease creeps through my body and then I breathe out a sigh of relief. Just to be away from the two men downstairs helps me catch a breath.

My heart pounds as I quickly change into my sleeping shorts and tank top, then I slowly open my window so it won't creak. The moment I climb out, I find Rafael waiting for me. He is lying on his back staring at the stars, but when he hears me, he turns his head and watches my every move. I smile and try not to be self-conscious from the look in his eyes. They tell me he likes what he sees. His gaze darkens as he looks at my chest before he turns his head and stares up at the stars again.

I give him a slight smile as I lie beside him. My hand searches out his and our fingers intertwine. His hands are that of a man, not a boy—large and strong. The way he caresses my thumb with his creates tingles of pleasure that run all the way to my belly. He gives my hand a squeeze and asks, "Who came for dinner?"

We turn our faces toward each other, and my eyes search his. The way his presence affects me tells me to trust him. I feel my need to trust him. To have someone I can talk to about anything at all that comes to mind or worries me.

"Peter Wild." I swallow hard, and admit, "It was just awful having to eat dinner with them both. They kept looking at me weirdly. The kind of way that made my skin crawl. Peter Wild constantly *looked* at me." I shiver.

"You're cold?" Rafael wiggles closer and wraps me in his arms. His warmth seeps from his body to mine and I start feeling so much better.

Smiling, I duck my face so he doesn't see how pleased I am with his response. It has been so long since I've been held. In fact, the last time I remember it happening was with my mom, but it's more of a feeling of warmth and love than anything else, like wings of a butterfly tickling my skin. I lift my head and place it on his shoulder as his arm comes behind my back and settles on my waist. I snuggle closer and sigh.

He puts his mouth close to my ear. "You like being this close to me."

Heat creeps up my neck to my face, but I keep my face buried in his shoulder. "Maybe I do like being with you."

He quietly admits, "I like having you this close, Wren." He pauses. "How was school?"

"Same as usual. I missed you being there."

"It took a bit longer than planned. Dad had some things to do." He rubs my back and I feel tension in his body. "I wanted to go and talk to Mom." He hesitates. "It helps talking to her. I know she can't talk back, but it's all I have."

Tears spring to my eyes at the sorrow I hear in his voice. I slowly slip my arm over his stomach and hug him. "I'm sorry, Rafael. Can't you talk to your dad?"

"I do." There is a smile in his voice, and he caresses my arm on his belly. "It's just weird talking to him about *you*."

"Me?" I raise my face and stare into his eyes. "You talked to her about me?"

He lifts a hand and wraps a piece of my hair around a finger. "Yeah, I told her about you. I told her about the butterfly girl with long dark brown hair." His gaze lifts to mine and I feel our connection grow.

The next few minutes pass in silence as I settle down on his shoulder, against his warm body. I feel happy right now. Truly happy. I want to continue to feel what I do when I'm with Rafael, but I know it will end. The moment he leaves to go back to his house, I'll be alone.

"I drew you another picture." Rafael sits up and tugs me with him. He offers a smile as he slips a piece of paper out of his back pocket. "I hope you like it."

I catch my breath as I unfold the thick piece of drawing paper. The pencil drawing takes my breath away. It's of me reaching up to a hanging basket outside of the glasshouse. Rafael has captured every detail, and my heart thuds in my chest. Looking at the drawing makes me see myself through his eyes, and I am, "Beautiful."

"You are," Rafael whispers. "The first day I saw you, I thought it was my imagination playing tricks on me. The butterflies loved you. It was absolutely amazing to watch." He smiles. "My dad kept looking at me. He knew you'd caught my eye."

"I've never had anyone to talk to before. Tonight, is the first time I remember being held in so long." I pause. "I don't really remember my mother because she left when I was a child."

Rafael places his arm around me and inches closer. "I'll always hold you, Wren."

"I'd like that." I let my head drop to his shoulder and sigh.

"What should I do at school? I want to be around you, but I don't want the Reverend to punish you for it."

"It's best if we keep our friendship a secret." I pull my lower lip between my teeth. I hate that I can't be with him in the open, but I need to keep him—us— safe. "I don't want to see the basement again any time soon."

He stills. "Basement?"

"I mentioned that the other day."

"No, you didn't." Rafael's jaw tenses. "He locked you in the basement, didn't he? That's what you let slip."

"It's okay." I turn and cup his scarred cheek. Our eyes meet and my fingers flutter over the red puckered scar. He gulps and holds still while I touch him. My heart goes out to him at this moment and I lean forward and press a kiss to the end of the scar on his jaw.

"*Wren,*" he groans and catches his breath.

"Shush." I smile close to his mouth. "Let me touch you like this." I hold his gaze and kiss along the scar, then I move to the one above his brow. "You make me feel good when you touch me. I want you to feel good too."

"Wren, you don't know what you're saying."

I chuckle. "I know exactly what I'm saying even though I've never experienced anything like I am with you before."

Rising up on his knees, Rafael places his hands on my hips to keep me steady and holds me tightly. "I think I should go before we get caught up here."

"Yet you're not making any move to leave."

"I don't want to leave. You make me feel whole, Wren. When I'm with you, everything that holds me in darkness dissipates and I feel...*happy.*"

Feeling brave after I hear his words, I lean forward and quickly press my lips to his. It's a very brief kiss. If I knew what I was doing then, maybe, I'd have kept my lips pressed to his longer. I don't really know what to do with a boy. I read a book that the girls had passed around at school. I'd found it shoved in my locker and had been too curious to ignore it. I'd snuck it home and hid it. Read it in the dark of night when I knew the Reverend slept. It had been *very* detailed. I'd been too scared to keep it in my bedroom, so I'd burned it by the river, then kicked the ashes into the water. I haven't thought about the book in a while, but now that I find myself drawn to Rafael, I want to remember it.

"You're really blushing," he comments. "Shit! Sorry!" He slips a bit and I reach out to grab him, and he adds, "I think I better go."

"Really?"

He moves away but slowly comes back to me and presses his lips to the corner of my mouth. "I feel everything you do, Wren," he whispers against my mouth.

He's gone and I see his figure in the distance as he climbs his back porch. I can't move and my hand stays covering my mouth, touching the kiss he placed there. I'm not sure what is happening between us, but I love the way I feel with him.

23

RAFAEL

My body feels tight and uncomfortable as I climb up my back porch. I turn my head and see Wren still sitting where I'd left her. I can't take my eyes from her and watch in the moonlight as her butterflies hover around her like a halo.

Instead of heading inside and up to my room, I slip into the dark shadowy corner of the porch and watch her. I tell myself it has everything to do with her safety, when, in actual fact, it has everything to do with my heart.

Every nerve ending feels alive and buzzes with electricity, tempting me to go back to her. I want to teach her how to kiss a man—me. The way her words wrap around me drives me crazy. She has no idea what she does to me.

While my head is filled with Wren, I watch as she moves back inside her bedroom, only taking the blanket with her at the last minute. Her dark brown hair shimmers under the stars in waves as she disappears, and I'm thankful I can no longer see her.

The night has grown cold and I shiver in my t-shirt as my body begins to cool from the world of heat Wren has created. The blood stops swirling in my head and I begin to hear the sounds of night crickets chirping, mosquitoes whimpering, small animals rustling in the underbrush, and the trees of the forest creaking as the wind picks up. All sounds that I usually ignore until I really listen.

The silence of the night stills my racing heart, even when Dad silently joins me on the porch, everything is still. The whack of a door banging against its wooden frame draws my gaze back over to Wren's house. The Reverend and Wild stand on the back porch chatting, their attention on our house.

"Don't move, Rafael," Dad says under his breath. "They can't see us."

"That man scares Wren. We have to do something to

keep him away from her." My eyes never leave Wren's house. "She doesn't know anything, Dad. She knows something is wrong with the Reverend and with what has been going on, but she doesn't know anything."

"I saw you *talking* to her," Dad states, and I know he witnessed our kiss.

I'm not sure what I feel for Wren. I certainly feel like her protector. I frown wondering if it's love to desperately want to keep the girl as mine and mine alone. What I feel for her is certainly close to the word "love."

"Everything about me is a lie."

"No, it isn't, son. What lies have been told can be explained, and Wren will understand in the end."

"I'm twenty pretending to be eighteen. That's a big problem, Dad," I hiss in frustration.

He pauses. "Ah, that's what you mean." I glance at him in the dark and feel my face heat at his amusement. "I get it now."

Without offering advice or even one word, Dad quietly disappears inside. *Nice one, Rafael!*

My face continues to feel heated as I watch the two men on the opposite porch finally move away to Wild's vehicle. The bastard wastes no time in getting in his car and driving off, his tires spewing gravel at the speed at which he leaves.

The Reverend has his hands on his hips as he watches Wild disappear down the road. When the headlights from the car can no longer be seen, the Reverend shakes his head and offers a quick glance in my direction before he disappears into his own house.

I stay outside for another ten minutes wondering what the men had been talking about. One of their topics would have been Wren, if I had to guess. It wouldn't have been their only topic. That I know.

Slipping inside the house, I go up to the attic and spread out on my bed, too tired to do anything else.

I'd sleep on it. Sleep on it all.

24

WREN

THE HOUSE IS SILENT AS I WALK DOWNSTAIRS FOR breakfast. It's always this way on Saturday mornings because the Reverend likes to be at his church early. Not much happens as a town, but there are always a bunch of cars parked in the lot. I'm curious, but not curious enough to risk asking.

I pull out a box of muesli and chop a banana to go on top, along with a spoon of natural yogurt. I pour half a cup of milk and take my breakfast to sit on the back porch. The day is humid, and the sun is out, which means it will be uncomfortable to be outdoors soon. My denim shorts and tank top are appropriate for the weather, as long I don't leave the property. I eat my muesli.

I munch on my cereal as I look over at Rafael's house and it looks quiet. I smile as I remember last night on the roof. It had felt good to press my chest against his side when I'd used him as a pillow. He'd certainly warmed me up in more places than I cared to admit.

Movement suddenly catches my eye and I watch as Rafael stands and stretches on his back porch. My mouth hangs open at the sight of him. He's only wearing black jeans, his chest bare. The tattoos are all over his back and torso. I can't make them out from this distance, but I certainly enjoy the view. His jeans dip low around his hips, which my eyes find difficult moving from. It's only when I manage to move them upward that I realize he's watching me. He leans with his arms on the porch railing, his gaze unwavering.

My mouth goes dry and, the muesli gets stuck in my throat, hurting when it finally goes down like a ball of bird seeds. It's only my butterflies that draw my gaze away and I realize I can't stare at the boy next door all morning. I have to water the plants around the glasshouse and inside.

With one last glance toward Rafael, I take my bowl inside and, after I've quickly washed and dried it, I grab a T-shirt and head to the side of the house. The hose is wrapped on a wheel, the end of which is attached to a water tap. I unravel the hose and turn on the water and let it dampen the garden before I move over to the glasshouse. I feel the humidity coming from it as I pass the door and water a few plants around the entrance. The plants get dry so quickly in the heat, so as water lands on the soil, they seem to come back to life in all their color. Different shades of green look so pretty all bundled together. The butterflies follow me and land on the plants as I move on.

Moving back toward the front door, I stop when I see Rafael standing waiting for me. He's covered up with a black T-shirt now, his hair just as messy as usual. I can't keep the grin off my face if I tried because I really am happy to see him here. He looks adorable all rumpled and quickly pulled together.

"I saw *he* wasn't here, so I took a chance." He hesitates and then moves forward, taking the hose from my hands. "I'll help you."

"Oh, yes." I laugh. "Sorry, I'm just surprised to see you here. It's a nice surprise, though."

"I know that." He smirks.

I nudge him with my hip. "I'm a tyrant of a boss. Follow me." I lead him to the opposite side of the glasshouse and enjoy the view of him watering the plants. The muscles of his back ripple when he moves, and I'm fairly sure he does it all the more because he knows I'm watching him. The slight smirk on his face gives him away. "You know?" I place my hands on my hips and wait to have his full attention. I have to clear my throat when his eyes darken as they leave a trail of heat over my skin. "You watch me just as intently as I watch you."

His smirk turns into a full grin that lights his eyes. "You admit to watching me *intently*, huh?"

"Ugh," I mutter. "Trust you to pick up on *that* word."

"I'm a guy, of course I picked up on *that* word." He glances at my legs and back to my face. "I can't help staring at you *intently* when you're in those shorts, showing off your legs. I also can't keep my eyes off you. You fascinate me, Wren Jacobs."

A blush coats my cheeks, but I find myself frozen in place by his words and the sincerity behind them. "You fascinate me too," I admit, the blush growing deeper in color. Turning my back, I head into the glasshouse. "We need to water everything in here." I pick up a small watering can I'd filled yesterday. "I'll water the strawberries with this, and you water everything else with the hose." I look over my shoulder. "Then, I'll show you the stream."

"Dad said there was a stream."

"Yes. It's ten minutes away through the trees at the back." I nod toward the back of the glasshouse. "I like spending time there on the weekends when the Reverend is at church."

"Do you swim in it?" Rafael asks, moving closer to me as I reach up to the strawberries in the hanging baskets.

I shake my head. "No. I'm not allowed." I place the watering can on the floor and turn to face Rafael. "I have dipped my toes in the water a few times, though."

Rafael steps into me until the tips of our shoes touch. He is taller than me and my eyes meet his collarbone. I am so tempted to ask him to remove his T-shirt so I can see the tattoos up close, but I don't. With the way he has drawn me, I know the artwork on his body will be just as impressive. I slowly lift my gaze upward and find him looking down at me with a look on his face I can't decipher. I swallow nervously but don't step away. I like being close to him. I like the way he makes me feel when he is. He gives me his trust, as I've given him mine.

He licks his lips and stares at me before he closes his eyes and takes a small step back. "I think they've had enough water for today. Go turn the water off and I'll help you wind the hose back up."

"Hmm."

He bends and whispers into my ear. "Unless you want to do something else." Then I feel his teeth nip at my earlobe.

A shiver of pleasure runs through me, and Rafael's eyes darken. "Water. Off. Now." Rafael turns and quickly moves with the hose to the side of the house.

I run after him with a quick glance toward the church to make sure the Reverend's red car is still parked there. It is. "I'll turn the wheel, if you guide the hose so it doesn't get twisted."

"Okay."

We work in silence for a few minutes as everything is tidied away. I don't say anything and walk toward the trees at the back of the property. Rafael follows behind me while my heart thumps wildly. If the Reverend finds out about Rafael being here with me there will be a lot of trouble. Associating with boys isn't allowed, and I'm starting to realize it's because he wants me for someone of his own choosing.

"You've gone tense," Rafael comments, moving in beside me. "Why?" I wasn't sure how to answer and, before I can come up with something, he asks, "Is it me?"

"No." I lead him over the uneven ground toward the water just in the distance. The boulder I always sit on while I contemplate life looks appealing as I take Rafael's hand and lead him onto it with me.

I move in beside him and sigh feeling at peace. Rafael just being close has started to settle my mind and anxious belly. "Before—" I pause. "I'd been thinking about how you make me feel and how the Reverend would react if he ever found out. I think he's planning on giving me to Peter Wild."

"No way is that happening." Rafael runs both hands through his hair. "You can't just be given to someone else. It doesn't work that way."

A tear slips free. "You don't know the Reverend and his followers. His word is law around here and people are too afraid to stand up to him." I meet his eyes and let my tears fall when he cradles my face in his large hands. He makes me feel warm where my soul is used to being cold—so very cold. "Before I met you, my world was mostly silent. No one talked to me. The Reverend only ever issued orders. But you,

you've made me crave something I hadn't known I wanted or needed. That's you, Rafael. I craved having a friend like you."

He wraps an arm around my shoulders and pulls me in against his warm body. "Is that all you want, Wren? A friend?" He whispers the question against the top of my head. "Because I like you a lot more than a friend should like another friend. Before you, my world was full of darkness and blood. You've given me light, and I long for it. I long for you." He kisses my forehead.

He deserves me to be honest no matter how embarrassed I will be. "I like you more than a friend should. My body swells and feels good whenever you're close or when we touch. I want to continue feeling that way."

A garbled response that I can't make out is the only reply he gives me. Then his arm is pulling me closer. I feel his heart thump against my ear until it slowly settles into a steady rhythm.

"It would have been my brother's birthday today," he admits quietly. "He should have been turning eleven."

"Oh, Rafael. I'm so sorry." I wrap myself around him and hold on while his sorrow overwhelms him. I feel it in the tense way he holds himself, and the way he breathes deeply to keep himself in the moment instead of in the past. "I really wish I knew how to make everything better for you."

His hand tangles in my hair and he tips my head backwards so that our eyes meet. "The fact that you want to, means everything to me." He glances at my lips and slowly lowers his head. "I'm not going to hurt you," he whispers, and glides his soft lips across my own. His head lifts and his lips twitch into a smile while his chest is heavy against mine. "You have no idea how beautiful you are." He kisses the tip of my nose and my breasts ache. "I want to do really naughty things with you that I haven't done with anyone."

"Oh! You feel this too?"

He offers a strangled laugh. "Give me your hand."

I look at him in confusion as I offer him my hand. He inhales deeply and moves my hand to the large bulge behind his zipper. He keeps his hand over mine and urges my fingers around the shape. Rafael hisses. My eyes immediately snap up to his half-lidded ones as I realize I'm squeezing his throbbing length.

He removes his hand and I leave mine there while I search his gaze. His cheeks have a deep red blush, as

I'm sure mine do. I know a man's penis swells hard and thick when he's aroused, but this is the first time I have had any experience with one. I'm curious as I squeeze my hand around him and feel his flesh jerk. He breathes deeply and his whole body is tense, so I release him from my grip. It isn't that I want to let go of him, it's more about what I need to do.

"Are you okay?" I ask, trying to ignore my embarrassment.

He swallows hard and nods. "Yeah," he mutters, stumbling over the words. He coughs and clears his throat. "Remind me not to put your hands on me in that way again."

"Why?" I'm hurt he doesn't like my touch.

"Why? Wren." He groans. "I enjoyed it way too much. I only intended to show you that I react to you as well. I didn't mean to keep your hand there, but it felt too good the way your fingers squeezed me."

"I don't know anything about boys or my own body, but touching you down there felt really good down there on my own body. I liked how it made you feel too."

"You're killing me."

"Can we do it again sometime?"

"God!" He jumps up from the boulder and starts

pacing. "My dad will kill me if he knows what we just did." He pauses. "The Reverend *will* kill me."

I follow him down and stand in his way. "They will *if* you tell them."

"Wren, we can't be like that again. We just can't."

"You didn't like how I touched you?" I back away and find myself caught by him.

He has his hands on my hips while he holds me steady. "I *loved* having your touch on my body. You're seventeen. I won't take advantage of you."

"But you want to? Take advantage of me, I mean?"

He stares deeply into my eyes and licks his lips before he answers. "Yes. I want to feel your touch on my skin. I've dreamed about touching you." He glances down. "I want to lick the tips of your breasts that poke through your T-shirts, like they're doing right now." He closes his eyes and steps away, the loss of his touch not nice.

"Oh," I mumble and follow. "You *do* like my touch." I stalk him as he moves around the clearing. "You're afraid of how you'll react when I touch you, skin-to-skin, huh?"

He moves quickly. "Stop talking."

"No. What would you do if I took my top off? I'm naked underneath." His honest reaction to my touch gives me the courage to be bold. Never in my wildest dream have I thought I would react to a boy the way I do Rafael. I want to be under his skin and to know that I make his body react in the way mine has.

I don't miss his eyes on my chest before he turns away. I smirk and move even closer and lay my hands on his back. "I saw you on the porch this morning. I noticed the ink that covers your skin, and I especially noticed how low your jeans rode on your hips. I wondered how you'd react if I licked around the skin just visible above your jeans, or even how it would feel if I dipped my tongue below the button that held them up. I really like the idea of licking you all over." I frown. "I'm not sure why I want to do that, but the thought makes me feel swollen and tingly."

Rafael reaches to the front of him, and then mumbles, "You, *please,* need to stop teasing me." His hand stills on the front of his jeans.

25

RAFAEL

"Okay," she agrees, her head tipped to the side as she watches me through half-lidded eyes. "I'll stop teasing you. I'm not sure what has come over me today. I've never acted like this with anyone before. Only you. You make me ache, Rafael, and it scares and excites me all at the same time."

I swallow hard and know I have to be the responsible one, because Wren sounds confused about what is happening to her body. I know what's happening, though. She needs my touch to ease the burning ache deep inside of her, just like I need hers.

"It's okay, Wren." Moving my hand away from the front of my jeans, I let her see how big my ache for her is. Her eyes widen and stay on my groin, until I step closer and reach for her hand. I intertwine our fingers and lead her toward the stream, pulling her down beside me.

The sound of water is soothing and helps me get my body back under control as we sit in silence. I'm glad because the silence is welcome. I'm almost scared of what Wren will say next.

"Are you angry with me?"

"What?" I snap my head to be able to see her. "Why would you think that?"

"You went quiet."

"I needed to calm down." I offer her a smile and let her see the mirth in my gaze. "You and your words wound me up. I'm good now."

"I wish things were different," Wren says, a forlorn expression on her pretty face.

Untangling our fingers, I slide my arm around her shoulders and hold her close. "I do too." I kiss her brow. "No matter what happens, I'm here for you. No matter what."

Her eyes search mine, and she says, "Why does that sound like you know what's about to happen?"

"I don't. I just know something isn't right in this town and the Reverend is at the center of it all."

"I know." She sighs heavily. "Will you tell me about life in New Orleans? I haven't been anywhere."

"You've never left the town?" I find that impossible to believe.

"I don't remember much from when I was younger, but I think I was born somewhere else. Since I've lived here, I haven't gone anywhere. The Reverend won't allow it." She blushes. "He doesn't like me being with anyone but him." She shrugs. "He never leaves, so I never leave."

I don't want to push Wren to remember things from her childhood, so I tell her about mine. "My birth mom died when I was a baby, so I don't remember her at all. Sarah, my mom, only came into my life when I was ten. I didn't need or want anyone else in my life. I had Dad and he was enough. Or so I thought." I chuckle. "Sarah was nice to me. No matter what I said or did—sometimes I was horrid—she told me she loved me. I loved her too, and Roman. They made us a true family and I miss them."

"Roman—"

"He was one year old when they came to live with us." I stare out over the stream, realizing I should have kept my mouth shut. She has no one to tell, so I continue, "They'd had a rough time of it beforehand

and Dad wanted them safe, so he brought them to our home. It turned out to be the best thing he did."

To my surprise, Wren swings a leg over my legs and settles on my lap, her arms wrapping around my neck, really holding me tightly. "I'm so sorry, Rafael. I wish I'd known them. I wish I was there for you when you lost them."

My arms tighten around her and I bury my face in the curve of her neck. It feels good being held by her and being able to hold her too without fear of the Reverend catching us. I haven't forgotten he's close, but I know Dad will alert me in some way if the Reverend moves closer.

26

WREN

Church on Sunday isn't optional for anyone, especially me.

The house has to smell like polished wood, blended with the aroma of roasting chicken in the oven. It's on low so that it will be ready when I arrive home from church. That will give me time before the Reverend arrives to prepare the potatoes and vegetables. It has become routine rather than a chore in the years since I've been tasked with doing it.

The one thing to change has been me. I've grown in more areas than just height, and my Sunday dress has had to be replaced more than once. That hasn't pleased the Reverend because he hates spending money on clothes for me. My new dress is pink with a fitted bodice and flared skirt that rests below my knees. It's made from cotton and feels cool against my skin, which is good in the heat of the day. The style with its flower-shaped neckline is nice and I think I look pretty in it. I've brushed my hair for longer than usual and have left it down. I do this for Rafael's benefit even though he won't be at church. As I slip my feet into matching pink ballerina shoes, I hope he will see me when I step outside the house.

The Reverend has been talking on his phone, but he stops mid-conversation as I appear, and his eyes sweep over me in a lingering glance. I feel sick being looked at in that way and it worries me. He's only looked at me so strangely since Marcel and Rafael have moved in next door. I don't think it's connected, more of a coincidence, but either way, I *really* don't like it. He indicates for me to get in the car.

Tempted to climb into the back, I resign myself to the front passenger seat, relieved the hem of my dress is long enough to cover my legs. We don't exchange words and, as soon as we arrive at the church not five minutes later, I'm left sitting like an idiot while he is already inside his church. Sighing, I climb from the vehicle and make my way around the side of the large, white building to the Sunday school entrance. I hate this part of my Sunday. I'm still expected to partake in the church day, so I've opted to stay in the school part for the younger children. The Reverend is happy with my choice because he thinks I'm teaching his words to the children. What I really do is sit at the back and daydream. I do help with the children, but only to keep them settled.

Agnes Mercer is the Sunday school teacher and her whole attitude is just like the Reverend's. She scares me when her beady eyes focus on me. I've learned to hide it well over the last couple of years. She hasn't liked that, but for now, there is nothing she can do about it. The younger children fear her too, maybe they sense the meanness in her. I always watch myself around her because one day she will knife me in the back as easily as she will say good morning to someone else. I think she is a bitter old spinster, but there is more sinister in her than spinster.

I want to be elsewhere—somewhere with Rafael, away from eyes like hawks watching us. It would be nice to spend more time with him down by the stream. I really enjoyed our time together there. I enjoyed it a lot more than I should have. So had Rafael. I want to touch him again like I had. I want to do that without his jeans being in the way.

The hour passes quickly and by the time the children start to put away their prayer books, my cheeks are on fire. Agnes watches me with an evil smirk on her face. She makes me angry and I want to slap that look right off her face. Of course, I don't. I sneak out the door that leads to the hallway to the main part of the church.

As soon as I step through, I hear the Reverend's voice rise with his sermon. I've heard this so many times before—about how daughters should be obedient and how sons should grow into strong able-bodied men to keep their wives in line. He is in his element preaching to the masses about obedience. It's like he's obsessed with it. He certainly has obedience from his followers—the journals, the uniforms, the removal of the computers from the school. Everything that has been done recently has all been agreed on by *his* followers. Not that they had a choice.

The Reverend finally starts to calm down and his words become softer. I take that opportunity to slide along the hallway so I can see more of what is going on. I wish I'd left instead, because as soon as I'm in view, my eyes land on Peter Wild who has a smile on his face. His eyes keep going up and down the length of me and I want to puke. My skin crawls as though a million insects run over me. Feeling the urge to flee, I turn and head toward the back exit, only to hear Agnes talking on the other side of the door.

If I remember correctly there is a way of getting to the side exit without being seen by going through the basement. Perhaps, I'm being a bit dramatic, but I really don't want to have to see Wild or Agnes. Both of whom would gladly tell the Reverend about my strange behavior.

Basements scare me, but at least I know the Reverend isn't punishing me right now, and he is distracted with his followers after the service. The cold seeps into my bones as I get further down the steps, but that's as far as I go.

In front of me is a door I haven't seen before. A fire door. It's thick and solid and has been left ajar. Through the gap I don't see one computer on a desk, I see five or six very familiar looking computers. Are they the ones removed from school? What are they doing here? I take a step closer and freeze with my heart in my throat as I hear voices. A man I don't recognize moves into the doorway as though to exit and is startled to see me.

"What's wrong?" another guy questions from the side.

The man shakes his head, his eyes on me. "Nothing." He moves his eyes upward, and that's my cue to get the hell out of sight

I turn and flee up the stairs and straight outside. Agnes is gone, thank God! I glance around and not seeing anyone, I hurry around the side of the church to the front so that the men coming out of the basement don't catch me loitering. Grabbing onto the railing at the front of the church, I breathe deeply to try and calm my racing heart. The sun shines down on me, so I lift my face and soak up the rays. It works a little but my heart still pounds with fear as I start walking home.

Today is turning out to be a bad day as I hear the unmistakable sound of Wild's car coming up fast from behind me. I don't have time to hide before Wild pulls the car to a stop directly in front of me—the way forward now blocked. All I can hear in my head is my pulse thumping as fear slithers like a snake down my spine.

Peter Wild steps out of the car and rests a clenched fist on the roof of his sedan, his eyes look glazed as though he's been drinking.

"Thought you could leave without saying anything, huh?" He grins. "A pretty little thing like you walking home alone." He shakes his head. "Anything could happen to you. I'm not about to let that happen. I don't want to lose you to someone else."

"Lose me?" I take a step around the back of his car as he moves around the hood.

Keeping the distance between us is at the front of my mind but a car coming up fast from the opposite end of the lane causes me to stumble and Wild grabs my wrist. His grip is tight, biting into my skin. I can already see an angry red welt on my pale skin that will definitely bruise. I want to puke as I feel his weight against my back.

"Behave yourself, Wren. You wouldn't want the Reverend to know how bad you've been," he hisses, and grabs hold of my other wrist.

I struggle to free myself from his grip, but his fingers refuse to budge. "I haven't done anything wrong. The Reverend will kill you for touching me."

He stops at my words and I see his reflection in the back window - the Reverend doesn't scare him.

I hear the car come to a stop and Wild wheels us both around to watch Marcel climbing from the large black beast of a car. He slams the door—loud in the silence—almost like a gunshot. Rafael jumps from the passenger seat and starts toward me. "Let her go."

"No." Wild tightens his hold. He's sweating like a pig in the midday sun and the smell is not pleasant at all.

"It will take Rafael two minutes to run to the church and tell the Reverend that you are mishandling his daughter." Marcel takes a step closer. His body language is controlled but I can tell there is anger just below the surface. He's clearly ready for anything Wild attempts. Knowing that Marcel and Rafael are here reassures me that I will be okay. The Reverend won't see it that way.

"You don't know anything about the Reverend." Wild sneers as though he knows something we don't. "Or me."

Marcel's jaw clenches tightly and he takes a deep breath. "How about you let her go and I'll let you live." He takes a threatening step toward Wild, who loosens his hold.

The opportunity rises and I take it. I stomp hard on the front of Wild's shoe. He curses and loosens his grip even more as I try to stay balanced. I'm so angry and now that I have the advantage over the tall man, I turn and knee him in the groin. He gasps and his eyes shoot fire as he goes down to the ground, cupping himself. The moment I'm free,

Rafael pulls me away and takes me straight to his father's SUV.

Rafael opens the back door and, grabbing my hips, lifts me inside the car. I shuffle over and sigh when he follows in behind me. "Let me see what he did." Rafael gently takes hold of my hands and glances out the windshield to check on his father before he turns his attention to the discoloring on my skin. "I hate this. I hate that you're in this situation and there's nothing I can do to help you."

"No. Please don't say that." I wince as I pull my hands free and jump into his arms, straddling his lap. My arms wrap around his neck as his go around my middle. We hold each other tightly. "You help me more than you know. Just by being here for me, you help me." I nuzzle into his neck and feel pressure between my legs. It takes me a moment to realize what I feel, and I smile and brush my lips against the scar on his cheek.

Rafael wraps his hand in my hair and tilts my head backwards so that our eyes meet. "You are asking for trouble." He shudders and lifts me from his lap. He inhales and quickly rearranges the bulge in his jeans before he lifts a knee and turns to me. Just in time too as Marcel climbs into the driver's seat and glances between the two of us. His eyes say he knows exactly what was going on between us, but his words are filled with concern.

"We have you, Wren. He won't touch you again or I'll kill him."

"Thank you for coming to my rescue." I squeeze Rafael's hand. "But please, you can't get involved in anything that involves me or the Reverend. You just can't."

"Hey, don't cry." Rafael wipes a tear from my eye even though more fall. "We're not going to let anything happen to you, Wren. We know there is something very wrong here." Rafael looks at his father, who meets his son's eyes in the mirror. "I'm not going to leave you to him. Ever." His eyes blaze with promise, and so much more that my young heart struggles to grasp.

This boy, who I haven't known that long, will protect me with everything he has. We've already established that we are attracted to each other, and now, I realize his attraction toward me is so much more than I could ever have hoped for.

Inside his house, Rafael leads me up to his room, and holds my hand as I sit on the edge of his bed. He crouches in front of me, and says, "I've never had a girl inside of my bedroom before." He smiles. "But I want you in here and I don't want you to go back to the house next door."

I dip my head. "I have to go back. You know I do." I reach forward and press my hand to his neck. "It doesn't mean I don't want to stay here with you. It just means I don't want any trouble coming your way."

"Trouble is going to come here because we helped you."

I shake my head and reach for him, pulling his face so close to mine that we breathe the same air. "The Reverend will be angry that he didn't stop *him*. He won't be angry he was stopped because that isn't how the Reverend is. I'm his property, and anyone who dares to touch me will have wished they'd never heard of him, or me."

Rafael frowns. "That sounds rehearsed."

"It's his quote." I sigh and brush my lips across his before I lick mine. "Will you take the memory away for me?" I ask knowing that he wants to follow my lead—the lead that I have no idea where it came from.

His eyes stare at my lips and I tease him again with a swipe of my tongue across them. I watch his chest move in and out as he takes heavy, deep breaths and my body shivers in delight when a groan rumbles in his throat. I feel claimed as he pounces forward and presses me against his bed. His lips crush mine and my calm completely shatters with the hunger of his kiss. I forget everything as his tongue pushes into my mouth and sends shivers of hunger racing through my body that land straight between my legs. I moan and wrap my legs around his hips feeling wonderful and needy. I can't stop rubbing myself against the hardness of his lower body. Rafael grunts and tries to pull away, but I cling to him, gripping his hair and angling his head to accept my eager mouth.

I should be embarrassed by my response to the touch of his lips, his body, but I'm not. He is every-thing I want in one delicious package and I never want him to stop touching me. The touch of his lips sears a path down my neck, my shoulders, and then I feel his tongue tracing along my collarbone. My insides melt and when his hand reaches up and outlines the circle of my breast, I can't help my wanton response. Rafael growls and bites down on one of my nipples and I squirm beneath him. His body is so hard and strong above me. I feel the throb of his penis at his groin as he grows larger and harder against me. My body burns from the inside out and I don't think I'll be able to stop. I need more and I need it with Rafael. My mind knows something out of this world is about to happen, but I have no experience and don't know how to get it.

"Rafael," Marcel shouts. "Can you come downstairs a minute?"

Rafael pants hard as he raises his mouth from mine and gazes into my eyes. He brushes a gentle kiss across my forehead, and whispers, "I want you." His last words are smothered on my lips.

"Rafael?" Marcel shouts again.

I pull my mouth away and bury my face in his neck, where I place a kiss. Rafael shudders and with reluctance in every slow move he makes, he unwraps himself from me. His eyes swirl with desire as he takes his time looking at my body spread wide open on his bed. I push up on my elbows and look down and my cheeks heat. My skirt is around my hips and my pink panties are visible. "Wanton" is the only word to describe how I look.

"Rafael, dammit!"

Rafael takes a deep breath, and replies, "I'll be down in a minute."

"Okay," Marcel shouts after a lengthy pause.

"About damn time," I hear him mutter as his voice trails away.

Rafael kneels between my spread legs and I watch as his hands explore my thighs before moving to my panties. His eyes glitter and stay focused between my legs as he teases by rubbing up and down my groin. Without thought, my hips wiggle closer to his hands and then I feel him drag a finger between the lips down there. I gasp in pleasure and drop back to the bed.

"I don't want to stop touching you." He rubs and draws circles on me, and I've never felt anything like it. "It drives me crazy knowing you want me."

"I do but how can you tell." I laugh. "I mean apart from me throwing myself at you."

His finger stops and then his hand cups me as his eyes lift to mine. "I know because your panties are soaked with arousal." He breathes heavier. "You smell good, too." He swallows and his voice comes out husky. "Touching you makes me hard, Wren. Do you understand that?"

"Yes. I want to see you." I blush deeply.

"I want to see you too, but not while my dad is waiting impatiently for me downstairs." He stands again and begs, "Will you pull your skirt down so I can't see." He glances at his own body and a shudder ripples through him as he tugs on the ends of his hair. "I can't go downstairs like this." His hands rest on his hips while he tilts his head and stares up at the ceiling, his breathing becoming slower.

My eyes go to his hips and I immediately wonder if he will ever fit inside me. My cheeks burn and I have no idea where the thought came from. I might be clueless about how exactly the pleasure bursts from my body, but I know that a man's penis is supposed to fit inside a woman's vagina during sex.

Rafael chokes on a moan and gives me his back. "If you keep looking at me like that, I'm going to be embarrassing myself." He runs his hands through his hair. "I'm too old for that," he mutters under his breath. His feet are heavy on the floor as he moves toward his bedroom door. He stops and looks over his shoulder. His eyes linger on my sprawled body on his bed. "Stay up here, okay? I'll find out what my dad wants and then come back up."

I nod and watch his perfect ass move out of the room. My head feels heavy on my shoulders as I drop it to his bed and stare at the ceiling. His bedroom is large and takes over the entire attic. The ceiling slips upwards into the roof of the house and is lined with hardwood and rafters. It would be nice to have twin-kling lights wrapped around the beams. That would be the girly thing to do, and Rafael is anything but girly. He is all man.

When he'd looked up at me from between my legs, he hadn't looked like an eighteen-year-old boy, he'd looked older, and wiser. What really makes Rafael DeLacroix tick? Wanting to make the most of my time alone in his room, I force myself off his bed. The area by the window attracts my attention. He has an armchair set by the window and beside it a small table holding a sketchpad and a pot with a few pencils in all black. I curl up in the chair and that's when I see them. His drawings. They take my breath away. He's captured me with my butterflies in different spots around the garden—in the door of the glasshouse, watering the plants on one side, in the middle of the garden with my arms outstretched. The latter drawing is on a larger scale than the one he'd given me. It's the first time he'd seen me. The first time I'd seen him.

Unable to move my eyes from them, I slowly stand and pad over to the wall covered in Rafael's artwork. His dedication to detail astounds me. My eyes linger over the pieces and freeze on the one of us both on my roof. I'm in Rafael's arms with my head resting on his shoulder, a butterfly—Tiger Lily—in my hair. I have to swallow around the lump in my throat at the sight of us together. My fingers softly trail over the outline of us. The boy has worked his magic on me from the moment we met—a connection between us that continues to pull us together.

From behind, hands squeeze my hips before Rafael wraps himself around me and rests his chin on my shoulder.

"How long were you watching me?"

"Long enough to know how much you like my sketches." His deep voice rumbles from his chest and vibrates against my back.

"These are more than sketches, Rafael." I continue tracing the lines. "You're really talented."

"Hmm." He sighs. "You don't think it's creepy they're all of you?"

I think about what he said, but they don't freak me out, I'm delighted he's drawn me. "No." I give him my answer. "I love how you've captured me, and the delicate butterflies. However, most of all, I *really* like this one of us both. It says so much that I don't think words would ever be able to justify."

"It's one of my favorites, but this one"—he reaches

forward and taps a finger to the one of me in the middle of the garden—"is my absolute favorite. You took my breath away, Wren. I thought I was dreaming when I saw you covered in butterflies." He nuzzles into my neck. "You're my beautiful butterfly girl." Rafael's lips are on my neck before he slowly pulls away, his words, "The Reverend is home," sends fear down my spine. "That's what my dad wanted to talk about. He wanted you to know that we'll go home with you and explain what happened on the road. You don't have to do it alone."

"I'll be fine." *I hope.* "He'll be angry but, hopefully, not at me." I shrug, feeling anything but relaxed.

"You know we'll both be here for you, right? I mean it, Wren. I'm not all talk and no action. You need us, and we'll come." Rafael cups my face and presses a lingering kiss on my forehead.

Feeling choked up with emotion, I hug him tightly. "That means everything to me," I whisper against his warm body. "Please don't worry."

"I will regardless." He gives me one last squeeze. "You better go before he gets angry for you not being there."

"Will I see you later?" I ask as he takes my hand and leads me downstairs.

He briefly meets his dad's eyes, and then whispers, "No. We have to run some errands." I frown when he won't meet my gaze.

Turning to his dad, I say, "Thank you, Mr. DeLacroix, for coming to my rescue."

He smiles. "You know my name is Marcel." He takes my hands into his.

"Thank you, Marcel."

"You are welcome. I hope my son has told you we are here if you need us."

I glance at Rafael. "He has."

Marcel nods and Rafael walks me to the front door. "I'm not going to risk him seeing you with me, so I'll see you at school tomorrow." He kisses my forehead and practically shoves me outside.

And as I cross to my house, I remember the computers in the basement of the church. I'll have to remember to tell Rafael.

I ARRIVE HOME TO DISCOVER I HAVE NOTHING TO worry about, at least, not then. The Reverend is locked in his office and has left me a scribbled note on the kitchen table saying to serve Sunday lunch in an hour. Nervously chewing on my bottom lip, I slip upstairs and close my bedroom door, sagging behind it. My body is still hot and tight after Rafael had his hands and mouth on me. His touch has ignited something within me that has only cooled, but not gone out completely. I'm unsettled and irritated not knowing what to do to take the heated flush from my cheeks. My heart thumps behind my breastbone and I want to run over to Rafael's house and demand he finishes what he started. "Frustrated" is the word I'm looking for to describe how I feel. Frustrated.

In a bit of a mood, I tug my Sunday dress off and pull on a pair of comfy sweatpants and a T-shirt. The shirt is plain and baby pink. I'm not allowed anything with a slogan or emblem on it. My neck is heated along with my face, so I grab an elastic and spend ten minutes braiding my long hair. I'm cooler for it. My eyes linger on the closet, and I know why. I have to take another look. I'm addicted to the boy next door. I shove my clothes to the side and sigh when I see the artwork Rafael has given me. I've hidden it to be sure the Reverend doesn't catch sight of them. I still can't get over the gift of them. I haven't received anything as beautiful before. Rafael sees me like no one else and I can't believe how happy that makes me.

I want him to see me in the way he does. I think sometimes he sees part of me that I want no one to see and feel sorry for. The part where I'm alone and live in a world of near silence before he moved next door. I've had my butterflies for company and nothing more. Well, I'm not really sure what I have, but it certainly makes me happy.

Then unfortunately, I remember Wild and that the Reverend will demand an explanation from me when I take myself back downstairs. My good mood disappears. Grabbing a sweater because of the sudden chill, I slip it on and move slowly through the house to the kitchen. The meal has been ready for around an hour, but the stove has kept everything warm and just right. I've added freshly picked baby tomatoes and zucchini to the pot with the chicken. It smells divine and my belly rumbles. At least my appetite hasn't deserted me. However, there is still time for that.

Not knowing exactly when the Reverend had written his note about when he expects lunch, I quickly set the table and make the adjustments needed. I pour water from the large bottle in the fridge and set the glasses to the side of our plates, four inches to the right from the tip of the knife.

"Lunch smells good, Wren."

I jump at the sound of the Reverend's voice and turn to face him. "Are you ready to eat?"

His eyes trail over me and his mouth turns into a frown. "Why have you changed so quickly?"

I can do this.

"Peter Wild followed me home and tried to get me into his car." I rush the words out, and continue, "He wouldn't leave me alone and wanted—" Tears fill my eyes. "He wanted to touch me. Said he was done with waiting." I wipe a tear away but keep my eyes on him. "Marcel and Rafael DeLacroix came to my rescue."

As I speak, the Reverend's face bulges red. The angrier he becomes, the deeper the red on his face turns. He looks about ready to blow a gasket. His fists clench on the table and I force myself not to move.

"I didn't do anything wrong," I blurt in panic. "He came after me. You said I looked nice in my dress. I told him you'd be mad if he touched me, but he said he wasn't bothered. Please don't blame me. I promise I tried to get away from him. I wouldn't have managed if the neighbors hadn't helped."

The Reverend still doesn't say anything—only stares at me while he breathes in and out like a bull ready to charge. He rarely lets me see him so angry, but now I really pray it isn't me he's angry at.

"You know I do not like the new neighbors. I told you to stay away from them. WREN!" He slams his fist on the table and the dishes rattle. "Stay away from them!" He holds my gaze and all I can do is nod as fear skates down my spine and lands in my belly like a rock. "I will deal with Wild." He glances at the table. "Put the lunch out. You eat yours. All of it. Place mine in the stove to keep warm and I'll eat it later. Don't wait up for me." He turns and slams out of the house with only one glance toward me.

27

RAFAEL

"SHE'S IN LOVE WITH YOU," IS THE FIRST THING DAD says to me the moment Wren leaves.

I drop my head and close my eyes not knowing what to do. Wren isn't the only one who is feeling this thing between us. I want her for myself and wish I could take her away from this place and never return.

The sweet taste of her on my mouth lingers and I crave her more than words can say. Wren is beautiful inside and out. I love talking to her. I could listen to her voice all day long and not get bored. When I'm close to her, my body fills with warmth and I crave the touch of her pale skin. I imagine joining her freckles with the tips of my fingers. I want to tell her everything I know about the Reverend and why we're in town. The only thing stopping me is the vengeance I want for Mom and Roman. The only thing. I hope when she does know everything that she'll understand and forgive me for lying to her.

"You love her too," Dad states, moving into my line of sight, a stoop to his shoulders. "We have something to do now, but once we're back, we need to talk."

"Why do I get the feeling we're not going shopping?" I ask when Dad passes me a flashlight.

"Because you would be right." Dad walks out of the house into the warm sun and I follow with a frown on my face. I'm confused.

"Where are we going?"

Dad indicates for me to get in the car. I'm tempted to go back inside the house, but I'm curious. We've been out into town for supplies and had no plans to go out again today.

Turning the engine on, Dad says, "We got information telling us to look around the old schoolhouse."

"Is that the place we snuck around before we moved here?"

"Yes." He rubs his mouth, and adds, "It's been closed for years."

"Something else is bothering you." I turn in my seat so that I can watch him closely. "I told you I wouldn't screw this up because of Wren."

"That isn't what's bothering me. At the moment anyway." He swallows and gives me a sidelong glance. "A note was shoved under the back door with the information. All it said was to check out the old schoolhouse. I'm not sure whether it's a move to get us there—a trap. Or whether it's someone inside the Reverend's fold, who also knows who I am and is trying to help."

"But you're curious enough to want to go look."

"Yes."

I think back to the night I was caught watching the computers being unloaded into the church and the man who told me to leave. He hadn't given me away.

"The man," I start, "who told me to go. You don't think he's law enforcement, do you?"

"I'm still waiting on confirmation as to Silas's status." He slams his fist in the middle of the steering wheel. "I have a feeling he's alive and going after the Reverend on his own."

"Not alone. We need to compare his handwriting

to that on the flowers. I bet he sent the note, which means he's asking for our help."

"What worries me is, if he isn't Silas, then who is he?"

"I don't know." I shrug.

Deep in thought, Dad doesn't say anything while continuing to drive along the country road that leads directly to the schoolhouse. We'll have to trek through the long grass to get to the building as the driveway has been covered up and left to go crazy. Foliage covers everything in sight. The wrought iron gates are falling to the side of the entrance.

I don't see anything out of place or different than the last time we were here. Dad parks out of view of the road, using the foliage to cover us from any passersby.

Jumping from the SUV, I'm not sure I agree with his reasoning for being here at his point. It's too damn hot to be looking for something when we don't know what we're looking for. Dad thinks we'll know when we see it.

Hours later, after searching the immediate area and coming up with nothing, I'm exhausted. Sweat runs down my back and stomach, dropping into my jeans. I discarded my shirt a while back, but fuck, my balls feel like they're baking trapped in black denim. Part of me regrets living in jeans at this moment in time. Maybe I should have had the sense to wear the khaki shorts Dad had tossed me a few days ago, I'd be a lot cooler at least. Sans boxers would be good too. A nice breeze to keep my dick cool.

I glance toward the water, fighting the temptation to take a swim. The thought that there may be a dead body or two in the water puts me right off. I have a healthy imagination that sometimes takes a turn on the dark side, like now. I mentioned to Dad that there were probably dead bodies all over the place. He didn't find it amusing. I'm not amused, just convinced I'm right.

Darkness has settled in as I climb into the car with nice air conditioning. My pulse pounds through my head as I go from melting into a puddle to a pleasant coolness. It caresses my skin while Dad sits staring off into space. I just want to get out of here for something to eat and a cold drink. Thinking about ice-cold liquid sliding down my throat makes my mouth water. What I want most though, while I'm all hot and sweaty, is Wren. She'll be a firecracker once she gets started, and I'm going to be the one to see her that way. No one else.

Shifting in my seat, I let out a heavy lungful of air willing my arousal down a notch or two...or maybe five. My head needs to be filled with something other than the girl, otherwise, I'm going to become an embarrassment.

I look at Dad again and he hasn't moved, his eyes focused on a spot near the river on the left side of the schoolhouse. His hands are wrapped tightly around the steering wheel and his fingers flex.

"Dad?"

"I think there's someone moving around over there."

"What?" I stare in the same direction, and it takes me a few minutes to really concentrate with the sweat running down my back. When I do, I realize he's right. "More than one person." I reach for the door handle, but Dad grabs my arm, indecision on his face. "We have to go and see what they're doing?"

"It's dangerous," he hisses, and curses under his breath. "I need to remember you can handle yourself."

"I can. Now, let's move it before we miss what they're doing." He doesn't restrain me now that he's come to the same conclusion as I have.

Slowly, we slip from the car and straight into the tall grass. It blows softly in the welcomed light breeze. Insects buzz around us, and not that I'm religious, but I'm fucking praying right now that I don't meet a snake. I shudder at the idea, but continue to creep forward, watching Dad and his movements. He stops. I stop. He moves. I move. He hadn't just insisted on martial arts and self-defense training after Mom and Roman died. He made sure I was ready to be here with him. He'd known I wanted the bastards responsible for their deaths to pay as much as he did.

Dad quickly touches my arm and I still and listen when he touches his ear. The first noise I hear is plopping sounds, like something hitting water. I frown wondering what the hell I'm listening to and then remember we're next to the river. About a foot to my left and I'll be swimming. I think we've spooked the frogs because that's what I hear, their croaks loud in my ears. I keep my head down and crawl away from the nest or whatever you call where frogs live. I'm out of the way with seconds to spare as one of the men we saw moving around stands where I was a few seconds ago.

It was close.

I hold still while my heart pounds against my breastbone and something jumps onto the back of my leg. I desperately want to shake my leg to get it off. It just sits there, the urge to move getting stronger by the second. A frog maybe. I don't turn my head because I'm keeping my eyes on the asshole looking around him. Luckily, his main attention is focused on the river.

Sweat drips down my face and between my shoulder blades. I'm afraid to move the slightest bit in case I attract his attention...and then, just as suddenly, he's gone, and I hear his boots squelching in the mud. I stare and wait, but he doesn't return. I drop my head in relief and feel the creature on my leg get knocked off. It croaks and disappears into the water.

Thank fuck it was only a frog.

Shuddering, I turn my head and indicate for us to move closer. Dad shakes his head, and whispers, "Wait."

I don't want to wait. I'm impatient to see exactly what they're up to. Lifting my head so I can see above the grass, I frown. There are three men standing around an old rusty bathtub. With how their attention is focused, I think we should have looked more closely.

Dad moves in until he's pressed along the side of my leg, and leans in whispering, "The Reverend."

"I recognize him. I don't the others."

"I can't get a good look." Dad makes a move to get closer just as a whoosh followed by flames fills the distance. Seconds later he dives on top of me. "Stay down."

"What the fuck?" I try to shove Dad from me, my heart racing with fear from being held down.

"Fuck," he curses and rolls from me. "I'm sorry, Rafael." He crouches down and I follow, trying to calm down, but I can't hear anything because of the blood rushing through my head. He rubs my back with a gentle hand and my breathing finally slows. I haven't had many panic attacks since I was attacked trying to go to Mom and Roman's rescue, so I'm surprised one hit me now. Not the most convenient of places to have one.

Dad indicates the direction to move in as I glance at the blaze happening in the tub. I know we need to move away, but I want to see what they're burning. It could be evidence. Incriminating documents. Dad shakes his head, knowing exactly what I'm thinking. "I'll come back tomorrow and check it out."

I take a step to follow but stop and listen. The hull of a boat sluices through the water moving away from us. They've gone and left the fire? No, a man has stayed behind and watches the flames shoot high.

"Move," Dad hisses, taking my wrist and tugging me with him.

He lets go and I continue to follow. "We can't leave until he's gone. He'll hear the car."

"We'll roll backwards down the hill before I switch the engine on. It should give us enough time to get out of here before he knows we were watching." He quietly shuts his door, and adds, "It's the Reverend standing there. He'll presume it was us, but he won't know for sure." With that, Dad releases the parking brake and eases us down the hill. Not before long, we're racing back to the house.

28

WREN

Hours after the Reverend's outburst, I'm in the kitchen with the ladle in my hands, which shake at the memory of earlier. He hasn't been angry like that in a few years. Inhaling, I scoop a piece of chicken from the pot and then top it on my plate with the vegetables. New potatoes have cooked well in the pot, so I place them around and admire the meal. It looks pretty with the different colors. It certainly smells good.

I'm not sure if I'll be able to eat it with my tummy rolling. He really frightened me with the slamming on the table. He is strong in his beliefs and rules his home with an iron fist, and perhaps those around him fear him more than I thought. Wild hadn't unless he'd used false bravado when he'd been after me. That man is dangerous. It worried me the way the Reverend had stormed out of the house. There is a part of me that hopes he's gone to teach Wild a lesson, because then maybe, the Reverend will get in trouble with the law and won't come home.

Sighing heavily, I decide not to dwell on something I can't control and use another plate to cover the Reverend's food before placing it in the oven, leaving it on the lowest setting. Mine looks lost on the table alone. I pull out the wooden chair and take my seat, pulling my dish closer. My belly lets out another rumble and I smile. I'm going to enjoy this! I get to eat a meal alone and take my time without the Reverend glaring at me. The vegetables are from my garden and that is an accomplishment. Delight fills me as I place a small piece of chicken and a baby tomato into my mouth. The tomato tastes fresh and juicy, while the chicken has been cooked to tender perfection.

Before I know it, I've eaten everything on my plate. Once the dishes are washed and put away, I decide to head outside. A light breeze ruffles the loose hair around my face as I glance next door. Marcel's SUV is still missing, and the house looks quiet.

The moment I feel the butterflies waking from where they've been perched, I smile and close my eyes with my face tipped toward the setting sun. The flutter of tiny wings tickle my nose and I sneeze and laugh after the fourth one. Tiny wings of all colors dance before my eyes. If I didn't know any better, I would say they laughed at me. These beautiful creatures who have become my friends are so delicate. And each are so different with varied sizes, shapes, and colors of wings. Sometimes I wish I could capture the essence of them so that I will never forget how they were here for me. Rafael had captured their beauty with his drawings. He sees what no one else ever has. It makes my belly tingle and dance with how he sees me. He not only sees the young girl with long dark brown hair, pale skin with freckles over my cheeks, but he also sees inside of me to the loneliness.

I hold my hand out and watch as Tiger Lily lands on my thumb and another follows along my finger. Butterflies do not have a long lifespan and I know it's only a matter of time before these beauties will become a memory. More will take their place, they always do, but Tiger Lily is special to me, and I will miss him.

The sun finishes setting as I move toward the

glasshouse and the humidity that meets me there. It's tropical inside, which is how my delicate friends like it. They thrive in the heat and moisture. I have four watering cans that sit under my small workbench that are already filled and waiting. I grab the first one up and start to water the plants that not only the butterflies rely on, but me as well. I love being able to come out here and collect fresh fruit and vegetables. As for fruit, we only have strawberries at the moment, but I am hoping for an apple or pear tree in the garden. Or maybe even some small ornamental orange trees in the glasshouse. However, my future isn't here. I know that with every breath I take. I can't stay here, not for anything. One day I'll have to leave my greenhouse and my butterflies, and the thought is bittersweet.

The town of Port Michael isn't home and I'm not sure it ever has been. The people are weird and now, with the journals and uniforms, I'm scared of what plans are already in motion. The Reverend knows. He's in charge and others come to him for advice and guidance. Over the years he's brainwashed them until they only want to please him.

Tonight, he has gone after Peter Wild. I know this and it doesn't bother me because the man scares me to death. I'm just not sure whether the Reverend went after him because the man had tried to touch me, or because Wild hadn't given a hoot about the Reverend's world. It's probably the latter.

"Oh well, Tiger Lily," I mumble. "Wherever I go or whatever happens, I'll always remember you." I blow him a kiss and make sure he's settled on his favorite flower, the purple coneflower. "Good night, my angels."

Stepping outside, my tank top clings to me from the heat. As I stretch, my attention zeroes in on the side of the house. A man is standing in nothing but his shorts as he uses a hose to spray himself down. I falter, my mind stumbling over my confusion at the tall man standing there undressed and in disarray. The Reverend! My stomach knots into a huge lump and I feel sick. Why would he need to do that? He has a shower off his bedroom. It doesn't make any sense. Something bad must have happened. On instinct, I step back into the shadow of the glasshouse and keep watching. The last thing I want is for him to know I've seen him. My mind wanders while my heart beats its scared rhythm if he's done something to that Wild man. I hope he has, but what I'm witnessing is so much more than what I expected. Surely, he hasn't blooded him up enough that he needs washing outside first. Can I imagine the Reverend doing something like that? Yes, I can.

No way am I about to walk through the house now. I'd hoped to be in my room before he arrived home. This isn't late by any means. As panicked thoughts run through my head, I know I'm going to have to climb onto the roof to get to my bedroom. I'm pretty sure I've left my bedroom window open slightly.

The moment the Reverend steps inside the house, keeping the lights off—another unusual behavior for him—I dash across the garden with my heart in my throat. Once I have the cover of the house to protect me, I move around to the side and grab hold of the wooden trellis. It isn't as though I haven't done this before, just not for a year or so. It will hold my weight because this is how Rafael gets onto the roof and he's a lot heavier than me.

Tightening my grip, my fingers ache on the wooden slats. I slowly pull myself up, only just getting my feet into the spaces as I get closer to the roof. My legs tremble, which makes climbing that much more difficult. It takes me longer to reach the roof, but when I do, I take a minute and sit. My hands hurt from where I've clenched tightly to the wood, my neck hurts a bit too. I must be tenser than I thought. Feeling sweat running down my spine, I crawl on my hands and knees to my bedroom window, sighing in relief when I find it open. I lift it all the way up and climb inside, knocking the pen holder off my desk with a foot. It crashes to the floor in a scattering of pens and pencils. It's loud enough that I freeze and wait.

The Reverend obviously decides against checking on me, either that or he's too lost in thought to have heard. Whatever the reason, it's welcomed.

Righting everything, I quickly get ready for bed and slip between the sheets. Unfortunately, my mind won't switch off and all I can think about is what the Reverend had been up to.

MISERABLE!

That's how I feel today.

It started with the Reverend banging around downstairs as though he was trying to catch a rodent or something. The slam of a cupboard. The sound of the silverware drawer being shoved in and out of the slider. The sound of pots crashing gets me out of bed.

He's in a right temper as I quickly pull on my uniform and dash into the bathroom. Five minutes later, I'm standing in the kitchen doorway. The table is a mess with spilled cereal from a large bowl that lies on its side, milk drips onto the floor where clumps of soggy cereal lie. I even spot coffee granules floating in the milk.

"Don't just stand there," the Reverend snaps, grabbing my arm before yanking me into the room. "Get this mess cleaned up. It's your fault I'm in a temper."

He leaves the house.

I stand staring at the mess while my pulse pounds in my ears. What did he do last night? I bet this morning's antics have everything to do with it.

I need to talk to Rafael, and I can't believe I'm even thinking this, but I want to check on Wild. Something isn't right and it's going to play on my mind until I know what is going on.

Hurrying to clean the mess up, I glance at the old white clock on the wall. I have twenty minutes before school starts. I run out the front door with a couple of apples and a banana in my hand, which I shove into my book bag.

As I enter the school there is an eerie silence in the air. I can't wait to get away from this place. Other students stare at me like I've done something wrong, and they give me a wide berth. It's something I've grown used to, but it feels different. The glances aren't friendly but accusatory. What I've done to deserve today's torture, I don't know. It isn't nice and it makes me jittery on the inside. On the outside, I make sure I look indifferent.

I walk to my locker and see Rafael standing close to it with three girls talking animatedly to him. He smiles and nods at them. My heart cracks at the sight and tears hover on my lashes. One of the girls takes his arm and glances over and smirks. I duck my head because I refuse to let anyone see how much Rafael's inattention bothers me. It's difficult to breathe as I open my locker. I blink back the tears. I won't cry. I won't.

Then I feel his presence beside me and know that I must ignore him. It hurts. I want to be open with him, but I can't. I can't even be seen talking to him.

"Meet me around back at break," Rafael whispers as he moves past me slowly. I give him a sidelong glance and notice his fan club has left.

"No," I hiss, keeping my head averted. I'm not sure why I'm acting like this with him when I want to spend time with him. I want to spend all my time with him—to show him my butterflies and my favorite places. I want to confide in him about last night.

I feel him tense and turn his head. I even know when his gaze turns into a frown, and the way there is hesitation in his body before he moves to class. I swallow around the lump in my throat and try to forget about yesterday in Rafael's bedroom. That had been real. I know it.

Slamming my locker closed, I groan. I've just experienced jealousy. I'm jealous of the open friendship he can have with others. I only need to be near him, and the Reverend will know. Someone in the school will tell him—they all believe in his word.

"Miss Jacobs." I still at the sound of the principal's deep rumbling voice directly behind me. "Why are you at your locker instead of in class?"

I gulp and turn to face him. "I felt a bit dizzy, but I'm fine now." He stares into my eyes, daring me to say more. I don't think I can, even if I want to. My mouth is dry, and I feel like a panic attack is imminent.

"Tardiness will be written in your journal. Get to class."

On edge, I scuttle away and feel Principal

Dobson's eyes on my back before I disappear into the classroom. I'm then faced with all eyes on me from other pupils and Mr. Bradshaw. I catch Rafael's gaze and he indicates for me to move with his eyes. His jaw pulses with anger as his eyes stay focused on the teacher.

I hate this. It is me against them. Or maybe it is Rafael and me against them. I don't know anymore. This new regime is wrong. Even though I know of nothing outside of Port Michael, I know the way we are treated is wrong. School shouldn't be so strict with rules not to be broken. Journals are not meant to be filled with reasons to be punished, or reasons to be praised. I don't understand why things have suddenly changed, not that they had been any better before. At least we didn't have to write everything down. The others seem too accepting, as if they knew this was about to happen. Nothing makes sense.

Once I've taken my seat, I keep glancing at Rafael from the corner of my eye. He watches me too. The sidelong glances from him make me feel funny inside. His eyes are deep as he watches me, the black darkening to orbs with flecks of gold. Mr. Bradshaw suddenly appears between us, cutting off our view of each other. His face is red with anger as he holds his hand out toward me. I glance up at him and back to his hand, not knowing what he wants. Rafael shakes his journal behind Mr. Bradshaw, which I luckily catch sight of. I shuffle through my little belongings and, grabbing the journal, hold it up. Mr. Bradshaw snatches it from me. "I will write in this." He turns to Rafael and takes his. "And this, while you get on with the instructions on the whiteboard.

He abruptly turns and moves to his desk at the front of the classroom and drops into the seat. My eyes narrow as he opens my journal and rapidly writes inside it. My heart sinks because whatever he writes, I know the Reverend won't be happy about it.

I pass a quick glance at Rafael before putting my head down and writing the essay as instructed. I find it more difficult than normal to concentrate. My mind is on the journal in Mr. Bradshaw's greedy hands. He never glances up, just scribbles angrily before he switches to Rafael's book.

All through class I feel eyes on me and know it is Rafael. He wills me to look in his direction, but I refuse. I'm hurt that he can't acknowledge me properly after what transpired between us in his bedroom. I know we have to stay apart in public, but I don't have to like it, and he certainly didn't have to consort with the enemy!

"Class," Mr. Bradshaw snaps, followed by the slamming of journals on his desk. "After break you have a free period, which is to take place in the library." His eyes land on each and every one of us before he says, "Dismissed." He gives Rafael his journal back and watches the class leave. I'm all fingers and thumbs as I try to put everything away. His brows draw into an angry frown as he focuses on me and indicates with his finger that I am to stand in front of his desk.

I swallow hard and my palms feel clammy as I approach. My book bag is clutched tightly in my arms while I wait for him to speak. All he does is glare at me and smirks when he knows he's gotten to me. I want to scream and hit the asshole. I do nothing.

"The Reverend needs to see your journal this evening." He holds it out and when I grab it, he won't let go. "He won't be happy, Wren."

I snatch the book from his hands and dash out of the classroom and right into Rafael. He grabs my arm and pulls me out the back of the school and into a quiet spot—the same one as the other day.

"You refused to meet me, so I had no choice," he

grumbles, and paces back and forth. "We need to stick together, Wren."

"That's what I thought too." I narrow my gaze so that he is aware I'm unhappy. "You were the one smiling and flirting with *them*."

Rafael comes to a sudden stop, and I watch as his mouth slowly splits into a grin. "You're jealous? *Again*." He smirks, and before I know it, he is directly in my face, mere inches separating us. "I only see you, Wren." His eyes land on my mouth, so I stick the tip of my tongue out and rub it along my lips. Rafael catches his breath, but he stays focused on what I tease him with. My body comes to life as I breathe in his scent. My breasts lightly touch his chest with each deep breath I take. Our eyes finally find each other's, and all sound disappears, replaced by a pounding in my ears as blood rushes through my head. My eyes wander to his mouth and I desperately want him to kiss me. He wants it too.

His hands land on my waist, warm and secure, and I feel that slight tug as our bodies become flush. I briefly rub against him and feel how hard and solid he really is. A moan slips from between my lips as I allow my eyes to fall closed and for my body to just feel. I want to feel Rafael against me in this way. I want to learn everything about this boy that makes me smile. I wiggle my hips to Rafael's surprise, and reaching up, I wrap my arms around his neck. I nuzzle against his warm skin and sigh.

Rafael is surprised at my spontaneous hug but, seconds later, he has his face buried in my neck and me wrapped tightly in his arms.

"We need to talk, Wren. I'll come to you later." He kisses the curve of my neck and leaves his lips there, softly brushing over my skin.

In that moment, I'm happy.

Truly happy.

MY HAPPINESS DOESN'T LAST ONCE I GET HOME. THE Reverend is waiting for me, his face barley able to contain the fury I see there. He sits at the wooden table in the kitchen and indicates for me to move closer to him.

I drop my book bag on the floor and do as he says, even though I'm terrified of him right now. He looks angry, as if the slightest movement would make him snap and come at me. My eyes go nervously to the leather belt in the middle of the table as I wait, trembling, my mouth dry.

He stands slowly and moves closer, his breath hitting me in the face. I try not to gag at the sour smell. "You didn't listen to me," he hisses through clenched teeth. "You are friends with the boy next door when I told you to stay away from him." He puts his face to the side of mine. "Has he touched you, daughter?"

I swallow hard, and answer, "No, sir. No one has."

"I don't believe you," he snarls. "Maybe I should let one of my men fuck you to see if you're stretched, huh? Something tells me you wouldn't like that?" He grabs the belt from the table and whips it across the old surface. "Maybe if I tan your bare ass, you'll finally listen to me."

Before I have time to think, his hands are on me and I'm face down on the hard surface. "No," I gasp, the tears no longer staying in my eyes. "Please! I promise he didn't touch me. I'm still a virgin."

He growls and lifts the back of my dress up over my bottom. "Virgin, you are not! Because of your stupid antics, you popped your own fucking cherry! I can't sell you as a virgin, Wren. You're not worth much to me anymore. I only keep you around because—" He stops himself.

I pray to God he doesn't carry out this punishment. He's losing his head and I'm scared and want Rafael. I want to run away with him.

My skirt gets yanked down and I'm lifted from the table and shoved toward the stairs. "Go to your room and stay there until morning," he says through his anger. "If I hear one word, Wren—one word—that you've been anywhere near that *boy*," he spits, "I will continue exactly where we left off."

He turns and stalks to his office, slamming the door so hard the house shudders.

I can barely move as fear races through my blood.

What is going on with him?

My eyes focus on the table before I turn and head upstairs and wait for Rafael to come to me.

29

RAFAEL

I watch the lights go out downstairs at Wren's house and continue watching until a faint glow appears in her bedroom moments later. My view is clear from where I lounge on the back porch of my house.

The Reverend is still inside. Probably in his office on the other side of the house plotting what is to happen next in his grand plan. I should go with my dad to find out what was going on last night, but I can't bring myself to leave Wren. I need to go and spend time with her. The ache I have in my chest hurts being so close yet so far.

My father comes outside, a beer in his hand as his

gaze wanders over to the house across the way. "You're going to tell her," he says. "It's been written all over your face since the moment you met her."

"She's innocent in all of this." I sit forward and place my elbows on my knees, getting tired of repeating myself to him. "I don't want her to get caught up in whatever happens. We have to keep her safe." I look at the beer again and he catches me.

"I'm not going anywhere. There's a car hidden on the road, watching the front of our house." He shrugs as though it's no big deal. "Jeremiah and Ken are going to check out the schoolhouse." He slugs the beer back. He focuses back on Wren's house. "I still think the only way to keep her safe is to stay silent. If she's clueless, then she won't be curious. If she isn't curious, then she won't risk getting caught snooping."

Moving forward, I pace along the porch full of energy. "I love her. I don't want any lies between us." I stand in front of him, holding his gaze. "I trust her."

Dad blinks sharply and a slow smile spreads across his face. "Then tell her." He hugs me close and goes back inside the house.

An urgency to get to Wren overwhelms me, but I pause as I jump from the porch. Movement to the side of Wren's house draws my gaze. I recognize the figure—the Reverend. He gets in his car and drives away in the opposite direction of the church. At least the coast is clear for me to go to Wren. I quickly pull my phone from my back pocket and message Dad that the Reverend has left and which way he headed. The last thing I want is for him to stumble upon Dad's friends moving around the old schoolhouse. Dad acknowledges my message, and I shove my phone away.

I can now focus on Wren. Her smile always makes my heart feel much lighter, and just the presence of her is enough to get rid of the darkness inside of me. She lights me from within and my first instinct is to take her back to the city so no one can find her. It's only a dream because they'd find her in the end. The Reverend would make sure of that.

Shaking off the sudden feeling of pending doom, I hoist myself up and onto the roof. Wren's window is ajar as I watch her favorite butterfly enter the room.

I crouch beside the window and listen.

"Hey, boy," she whispers, her feet softly padding closer to the window. "How was your day?" I watch as she offers her hand to Tiger Lily. The butterfly flutters his wings as he moves his tiny body onto Wren's finger. "I really hope it was better than mine."

From the corner of my eye, I catch three more butterflies enter the bedroom. They settle with Tiger Lily and the sight of them causes me to smile. My butterfly girl. They are so beautiful and trust her to care for them. It's as though she holds some kind of magic over them. I have no idea how or why they've attached themselves to her and I don't think she does, but she will be lost without her butterflies.

The sudden flutter of wings as they take flight toward the window draws her attention to me. She only pauses for a moment before she moves to help me into the room. It isn't until I stand to my full height and look around her room that I realize how bare it is. My eyes soon drift back to Wren and I slip my tongue between my lips as her eyes follow. Her body heats up and her breathing becomes heavy, as does mine.

"I want more of what you did to me the other night. I want to feel that unbearable heat all over again." She blushes heavily the moment the words leave her mouth. It makes me feel good to know she feels a deep ache too. "I want us to do what the Reverend accuses me of."

Wait! What?

"Wren?"

"It doesn't matter," she says with tears in her eyes.

"It matters. Did he hurt you?"

She inhales and pulls herself together. "He was about to, but he stopped himself. He accused you of touching me. I really want to do what he insinuated. Right now."

She's not telling me something, but with the look on her face, I dip my head until our faces are so close that I can see the ocean blue in her eyes. I gently cup her face and brush a soft kiss across her lips. "I wanted to do that all day," I whisper, and press my lips to hers. My lips turn up into a smile before I kiss the tip of her nose. I back up a step and sit on the end of her bed. "He went out, so I figured it was safe to come in here." I smirk. "In case you wondered."

"I heard him leave."

"Talking to your friends." I smile, which slips when I watch her.

She sits next to me, and fidgets before she blurts, "I think the Reverend did something to Peter Wild."

"What?" I rest my arms on my thighs as I lean forward, my head tilts toward Wren.

"Last night I saw him taking a shower with the

hose. It was dark so he didn't see me, but I don't understand why he'd need to clean up outside. He's never done it before."

"Then tomorrow we'll go to Peter's place and have a look around," I say, as though it's a regular occurrence to go snooping around someone else's house.

"I don't like that idea." She chews on her lip. "But I won't stop worrying until I see the man for myself."

"You really are worried about him after what he tried to do to you?"

"I'm only worried because I think the Reverend was covered in someone else's blood. I wanted Wild away from me, not…well…dead."

Frowning, I say, "You don't know he's dead."

Was that what the Reverend and the other two men were doing last night? Getting rid of Wild.

"I have a really bad feeling a lot of stuff is going on that we don't know anything about. I'm not sure I want to know either."

I stay silent and lean back on the bed, staring at the ceiling. "We'll find out." I pat the space next to me. "Lie back with me."

The moment she does, I bring her into my arms. I feel good having her so close, and it makes it difficult for me to leave.

Glancing around her bedroom to try and think about something other than the gorgeous girl in my arms and how much I want to keep her with me, I really take notice at how bare the room is. "What did you do with the drawings I gave you?"

She smiles against my chest. "I put them up in the back of my closet so he wouldn't see them. He wouldn't have liked it and you have no idea how much I cherish them."

I hold her closer. "I do know. I also know why they're in your closet and not out in the open. You don't have to explain anything to me about him."

Tears hover on her lashes as I gaze at her beautiful face.

"I want to tell you, Wren." I meet her gaze before I stare straight up at the ceiling. "I want to tell you what happened to me."

"I'm here, Rafael. You can tell me anything, and you know I don't have anyone else to repeat it to. I wouldn't anyway."

I offer her a reassuring hug. "It isn't pretty, so just let me get it all out, okay?"

She nods against me.

I know I have to give her something else before I tell her my story. "I'm not eighteen, Wren. I'm twenty." She pulls her brows into a frown, so I reach with my fingers and stroke them away. "I will explain later, but I need you to know my real age because I have strong feelings for you."

"I thought you looked older." Her eyes search mine. "Tell me your story, Rafael." She tugs me close and kisses my lips before we settle back down on the bed.

"One of my teachers hadn't shown up for class, so a few of us went over the back wall and ran off down the alley. I knew Mom and Dad would be angry with me, but I hadn't wanted to stay at the school and be bullied and teased for staying. So, I went over the wall.

"We all went our own way once we were clear of the school. A few stuck together. But not me. I decided I had to come clean to my parents, so I went home. My younger brother was in a different school because of his age, plus, he was autistic and needed more help than my school could provide. He was at home sick that day, which I didn't know at the time.

"It didn't take me long to get home, but as soon as I walked up to the front door, I knew something was wrong. It wasn't anything in particular that stood out to me, just a feeling.

"The old wooden front door was ajar." I smile. "My mother loved that old door and wouldn't have it replaced. She said it was the door that made her fall in love with the house. My dad loved her and would have given her the world if he could. I loved her too. She was the only Mom I knew. My birth mother died when I was a baby. I think I told you that already."

Wren nods.

"Anyway, Roman was her son from a previous relationship, but we loved him. He was such a loveable kid that I never once regretted having Sarah and Roman join our small family." I sigh. "Sometimes I wish the clock would turn back to the day before so we could do something different the day they died—they wouldn't have been home."

Swallowing hard, I continue, "I remember opening the front door and seeing what I thought at the time was red paint. So much of it in the hallway, the walls, the floors, handprints on the cream carpet on the stairs, splatters on the ceiling. I remember thinking Mom would go nuts and kill Roman when she saw the mess he'd made.

"It didn't smell like paint, though. I stood frozen in place when it slowly started to dawn on me that it wasn't paint, it was blood. I struggled to comprehend what I was seeing while my heart pounded like it was going to jump right out of my chest. I fumble with my cell phone and it ends up flying out of my hands and hitting the ground. I remember fighting the urge to run and I shouted for Mom. Seconds later, I heard a loud crash and then Mom screaming for me to run.

"The sound came from the back of the house, and without thought to my own well-being, I took off toward the kitchen. And that's when it all happened. I was grabbed from behind by a giant of a man. Strong as fuck too. I tried to fight to get free, but his hold was too strong. At the far end of the kitchen a man was crouched over Mom who was surrounded by blood. She was on her knees. Roman was held back by another man. Crying and shaking, also covered in blood. The men wore masks, and the one in charge waved around a fucking sword. He laughed and went to use it on Mom, but in a split second Roman broke free, screamed, and threw himself at Mom. I think he was trying to shield her. The sword passed through both of them. The man screamed in rage, his eyes blazing with savage hatred.

"I don't remember much after that. I woke up in the hospital while Dad cried and held my hand."

My stomach rolls remembering that day, but I'm

relieved to have told Wren. She's important to me, and to finally have told her the truth about my age, and about the worst time in my life, I feel as though a weight has lifted from my shoulders.

"After he pulled the sword out of Roman and Mom, the guy turned toward me. All I can remember is that damn sword and the guy's cold voice, 'Shitty break, kid', then he swung, and everything went black. They said it should have killed me, but he didn't swing hard enough. For a long time, I could only smell blood and the sight of even a small scratch would make me physically sick. I went out of control and hung around with kids I shouldn't have ever had anything to do with. I got the tattoos because I liked the pain that came with them." I sigh. "But after getting in trouble one too many times, Dad intervened." Her hand cups my chin and she brings my face down to hers. "Dad's intervention brought us here to Port Michael. It brought me to you, Wren."

She lets her tears fall. I use my thumbs to brush the tears away, but they flow like a faucet. She shakes her head and crawls completely into my arms before wrapping hers around my neck. "I'm sorry." She sobs into my neck and hiccups. "I tried not to cry. But I can't help it."

"Let it out. I'll hold you." I run my hand down her back and it's only when my hand sinks lower that her tears stop and I feel a change come over her.

There is more to tell her, but I don't want to break whatever is going on in her head right now.

I like the feeling too.

30

WREN

"R AFAEL ," I WHISPER . "W ILL YOU SHOW ME YOUR tattoos?"

He stills beneath me, so I take the opportunity to sit up and straddle his hips. His eyes flare with heat as his hands land on my bare thighs, his fingers gently digging into my flesh. I smile. "You were about to show me your tattoos." I wiggle my brows.

With reluctance he removes his hands from me and tugs his T-shirt up and off, dropping it beside us. I catch my breath at the beauty before me. The artwork is amazing, all fine black lines and shading over his bronzed skin. I reach out and trace over the lines of a dragon with my fingers. His skin ripples beneath my touch, making me bolder. I trace over the lines of the mandala art up on his chest, my fingers swirl around his hard nipples—not touching—teasing.

"Please, tell me about them," I whisper.

His eyes fill with anger before they soften. He swallows hard. "The needle of the tattoo machine going into my skin helped to numb the pain I refused to let out. It was eating away inside of me after Mom and Roman were killed." He pauses. "The artist saw that I fought demons, so he helped me design the masterpiece on my back." He smiles. "A phoenix rising from ashes. It covers my entire back and the project helped me come back into the living in a way." He touches the roses protecting his heart. "The yellow is for my mother, and the green for Roman. Their favorite colors."

I caress over the flowers, holding his gaze. "I love how you chose to honor their memory, Rafael. You're a good person with a body full of amazing artwork."

He smirks, lightening the conversation. "I thought you were going to say something else about this fine body."

I chuckle. "Hmm, you already have a big head, so I think those words can wait." I slip my fingers under the slim, gold chain that holds a ring and a locket around his neck.

"My mother's," he whispers.

I hope he'll tell me more about them one day but, for now, I don't want the pleasure to fade. My fingers continue exploring him, and I love watching the goosebumps appear on his skin and the way his muscles move under my touch. His hands tremble on my thighs and slip under my dress to my hips. When his fingers spread over my bottom, he squeezes and brings me forward.

I gasp, my eyes closing at the sudden bolt of pressure between my legs when Rafael settles me on the bulge behind his zipper. Pleasure pulses where we touch, and I struggle for breath.

"I feel it too, Wren." Rafael rocks me on him and hisses. "You feel good."

"I've never felt like this before." I blush. "I want you to teach me more."

He snaps his eyes closed and moans. "You can't be saying that to me."

"My body feels swollen." His eyes snap open and darken as I talk. "Like it did the day in your bedroom. When I'm close to you, I ache, and my body feels on fire." I wiggle on his penis knowing that I make him bigger—harder. He feels good under me.

It's my turn to moan as his hands slip into the back of my panties and he squeezes my bottom. He moves me on him and there is no way he won't be able to tell how wet my panties are. I want to make Rafael squirm under me, so I finally move my fingers those few steps and press them back and forth over his nipples. He arches and gasps, and when I pinch the hard nubs between thumb and finger, he shoots upward from the bed, his hands clenching my waist.

"Wren," he groans, "we need to stop."

"I don't want to." I wrap my arms around his neck and lock my ankles behind his back so I can rub my body on his.

My breasts feel swollen and tight, only getting relief as they rub against Rafael's chest. His hands slip into the back of my panties again and spreads the cheeks of my bottom open, which creates more friction between my legs. I'm really sensitive there and the pressure increases in time to the fast pace of my hips as I frantically move them up and down Rafael's erection. He feels really hard and big and I can't stop chasing my pleasure. I feel like something else has taken over my body and only Rafael can save me.

He wears a deep blush on his cheekbones as his breathing becomes as heavy as mine. Our lips crash together and we kiss madly - all teeth, tongues and lips - uncoordinated as our desperation for each other grows. I'm not sure how much time passes but I find myself on my back with Rafael looming over me.

"I want to touch you." His chest heaves. "Will you let me, Wren? Will you let me touch you?"

"Yes. Touch me anywhere," I beg.

Rafael chuckles as he untangles from me and tosses the dress I'm wearing up to my waist. "I want to touch you here." I nearly jump from the bed as he presses a finger between my legs.

Wantonly, I spread my legs further and Rafael curses under his breath. "You are gorgeous." His eyes briefly lift to mine. "Touching and wanting you in the way that I do feels right, Wren. The way you react to me drives me crazy."

I trail a finger down his chest and dip it into his belly button. I smile slightly when his belly quivers. "I wondered how it would feel to be like this with a boy, and I always thought I'd be too embarrassed to do anything. I'm not, though. You make me feel good." I pause. "I trust you, Rafael DeLacroix."

"I trust you too, and I don't trust easily…but you—

" His words drift off when he bends and kisses the inside of my thigh.

My body trembles and when his lips graze my skin, heat pours into every part of my body. And then his fingers tickle up my thighs to slip into the band of my panties. My breathing heavy, I raise my hips up and feel the material being taken down my legs. He doesn't give me time to think before he spreads my legs further apart and settles his shoulders between. He presses an arm over my hips to keep me still and then blows a breath onto my swollen vagina. His mouth is next. His lips brush over my skin before his tongue darts between. Rafael moans and starts licking and nibbling at me. I can't think straight as my whole concentration is centered between my legs. His mouth is hot. His tongue wet. I feel something climbing higher and higher inside of me as small whimpers leave my lips. I try to move my hips but can't because he holds me down, and then he pushes his tongue inside of me and I burst. My body shakes from the pleasure that runs through me. It's an explosion of fireworks, and I'm only vaguely aware of Rafael's grunts and groans. I certainly feel the vibration between my legs.

The pleasure starts to subside, and I watch Rafael

as he lifts his head and holds my gaze. He wipes his mouth on my dress as he raises himself above me. His hair is messy, sexy, and his eyes dark and sparkling into my own. I reach up and slip my hands into his hair. He sighs heavily and scoops me into his arms, holding me tightly. I wrap my legs around his hips and enjoy the feel of us together in this way. He is beautiful and sexy and makes my heart turn over with so many feelings that it wants to burst right out of my chest.

What we've done has been daring with the chance of the Reverend returning at any time but, for once, I don't care. I had actually forgotten about the Reverend the moment Rafael climbed into my bedroom. All my thoughts have been on Rafael and how good he looks without his shirt on and only in black jeans. His breath against my neck reassures my racing heart that he is real and plans on going nowhere. I'm totally okay with that. I want him to stay with me and, with the way Rafael has relaxed, I'm fairly sure he has no wish to move.

In the position we are in, I feel the ridges of his back that flex and quiver as my hands and fingertips find them. I love the feel of his skin against my own. I love the way his body reacts to my touch. It makes mine come alive and I want his hands all over me. After what he has just done with his mouth, I want to feel his kiss all over.

"What are you thinking so hard about?" he whispers against my neck before he lightly bites down in the curve of my neck. His nose runs back and forth over the sensitive spot there. "I bet I know."

I slip my fingers into the back of his jeans and scrape his butt with my fingernails. Rafael shudders hard and grunts while I laugh. "It's really hot having you react the way you do. I never knew what power over a man was until now." I smirk and meet his narrow stare as he turns his face to me. "I've never had power to do anything before, so this here with you, makes me happy." I press my nails into his skin knowing that his body is reacting to my daring touch. I feel him growing hard, pressed between my legs. "It makes me dizzy that you want me. I'm nobody. The weird girl in class, yet the new bad boy wants me."

He smiles and nuzzles along my jaw before a large hand holds me still. I can't move, not that I want to.

"Now I've tasted you, you can't be letting anyone else near you. Ever, Wren." He drops his forehead to mine. "I never knew I was possessive until now."

"I'm glad." I run my fingernails up the sides of his body and realize that he is ticklish. He wiggles and tries to catch my hands, but to no avail. "Have I discovered something else about you?" I murmur as I tickle him some more and can't keep my hands to myself. Curiosity at this much lighter side of him gives me courage to slip a hand down the front of his jeans. It happens so quickly and the moment I reach inside, and my fingers connect with his penis, he rears up and presses himself into my hand. I'm not sure that was supposed to happen, but that's how I end up stroking him.

"Wren," he groans. "I'm sticky." A blush covers his cheekbones.

"I can feel." I grin and tighten my grip, the tip of him leaking onto my wrist.

"I'm not sure I can handle you like this."

"I'm enjoying *handling* you." I tease.

Rafael laughs, which turns into a groan. He briefly closes his eyes and shudders before he gazes straight at me. Seconds later, he shoves his jeans and briefs down, and quickly repositions us.

My belly quivers from sitting astride him, and when his hands grab my butt, he moves me directly over him. My eyes roll when my sensitive parts meet his hard length. The hair covering the root of him tickles me.

He holds me tightly and waits for me to meet his gaze. "I thought you would be shy when I got you like this. When I touched you. I never expected you to put your hands on me without encouragement. It's hot."

I smile. "So, you've thought about me naked, huh?"

"Maybe." He wiggles his eyebrows and my grin widens. "I'll never tell," he adds.

"I bet I can make you tell me anything."

"No way."

"Yes, way."

His eye glitter with excitement. "Make me, then"

Nerves flutter in my belly, but another kind of flutter starts between my legs. Before I can change my mind, I grab my dress and toss it to the floor, followed by my tank top.

Rafael offers a garbled response as his eyes take in my firm breasts. I look down wondering what holds his attention. I'm on the larger side but my nipples look big and feel tight. They tingle and ache the more he stares. My eyes drift down and I catch my breath at the sight of his penis stretched up to his belly button with my pussy lips open to him. It's a naughty sight, but I can't look away.

I reach out with a finger and circle the head. Rafael curses, his stomach trembles and his penis twitches, leaking onto his belly.

"Dark and light," he whispers hoarsely. "I'm going to come if you keep doing that. Having you on display above me has lit a fire inside me."

"I want your hands everywhere." I move mine up his sides and rest my hands on his chest. I slowly slide up and down his penis, my breasts swaying.

Rafael suddenly sits, his mouth latching onto a nipple while his fingers play with the other. I squirm on his lap, desperate for so much more. I grab a handful of Rafael's hair and pull his head backwards. I wait until he meets my gaze and tell him, "I want you to make me a woman, Rafael. I want to feel you moving inside of me."

Slipping a hand between us, I wrap my fingers around his length, watching as Rafael's eyes flutter. "You like my hands on you?"

"Fuck, yeah!"

I jerk him a few times, enjoying watching the tip leak with his excitement, and the way his breathing has become heavy. The way he trembles under me. I do have a confession to make, though, so he doesn't get the wrong idea. "I've never done this before." I lick my lips while continuing to slowly stroke him. "I've never had sex, but I don't have a...barrier."

I feel a blush start but push through it. I mean I'm sitting naked on top of him. I shouldn't be embarrassed. "A few years ago, I was up in the rafters of the church. I shouldn't have been up there but, anyway... I always wanted to do gymnastics, so I was walking the 'beam,' otherwise known as the rafters. The Reverend suddenly appeared and yelled up to me. Furious. He made me jump and I lost my balance." I wince. "I slammed down so hard that I saw stars and nearly blacked out from the pain. I was lucky that I didn't actually fall under it. But the force with which I fell broke it."

Opening my body to him, I push the tip inside my vagina. Rafael quivers and his hands grip my hips. "I can't think with you wetting my dick." He pants. "I am glad I won't be hurting you, though."

"Me too." I nervously lick my lips again. "Will you distract me?"

His eyes darken to granite and, the moment his wet mouth connects with my nipple, I slide down, pushing myself on him. I'm really full as my body spasms and tries to push him out. Rafael curses and hisses and then he thickens, spilling inside me. His body quivers and trembles and his hands squeeze my butt.

Grunting and panting for breath, Rafael buries his face in my shoulder and holds me tightly. "I'm sorry. Too excited. Couldn't wait," he mumbles. "Make it up to you." He turns and captures my lips with his. The kiss is warm and deep, soon turning to heated.

Rafael flips us so I'm on my back and starts to slowly move over me. His chest rubs my breasts, the pleasure going straight between my legs.

My breathing becomes heavy as I try to move, but Rafael holds me down with his hands on my hips while he continues to move. He doesn't stop, even when lights explode behind my eyelids, he continues. My pussy squeezes and quivers around his penis as I lose myself in him.

"Oh," I murmur, clutching him tightly.

Rafael pants into my neck and chuckles.

Ten minutes later, we lie on my bed pressed together, his heart beats steadily against my ear, which is relaxing. Then he says, "We didn't use protection."

I frown wondering what he's talking about, then it clicks. "Oh."

"I never thought about it, and I should have. It was

my responsibility to make sure I was wrapped." He sits up and tugs at his hair, his eyes full of apology.

Crawling back into his lap, I say, "I'm as much to blame as you. I know I haven't done this before, but that's not an excuse."

His eyes bore into mine as though he's trying to tell me something and his Adam's apple bobs when he swallows hard. "You're my first time too, Wren," he admits. "I've jerked off countless times." He gives me a wry grin. "But I've never stuck it in anyone until you."

I gasp and, laughing, push him away. "You stuck it in me, huh?"

He grabs me around the waist, and we fall on the bed in a tangle of arms and legs. Laughing, Rafael pulls me up until my head is on a pillow and then he's on top of me, cupping my face between his large hands. "I may have *stuck* it in you"—he smirks and then becomes serious—"but I made love to you, Wren. All of this was me loving you."

Sliding my hands up along his neck, Rafael shivers and closes his eyes. I pull him down to me and take my time kissing his eyes, the tip of his nose, along each cheekbone, paying special attention along the scar. He sighs and settles further down my body, his head resting on my chest.

"I love you too, Rafael," I whisper softly, sliding my hand through his hair. "I liked you being inside of me with nothing between us. It felt really good when you came. Warm."

His head lifts before he swoops down and kisses between my breasts. My pulse quickens as one of his hands slides down past my stomach and over my sensitive mound before I feel his arousing touch between my legs.

Heaven.

31

RAFAEL

THE TASTE OF WREN LINGERS ON MY TONGUE AS I TRY
and softly move up the porch and slip into the house
without Dad catching me. I smell of sex and I never
want to shower again. I grin like a fool becoming
aroused all over again thinking about the girl. Her
response to me had been nothing like I'd expected.
I'm not sure what exactly I expected, but eager and
wanting to lead hadn't been it. I turn and glance
through the kitchen window over to Wren's
bedroom, and I see her silhouetted in the moonlight
just before she closes her curtains.

"You had sex with her." Dad accuses, and I tense.

It doesn't bother me that he knows. I'm twenty,
soon to be twenty-one. However, it's the way he said

it, as though she's beneath me, or maybe he's saying she's too good for me. Shaking my head, I turn to face him, shutting out my previous thoughts. Dad knows me better than anyone, so he knows that my heart is involved. So is Wren's.

"What if I did? You know how I feel about her." I grab a bottle of water from the fridge and sit at the table with him. We keep the lights off so not to be seen.

"She's seventeen and—," he hisses between his teeth before taking a large inhale. "Never mind. What's done is done."

"I told her my age and about that day. It wasn't easy but easier than it has been in the past when you made me talk to a shrink."

"You used protection, right? Because I have not seen you buying condoms."

Oh fuck!

"Instead of getting on my back about Wren, what happened with Ken and Jeramiah?"

"Clever." He tilts the neck of his beer toward me. "I noticed you didn't answer, which means no." He clumsily places the bottle on the table and leans closer. "You are an idiot. If you have sex, you wrap it!" He rants. "How many times have I told you?"

"Fuck." I push away from the table and lean over. "You've told me lots of times." I run my hands through my hair and tug. "I wasn't thinking, okay?" I admit. "I love her, and I didn't think. I'm an asshole." I drop my butt down into the chair again silently cursing myself. "She's mine anyway, so it doesn't matter."

"Doesn't matter," he repeats, good and mad. "You are twenty. She is seventeen. You do not want a baby. Are you nuts?"

I'm angry now too. "No," I shout, getting in his face. "I'm in fucking love with her." I slam a fist on the table and his beer tips over. The liquid trickles out of the half empty bottle. "I love her," I whisper. "I screwed up, okay? We've already talked about it."

His eyes remain on me and he sighs. "I know you love her, son." He adds, "And I love you. I don't want to see you get hurt."

"You're not so bad yourself." I offer him a wry smile. "I won't get hurt as long as Wren is okay."

"I'm too old for this." Dad rubs a hand over his face. "I worry that we're in over our heads."

"That's not like you."

"I don't usually have anyone to worry about when I'm working other than my partner. I have my son and his girlfriend to think about." He sighs and stares at nothing, his mind not in the here and now for a few seconds. "They found the remains of a body in the tub."

My eyes snap to his. Surely, I didn't hear him correctly. "A body?"

"Yes. The guys moved it and took it to the coroner in the city. They'll keep it hush-hush for now. Although I suspect someone will be looking for it real soon."

"Is it Wild?"

He winced. "No idea. Haven't seen him around but, then again, he tends to keep to himself so that isn't news."

"Wren wants to go and look for the man tomorrow. She caught the Reverend washing behind the house with the hose last night. He took off after she'd told him about Wild." I sigh. "She's worried the Reverend has done something to the man." I groan and drop back into the chair. "I don't want to take her there, but maybe, if she's with me, it will be easier to explain later about what is going on here."

"Be careful. Out of the two of you, I suspect Wren will be the safest. Come back here afterward and I'll talk to Wren, okay? I also need to know you're both okay."

I raise a brow, knowing exactly what he's going to do. "Don't let the mosquitos get you when you follow us."

"Go to bed, Rafael."

Laughing, I rise out of the chair and give him a hug. "I love you too, Dad."

As I ascend the stairs to my room, my feet consume the distance without a backward glance. I'm going to be really sorry to see this house go when we've done what we've set out to do. One of the reasons is that I can imagine Wren here with me. Spending our time cuddled up on the armchair in my room in front of the window together, watching her butterflies dance and hover at the open window. No matter. Wherever we go after this, Wren will be with me.

32

WREN

ALTHOUGH IT IS REALLY GOOD TO BE IGNORED BY THE Reverend, it worries me. Once again, he signed my journal and dismissed me—no anger at the words Mr. Bradshaw had written the day before. Dinner, he said, would be eaten elsewhere, and I'd been left to my own devices. A quick sandwich washed down with milk satisfies my hunger after the even stricter day of school.

Now it's time to visit with my butterflies and wait for Rafael. Our mission tonight is to go and check on Wild. I'd planned on sneaking out of the house, but now I don't have to. It would have been tricky because we're going before nightfall so we can see around us. I hate being in the forest in the dark. I find it spooky.

My butterflies love my attention, but their needs aren't demanding—all they need is the food plants, and they are plentiful around the glasshouse, and inside.

In my eagerness to spend time in my glasshouse, I jump down the back stairs and startle. My body is different after what Rafael and I did the night before.

Smiling, I step into the tropical paradise I've created and inhale the scent of the tomato plants. To some, it would probably be overwhelming but, to me, it's home.

The more I look around, the more butterflies I count. At least fifty are inside either feeding or sleeping. They watch me and flutter their delicate wings.

"I've never seen anything as beautiful," Rafael whispers, startling me.

My heart thumps heavily against my breastbone as I slowly turn and see his gaze is on me and not the butterflies. "Oh."

He smiles. "They're beautiful, too," he adds. Stepping closer, he turns me in his arms so that my back is against his front. "No one is as beautiful as my girl." He kisses my neck. "How are you feeling?"

My breath leaves my body in a rush as heat travels through my limbs. His mouth tickles my ear as he whispers, "I feel the same rush you do when our bodies touch." He slides his hands along my arms and catches hold of my fingers, lifting our joined hands out to the sides. My butterflies hover and then land along our outstretched arms, shoulders, and of course, Tiger Lily on the tip of my nose.

Rafael chuckles. "I'm almost jealous."

"Almost?" The butterflies are sensitive to noise and the last thing I want to do is scare Tiger Lily.

"Hmm." Rafael sighs. "I get to feel you against me." He kisses my ear. "So yes, I'm *almost* jealous."

"You're sweet."

I feel the stillness in him. "I'm not sweet, Wren."

My brows draw together in a frown because his voice sounds flat. I gently move my arms and when the butterflies fly back to the plants, I turn and face Rafael. My breath catches at the sorrow written all over his face.

Instinct has me reaching out to him. My hands cup his face and I search his eyes for a sign of what is going on with him.

"My mom used to say that to me." He swallows hard and tries to pull away.

I won't let him and wind my arms around his neck. "She loved you, Rafael. You have to remember that, and I'm sorry my words brought back memories."

He wraps his arms around my waist and holds me tightly. "I try not to think about her and Roman because I get a really bad pain in my stomach. It's like fire and I don't know what to do with it." He sighs and keeps his face buried in my neck. "She would have loved you."

I move slightly so that I can see his face. "Knowing you, I'm sure I would have loved her too." I offer him a small smile and clear my throat. "So, are we going snooping?"

His eyes roll and he laughs, but I sense there is something in the hidden depth of his gaze. He looks almost wary. "We have to be careful, Wren. We both know there is a lot going on in Port Michael they don't want anyone else discovering."

"Your father appears normal." I wince the moment the words leave my mouth. "I mean, different than the Reverend."

Rafael laughs and continues to chuckle. "Wren, I hate to break this to you, but not many people are like the Reverend."

My eyes roll at the amusement I see in his. "So, back to my original question. Your father is cool?"

"Yes, my father is cool." He takes my hand and intertwines our fingers, pulling me out of the glasshouse. "If we find anything we need to share, then we can go to my dad, okay? He'll know what to do." Rafael won't meet my curious gaze as he continues walking.

Our feet crunch on the mulch in the forest at the back of our properties as we make our way toward Peter Wild's house. The man lives in a small cabin on the outskirts of town, which the Reverend had once said was just what the man needed. Now, I'm not sure exactly what he had meant. Is it what Peter Wild had needed, or the Reverend? And what for? I hadn't given it much thought at the time, but after the weird comings and goings of the Reverend, I wonder.

"Are you okay?" Rafael looks over his shoulder.

"Thinking."

"About?"

"I'm getting a bad feeling in my belly about this."

Rafael hesitates and reels me in. "This whole town gives me a bad feeling." He runs his hands through his dark hair, which is damp with sweat. It might be evening but it's warm and humid. "We'll check the cabin out and then go to my house. My dad should be home."

"Providing we find something bad," I whisper.

"I'm expecting to find something bad, Wren."

"I am, too," I admit. My hand is once again engulfed in Rafael's much larger one as I follow him like a lamb being led to slaughter.

It doesn't take long before we arrive at the gravel road leading up to Wild's cabin. I swallow hard in nervousness and get dust in my throat. I cough and inhale through my nose, the dust finally disappearing. A bottle of water would have been useful. We didn't think to bring anything with us but, then again, we're not expecting to need anything. Barbed wire fencing looks old and rusty as we walk up toward the cabin. Wild's mailbox leans to the side and is nearly lost in the weeds. It's quiet except for the sounds of crickets and grasshoppers whirring as they keep us company.

Glancing around, I'm thinking that we should have approached through the tall grass and weeds so as not to be seen from the cabin if anyone is inside. However, I'm not really all that keen on that idea. The thought of stepping on a snake chills me. Hopefully we haven't made a mistake going up the driveway. It looks like it's rundown and has been for a while. It surprises me because Peter Wild hadn't appeared to be anyone who the Reverend would associate with. Not if the driveway is a sign of what we see when we round the bend in the road.

"Is this the right place?" Rafael asks, looking around.

"Yes." We'd discussed it at school during our short break when we'd snuck away. The sneaking wouldn't last because others would know and report us. It was only a matter of time. "Different than what you expected, huh?"

"You could say that." Rafael continues glancing around. "It's as though he hasn't been home for a long time. It has that feel about it." He pauses. "We know that isn't the case."

"I got the impression from the Reverend that Wild had money. I don't see any sign of that."

Rafael shrugs and intertwines his fingers with mine. "Watch the steps."

My heart pounds while I follow Rafael. The steps creak, as does the porch beneath my feet. Goose-bumps and cold shivers run down my arms when

Rafael tries the front door. It won't give, which makes me feel a bit better, but then he steps back and kicks in the door. I don't move. I can't. I'm shocked that we are here doing this. I've never broken into someone's home before. I'm a good girl.

"Wren?" he questions, his focus on my face. "We have to go inside."

Nodding, I take a step forward and swallow hard. "I know. I have a bad feeling about this."

"There's no one here." He takes my hand again and keeps me close to his side. "I want to see if there's anything lying around that he shouldn't have." He averts his gaze.

Frowning at Rafael's odd actions, I take in Peter Wild's home. It isn't much and very basic. One chair in front of a large television that is hooked up to digital equipment, and a coffee table with tipped over bottle of beer close to the edge.

The front door slams shut, scaring the life out of me. I whip around and see Rafael standing in front of the closed door with an apology on his face while my heart races. I shake my head. "What kind of stuff are we looking for?"

I have a perfect view of Rafael's back and something tells me he knows more than he's told me. His action speaks loudly of that. I just don't know what he knows or how he can know it.

While heading toward the back of the house, the sound of a car approaching the house causes me to pause. I glance at Rafael in panic.

Sweat beads on his forehead, but he seems to be the calmer of us both. The moment the car comes to a stop outside of the cabin, Rafael moves and shoves me toward the back. "Keep moving, Wren," he whispers, not that we have a choice.

Before I know it, we're in the bedroom, which is where I freeze, and Rafael bumps into me. He shuts the door with more finesse than the front one. "Wren, what's"—he stills beside me—"wrong?" he whispers. "The *fucking* son of a bitch," he hisses between his teeth.

That about sums it up. The walls are covered with images of me—floor to ceiling. The images are all sizes, some like posters. Close up and from a distance. Although I struggle to comprehend what this means, Wild has been stalking me for the past few years. Images with my butterflies, in the glasshouse. The ones that really creep me out were taken of me inside my bedroom. My cheeks heat with embarrassment and anger at the ones of me with next to no clothing on. He even has a blurred image of me fully nude. I suppose I should be grateful it's blurred. I laugh in disbelief at my thoughts. There is something wrong with me if I'm thinking about blurry naked images of me.

A hiss from Rafael draws my attention and I feel sick that he's seen the nude photograph of me. He notices the horror in my eyes. Moving to me, he gently holds my cold face in his hands. "If someone wasn't about to enter the cabin, I'd take every photograph down and burn them." He kisses me hard and deep. "The asshole is lucky he's already dead, otherwise, I'd kill him."

The front door slams open before I have time to question Rafael about his comment. Does he know something I don't?

"Later. I promise, Wren, but right now we have to get out of here." He jimmies the old window open and starts to climb through when he grabs for me. "Come on, Wren. I'll lower you down."

Footsteps moving down the hallway light a fire under me. I use Rafael to steady myself and I'm out of the window before Rafael can help me. The drop isn't too far, although, the impact shoots pain up the back of my legs, I'm okay. Rafael drops beside me and when I move to run, he wraps an arm around my waist. "Under the window," he whispers, and gets us there just as the Reverend shoves his head out of it.

My heart pounds and the sight above my head scares me more than snakes. A whimper works itself up from somewhere deep inside of me. I force my lips to stay tightly together while the horror of being so close to the Reverend is written all over my face for Rafael to see. *What the hell is going on?* He tightens his hand around my much sweatier palm and holds my gaze until we hear the window close. My body sags against Rafael who leans close and presses a kiss to the top of my head.

"Follow me, okay, Wren?" he whispers. "If we get to the tree line over there"—he points—"we'll be able to watch what they're up to."

The moment the words leave his mouth, he tugs me away from our hiding place, and we run. Fear makes me run faster and harder than I ever have before, and as my feet crunch over weeds and shrubs and things I don't even want to think about, I become breathless. The tree line is directly in front of us as I slowly start to fall behind Rafael. I can't keep up with his pace any longer. His legs are longer than mine.

Even when I hear voices from the cabin, I can't move any faster.

Moments later Rafael catches me up against his chest. His breathing is as heavy as mine while we stand together trying to slow our racing hearts. "No one saw us," he tells me. "It's okay, Wren. I have you."

His words take a few minutes to penetrate my fuzzy head, and that's when I realize I'm shaking. My whole body is full of goosebumps, my skin feels sweaty, and I'm fairly sure my face is bright red. "That was close."

"Look." He turns me to face the cabin. "They're clearing the cabin of electronics." He shakes his head. "I don't see furniture."

Wiping the sweat from my eyes, I stare and watch as the Reverend and two of his friends fill up the back of an SUV. There's some shouting and then the two men start throwing liquid all over the porch and outside walls.

"They're about to torch the place." Rafael squeezes my shoulder. "No one will ever see the bedroom, Wren."

"I feel dirty having seen that room." I shudder at the thought of what Wild got up to in that room.

"You haven't done anything wrong." Rafael pulls

me to him and tilts my face up to his. "We won't tell anyone about what we saw. Not even my father. I promise, Wren." He kisses my lips quickly. "We need to get away from here."

"We need to call the fire truck."

"No. They'll know we were here…and there's no fire yet."

"But the fire will spread to the trees."

"I don't think they'll let it get that far because if they do, the Reverend would be risking his house too. After one more glance toward the cabin, we turn to leave.

Our fingers intertwine and Rafael leads me through the foliage until we skim the outside of my house. We don't stop there and keep going to his house. I nervously glance over to mine but know the Reverend isn't there. He's at Wild's home. I allow Rafael to shove me in front of him and into his house.

We look at each other and Rafael gives me a wry smile. "We need to get cleaned up." He smiles and I follow him as he takes me to his room. He releases my hand and I stay by the door.

Rafael moves around his room. "My dad will be back soon." He pauses when he sees I haven't moved. "Wren?"

Swallowing hard, I shuffle further into the room. "I don't want to go home." I blow out a large breath and drop to the edge of Rafael's bed. I wince when dust lifts from me. "Sorry. I didn't realize I'm covered in dust."

He grins. "That's why I suggested we get cleaned up." He holds out his hand to me. "Come on. I'll show you my bathroom."

I laugh. "Oh, really?"

He rolls his eyes and laughs. "If you're willing to share my super large shower, then I'm not going to object."

"I've never shared a shower before." *And I need my mind distracted from everything that's happened.*

"First time for everything." He grabs my hips and lifts me to the bathroom counter. "We need to talk first." He glances at the shower and sighs before he meets my gaze. "I'm worried because I didn't suit up last night. I know I said it then, but it bothers me that I didn't take care of you."

"Suit up? And you did take care of me."

"I didn't wrap my dick, Wren." I see the humor in his gaze. "It felt incredible being inside of you without wearing a rubber, but the last thing we need is for you to get pregnant."

The light bulb goes off in my head as to what he's telling me. "I could be pregnant?" I smile, not opposed to the idea. Although, I should be at my young age.

Rafael lifts a brow. "Wren?"

"I'm not sure I like the idea of you being inside of me wearing something. You felt really good last night."

He swallows hard and drops his forehead to mine. "You don't know what you're saying."

I laugh and drag my fingernails down his chest to his belly, which quivers at my touch. "I know exactly what I'm saying. I loved feeling you come inside of me—feeling the warmth of your release."

"Fuck!" His hands tremble as he slowly starts to unbutton my shorts while his eyes hold mine. "You're my girl, Wren."

I rise and he pulls my shorts and underwear down my legs before settling back between them. His hands grab my bottom and he brings me to the edge of the counter. I gasp when my sensitive lips rub up against his jeans where his penis throbs. "You're mine too." I chew on my lip debating what my next move should be. All I need is to see the emotion in Rafael to know I need to touch him. I need him to feel what he makes me feel.

As his mouth captures mine in a toe-curling kiss, I slip my hand down the front of his jeans. He moans into my mouth when my fingers first touch his cock. The tip is wet and the flesh jerks as I wrap my fingers around it. He presses deeper with his mouth, his tongue exploring every bit of space in my mouth and dancing with my tongue, slipping and sliding together.

Rafael lifts his head and removes my hand from his jeans, and then my top disappears to the floor and my breasts swing free. All pleasure shoots between my legs the moment he cups me and rubs his thumbs back and forth over my sensitive nipples. I arch, throwing my head back, and moan when his hot, wet tongue laps at each in turn. My fingers run through his hair and I hold him close. I never want him to stop doing what he's doing. My body feels alive and desperate to feel him pushing between my legs like he had the night before.

"Wren," he whispers, his voice deep and husky, "you have no idea how sexy you are right now. It drives me crazy how you react to my touch." His hands massage my breasts, my nipples rubbing against his palms. Rafael licks between my breasts and moves his head downward, swirling his tongue around my belly button before he dips lower. He quickly releases me to remove his own clothing.

Before he drops to his knees, I catch sight of his hugely erect penis. It looks hard and throbs with a wet tip. Then I don't have time to think of anything else as Rafael touches my pussy. He spreads my lips and moves his face so close that I feel his breath on my mound where he kisses me. The first touch of his tongue causes me to tremble. It feels so good. He does it again and I push against his face, his loving driving me up and up to dizzying heights.

I throw my head back, opening my legs wider as I tilt my hips forward, so close to that moment of ecstasy, when Rafael gets to his feet. He's crazed and growling, his mouth captures a nipple, sucking and nibbling. The moment he switches breasts, he breaches my opening. I'm so wet that he's inside with one thrust. My breast drops from his mouth as he gasps in pleasure, his eyes finding mine. He slowly moves his hips and I relish the feeling of him filling me.

My body knows Rafael and I wrap my arms around his neck, pulling myself up against him. His arms go around my waist, and he holds me steady. The crest I'm desperate for suddenly reappears on the horizon and I moan into his mouth as he captures mine. I clench and pulse around him as he pumps into me, spilling his release.

Holding each other, our bodies slick with sweat, Rafael cups my face and gives me the sweetest kiss. "I love you, my butterfly girl."

33

RAFAEL

WREN LOOKS REALLY GOOD WEARING MY BLACK T-shirt, which comes to her mid-thigh. Her legs are bare, and I have to turn my back. I reach up and hold onto one of the rafters as I stare out of the window and think.

Dad waits downstairs for us. I'm relieved he's given me the privacy to be with Wren, but I'm hesitant to go down, even though I need to talk to him. Once Wren knows everything, I know this peace we've created between us is going to be shattered. At the end of the day, the Reverend is her father, and that has to mean something. At least, I would think it would.

I tense when I feel the gentle touch of Wren's

hands on my back. Her fingers are like tiny butterflies walking over my skin, and when she presses her lips against my back, the rest of my body goes tense. Turning, I wrap the enchanting girl up in my arms.

I can see the concern in her eyes but before I can ask, she mumbles, "I thought you regretted having me here."

"What? Hell no!" I squeeze her tightly and then move to cup her face. I rest my forehead against hers and hold her unsure gaze. "I want you here, Wren. I don't want you ever to go back next door. I want and need you to stay with me. I know that can't happen until you're eighteen, but, as soon as you are, we're leaving. Dad, me, and you."

Her face crumples and then her tears flow while she buries her face in my chest, her arms wrapping tightly around my waist. "I didn't know how I was going to leave. I have nothing, Rafael. I'd always planned on leaving but I'd never been sure how to do it. Are you really going to take me with you?" She lifts her tearstained face.

I wipe at the tears, and tell her, "You are my beautiful butterfly girl. I'll never leave you, Wren." I kiss each lid and then her cheeks and place a softer kiss to her lips. "You need to get dressed so we can go and talk to Dad. He has some things to tell you." I hesitate, and add, "Please remember that I love you."

She frowns. "You have me worried."

I shake my head and try to lighten the mood by smacking her ass. She gasps and wiggles, trying to move out of my hold. Unable to resist, I grab her up in my arms and sigh when she wraps herself around me. My hands slip beneath the shirt and cup her bottom. Bad idea. She hasn't put panties back on yet. Then I smile and take advantage of that, moving us so that her back is against the door. I use my hips to keep her steady, bringing her arms above her head and holding them up there with one hand on her wrists. Our breathing becomes heavy, more so when I circle a hard nipple through her shirt. I pinch and roll it between my finger and thumb and wonder what I'm doing getting us all worked up again.

Dad's waiting.

Wren moans and my balls ache.

Panting into her neck, I hiss, "We have to go downstairs."

"No," she mumbles, rubbing herself on me.

I'm going to be in pain, but the least I can do is make sure my girl isn't.

Turning, I drop her to the bed and, before she can

grab me to her, I drop to my knees on the floor. I tug her legs and shove them over my shoulders as I settle between. My eyes focus on the arousal leaking from her body and I desperately want to be inside her again.

There will be time later.

The moment I tickle her pussy with the tip of my tongue, she nearly jumps from the bed. I use an arm to pin her down and continue teasing her, getting her wetter. With my tongue, I search for the small opening into her body and my eyes close at the taste and feel of her on me. The moment I'm loving her with my tongue, she arches upward, her head flat to the bed, and shudders against my mouth. The walls of her pussy convulse and try to suck my tongue further inside of her while she pants through her orgasm. She's fucking sexy when she lets go in this way.

I glance up at her from between her legs and grin at the dazed look on her face. I make sure to keep her eyes on me while I yank the shirt from her body and use it to wipe my face. My eyes snap closed at the naked beauty before me. "Will you please get dressed? My dad won't wait all day."

"Hmm. I'd rather stay in bed with you all day."

Don't open your eyes. Don't open your eyes.

I do and watch her disappearing into the bathroom where her clothes are.

My body is strung tight, my cock ready to burst out of my jeans, but I do nothing. That was about Wren. I wanted to reassure her that she's mine and goes where I will. Except, I don't want her thinking—

"Wren." I moan as she comes out of the bathroom a few minutes later dressed in another black T-shirt of mine and her shorts. She has no clue as to what she does to me, which I try to ignore and remember what I'd been about to say. "You know I want *you*, right? Not just the sex. I want you as a person. I've been enchanted since the moment I laid eyes on you."

She smiles softly. "A boy who draws me amazing pictures, and who climbs on my roof to deliver them to me, and risks the wrath of the Reverend, has to like me for more than sex."

I splutter and end up coughing and wrap an arm around her neck to pull her close. "I don't just like you, I love you, Wren." I kiss the top of her head and grab a shirt from the set of drawers by the door on our way out of the attic.

"Wait," Wren says. "I want you to know that I'm not looking at you as my savior. I mean you are going to get me away from *him*, but my heart is involved,

Rafael. I don't ever want to lose you." She nibbles her lips.

"You won't." I kiss the lips I've been imagining a lot, a chain of thought I need to stop now before it becomes embarrassing. "Let's talk to Dad and then we can figure out what's next, okay?"

The look on Dad's face as we appear causes me to grin. He's embarrassed, which also means that he knows exactly what we've been doing upstairs. I don't care.

"Remind me to give you something once our talk is over," he says and looks at me with meaning.

I have no clue what he's talking about until his eyes flicker between Wren and me. The lightbulb goes off in my head. Condoms. Now it's my turn to blush.

Clearing my throat, I usher Wren into a seat at the kitchen table and, after unscrewing the cap for her, hand her a bottle of water. She takes a long drink as I pull up a chair beside her. I don't want her thinking she's alone.

Dad sighs, sitting opposite. "I don't know how much Rafael has told you."

"Only about what happened *that* day," I insert.

Nodding, Dad continues, "I'm a former DEA Agent, Wren. When I lost my wife and son, I tried to find a lead, anything, to find the person responsible. Then I found a thin thread that linked the Reverend. You see, he had disappeared ten years ago and hadn't been heard of until after Sarah and Roman were laid to rest. I knew. Sarah had always said the Reverend would find her one day, and he did."

"You're saying he killed your mom and brother?" Wren turns watery eyes toward me. "How can you like me?"

"Wren, you're just as innocent as they were." I squeeze the hand on her lap.

"It wasn't the Reverend's hand that carried out the killings. Peter Wild, I'm guessing was the killer. Another man was present. I don't know who." He clears his throat and his eyes flicker to me, as he adds, "Sarah owned this house."

I snap my head up and stare at my father in surprise. "What? You told me Jeremiah had managed to set it up as our background. Bought the place."

"I didn't want you asking too many questions, so I left it at that." He winces. "I'll explain that after, but, Wren, I need to ask you if you've seen any drugs? Any suspicious activity going on? Because the DEA thinks there are drugs being distributed from here. They've watched for over twelve months and so far, they have nothing concrete."

Wren looks pale while she stares at my father, taking in everything he said. She releases my hand and wraps her fingers around the water bottle. Nervously licking her lips, she says, "There is always something going on that makes no sense to me, but it's not new. I mean everything is the same as it's been for years. The only new things are the uniforms, journals, and the removal of all thirty computers from the school."

"You're sure on the number?" Dad asks.

"Yes. When they arrived at the school, I was thirteen and the Reverend asked me to count the large boxes as they went inside. I've always remembered that because he had never asked me to help in any way before. Even if it was to distract me." She shrugs. "I don't know anything about drugs, though. I guess they could be in a cupboard in the house for all I know because I don't know what they look like."

"The DEA got a tip, which had put the Reverend on the watch list, that it was heroin. The only reason the Reverend stayed on the watch list was because of his connection to the raid in Amarillo. That's how I found him this time."

"Didn't you save Mom from that raid?"

Dad looks at me and gives a resigned sigh. "Sarah was married to a Lucas Jacobs in Amarillo."

"What the fuck!" I jump up and glare at Dad. "Are you telling me what I think you are? Because if you are, then you fucking lied to me! You told me her husband died during the raid."

"I'm confused," Wren says.

I can't respond because my head is full of disbelief and even grief. "How didn't I figure it out?" I question in a soft voice. My throat feels like it's full of glass as I chug Wren's water.

"What is going on?" Wren holds my gaze and I can't look away as I fall back into my chair.

"Dad?"

Dad runs his hands through his hair and sighs wearily. "Sarah DeLacroix was Joy Jacobs. Your mother, Wren. Roman was your brother." It takes Wren a few moments of silence to understand what Dad is telling her.

She shakes her head while tears run down her face. "Are you sure my mother's dead? The Reverend never said that."

"I'm sure, Wren. I knew her while she was married

to him. She helped us, but unfortunately, your father looked clean as a whistle."

"She left me with him." Wren glances at my father before staring in shock through the kitchen window. I'm not sure she's seeing her house, but she's certainly thinking about something.

"She didn't leave you. She thought you were dead."

"And she never checked?" I ask the question.

"The night of the raid, Sarah wasn't where we'd agreed to meet, so I went looking for her. She was distraught, she said you weren't breathing. There was a fire, set by the group not wanting to be taken alive. We thought the child that had been recovered was you. It eventually gave her relief knowing you hadn't suffered in the fire because you'd already been dead." He pauses. "It wasn't until after her death that I discovered you were alive. I'm just as confused as you are as to what happened that night. Why did she think you were dead? The only person who can answer is the Reverend."

"Why can't I remember her, my brother, anything from then? I would have been, what, seven, almost eight? I should remember something."

"I don't know, Wren." Dad looks gray, and Wren is even paler than usual.

I want to hold her to me, comfort her, but I don't. I'm scared she'll push me away now that she knows the truth. I still can't believe I never worked it out. I feel like an idiot. I'd known Dad was keeping things from me, I just had no idea it was that. The woman I'd considered my mom, and the boy I considered my brother, had been Wren's true parent and sibling. I didn't know whether to rejoice or be jealous. I shake my head. I have no reason to be jealous. When I think about it, I'm angry that Wren was left behind.

"Rafael?" Wren whispers my name and slowly reaches out for my hand.

My heart races as I grab it up in mine and hold on. "I don't know what to say."

"Don't say anything, son, just sit back down because we need to end whatever is going on and leave town…with Wren."

"I'm not going anywhere," she states in a firm voice.

My heart slowly starts to sink when she squeezes my hand. "I need to know what happened to me in Amarillo and why my mother left me for dead. I can't leave. The need to know the truth will eat me alive."

"I get that, but it might not be safe for you to go home."

She ignores Dad's comments and asks, "How do you know Peter Wild is dead?"

Surprised, Dad quickly looks at me before he shakes his head. "The Reverend and two other men killed him the other night. My contact at the DEA wants the drugs."

"I don't know anything about drugs. I told you already. I do know that Peter Wild was a disgusting pig. He had my photographs all over his bedroom." She shudders. "Sick."

"The Reverend was in the process of pouring accelerant over Wild's cabin when we left," I add.

"You mean you were nearly caught, again." Dad raises his brows.

"Please tell me about the drugs. What do they look like? What kind of place would they need to store them?"

"The DEA suspects that they're either getting their opium from elsewhere or they're growing it themselves. Ariel footage doesn't show sign of the latter, but that doesn't mean it's not happening."

"How do you grow your own?"

"Poppies," I tell her. "Papaver somniferum is the type of poppy that produces opium. The quick explanation is that the opium is removed from the pod of the flower. It's then refined to make morphine, and then further refined into different forms of heroin. The market value for a kilo is around forty-five thousand dollars."

"That's a lot of money." A frown creases Wren's brow and when I've finished explaining, she says, "So they'd have to keep them hidden but still have them outside."

Dad pauses and sits forward. "What do you know, Wren."

"Stop pushing her."

"It's okay," Wren says. "I do know where poppies are growing. It wouldn't be viewed from the air because it's covered."

"Covered? How?"

"The forest goes on for miles. If you head toward the stream Rafael has seen and keep going straight, you'll come to them. The trees hide them from view." She shrugs. "I don't know if they're what you're looking for, but they are red poppies. Pretty. The Reverend told me never to enter the area where they are because I could get sick." She tilts her head. "Thinking about it now, the butterflies never went close either. Some would follow me, but they'd always stay back. I haven't been for months."

"At least he warned you away, and you listened." I offer her a wry smile.

"I do listen sometimes." She sighs. "I want to remember my mother and Roman."

"We'll try and help you remember when this is over and you're safe. First though, you have to act as though you know nothing. He can't know, otherwise, he'll flip."

"I've been acting all these years."

"You go home, Wren, before the Reverend gets back. When it's dark, Rafael and I will go and find those poppies."

"Be careful. The Reverend knew the last time I went. I don't know how. Maybe he's put cameras up or something. But he knew I'd been there."

Dad nods and I pull Wren into my arms, and whisper, "You be careful. If you need help, run over here and hide, okay? I'll find you." I kiss her pale cheek and watch as she leaves, her shoulders slumped.

"Do you think I should go with her?" I ask Dad. "She doesn't look right."

"She's had a shock."

"I thought she was okay."

"Son, you're not okay after finding out you were left for dead by the person who should protect you."

"Fuck! I'll go to her."

"Not now. Later. Give her time alone to process everything."

"What if she decides she doesn't want any part of us...of me?" I lean against the sink and watch Wren enter her own house. I feel as though I've been punched in the gut. I just can't bring myself to believe she wouldn't want to be with me. "I won't let that happen."

Dad pats me on the back. "I've seen the way she looks at you. She won't change her mind, which reminds me—" He grins and reaches into a cupboard, then places a large box on the counter. "Bought you some rubbers. Use the fucking things, Rafael."

On that note, he leaves me to my own embarrassment and disappears to the front of the house.

34

WREN

As soon as I'm in the house, my feet pound upstairs and I hide in my bedroom. There are so many things churning inside of my head that I can't concentrate on just one. The main thing is how could my mother have left me? That hurts. It more than hurts. It feels like I've been cut somewhere deep and I can't stop the wound from spilling out inside me. I don't know what to do. I want to scream and shout. My breath is difficult to catch as I slump in a ball on the floor. All this time, I thought she was living her life elsewhere. Not dead. Now I'll never get to know her. Or my brother. How could I forget I had a baby brother?

I'm glad Marcel had given me something else to

think about because it gave me time to pull myself together. I honestly thought I was going to fall apart in his kitchen. No matter what the truth is, it doesn't change the past ten years that I've lived under the control of the Reverend. Nothing changes that.

Dragging myself up from the floor, I crawl onto the bed, and roll onto my back. My heart hurts and I don't know what to do about it. I was unwanted.

That's not true!

Why hadn't I told Marcel and Rafael about the church basement and the computers that I'd seen? I should have told them. The same can be said about the basement under the house. After what they told me, I wonder about the door and whether or not there is something behind it. Do I want to know?

I have buried my head for years not wanting to snoop too closely because I knew I would get caught and punished. I can't get away with anything in this town.

"Wren?" My name yelled from downstairs has me frozen to the bed.

The Reverend is home and I didn't hear his car. Strange. It makes the loudest noises. I remain motionless and wait.

"Wren, are you home?" he calls again.

I'm tempted to shout back, "No." However, I stay silent.

Doors slam around downstairs and then I hear the front door rattle on its hinges as its closed. "What is he doing?" I mutter, wishing my bedroom was at the front of the house so I can see if he's left. I don't hear anything else downstairs, even though I lie still for maybe twenty minutes. Still no sound. So, he's left.

I want to know about the door in the basement. At least, if I check it out first, and make a big mistake by getting caught, the punishment won't be as bad as what he might do to Rafael or his father, right? That's my way of thinking. Not that I want to be punished.

Sitting up on the bed, I glance around and continue to listen for movement downstairs, but there is no sound, just the usual creak of the old house. I quickly change into a dark pair of jeans and my flat-heeled boots. They lace up to mid-calf, so they'll keep me warm in the basement. I toss my own T-shirt off and give a secret smile when I look down at the black one of Rafael's that I've borrowed. It smells of him, so I want to keep it close. I intend to wear it the next time he sees me. I hadn't missed how his eyes had heated when he'd seen it on me.

A wave of sadness washes over me as I think about

the boy who holds my heart. He got to spend close to seven years with my mom and brother—the family I can't even remember. It hurts a lot, if I'm honest, and there's also jealousy trying to get out. However, I'm more than aware the Reverend is the one to blame. The one to hold responsible for my loss, and Marcel and Rafael's gain, and then, eventually, their loss. He's an evil man who will soon get what he deserves.

Anger eats at me as I yank a sweater over my head and move across the room. My bedroom door creaks at a certain point, so I only open it enough to allow me to slip through.

I know which floorboards to miss so I don't make a sound as I make my way downstairs. I walk quietly from room to room, but the Reverend really has left. I glance through the front room window and then the kitchen and see no sign of his car. I frown because I really did not hear his car when he arrived or left again. Surely, he didn't walk from the church because that is unheard of.

Instead of wasting more time, I place my hand on the doorknob leading to the basement and my belly fills with nerves. I haven't really thought about this. I hate it down there. I snatch my hand back and step back. Swallowing around my growing nervousness, I quickly move and grab a flashlight from the junk drawer in the kitchen. I check to make sure it works and then yank the basement door open before I can change my mind.

You can do this. One foot in front of the other.

The flashlight is bright as I move forward and close the door behind me. My heart races as I move the light around to check that I'm alone down here. I then focus on where I saw the door, and I discover it's real. It's solid wood and I blink when I focus on the padlock. It's hanging open and the door looks slightly ajar. At least from my view at the top of the stairs it does. Telling myself I can do this, I slowly move down the old stairs, hoping they're not making too much noise. I can't hear anything with the blood rushing through my ears.

With my feet on the ground, I move forward, ignoring the scratching noise coming from behind. Vermin. That sound I am used to down here. My nose twitches from the foul smell the closer I get to the door. I tuck my hand inside of my sweater and cover my mouth and nose while my other hand trembles holding the flashlight.

Forcing my feet forward, I reach for the edge of the door and pull it toward me. It opens silently and I find myself staring into a dark tunnel. Questions tumble through my head as to how I didn't know this was here, and I can't help but wonder where it leads. I thought I was observant. I knew who was sneaking around with whom. I even knew who the Reverend slept with on which particular day. However, I had no idea this was right under my nose. Clueless!

I shine the flashlight inside and the ground in the tunnel appears to gradually slope downward. "You can do this," I whisper to myself. "I can do this," I say more determined. I'm not going to chicken out, no matter how much I hate being down here.

Inhaling deeply, I step forward and then stop with a last-minute thought. I quickly remove the padlock and shove it into my back pocket. If I have it, then I can't be locked in here.

I move into the tunnel with only the flashlight to guide me. The walls and the roof are laid out with wood. Hardwood maybe. I don't really know. Something strong, I imagine. My steps are slow and as I put distance between the basement, I nervously glance behind me. The doorway is getting smaller.

I slowly turn my head back toward the dark tunnel and scream. A large arm wraps around my waist while his gloved hand covers my mouth. I try to bite him, but it's impossible with how tightly he holds me. He grunts as I kick him in the knee. We move back toward the basement and I continue to fight him. My hands grab his jacket, I try to lift my arms and grab his face, but he's too big to reach.

"I'm not going to hurt you," he hisses. "Wren, stop fighting."

"That's what killers say before they kill you," I mumble, my mouth still covered.

"I'm your uncle," he says quietly.

Hell no!

I start wiggling again and just as he pushes us through to the basement, I trip him and we both go down. My heart is pumping, and I know I have to fight, but he has my legs. I can't even kick him in the face.

"Not related to your dad. Your mother, Wren."

I still at his words and swivel my head to his face. "My mom?" I see him nod in the glow from my flashlight.

"My name is Silas Mathis and your mother, Joy, was my sister. I'm here for you, Wren."

"I don't know what to believe."

He releases my legs and pulls himself up, offering

me a hand. I hesitate, and he says, "If I wanted to hurt you, I would have done so."

I take his hand.

"Marcel knows about me, or rather, he knows that Joy had a brother who died. My death status had been a mix up. However, in the end, it meant I could work as a ghost...*for others*. It became easier to let everyone believe I was actually dead. Eventually it worked to my advantage because it meant I could work toward finding the men responsible for Joy's and my nephew's deaths. I've only been back in the country a few years. Until then, I had no idea what had happened." He runs a hand through his hair and admits, "Rafael has seen me too."

"Wait. You're the one who told me to leave in the church basement." I wince. "I'm always meeting you in basements."

"You have to stop snooping, Wren." Silas pushes the door closed to an inch and turns to me. "This thing that the Reverend is involved in is bigger than you and me, and your friends next door."

"They have help." I dust myself off and look around for the flashlight. I find it under the stairs with the battery lying next to it. While distracted putting the thing back together, I add, "They believe heroin is being produced here." I look at him and notice a tick beside his jaw. "They're right? Are the poppies in the field opium ones?"

"You know a lot."

"Not really. I had a crash course not long ago. I've been blind my whole life, it seems."

Silas moves closer and, reaching out, brushes a lock of hair from my eyes. "You remind me of your mother." He turns sad, and his eyes look like he really isn't here with me. "I wish I'd known what was happening back then. I'd have helped her, or at least tried."

"The only person to blame is the one who took their lives, and the one who requested that it be done."

"You're older than your years, Wren."

"Not really."

"Wild was one of the men there that day," he says quietly. "I don't know who the other man was yet. I will, though. From what I've heard, the Reverend wanted his son back. Roman wasn't supposed to be killed. Just taken and brought here. To *him*. I hadn't seen the Reverend so angry until the day he learned of his son's death."

I gasp. "What?"

He ignores me and orders, "Tell Marcel to leave with you and Rafael before someone gets killed. They don't like interlopers, which they believe the DeLacroix to be. If the Reverend knows you're in love with Rafael, there will be bigger trouble than you can imagine. He's unhinged, Wren. Don't push him because he will push back harder than ever before."

"I want to know about my mom," I say fiercely. "And Roman. I can't remember either of them."

"I'll tell you what you want to know, but not now. You need to go upstairs before the Reverend gets back. He went to the church via the tunnel."

My eyes widen and Silas curses. "Be careful, Wren. You're the only family I have left." With those words, he leaves through the tunnel.

I feel pale and drawn as I stare at the closed door. Part of me wants to follow him and demand he tell me everything. The other part, the scared part, has me putting the padlock back into the ring and finding a hiding place for the flashlight. I avoid leaving it close to the bed because that would be the logical place for the Reverend to look for it. Instead, I decide to leave it in the open and place it face down beside the doorframe. It's in view but not obvious. Maybe he'll think someone else left it there if it's discovered. I can only hope.

Leaving the basement as quietly as I entered, I go and hide in my bedroom and wait. For what, I'm not sure. Maybe the Reverend to come back and tell me he knows what I've been doing this afternoon. Or maybe for Rafael to come and tell me about my mother and brother.

I desperately want to remember them. I do remember a woman singing me to sleep when I was little, but the memory won't come into focus. I've tried hard over the years to remember the face of the woman who I have always assumed to be my mother. I've never known for sure, and even now I don't know because I can't remember.

Then I remember I'm still expected to have dinner on the table.

35

RAFAEL

UNSETTLED SINCE WREN LEFT, I CLIMB UP ONTO HER roof, keeping low so I'm not seen as the sun sets. She's in her room. I see her shadow moving around, as though she's pacing back and forth. I've given her enough space to think about what was said and I'm only hoping she doesn't blame me for anything. My main concern is her thoughts on her brother and mom—the ones I had for seven years, the same length of time Wren did, but struggles to remember. She hadn't been the only one surprised at Dad's admission. All this time I'd never known Sarah had had a daughter. Was that why she'd sometimes looked sad?

Sighing, I gently tap on Wren's window and feel some of the tension drain away when she immediately appears, letting me in. It drains away completely when she wraps herself around me and shoves her face into my neck.

Picking her up, I move and lie down on the bed with her snuggled in my arms. We're as close as can be with our clothing on and I feel like she wants to get closer. "Has something happened between then and now?" I brush my lips across her forehead.

"I went to the basement," she whispers. "I should have told you before. I don't know why I didn't." She rolls away, but I'm not going to let her put distance between us.

My arm snakes around her waist and I pull her close, hovering above. "Tell me, Wren."

"I'm lying. I didn't tell you because I figured if we got caught then you'd be in more trouble than me. Now I'm not too sure that would be the case." She glances away, and adds, "I met my uncle."

"Uncle?" I watch her closely.

"I'll start from the beginning. I caught a glance of a door in the basement that I hadn't noticed before because it's dark and there isn't any light. I checked that the Reverend wasn't around and then I took a flashlight and went down there." She moves to her knees in excitement. "I was scared stupid, but there is a tunnel leading to the church. I didn't get that far. In fact, I didn't get far at all. Someone was in there and he grabbed me. I fought but he was stronger."

"Fuck, Wren!" I hiss.

"It was my uncle, Rafael. At least, he said he was. Silas Mathis. He said everyone thinks he's dead."

"It could have been someone *fucking* else, Wren!" I'm too agitated to sit so I start pacing. "What if it had been the Reverend down there? Shit!" I rub at my chest and calm down when I see her chin wobble and tears seep from her eyes. "I'm sorry. The thought of you down there—alone and in trouble—scares me."

"It wasn't the wisest decision I've ever made, but I met my uncle. I thought he meant the Reverend's brother at first and I got a good kick in then, but he explained he meant my mother's side of the family. He didn't confirm there were drugs around, but when I asked about the poppies, he was surprised I knew anything. He said for your dad to take us both away from here. It's too dangerous. Why do you think he's here?"

"The same as us. Vengeance." I rub at my eyes. "That's all I've wanted, Wren. Since I saw them die. I've wanted the bastards responsible to pay. That's what Silas wants too. He left flowers on Mom's grave saying as much."

"Then we have to find enough evidence of what they're doing here to get the authorities to act. Did you find the poppies? You went looking, right?"

"We didn't find anything."

"That's impossible." Wren frowns. "They were there."

"We walked for a while and couldn't find any flowers. But Dad thought we had found where they had been. The ground looked turned over, but that's about it."

"So, I was right? They were growing those type of poppies." Wren pulls off her sweater and tosses it to the bed while I grin at the sight before me.

"You're wearing my shirt." I move closer and tug her up, slipping my hands inside the T-shirt. She shivers when I reach the bare skin of her torso and hold her gently. "We're going to get him, Wren. I promise." I kiss her forehead.

"I need to tell you something else," she says. "Something is going on in the basement of the church."

"Oh, hell no! You are not going snooping there.

No way." I cup her face. "That is way too dangerous, Wren."

"I accidentally went down there on Sunday. I was trying to avoid Agnes, the Sunday school teacher. Silas was there and got me out of the way. Of course, I didn't know who he was at the time."

"What exactly are you on about?" I pull her down beside me on the bed. "You've been keeping things from me that could impact your safety."

She narrows her eyes. "Oh, and you and your dad haven't kept some pretty big things from me! Like the fact that you lived with my mom and brother for years." She stands, good and mad. "I've managed alone for years, so don't start getting mad when I find myself somewhere I'm not supposed to be."

Reaching out, I pull her onto my lap and hold her down when she moves to get up. "I didn't know Sarah and Joy, your mother, were the one and the same. I swear."

"I'm sorry." Her head touches mine. "I shouldn't have said that. I know it wasn't your fault. I need to know why I was left behind, Rafael. It's eating at me. Why didn't she want me?"

"I don't believe that for a minute. Want to know why,

because every now and again, Mom would get this look on her face, and I knew she wasn't really in the room with me. Now that I know about you, I'm thinking you're the one she was thinking about. You heard Dad. She told him you'd died. She wouldn't have lied about that. I know that beyond anything, Wren. Whatever happened, it made her truly believe she'd lost you."

"I'm so tired and my head hurts."

"I'll stay until you fall asleep." I move her onto the bed and follow her down, pulling her back against my front. "Close your eyes and clear your mind."

"Will you take my jeans off?"

I grin. "I'm game."

She chuckles. "No funny business."

Slipping a hand to the button and zipper, I peel the denim over her hips and off before I settle back down with her. She wiggles and pushes her bottom against my groin—not helping. Wrapping an arm around her stomach, I hiss, "Stop rubbing on me."

"I wish you could hold me all night," she whispers as I bury my nose in the hair spilling over the pillow.

"Soon."

She finally drifts to sleep, and I don't want to leave. I want to stay this way forever. Holding the girl I've fallen in love with. Instead, I gently unwrap myself from her body and pull the quilt over her. She mumbles something in her sleep and cuddles into the quilt.

I stand watching her, my heart aching to get back on the bed. I can't. The Reverend may check on her when he comes home. It's with those thoughts on my mind that I climb out of the window and tug it down softly behind me. I leave a small gap, so she gets some of the fresh air. I know she likes this weather, even though it's humid. As I turn, I'm surprised to see a group of butterflies hovering close, as though they've been watching us through the window - as though they sense the turmoil inside of Wren.

"She's okay for now," I whisper to her friends.

They hover and then disappear into the night. Probably to the glasshouse that Wren has created for them. I wish they were able to keep her safe for me while I can't be here.

36

WREN

Breakfast is quiet and it takes everything in me to not look at the Reverend as I eat. If I do, I know all the truth I've learned in the past twenty-four hours would be shining clearly on my face. Instead, I keep my eyes down into the bowl as I eat. The Reverend made me oatmeal, which I like, but he never makes me breakfast. I can't imagine why he would do this now, so my mind is churning as I try to figure it out. I don't have a problem eating it because he also put a spoon of strawberry jelly into the dish. He doesn't appear to be in a happy mood either, so this is bizarre. I always have to do what he asks, so it's not like he's trying to get his way about something. His

way is the only way. Or so I learned while growing up.

When the bowl in front of me is empty, I move
from the table with my dirty dishes and reach for the
Reverend's. He passes them to me and sips his coffee,
his eyes on me. "I want you to accompany me to the
church today, Wren."

A dish slips out of my hand to shatter on the floor.
I gasp and quickly get the broom and dustpan to clear
the mess, mumbling an apology. I dare not look at
him because he'll be angry. I've ruined good dishes.
They're not actually good dishes, but he likes to think
they are. Not one matches.

"Bring your schoolwork with you."

"Why am I going to the church and not school?"
The moment the words are out of my mouth, I cringe
inside and wait for his rebuff—it doesn't come.

"I'm leaving. Now, Wren." I turn and frown at his
back. There is something going on. One, I'm never
allowed to miss school, and two, he didn't yell or
react when I asked him a question.

"Wren!" He does yell this time.

Running through the house, I grab my book bag
on the way out to the car. The engine turns over
before I've even gotten in and then he's off. The speed

at which he leaves slams the door and me in the seat. I scramble for the seatbelt and my hands shake as I try and get the end into the slot. The Reverend laughs. "Feel that power, Wren. It makes me invincible."

What is he on about?

I stay silent.

"We'll be moving soon," he continues. "Somewhere that has cold winters and warm summers. You'll like that." He pulls up outside of the church and makes no move to get out of the car. "One day, you'll realize that everything I've done, I've done for you." He turns his eyes on me and I feel ill. "You'll run the next church with me. My daughter by my side. Wild has left, so I'm going to take good care of you." He grins and gets out of the car. "Agnes is in the office. She'll keep an eye on you today," he shouts over his shoulder.

Peeling myself from the car, I want to run through the trees and find Rafael. I don't like anything that is happening today. It's making me feel more uneasy than before. The Reverend isn't right. The sun shines off the car and blinds me, so I have no choice but to look toward the church where the Reverend waits. He's talking to a man who turns slightly, and I recognize him as Silas.

Seeing Silas reassures me that he'll be close because I desperately want to trust him. He's got me out of the way twice now, so I have to trust that. Trust him. He casts me a quick glance without missing a word with the Reverend as I walk by and into the church.

What would be good is if Agnes decided she had something better to do than babysit me. I know she'll be in her small Sunday school room, so I decide to head to the office outside of the Reverend's. Agnes actually scares me more than the Reverend does.

I dump my bag on the empty desk and take out books so that I look busy. He won't ask me to do stuff around here if I'm doing schoolwork. Then again, I never expected him to willingly let me miss a day of school.

With the pencil twirling in my mouth, I open one of my religious books, knowing it will please him, and then think about why he is talking about moving. It's out of the blue and makes no sense. Why would he up and move us when everyone in this town worships the ground he walks on? Does he know people are on to him? Does he suspect that people know about Peter Wild's murder...and the drugs...and whatever else he's done that has yet to be found? Is he about to go on the run? Is that why he is keeping me close? I would have thought he'd have left me here. I'm just a servant to him. Or am I?

He appears in the doorway with Silas, stops and stares at me, and then heads into his office. "Wren, I asked you to go to Agnes."

"I thought I could help you in here instead," I find myself offering, wincing as Silas turns his eyes on me. He's not impressed.

"Whatever, I'm busy and don't have time for this. Just stay out of my way." The door slams but not before I catch Silas nodding his head toward the entryway. He wants me to leave.

I want to leave, but I also want to know what is going on. I'm tired of being punished or having to watch my step so I don't upset *him*.

I'm in the church and the basement is where I saw the computers and a few men doing something to them. Maybe that is where I should start.

Thinking about going looking, I move toward the door and quickly run back to the desk. I leave a note saying I've gone to find Agnes. He might believe that or not, but I'm going downstairs.

Leaving the office, I lower my eyes so as not to cause suspicion. I'm always like this—I never meet anyone's stare. To others, I'm acting like I always do—shy and awkward. Nerves flutter in my belly as I walk past the statue of Jesus Christ, a replica of the one in Rio de Janeiro. It's always given me the creeps.

I don't pass anyone as I move downstairs, and then I find myself standing in front of the closed door where I'd first seen Silas. The computers from school had been in there and it had looked like they were setting them up. Why they'd need all those computers in the basement baffles me. If they are doing illegal stuff, I don't understand the need for everything they removed from school.

Leaning in, I place my ear against the door, not hearing anything. It's as though I'm the only one in the church because there really is no sound coming from behind the door or above me. I frown and glance up toward the ceiling wondering why it's so quiet.

The nerves are eating away at my stomach and I find myself taking a step toward the stairs as I stop. *I can do this.* I turn back toward the door, and with determination, I raise a hand to push the door open. However, I freeze with my hand raised, distracted when I hear a loud banging noise coming from the front of the church.

Now I hear movement. Footsteps running along the hallway above me. My heart pounds, and I turn to look for a place to hide. There isn't anywhere down here. Just the stairs and the door. More noise infiltrates my ears, so I use it to my advantage and run upstairs. Armed men come through the front door of the church wearing badges around their necks. I spot a few women amongst the men as more come inside. The word "warrant" reaches me as blood starts to pound through my ears.

What do they mean warrant? I thought Marcel was trying to get enough evidence to go to the DEA. I don't understand what has changed from last evening.

"Wren," snaps the Reverend.

I blink a few times and slowly make my way toward him on weak legs. I thought when anything like this were to happen, I would be with Marcel and Rafael. Not alone with all these strangers and the Reverend. I don't trust anyone in this room.

"Wren, we don't have all day."

The moment I'm within arm's reach, he grabs my wrist and pulls me into his side. "This is my daughter."

"We'd like to talk to her," one of the men says. "Alone."

The Reverend shakes his head. "She's a minor, so I have to be present."

The man who appears to be in charge tightens his jaw. I'm surprised because the Reverend can be an asshole. However, as sheltered as I've been, I know that's the law. The Reverend grins in a weird way and stands his ground.

"What are they doing?" I ask, not only surprising the Reverend, but myself. The words just blurted out of my mouth causing everyone to focus on me.

"We have a warrant to search the church," the man says. "I'm Special Agent Ken James with the DEA."

"Oh!" I mumble, watching them get sorted. "DEA? Drugs?" I ask, pretending I really am clueless.

"You know anything about that?" He raises a brow in question. "Because I can promise you protection for information."

"There is nothing to find, so stop filling her head with nonsense." The Reverend looks furious, but his voice is calm as he says, "Wren, please wait with Agnes while I make sure these agents don't make a mess."

He probably means, so the agents don't touch anything not covered in the warrant.

"Yes, sir." The man, Ken James, watches me move around him and the other agents to leave the room.

Unfortunately, for me, Agnes is already waiting in the hallway. She, too, makes a grab for me. However, I slip away. "Do not touch me. You're not the Reverend. No one touches me but him," I hiss, very pleased when she turns red in the face.

She's furious. I can't remember a time that I've ever spoken to her like that. It feels really good. Maybe I should have been sticking up for myself more, then I wouldn't have found myself in this situation. Even as that thought runs through my mind, I know I'm wrong. Nothing would have changed the way the Reverend has been toward me.

"You can't go in there," another DEA agent states.

Agnes bristles past me. "That is my office."

"Then you can enter and speak with the agents inside." He glances at me, his eyes dancing. "You can take a seat." He nods toward a row of three chairs like you'd get in a dentist waiting room—plastic and uncomfortable.

"I'll stand," I mumble and tilt my head to the side. "Do I know you?"

"No, ma'am." His eyes stay on the wall in front of him. Part of me wants to slide along the wall until I'm in front of him, because I really feel like he knows me. I don't mean because he's researched the Reverend, but like—

My eyes snap to his face, and I wonder aloud. "Marcel DeLacroix."

There is a slight flicker in his gaze, which I would have missed had I not been looking for it. He knows Marcel, which is how he knows me. The man sighs, and whispers, "Please just sit and wait," without moving his lips. "Cameras."

I hesitate for a moment before I collapse into one of the chairs, knowing when I get up it will hurt. The plastic always sticks to my legs when I'm in shorts. What a weird thing to think about when the DEA are crawling all over the church.

As time ticks on by, I start to fidget, and wonder what Rafael is up to. Does he know what is going on here? Especially that I'm here too.

"This is upsetting for my daughter," the Reverend hisses, suddenly moving down the hallway toward me. "I want you all to leave us alone. We haven't done anything wrong."

I want to say that it's not upsetting me but think better of it. They won't take me with them, which means I need to watch my mouth. Agent James casts a glance in my direction and refrains from saying what he really wants to. I can see in the agent's eyes that he's holding back, not easily either. "We'll be leaving soon."

The Reverend turns away from the agent and stares in my direction but doesn't really look at me. He's thinking about something before he snaps his fingers and moves back toward his office, the agent on his heels.

Shaking my head, I turn my attention to the agent guarding the door into the Sunday school room, and ask, "You're DEA, right? So are you looking for drugs, because I have to say, I've never seen any?" I pause. "But in truth, if I did, I probably wouldn't know it. I've no idea what drugs look like."

"*When* we find them, I'll show you."

I smile. "Then maybe I'll be able to help you find more if I know what I'm looking for."

He shakes his head. "No, you won't. You'll stay safe, Wren. Marcel will have my head on a plate if something happens to you on my watch. Not to mention Rafael." He grins before catching himself.

"You tell the Reverend the truth. That you asked me what we were looking for. Nothing more."

"Okay." I stare at dust that has gathered close to the baseboard opposite, and ask, "Are there cameras everywhere inside?"

"Yes," he whispers, and then clears his throat. "We're leaving."

"What?"

"We didn't expect to find anything." He offers me his hand. "Just wanted to let him know he's on our radar."

I slip my smaller hand into his and we quickly shake.

"You're not alone," he says so quietly that I only just catch his words as he moves past me.

I stifle a giggle, because although those words are true, I once remember reading a book during reading hour at school and that phrase was in it a few times. Only the book referred to alien life form, not someone's welfare.

My eyes follow the man as he strides down the hallway, and other agents seem to appear from different directions as they leave as quickly as they'd arrived. I'm so engrossed in watching them that it takes me a few seconds to realize Agnes is standing beside me. I quickly jump up from the chair. However, I'm not quick enough and Agnes grabs my arm and pulls me into her office. The door slamming closed behind us.

She releases my wrist and gets in my face. "I know what you're doing, Wren. You and that boy next door, or should I say man? The Reverend knows all about Marcel and Rafael DeLacroix, so I suggest if you care anything for them, you'll stay away."

"Get away from me," I hiss and shove her backwards.

"You little—"

"Wren," the Reverend shouts, opening the door and pushing me toward Agnes.

Managing to sidestep at the last minute, I catch myself before I fall to the floor, and then rush to the Reverend's side. He blinks in surprise and frowns before turning his eyes on the evil woman.

"What is going on in here?" he demands, his voice dripping with menace. "I've told you to leave my daughter alone. No one touches her."

"Does Wren know that?" she sneers. "You know she's letting Rafael touch her. Yet you do nothing."

The Reverend looks ready to blow a gasket from

how red his face is with anger. "I know nothing of the sort!" he roars. "You will stay away from Wren."

He grabs me tightly around the top of my arm before dragging me from the room. He's moving so quickly along the hallway that I stumble into the wall. It makes him angrier. Outside in the bright sun, he slows and looks around. Then we're off again and my feet hardly touch the steps at the back of the church as I'm dragged down them.

"You're hurting me," I cry, unable to prevent the sob from leaving my mouth.

"Do not say a word to me, daughter." He yanks on the car handle and curses when his hand slips off. He gets it on the second try and pushes me into the seat. "Get in, Wren," he snaps.

Terrified of what is going on, I tuck my legs into the car and curl up on the seat. The Reverend stares and I find I'm unable to move. He hisses and, leaning over me, snaps the seatbelt on. Seconds later, we're off down the road.

37

RAFAEL

FIVE MINUTES BEFORE THE DEA ARRIVED AT THE church, Dad received a message telling him what was about to happen. It hadn't been enough time for me to get Wren out of the place. I probably would have had time if I hadn't spent it arguing with Dad. Of course, we'd been arguing about Wren.

The binoculars have been glued to my eyes from the moment the black cars and one van had pulled up outside the church yard. Dad wants reports, but all I want is to catch a glimpse of Wren.

I wonder why the Reverend decided to take Wren with him today instead of sending her to school. Had he known something was about to happen? Why would he want her there? That made no sense. I believe everything Wren has told me, so the Reverend holding Wren back worries me.

"They're gone." Dad moves next to me. "Has anyone left after them?"

"No movement."

Finally placing the binoculars on the side, I stare out the back window to the tree line. "I want to find Wren."

"I know you do, son. She'll be okay for now."

"How do we really know that to be true? For all we know the bastard could already be hurting her. What if she didn't keep quiet about everything she discovered yesterday? She was really shaken learning about Mom and Roman. I could see it in her eyes last night. She wanted to ask the Reverend why he had them killed. I'm worried she doesn't care about her own safety now. She just wants answers."

Sighing, Dad hugs me close, holding on as he says, "She's as loyal as you are, Rafael DeLacroix. I mean she will do anything to protect you. That's why she needs answers from him. Not just for herself, but for you and, of course, that means me too." He kisses my forehead.

"Jeremiah is here. He will have answers. I hope,"

Dad says, nodding toward the man running across the backyard from the tree line.

With how silently he moved through the back-door, you wouldn't think he'd run with any speed. "She's okay." He glances at me. "Before you ask."

I nod.

"Why now? I thought we needed more before they'd go in." Dad passes him a bottle of water from the fridge.

"Ken wanted to shake him up. Found nothing, but he didn't expect to. Wanted to let them know we are watching." He takes a long drink, and adds, "The Reverend kept his cool and, to my surprise, the man actually appeared protective of Wren."

"How?" I ask, itching to go and find her.

"He wouldn't let her talk and showed real concern about her being left alone. As to Wren, she was nervous and curious. She wanted to ask questions but kept quiet because the Reverend was within earshot. Agnes Mercer, the old woman who runs the Sunday school, wasn't pleasant and I sensed Wren was scared of her more than the Reverend." He shakes his head. "The people there all look for guidance from Lucas Jacobs."

"We can't leave Wren with them."

"Rafael, your girl is safe where she is at the moment. If you take her from him, things won't go as planned. You have to be careful. The less the Reverend suspects of Wren's involvement with you, the safer she'll be. There are agents watching. They know Wren is innocent in all of this and should be protected. The best thing to do is stay away from her for the next few days."

I frown and tilt my head as I watch him. Jeremiah knows something. At least that's the feeling I'm getting. "What's going on?" He stays silent and my anger rapidly starts to rise as I add, "Something is happening, right?"

Jeremiah finally admits, "We don't know any more than you do. However, we have been led to believe something big is going to be happening. We assume it's drug related."

"Dad?"

"I'm thinking."

Pacing across the kitchen, I try and shake the anger I feel. I desperately want to find Wren and leave this town. I came here for vengeance and never expected to fall in love with Sarah's daughter—the daughter of the woman I called Mom, and still do. I can't change anything—wouldn't if I could. I've fallen in love with Wren and I'll do anything to make sure she doesn't end up like our mother and brother. It's frustrating having to think before I go off and act hotheaded when I really need to stay calm and have a plan. A plan is what's going to get the bastard. Then I'll have Wren.

"The tunnels!" A bit late in the day to remember, but better than not at all, I guess. "Wren told me about them last night."

"What tunnels? Why are you just telling us now?" Dad shouts.

"It wasn't as though we could go snooping," I answer back. "It was late when I got back here, and I didn't think about it until now."

"Explain exactly what you mean, Rafael, please." Clearly, Jeremiah is the calm one right now. I can barely keep from pacing. Dad looks like he's ready to shake me, while Jeremiah leans back in his chair and calmly holds my gaze.

I run my hands through my hair and join him at the table. "She had seen a door in the basement the last time she was locked in there. It was only after we told her about Sarah being her mother and the drug angle that she decided to check out what she'd seen. It was open. She was caught snooping by Silas Mathis."

"What?" Jeremiah shoots up in the chair. "Say that name again."

Frowning, I repeat, "Silas Mathis."

Dad asks, "You know him?"

Jeremiah glances between us, his eyes flickering back and forth. "Yes." He sighs. "You cannot repeat this, and I'm only telling you now because you obviously know more than what you're telling me."

Dad shakes his head. "He made himself known to Rafael, not by name. He also left flowers on Sarah's grave."

"He's been working for us for a few years. He got back from overseas pretty banged up. The moment he discovered what happened to his sister, he contacted us. He wants the same things you two do but got talked into helping us in the process. He tends to do his own thing, which is why no one knows his exact whereabouts at the moment."

"Wren said she started moving down the tunnel, which seemed to slope deeper into the ground as she walked. Silas startled her and she fought him. He told her who he was and to stop snooping before she got caught. He also suggested we leave town and take her with us. For our own safety, apparently. She picked up from something he said that the tunnel leads to the church. I don't trust him."

Jeremiah's eyes light up with glee. "Silas is a good guy. He lives with a lot of guilt because he had no idea what his sister had gone through. Ken is worried he might go after the Reverend alone if it comes down to it. He probably will. I don't blame him. However, now you know he's working for us, I want you to try and make sure the Reverend lives to answer for what he's done. I don't want to have to put Silas away for murder. You hear me?" He pauses. "We need to find out about that tunnel. Maybe there could be more down there. I have a friend who is a historian. I'll ask him if he knows anything about tunnels around this area."

"Shouldn't you have already checked?" I ask.

"Not really. Tunnels between Mexico and the US are common. Not so much here as we're not exactly a border town."

"Regardless of tunnels, I want the Reverend to pay for killing Mom and Roman, but my priority has changed. Wren's safety means more to me at the moment. I need her safe."

"I've told you agents are watching her."

I frown at Jeremiah and ask, "What exactly do you mean by that?"

He winces. "The Reverend has taken her to Padre's in town."

"The bar!" I jump to my feet and concentrate on breathing before I say something I can't ever take back. Once I feel calm enough, I ask, "There are agents inside, right?"

"Yes. Ken put two agents in town just in case. They're posing as a couple. The Reverend may be aware they're agents. Strangers stick out like sore thumbs. But he knows he's being watched anyways because he knows your dad, Rafael."

"Can't they arrest her or something and get her out of town?"

"Rafael," Dad admonishes. "She is the woman you love. You cannot have her arrested for that reason without her prior knowledge. Jeremiah says she is not in any danger right now. She is probably safer with the Reverend while he unloads the drugs."

Moving away from Dad and Jeremiah, I rest my hands on the windowsill in the front room. I can hear them talking about the Reverend and the opium. Having grown his own will give him a very lucrative profit. How much depends on how many kilos he's been able to make. A more popular way is to bring in the opium from China or South America, but that costs a lot of money, and his profit wouldn't come close to what he gets from producing his own.

It was the drug trail that led us to the Reverend's location. He'd been a ghost until one of his men had screwed up. Within a month, Dad and I had taken up residence in the house Mom had left him—next door to Wren.

38

WREN

The moment we enter the bar, the Reverend makes me sit at a table toward the back before placing a cola in front of me. "Drink, and don't move." He turns his back, leaving me alone in this rough place. Apart from a couple near the entrance, I'm the only female in here.

My gaze drifts back to the Reverend and I catch sight of three men in the room he's entering before the door closes. At the last minute, a different man grabs the door from the Reverend and stares directly at me. My belly flutters with fear as I go hot and cold. That man is dangerous—tall, dressed all in black. Even the scruff on his face is black, but it's the look in his eyes as he focuses on me that I find terrifying.

"Ignore them," the bartender says, placing a bottle of water on the table. "You look thirsty."

Recognition dawns as I stare at the boy. "You went to my school, not long ago either."

He looks uncomfortable, so I mumble, "I'm sorry. I shouldn't have said that."

"I did go there," he whispers. "I was needed here." He shrugs. "So, I left. No big deal." He sounds sad. I'm guessing it was a bigger deal than he'll admit. "Just drink the water, okay? You look as though you could do with something stronger, but I don't think the Reverend would allow it."

I offer him a small smile. "Thank you." The bottle hasn't been opened, so I twist off the cap and take a really long swallow. The water is cold and wet and feels nice going down my parched throat. I shouldn't allow my nerves to get the better of me. But it's difficult. There is an uncomfortable feeling in my stomach because of how quickly things are happening out of the norm.

My life hasn't been a happy one, I will be the first to admit that. But it had a steady rhythm to it. I knew what to expect. I always had food on the table, and a warm bed to sleep in at night.

All these years, I've ignored what has been going

on under my nose, and I can't even say there had been any signs there. It only became apparent that something was going on after Marcel and Rafael had moved in next door. The Reverend knew who they were from the start. Is it because of them that he's planning on moving on?

I glance around the bar remembering the barman's name. Andrew Chatsworth. He rolls his sleeves up as I watch and pours drinks into glasses at the bar. Four men occupy the seats, ignoring Andrew.

The smell of cheesy nachos reaches my nose and makes my taste buds water. It's been so long since I've eaten them—it isn't a food the Reverend likes.

"Wren?"

Sighing, I ignore the voice in my head calling my name and think about Tiger Lily. He won't be here for much longer. Another will appear in his place, but it won't be my Tiger Lily.

"Wren?"

I wish the voice would shut up.

"Wren?" My name is shouted, followed by hands clapping in my face. I blink, snapping my eyes up to the Reverend, who looks ready to blow a gasket.

"I'm sorry. I don't feel well," I mumble as an excuse.

He sees through me but lets the lie go.

"Come."

Grabbing my arm, he hauls me out of the chair, none too gently either. A beer mat falls from my hand that I'd been absently picking at before the Reverend ushers me toward the back room. My stomach rolls at the thought of being in that room with the scary guy. I try to dig my heels in, but the Reverend is stronger, and I get nowhere other than propelled forward.

The door opens and closes with me inside before I can catch a breath. I feel hot and flushed as my nerves dance. I wipe the sweat from my palms only to feel them coated again. I can't help it. I'm scared. The man with the scar on his face, whom I think is in charge, stares at me as though he's debating something. A sense of evilness comes off of him and I want to run. Maybe if I can get the two bricks in my shoes to move then I will be able to. I feel sluggish and I know it's because of how scared I am.

I'm left propped up against the grungy wall so the Reverend can go and whisper to the man. They mumble amongst themselves with two other men joining in. I sense someone close and when I turn my head to look, it's Silas. I'm surprised to see him here and when I catch his eye, I know I don't have to say anything. Knowing what I know, he can't be here as himself. The Reverend wouldn't trust him at all if he knew he was my mother's brother.

"Wren can go!" The Reverend volunteers. "I'll go with her."

Hearing my name, I turn my attention back to the other men in the room. They are all staring at me. My heart leaps into my throat and air rushes out of my lungs. Panic races forward, and I try to will my legs to run—only they're not listening. Silas goes tense beside me as though he's expecting trouble. I should be saying something right now, but nothing will come out of my mouth. I can't even think of words to say. What am I being volunteered for? It can't be good if these men are involved.

"Jonas." The evil man looks at Silas. "You go with Wren and make sure she does as she is told. No funny business."

"What?" the Reverend hisses, and I can tell he is angry.

Finally! He's standing up for me.

"I do not want Jonas going."

I should have known.

"He is going with your daughter." The man has spoken and from the look of defeat on the

Reverend's face, it is clear who is really in charge in this room.

My hope has completely disintegrated for any chance that the Reverend cares about me. None. Gone. The knowledge must be clear on my face because the Reverend takes a second glance at me before he turns to the man.

"Ezequiel"—*he has a name*—"I do not want him anywhere near my daughter."

The man, Ezequiel, laughs. "You do not trust Jonas with your daughter." He laughs some more. "That is funny, my friend. Tell me." He runs his eyes over me, becoming serious. "Would you trust me with your daughter?"

I can tell it's on the tip of the Reverend's lips to argue and tell Ezequiel hell no, but he stays silent.

"I thought not." Ezequiel continues to stare at me, and I focus on a red mark on the wall over his shoulder. "You killed Wild for being obsessed with precious Wren, you don't have the balls to *try* and kill me, huh?"

The Reverend is bright red and furious, but he still does or says nothing.

Ezequiel is most certainly in charge.

Silas steps closer to me, and says, "I will protect her and get the job done."

"I like you, Jonas. Do not screw this up." Ezequiel moves away from the Reverend, which I think is for the best as he looks like he's ready to do *something.*

Ezequiel's men must think so too as they have their hands on their weapons at their sides.

"Are we good Reverend?" Ezequiel asks.

The Reverend swallows and breathes deeply before he answers. "My daughter won't let you down." He glares at me as he says this.

I see the promise of retribution in his eyes if I screw this up—whatever this is.

"I'm done with this discussion." Ezequiel snaps his fingers. "Diego, bring the packages in here." To me, he asks, "You have a book bag for school?"

Swallowing, I nod.

The Reverend adds, "It's in the car." He disappears from the room.

"What am I doing?" I ask, my words barely a whisper.

"Something very important," Ezequiel says. "Give us a few minutes." With that said, he walks out with his men, leaving me and Silas alone.

Finally, able to breathe properly, I turn to Silas,

who subtly shakes his head. While I search his eyes, he moves them over to the desk and back to me. He does it two more times and then it hits me.

"Oh!" The room is bugged or something close to it. At least, I'm assuming that's what he meant with the weird back and forth.

Silas offers a wry smile.

"You know what they want me to do?" I ask knowing he does. It will look weird if we don't say anything.

"No."

"You wouldn't tell me if you did know." I push.

"You're right."

I wrap my arms around my stomach. "Did the Reverend really kill Peter Wild because of me?"

That does get Silas's attention. "That was the first time I'd heard anyone admit Wild disappearing had anything to do with the Reverend."

I believe him.

"He gave me the creeps."

Silas nods and quickly moves to lean back against the wall beside the door. A quick escape, no doubt. I want to ask *other* questions and it's frustrating knowing I can't right now. I also want to tell him about Wild's house. I don't exactly want him to see what Wild had done to his room, but I think he needs to know.

Frowning, I wonder about the house. Rafael had thought they planned on torching the place, but I didn't see any signs of fire or hear any sirens. There wasn't even a smoky smell in the air. What did they do to it? We certainly saw them dosing it with something out of cans. Trying to think of a way to ask Silas without anyone hearing me, I open my mouth but don't get the chance.

Silas overrides what I was about to say. "They're back."

The door opens and in they walk.

The Reverend tosses my book bag onto the table and helps Ezequiel transfer two packages into my bag. *Are they the drugs Marcel was asking me about?*

Ezequiel drops my bag on the old wooden table in the center of the room with a thud.

I lick my lips as all eyes turn to me. Sweat trickles down my back as I wipe my brow. My hair is damp with sweat and I feel like I'm going to be sick.

"Here," Silas says, passing me a bottle of water.

Staring at him and then the water, I ignore the smirk in his voice when he tells me, "It is a fresh bottle. Still sealed."

Blood rushes through my head and I can hardly think as Silas stoops so he can look into my face. "Wren." He waves a hand in front of my face.

"What?"

He smiles. "Drink."

I watch him twist the cap to open the water and then slowly I drink as he holds it to my mouth. The cold liquid goes down and helps to settle my thoughts. For a moment there, I felt like I was watching someone else in the room. That I wasn't really here.

Wishful thinking!

"Get away from her," the Reverend snaps at Silas. To Ezequiel he says, "I don't know why I can't go with her. She's my daughter."

"Stop whining like a baby." He shakes his head. "You are too stressed, my friend. First DeLacroix moves into town, and then the DEA raids the church. Your mind is on bigger problems and that will cause you to screw up. This cannot go wrong, so shut your mouth."

The Reverend snaps his mouth closed, and I want to laugh. This whole situation I find myself in is frightening, but witnessing the Reverend being told to shut up makes me want to laugh. No one dares to talk to him in that way, but he's taking it from the man they call Ezequiel.

"You know what to do," Ezequiel says to Silas. "Keep under the speed limit. Do nothing wrong. Wren is your daughter for the day." He laughs while my eyes go to the Reverend. He clenches his fists and says nothing, getting angrier by the second.

"I'll go alone," Silas says. "I don't need the girl with me."

"It is nonnegotiable. She goes. You are less likely to be stopped if she goes with you. You know this."

"She was there when they had the DEA crawling all over the church, which her father owns. You don't think they'll be suspicious?"

"All the more reason to take her with you." He slams a fist onto the table. "I am done arguing. Jonas goes. She goes. Now!"

Silas curses under his breath and swipes up the book bag before turning to me. "Let's go."

I don't need telling twice and rush from the room as Silas walks beside me. "I don't like this, Wren. Something is off."

"We could ask Marcel and Rafael for help," I whisper.

"No! It's best they stay in the dark. The Reverend

has a couple of men watching their house. He knows they're watching him." Silas opens the car door and places a hand on my arm, stopping me from climbing inside. "The Reverend knows about you and Rafael."

"I feel sick." The words escape before I can stop them. I don't think I'm actually going to puke but I don't feel too good as we get into the car and Silas drives us away from town. "I don't get how he knows. No one was around when we were together." My panic must show on my face.

Silas shakes his head. "There are cameras all over the place, Wren. Twenty-four seven. That's what you nearly walked in on that day in the basement of the church."

"Oh." I really don't know what to say to that bit of information while I try and remember exactly what Rafael and I have done outside. I don't think it's much —we may have been caught. "Oh no, they caught us at the cabin."

"Unfortunately, yes. They were planning on torching it until one of the guys watching the footage called the Reverend to warn him."

All color drains out of me at the thought of the house still standing. "The photographs," I whisper.

"Hey, what's wrong? What photographs?"

Sitting back in the seat, I concentrate on breathing in and out slowly, waiting for my panic to go so I can think clearly. Silas turns the air conditioning up, which helps, except I'm left with my skin feeling clammy.

"Wren?"

Slowly turning, I look at my uncle, and use my mouth but not my voice to question, "Is the car bugged?"

He shakes his head. "No. If it was, I'd have gotten a notification on my phone. There is GPS tracking, so they'll know if we deviate."

Nodding, I whisper, "Wild had photographs of me." Tears blind my eyes but don't fall. "They were all over his bedroom."

Inhaling deeply, I curl up in the seat and watch Silas.

His body is tense, and anger radiates from him. A few moments later, he curses and bangs his fist on the steering wheel. "Okay. Here's what we're going to do. We'll get this job done, then we'll swing by Wild's house and make sure they disappear." He grabs my hand. "I promise, Wren. We'll remove the images and burn the things. I won't let anyone else see them."

I tangle my fingers with his. "When this is all over,

can we spend some time together? You're the only family I have other than the Reverend, and I don't think he likes me being his family."

"You're wrong. I don't think he knows how to be a father, but he stands up for you with the men." He pauses. "The Reverend had promised Wild that on your eighteenth birthday he could marry you. Wild didn't want to wait. I had no idea the man was more than infatuated with you. Makes me wonder if that's why the Reverend killed him. But he didn't like the idea of me coming with you today. He doesn't like any man being close to you. The only reason he hasn't put a stop to you and Rafael is because of who Marcel is. Doesn't appear to be making any difference, though. The DEA still raided the church."

My head hurts with everything turning around inside of there, But I wouldn't go back to a time when I didn't know Rafael existed and I was clueless. I've changed because of him. My eyes are wide open.

Or maybe not. I straighten in the seat, and ask, "Are there really drugs in my bag?"

"Wondered if you'd ever ask." He gives me a side-long glance. "The less you know, the better."

"You've just answered my question," I announce. "We're delivering drugs for them. Where?"

Silas sighs. "The river."

"We're meeting buyers at the river." I shudder.

"It's abandoned. Secluded. The best place." The car starts bouncing over potholes in the old side road. "Stay close to me, and don't forget to call me Jonas."

"I'm nervous," I whisper. "Scared to death."

"You're safe, Wren." He frowns. "Having the Reverend as your father makes you safe around anyone in town."

"They're not from town, right?"

"No, they're not."

39

RAFAEL

Pressed up against the side of the Reverend's house, we pause to catch our breath and listen for movement. The house is in darkness and creaks with the wind. The agents watching in town say the Reverend is still in the back room there, but we have our doubts. If Wren slipped out with Silas, who's to say the Reverend didn't? He could have easily gotten to the church and then used the tunnel to get home.

The old house creaks as Dad indicates for me to follow him in through the kitchen door, which is unlocked. Staying low, we move over the linoleum floor. I stumble slightly and knock into a chair tucked under a wooden kitchen table. Dad heads to the basement while I keep watch. While I wait, I move slightly and look around the living room but find nothing homely. No photographs. Everything is very basic and plain—white walls, dark sofa, no television. A dark side table stands alone with three religious books stacked neatly to the left.

"Rafael," Dad whispers from behind me. "We're in."

With one last glance around the room, I slip into the basement. A shiver runs down my spine once the door closes behind us, and the cold of the room hits me. I know its nighttime and it gets cooler, but this feels wrong.

Dad passes me a small flashlight as we slowly make our way down the steps. Seconds later, he shines the light up into the corner of the room. "The frigid air is coming from there," he says. "If there are cameras around the town, what do you want to bet there are some down here?"

"This is all ending. They're going to try and move the drugs after the DEA's visit. I don't care about cameras anymore. I just want to find Wren, the drugs, and then get the hell out of this town."

"I hear you." Dad pauses at the door Wren had described. It's slightly ajar and Dad indicates for silence.

I nod and follow him into the tunnel. Immediately

we're hit with the smell of damp earth. I shine the flashlight around the narrow tunnel and make a note of the wood supporting the walls and roof. The walls may have a wooden support, but they're muddy. Water slowly drips from the tunnel roof, making large puddles on the ground. As I descend deeper into the darkness, I notice cobwebs attached to the support beams; these webs are laden with giant spiders, eager to consume.

I momentarily freeze when I feel something move over my foot. Quickly shining the beam downward, I catch sight of a rat scurrying away.

This place is hell and I feel like I can't breathe the further we move. Rolling my ankle slightly, I grab onto a rough-hewn support beam and curse when a sliver of wood wedges itself into the palm of my hand. Dad turns and takes a look. It isn't as bad as it feels. I shudder wondering what the hell germs are going to be spreading in my blood from this dirty as fuck place. No way am I using my mouth and teeth to try and get it out without cleaning up first. Dad grins and his white teeth flash in the dark before he indicates to keep moving.

Seconds later, we come to a crossroads in the tunnels—one forward, one to the left, and one to the right. The one in front of us must lead to the church, if I'm not mistaken. Not sure where the other two lead. I still sense we're alone and so does Dad as he shines his flashlight up ahead. I nod in agreement and continue to follow behind him. I don't particularly like being underground in case we get trapped down here, but I'm somewhat relieved that we're both armed. Dad hates me having a gun. However, he's aware I know what I'm doing. Won't be of much good if the roof collapses, though.

Stop thinking in that direction!

This tunnel is the same as what we've already moved through, except it appears to be where the majority of the rodent family are living. Ignoring the critters scurrying out of our way is the only way I can move forward. I hate the damn things. This tunnel isn't as long as the one from the house to the cross-roads and we seem to reach the end in no time. Dad shines the beam of the flashlight around the plain wooden door. Nothing unusual about it. We listen at the door but can't hear anything. Not one sound.

Closing his eyes for a few seconds, Dad opens them again and stares at me. They're filled with worry, but there is no way we're heading back without checking out what is behind that door. I shake my head and point to the lock. Dad works his magic and the door slowly opens.

Something wooden is blocking our exit or entrance, depending on which way you look at it. A bookcase? Dad moves in close and whispers directly into my ear. "Be prepared. We don't know who or what is behind that."

I take out my gun in response. He does the same.

We check along the edge for a locking mechanism and, not seeing one, I help Dad and push the object out of the way. It moves easily, as though it's free-standing. I'm also correct—a bookcase full of multiple copies of religious books.

We're also lucky because there is no one around. It's deadly quiet as I glance at Dad. He frowns and looks up the stairwell. I follow his gaze and confirm that we are in the basement of the church as I make out a statue of Jesus Christ in the darkness.

We came out at the bottom. There's a single door to one side and a long hallway on the other, which must be the one Wren said she had been heading to when she first saw Silas.

Which means, "Computers," I mumble. "They were taken into that room."

Dad keeps his weapon in hand while I slip mine

into the back of my jeans. The gray door opens with a slight tug and then we're inside a large room. Again, it's strange to find no one. Why isn't anyone here? It makes no sense.

The light has been left on in the room, which is filled with tables covered with computers. Some are still in the casings while others look to be in the process of being dismantled or put back together. I'm not sure which.

"Holy fuck!" Dad curses, startling me into motion toward him. He never curses. Well, hardly ever.

My eyes widen when I notice what he's holding. "Is that what I think it is?"

Without a word, he drops it to the table beside the computer and, using a screwdriver, makes a small hole in the bag. Licking his finger, he gets a smidgen of powder to stick to the fingertip, and then he tastes it. "Heroin." Wasting no time, he grabs his cellphone and snaps pictures of the room and what we've found. "It's a kilo." He moves on to more computers and grins as he looks over his shoulder at me. "They've removed the power source from the box inside the computer and replaced it with a kilo of Heroin. Clever." He checks all the open computers. "Just these eight computers alone, we're talking a market value of around three hundred sixty thousand dollars." He quickly counts the computers in the room. "If there's a kilo in each computer, then we're talking around one-and-a-half million."

He quickly sends the images to Ken and tells him that we need to talk. However, the message won't go through while underground. He curses. "It will send automatically when we're outside."

I'm going to be asking him where the hell Wren is. There are agents watching her, so she better be safe. "We need to leave." I suddenly urge. "This feels wrong. Don't you feel it?"

"This whole situation feels wrong, but you're right. We'll leave everything as we've found it." He shoves the drugs back inside the power source box and, making sure there is no residue on the table, we leave the room and quickly get back inside the tunnel.

Closing everything up, the darkness surrounds us once again until Dad has the sense to turn his flash-light back on.

"I want to check out one of the other tunnels while we're down here. Might not get the chance again." I tug him to the right as we reach the cross-roads. "If it's long, we can turn back."

For a second, Dad hesitates before he agrees,

insisting that he leads the way. I've yet to point out that trouble could come at us from behind, not just in front. Each tunnel is the same as the next, and it's obvious that whoever built them had spent time making sure the structures were secure and wouldn't cave in. The wood doesn't look new, but I don't think it can be all that old either. Maybe a few years. They've certainly got a good operation running, and it makes sense why the DEA has never been able to get anything on the Reverend. Nothing is moved from his home or the church. It's all done underground.

Lost in thought, I bump into Dad, who has stopped in front of me. I shine my flashlight around him and notice we're in a larger area. At a guess, it's about twenty by twenty feet. There is a built-up section in the corner with a door. The tunnel continues on past the room. Dad glances at me before he steps forward and gently tries the door handle. Something else I realize is that this part seems cooler than the actual tunnels. The air outside isn't cool, so it can't be from an air vent. Air conditioning—down here?

The door opens and a sound like a girl whimpering hits my ears. Dad must hear it too because he burst through the doorway and into the darkness behind it. I'm so in tune with my dad, that I follow on his heels instinctually, but I pause long enough to shine the flashlight into the room. What looks like a jail cell is in front of me. Inside are two girls huddled together in the far corner. It's hard to tell their age from how they are trying to hide themselves.

"We're not here to hurt you," Dad says. "¿Entiendes?"

"Yes, we understand," the girl with dark hair whispers. "You are not like the other men."

"No, we are not. We need to get you out of here."

Her eyes move to me, so I crouch down, and ask, "What are your names?"

"I'm Jessica and my friend is Ella. We just want to go home."

"I'm Rafael and this is my father, Marcel. We'll help you."

"How long have you been here?" Dad asks, trying to pick the lock of the cell, but he's not having any luck.

"I think two days, but I'm not sure. We don't have any light."

"Where did they take you from?" Dad curses under his breath, becoming frustrated with the lock.

"Omaha, Nebraska," the girl whispers and flinches when the soft sound of voices can be heard. "You need to go. They'll find you and then you can't help us."

"No," Ella whimpers.

"Shush. It's okay." Jessica meets Dad's gaze.

"I promise you we will be back for you both and, when we are, you will be leaving with us." Dad quickly snaps a photograph of the girls and adds it to the message waiting to send to Ken.

Heavy footfalls sound even closer when he closes the door. We take a second to determine where they're coming from - further up the tunnel, so we turn back toward the main tunnel. It's too dangerous to turn on the flashlights, so we use our hands for guidance and find our way back to the Reverend's house in silence.

I don't know what Dad is thinking, but my head is spinning. *Girls!* Does the Reverend even know about them? *Of course, he does.* He uses the tunnels, that I'm sure of, which means he knows about the room back there. And are there other rooms like that one in those catacombs?

What the fuck is going on?

40

WREN

THE SMALL DOCK IS QUIET EXCEPT FOR THE SLIGHT whoosh sound coming from the water. Silas would have preferred me staying in the car, but I felt safer sticking close to him. "I don't like this," I whisper into the dark night.

Silas squeezes my hand and let's go as a small fishing boat slowly slides alongside the jetty. I can't see who is manning the boat until he turns around and I'm surprised. The man has to be in his eighties with a medium build and height. He's wearing a black knitted hat on his head. He looks warily between Silas and me before narrowing his eyes. Silas speaks Spanish to him while my attention is caught on the green tarp at the bottom end of his small boat. It looks bulky.

Gasping, I quickly take a step back when I see a foot poking out. I'm caught by Silas who drags me in close to his body. He whispers, "Don't move," hardly moving his mouth.

"The girl." The old man nods in my direction. "Who is she?"

"Don't worry about her. Do you have payment?" Silas asks, his other hand is beneath his jacket where I know he has a weapon.

"The girl is Ezequiel's payment. That's all he wanted. The girl." The old man continues to stare. "Tell me who your girl is, or I leave now."

"She is a friend of Ezequiel. You wouldn't want word to get back to him that you scared her, huh?" Silas releases me with a warning glint in his gaze. "Go and get the book bag." He nods toward the car behind us. I really want to get in the car and drive away.

I don't.

Silas stays and I see them whispering back and forth. As I approach with the bag, he asks him, "Who is the girl? Someone special?"

The man laughs. "Ask Ezequiel." He shakes his head. "Pass me the bag."

Silas moves to take it from me, but the old man says, "No! The girl must pass it to me."

With barely controlled anger, Silas backs away.

"I don't know what I'm doing."

"Lean over and pass me the bag. I haven't got all night. The coast guard will be back soon." That certainly gets me moving, and the man snatches the heavy bag from my hands. If it hadn't been for Silas's quick reflexes, I'd have fallen headfirst on top of the girl.

"You have the packages, now I want Ezequiel's." Silas glances around and steps into the boat.

The tarp is moved and beneath is a dark-haired girl, maybe a year or two younger than me. Silas checks her pulse before lifting her to the small jetty and pulling himself up. "If you've double-crossed us, old man, the Reverend and Ezequiel know where you live."

The man gives a toothy grin. "It's what they ask of me. No problem."

He pulls a large container out of the water and opens it up before shoving the heroin inside and lowering it back beneath the dark waves. Hearing a clunk, I frown, wondering what goes on beneath the boat.

Hissing, Silas says, "Go to the car and open the back door, Wren. We need to go."

He collects the girl into his arms and places her gently on the backseat. I follow her inside and, after a quick hesitation on Silas's part, I'm shut in here with her as we speed away. I couldn't tell you where this place is because I haven't seen it before. Maybe in daylight I could have gotten an idea from what I've seen of Padre Island. In the dark, though, I have no idea.

"You didn't know about the girl, did you?"

"No," he growls. "There is a bottle of water in the bag on the floor. Use that to dab at her lips."

Following his instructions, I uncap the water and use the T-shirt in the bag to clean her face. I find a fresh part and dab it over her lips. She doesn't react and stays sleeping. "What's going on, Silas?"

"I don't know. I was expecting cash, not a girl." He glances into the back. "Okay, here's what we're going to do. I'll drive us to Wild's place and call Marcel. He can meet us there and take you and the girl away from here. Call in the cavalry. This is fucked."

"You have to come too, right?"

He stays silent.

"Silas?"

"Don't, Wren."

"You're my family, Uncle Silas. You have to come. They'll hurt you if you go back without us."

"Wren, listen to me. I have to finish what I've started, but I can't hand over a girl to them. You will be safe, for now at least, but she isn't. Ezequiel is unstable and I don't know what he'll do or how he would punish us if I don't go back with her. You hear me. I can take care of myself if I don't have to worry about you."

"I hate this. Why now? How could I have not known all of this? I'd been aware of everything going on in the town, or, at least, I thought I had."

"They didn't want you to know. That's why. It isn't your fault. Now, we have to get those photographs and burn them, and then get you away from here."

"Can I call Marcel now?"

"No. The car isn't bugged but I'm sure my phone is. I'll call once we have the photographs and leave you in the forest for Marcel and Rafael to find. It won't take long."

"I feel sick."

"This will be over soon. I promise."

His phone rings, and he curses.

"Ezequiel is calling." He slams a fist into the steering column. "I have to answer this."

He does and speaks rapidly in Spanish while casting a glance into the back. Our eyes meet and I know it isn't good. "Sí." He ends the call.

"We have to go and meet him. He says if I don't go back with you or the girl, that they have men watching Marcel's house."

"No," I cry.

"I don't know why he thinks 'Jonas' would care, but that's what he said."

"The photographs?"

"We know where they are. We'll get them. Just not right now."

"Can't we call Marcel and warn him, or go to their house? All of us can leave."

He shakes his head. "They are watching the tracker on the car, which prompted the call." He sighs. "I took the right fork in the road, which leads to Wild's place. The left is the one I should have taken. They knew. They called."

Silas looks worried as he continues to drive, cutting through a side road to get back onto the road he should have taken originally. The girl still hasn't moved, not even a snore. If she wasn't breathing, I'd think she was dead.

I stay silent in the car unable to think of anything reasonable to say. I know Silas is thinking too and I'm not sure I'd like his thoughts with how tense his body language is.

The trees and run-down houses pass in a blur as the car eats up the miles to wherever we are supposed to go. It isn't town. Making a sharp left, the tires spin on gravel. Glancing around as the car slows down, I recognize the old logging road. I've been here before. A few years ago, I think.

"Silas, stop!" He slams on the brakes and turns to look at me as I move between the front seats. "We can't go up there. This is the only road in and out. We'll be trapped."

"I've been here before. I know where we are. I'm not sure exactly what is going on, but we don't have a choice except to show up."

"I know you think I'll be safe because of the Reverend, but what about you? Plus, do you really trust Ezequiel?"

"I don't trust any of them, Wren. You shouldn't either." He glares and then starts the car up the dark road.

My belly is in knots the closer we get to the site. I don't remember much being there before, and as we come into view of the top of the hill, all I see is a wooden shack, and cars. I don't recognize any of them.

"I'm sorry you're involved in this, Wren. I should have gotten you out before I even got in with the Reverend." Silas reaches back and takes my hand. "Your mother would be so proud of you and, no matter what happens, I need you to believe that. She loved you. She didn't leave you, she thought you were dead. I don't know how he did it, but she would never have left you there with him. *Never.* You have to believe that, even if you don't believe anything else."

"You're scaring me more than those men right now."

"Listen to me. If anything happens to me, go to Marcel's house. In the corner, by the front window in the living room, pull the floorboard free. Inside is a lockbox. It holds pictures of me and your mom as kids growing up. Me in my uniform. Your mom as a young girl. There are letters that she wrote to me. Including the last letter I ever received from her. This is who your mother really was. Don't believe anything the reverend tells you." He parks and gets out of the car.

I'm dazed listening to him. Tears well in my eyes knowing that the situation we are in won't be ending well. Silas knows that too, otherwise, why would he tell me where to go to learn about my mother?

Silas opens the door as I wipe the tears from my face. A man in an expensive looking suit steps out of the shack, and Silas looks like he's going to be sick as his eyes meet mine. "When I tell you to, run. Don't look back. You run and hide. I love you, kid," he says, and turns to face the man who looks vaguely familiar.

41

RAFAEL

LOOKING FOR A PAIR OF STRONG CUTTERS IN THE toolbox is impossible. Dad's not the most organized person when it comes to tools. Giving up, I grab the metal box and upend it. The contents fall over the wooden floor, clattering on top of each other. However, I smile when I spot the cutters. I knock my hand with the wooden sliver in it and curse. Lifting my palm to my mouth, I nibble and suck on the damn thing. It's too annoying to ignore anymore. Luckily, it works and I don't have to go looking for a sharp needle to pierce my skin with.

That done, my mind returns to the girls in the tunnel. It spins at what we may have stumbled upon, and if that is the case, then the Reverend and his friends are going to be even more desperate to keep it to themselves. Dad hadn't even thought about human trafficking. Not once had it been mentioned from anyone. According to the DEA and John, Dad's friend with the FBI, the only whispers have been about drugs.

"Got the blankets," Dad announces, dragging my attention to him. "What's wrong?"

"Why doesn't anyone know about the girls? The two we've found can't be the only ones. Someone would have talked or suspected. You have contacts with the FBI and DEA and yet neither of them have mentioned human trafficking. Why? It doesn't make any sense."

Dad's thoughtful as he moves into the kitchen. I follow and place the cutters onto the table beside the blankets. Grabbing two bottles of water, I place them down while I empty the book bag I've been using for school. "I hate to ask this, but are you sure you can trust them?"

"Rafael." He sighs. "I've known them for years. Since before the raid in Texas. I've never known them to lie or mislead. There is the possibility that they did not know."

Mulling that over in my head, I realize I'm not as

convinced as Dad. They've been watching the Reverend for a while. They must have been for Silas to have gotten involved. Someone knew something, that I'm convinced of.

"Ken messaged back saying he's getting a warrant signed as we speak, and a team together. He wants us to stand down until they get here."

"No fucking way! We promised those girls we'd be back. I'm not leaving them." I shove everything into the book bag before swinging it onto my back. "We are going now. They can catch up."

Hesitating for a few seconds, Dad finally agrees and sends Ken another message telling him where we're heading. At least they'll know where to rescue us from if we get caught.

"I'm ready." He takes his weapon from the holster and keeps it pointed to the ground as we head out of the house and across the open area between our place and the Reverend's.

We're just as careful as the last time because of the tunnels, the Reverend could have made his way home without our knowledge. The last thing we need is to come across him before we have the girls, the drugs, and, most importantly, Wren.

This time, upon entering the tunnel, a distinct

odor can be detected. It overrides the smell of damp earth. My nose twitches, and I whisper, "Vinegar?"

Dad frowns. "Heroin has a distinctively strong vinegar smell." He pauses. "I don't know why we would be smelling it down here."

"Could someone be smoking it up ahead?" I whisper.

"Only one way to find out. Keep the flashlight off." Dad slips fully into the tunnel and uses the wall for guidance.

I follow behind and find the smell is stronger the further in we move. We turn left at the crossroads and then head quickly to the room. Not seeing or hearing any sign of anyone, Dad finds his way to the door, and curses. "It's not locked," he hisses, flinging the door open, his weapon up, ready for trouble. "Fuck, they've taken them."

Staring at the empty cell, it takes a moment for me to realize that they really have been moved. "There's cameras everywhere. We weren't bothered before because it's all ending tonight, but what if they knew we'd found them?"

"I don't know."

"That means they've probably moved the drugs too. We have to check."

"No!" Dad grabs my arm as I turn to leave. "We'll go back to the house and wait for Ken and the team to get here. This is too big for us. The girls could be anywhere."

What he says is true, but it's really bothering me that they were so quick to respond. Voices in the distance draw my attention. At least two people are moving in from the other end of the tunnel. Dad grabs my arm and gives me a slight push to indicate for me to move back the way we came. Rounding the corner, we pause and watch the low beam of a flashlight flicker in the distance. It hovers around the room where we'd just been. We wait and see what happens, but after a minute or two the beam moves back the way it came from.

Placing my mouth beside Dad's ear, I whisper, "Let's go along the other tunnel." Dad shakes his head, so I add, "We'll check it out and then go and wait for Ken. I won't do anything foolish."

He hesitates, then finally nods. I think he knew I'd go anyway.

This tunnel feels damper than the others and there is a lot more water on the ground. As we slowly move further along, the ground starts to slope downward and snakes left, and then right, before heading back again. "Water," I whisper. I don't even question myself because the soft lapping against the bank is distinctive. Either that or it's a small fishing boat sloshing through the water.

Moonlight filters through what looks to be the entrance of this particular tunnel, and that's when we notice water gently swishing in the entrance. The larger body of water is where the tunnel leads as we stay to the side and look out.

"Laguna Madre," Dad says. "Padre Island is across from us."

Again, I hear the swish of a boat traveling through the water. "It sounds bigger than a fishing boat," I think aloud as my eyes adjust to the night sky. "There!" I point south.

"A trawler," Dad comments, removing his phone. "I've told Ken to get the coast guard out here."

"Don't they have boats in these waters, being so close to Mexico?"

"Yes. The coast guard can only cover so much area." He pauses. "We need to head back."

Unfortunately, I agree as I follow Dad back to the Reverend's basement. The house is still dark without a sound other than the creaks that you'd expect from an old house. When we reach the kitchen, my feet refuse to carry on moving. I can't go. I need to find Wren. I've tried to put her from my mind while we helped the girls, but I'm unable to do that now. "I'm going up to Wren's room. I need to check."

"I'll wait here."

Shaking my head, I say, "You go back and wait for Ken. If the Reverend returns, I'll go out onto the roof."

Dad hesitates before he follows my lead and disappears into the night.

Moving upstairs, I head straight into Wren's bedroom and close the door softly behind me. I smile when I spot my shirt tucked into the top of her bed, no Wren, though. Footsteps downstairs cause me to freeze, and when I hear them on the stairs, I quickly get through the window. My heart is in my throat while I try to catch my breath. Wren's butterfly, Tiger Lily, appears before me. His wings fluttering as he hovers and watches me. "Can you find Wren?" I quietly ask. "She needs us."

The banging of a door close by—Wren's bedroom door—resonates in the window frame, and I quickly jump off the trellis on the side of the house. My feet touch the ground and I calmly walk toward my house. I don't care if he sees me anymore. He's going to be behind bars soon.

"Rafael," the Reverend yells. "I know you're there, Rafael. You'll never have my daughter." He laughs in a hysterical way, as though he's on the way to becoming insane.

As much as I want to go back and pound the asshole until he tells me where Wren is, I don't. I disregard him and continue walking toward my father, who is observing and waiting from the back porch.

I sigh heavily. "Wren, where the fuck are you?"

42

WREN

MY KNEES TREMBLE AT THE LOOK ON THE MAN'S FACE coming toward us. Silas is shocked speechless and moves to block me from view. The man laughs. "As though you can protect her from us." He shakes his head. "I have no wish to harm Wren."

"Why, Ken? I trusted you. Marcel trusted you." Silas places a hand on my arm. "Why, dammit?"

I slip around him, wanting to get a better look at the man—to remember who he is—if I have a future.

The man from the church! Marcel's friend.

"My wife was sick. We didn't have the money to pay for treatment." He shrugs. "In the end, it didn't matter, she died anyway." I truly believe those words.

He coughs and continues, "You should have stayed overseas."

"I've had enough of this reunion," Ezequiel snaps at Silas. "Get the girl from the car and bring her to me."

Silas hesitates, throwing a frown in the other man's direction before he glances at Ken, who slightly shakes his head without looking at anyone before heading back toward the shack he came out of.

"Girl. Now!" Ezequiel snaps his fingers, and his men point guns at us.

There are four men around the shack, two on each side of Ezequiel, and another eight spread out around the perimeter from my quick count. Those men face outward. Waiting for trouble. There's no point in running. They'd catch me or kill me within seconds. And who knows if there are more hiding in the tree line.

My body feels chilled in just my shorts and a tank top. It must be really late for the air to be this cool.

A hand nudges mine and I turn to face Silas. "Do as they say, Wren," he whispers. "I have a bad feeling."

"Me too." I move with him to the side of the car and hold the door while he gets the girl out. I'm not sure if I'm helping at all but I'm trying to protect his back. He doesn't trust these men, and neither do I. The only thing I believe is that they have no intention of harming me. *Intention.* Things could change.

Moving with Silas as he carries the sleeping girl toward the shack, I ask Ezequiel, "Where is the Reverend?"

"Home." He pushes me forward and I stumble up the wooden steps.

Silas pauses and casts a quick glance in my direction. He stays silent and enters the shack. I follow, scared of what is inside. It can't be much considering the size of it.

I'm mistaken.

There is a large hole in the ground with wooden steps leading down into the dark. Silas stops and refuses to budge. "What the fuck is down there?"

"Don't be a baby, big man." Ezequiel laughs. "I will show you." He steps around us and goes down the steps first.

The girl makes a slight noise, but when I step forward to check, Silas moves down the steps before I can touch her. I do the only thing I can do and follow. The stairs creak under our weight and the smell is horrid—sweat, musty earth, and my nose twitches before I reach up and cover it and my mouth.

Vinegar?

Towards the bottom, I look around and see a dented lantern hanging off a rusty hook. It's attached to a wooden post that looks to be keeping the earth above us from caving in. My heart pounds heavily at the thought of being trapped beneath the ground. Are we in a mining shaft, I wonder? The ground is uneven, and I feel sick at what else might be down here with us. I've had enough experiences with the basement back home and that came with rodents scurrying around. The last thing I want is to experience that again.

The tunnel snakes around to the right and then we come to a room. The men hold flashlights at the room. It's made of rusty old tin. I move forward and cling to Silas's arm. I don't want to be in here. I want Rafael—to have his arms around my body, telling me everything is going to be okay.

Silas hesitates and moves forward into what turns out to be a small jail cell. I freeze, staying at the door. Suddenly tense, ready for a fight, Silas turns to exit— then I'm shoved inside with him, and the door slams shut behind us.

I blink a few times and then scream, "Let us out. You can't do this." I shake the door. It doesn't budge.

"My men will have fun with you." Ezequiel snickers. "They'll loosen you up before giving you back to the Reverend. Make sure he doesn't double-cross me again." To Silas, he says, "And you, DEA Agent Silas Mathis, can spend time in this cell with your niece. A family reunion, yes?" His face hardens into steel. "This mess is caused by the Reverend." He turns his angry eyes on the girl in Silas's arms. "And *her* father." He waves and his men leave. "You might have fooled the Reverend, Silas Mathis, but you have not fooled me." Ezequiel walks away and leaves us alone in the dark.

Silas places the girl on a small bed in the corner of the cell before he turns to me and takes my hand. He pulls me into his arms and wraps his other arm around my shoulders—holding me tightly. I feel him kiss the top of my head. "Sit on the bed with the girl. I think she's waking up. I want us together in here." He keeps hold of me until my legs touch the frame of the bed.

Crouching down, I'm surprised when a small light appears. "They forgot to take your phone?"

"Yes, but it does us no good down here, other than the light." He moves it slightly, so it doesn't blind the girl. She's slowly starting to wake up.

The moment the girl becomes fully awake, she gasps and backs away into the corner, her knees up in front of her.

"We're not going to hurt you." I reach out, but she curls further in on herself. "I'm in the cell with you. I'm Wren, and this is my uncle, Silas. We're together in this."

She watches us closely, her eyes nervously sliding between us. "How did I get here?" She frowns. "Where am I?"

"You're in Port Michael."

She shakes her head. "I do not know where that is."

"Where are you from?" I try a different route to find out how far she's travelled.

"Mexico." She licks her lips, and continues, "Mexico City. I was visiting my abuela at the Panteón Español Cemetery. They killed my bodyguards." She sniffles. "They killed them."

"What's your name?" Silas asks.

"Maria Rosa Suarez."

Silas moves closer, cursing. "Your father is known for being untouchable. He works for Interpol's NCB?"

Maria nods, but I'm confused. "What is that?"

"National Central Bureau. They go after anything illicit—drugs, money laundering, trafficking." Silas goes silent, and mumbles, "So, why would Ezequiel kidnap you?"

"I do not know. I don't know about my father's work. Nothing."

"They're trying to get to him. Make him *touchable*." His phone goes dead. "Fuck."

43

—————

RAFAEL

JEREMIAH SLIPS INTO THE KITCHEN AS SILENTLY AS A ghost. Neither Dad nor I heard him approach. The man is sweating and disheveled and whatever news he has for us has put a frown on his face. He drinks down a full bottle of water before he says, "We have no idea where Silas and Wren are."

"What?"

"Hear me out." He waits before continuing, "The GPS tracker in Silas's phone worked fine up to what we presume was a drop off/pick up point outside of town at a small jetty. Nothing there apart from that. The tracker was disabled at that point. The cell last pinged when he used it on his way back to town.

Nothing since. They've just vanished, but we'll find them."

"I need to have your confidence, because right now I'm scared something has happened to her." I run my fingers through my hair as fear wells inside of me.

"Silas won't let anything happen to her. You know that, right?" Dad says, squeezing my arm before moving to the table.

"Let me show you the tunnels. I was about to try and match them to an actual map, see if we can work out where the left tunnel comes out." Dad gets engrossed with Jeremiah, discussing distances and theories.

All I can think about is Wren being alone and scared. The Reverend could have her locked up again. She hates the dark because of the years he's abused her. That bastard has a lot to answer for—and those girls—that's just really fucked up. "Wait," I snap, leaning on the table, "Did the coast guard find the girls?"

Jeremiah frowns. "What girls?" He glances between the two of us. "What girls, Rafael?"

"There's a team on the way, right?" Dad asks.

"I think I'm missing some information," Jeremiah says carefully, going silent.

My pulse pounds in my ears as the realization of what he's saying slowly starts to sink into my brain. I move my gaze to Dad and see the same look of shock on his face.

Dad slowly says, "Are you telling me that you have no idea about the drugs in the computers, or the two girls we found? Is there a team on the way?"

Jeremiah sits forward and holds Dad's gaze before turning to look into mine. Then he curses, and slams his fist on the table, causing pens to bounce. "You messaged Ken?" He shakes his head and paces. "I put his distraction down to his wife's death, eight months ago. But this, now, explains how he paid for the private health care she received. He said he'd taken out a loan. I didn't check because I fucking trusted him."

"We don't know for certain that he's done anything wrong. He could be on his way here." Dad is giving the guy the benefit of the doubt but, from the look on his face, I'm not sure if he believes his own words.

Jeremiah reaches for his phone, pulls up his contacts and dials before holding it up to his ear. He lets it ring for a while and then slams it down. "That asshole never misses a call."

"I agree." Dad stands. "It explains how the girls disappeared so quickly." He shakes his head. "I messaged him photographs I took with my phone of the drugs and the girls. They would have had time to move them while we were back here getting supplies together to go get them out of the cell."

Jeremiah looks confused, and I take pity on him and tell him everything about the tunnels, from what we found to the sound of a boat slushing through the water. The more I speak, the angrier he becomes.

"Send me the pictures. I'll get the warrant and the team, and the coast guard." He stands. "Send them now. I'm going to call the boss." He disappears into the front room, and we hear mumbling.

"I can't believe Ken would do this."

"You didn't want to believe a friend could betray you, Dad. Maybe he had no choice in the beginning and ended up being indebted to them. You don't know the circumstances."

"Nothing he can say will explain how he can be involved with these people. I know this happens. People with connections are the ones who get the majority of drugs into the country. Turning a blind eye here and there. I never expected it from Ken."

"He wouldn't hurt Wren, would he?" I ask, needing

reassurance. It doesn't matter, though, because no matter what Dad replies, I'll still worry until I have her with me.

"I wish I knew."

"The boss is getting things moving. He called the coast guard while I was on the phone, they've launched a search in Laguna Madre. If they're still between here and Padre Island, they will be found." Jeremiah pauses. "The Reverend is a little fish in the pond, and I have a feeling we are going to be catching much bigger fish within the next few hours."

"I can't sit here waiting. We have to find Wren and Silas. Because if Ken is involved, then he knows who Silas is, and who he's working for. That isn't good." I pace. "What if he's got them in the underground cell?" I stop and face them. "It would make sense, right? They move out the girls so we can't find them, and so the cell is free. They shove Wren and Silas in there. Only we know about the tunnels, or at least that's what Ken thinks."

Shaking his head, Jeremiah says, "By now Ken will assume you've spoken to me, and in turn, I've reported him to the boss. I don't think they'd be stupid enough to put them where they can be easily found."

"If they just want them out of the way for a short time, then it's the perfect place to keep them," Dad adds.

"I'm going back." I grab my weapon from the side table, but find my arm clenched in Jeremiah's hand.

"What happens if that's what they expect? We get ambushed." He shakes his head. "We have to think and be smart. They know we are on their trail. Three things that are distracting us from the objective at the moment are the whereabouts of Wren, Silas, and Ken's betrayal. Each one is important, but not the objective. You found two girls who have been moved by boat. We need to know if they are the only ones, who took them, what is their final destination. We know they are selling drugs in kilos, but we don't know where their destination is either. We don't even know who the key players are. There is so much unknown right now, and the only one who I bet does know all this, is living next door to you."

My eyes widen in surprise. "I should have thought about him." I shake my head disgusted with myself. "He's home. Let's go!"

Jeremiah winces and shakes his head. "He isn't there."

"Great! Do you know where he is?"

"Not exactly," he admits.

"Oh, fucking great!" I storm around the kitchen and kick a chair over, snapping its leg in the process. "Why the fuck does no one know where the hell everyone is?"

"Calm down before you break something else." Dad moves the chair out of the way.

"He was home not too long ago because he shouted to me from Wren's bedroom window." I pause. "He's gone through the tunnels," I whisper aloud. "I'm not going to sit here while he knows where Wren is. You can either come with me or stay here, but I'm going." I glare.

Dad sighs and then laughs. "You're as pigheaded as me. Give us a few minutes to get a plan together and let the team know where we're going. Then we'll go and find Wren. And Silas."

44

WREN

It's freezing!

If it hadn't been for Silas, I'd have turned to an icicle in this cave. Perhaps an overactive imagination with that thought but he really is keeping me warm. Maria is wrapped in Silas's jacket, while my uncle has an arm around my shoulders for body heat. He's a stranger to me, but something about him and the way he's being protective is a comfort.

I'm scared, though. Silas knows the man who was at the shack when we arrived. I've seen him too. No way will he let us go now. Why would these men need me to make sure the Reverend doesn't betray them? He wouldn't do anything to protect me. Part of me wonders if he really has been thinking about double-crossing those men. They sure are not anyone I'd want to do business with. One thing I know without question is that Rafael will be looking for me, along with his father. At least I have them to hold on to.

I've never been a fighter—apart from once or twice—I've always given in to the demands of the Reverend. Only because I figured it was safer that way. Now, though, now I have to fight to get out of this hole. That's what it is too. A hole in the ground with stale air conditioning that I'm sure has been set to artic.

Shivering against Silas, he tightens his hold, rubbing up and down along my arm. Because of our position, I feel him tense, then I feel the thud of men moving toward us through the ground. "Whatever happens, Wren, stay strong, okay? I have every faith in Marcel and Rafael. They will find you. Do not give up," Silas says, determination in his voice as the door opens and light floods the room.

I don't recognize the men, which means they must have arrived with Ezequiel.

"¡Vamos!" the taller man shouts, pointing at me and then Maria. "¡Vamos!" he yells, getting annoyed while the other man tries to get the lock opened. The moment it clunks open and the door swings wide, they point their weapons at Silas.

"¡Te quedas!" The same man says to Silas.

Why does he want Silas to stay, and us to go with them?

I cast a glance at Silas, and realize he knew this would happen. Without taking his eyes from the men, he whispers, "They can't let me go because I know who the other man is. I can do a lot of damage." He pulls me into his arms and continues whispering into my ear. "Remember that the Reverend also has something that Ezequiel wants." He growls, "But you are safe, for now at least." He puts me away from him and waves his arm. "They won't hurt you because Ezequiel will kill them if they do." He glares over at the two men in warning—a warning which they understand.

My legs are unsteady as I stand. Partly because I'm cold but mostly because I'm scared. Maria trembles hard, so I take her arm into mine and help her to move out of the cell. The moment we are clear of the door, I turn and glance back at Silas. "I love you, Uncle Silas." Tears drip from my eyes while the taller guy grabs me and the other one grabs Maria. My gaze stays on my uncle until I can no longer see him.

The smelly men laugh as they half-drag and half-carry us out of the dark hole. I only understand Spanish if it's spoken clearly rather than mumbled. So, I can't quite understand what they're saying now, which is frustrating.

As they push us out of the cave, I realize we've been down there for hours. The early morning sun is slowly rising on the horizon as we are led into the clearing. There isn't as much activity today as there had been last night. Only three cars and a handful of men that I can see.

To my surprise, the Reverend steps out of a black SUV not looking his usual put together self. He looks as though he's slept in the clothes he's wearing, and his hair is greasy. I frown as he approaches, tilting my head to the side as I try to understand what is happening or what he is about to do.

I don't flinch when he reaches out and wraps a loose strand of my hair around his finger before letting it go. He looks sad. That can't be right, though. Is he sad they have me? Or for some other reason? He doesn't look scared, which is what I am—not just for me, but for Maria too.

"Can I ask you a question?" I swallow hard and wait for his acknowledgement.

He slowly nods.

"Why did you give us all a journal and the uniforms on the same day? Why do it at all if this whole town was about drugs and trafficking?"

"A distraction," he replies absentmindedly. "I knew exactly who Marcel and Rafael DeLacroix were. They'd come sniffing around town because of Joy and Roman. I knew they would eventually find something. Since I am a man of God, and the town is under my influence, I decided to use that as a distraction. It worked long enough for me to finish off everything I needed to do." He shakes his head before his eyes meet mine and he searches my gaze. "I'm sorry, Wren. You could have grown up with a mother, but instead I let her believe you'd died all those years ago. I tell myself I got you and she got your brother, but I wanted you both."

"How?" I barely whisper as fresh tears slip down my face and drip from my chin.

The Reverend moves closer and cups my face in his hands, wiping at my tears. I don't have any strength left in me to move away, but the need for the truth is holding me in place.

"Please tell me why she thought I was dead. What did you do to make her believe that?"

He sighs. "I knew what was about to happen—the

raid. So that night I gave you a general anesthetic, which lowered your respiratory rate and made you extremely pale. The moment one of my men led her from the room, the doctor gave you a concoction of drugs to bring you around. I honestly thought my plan had backfired at first because you didn't respond." He offers a wry smile. "As you can see, it worked in the end."

The slamming of a car door forces the Reverend to step away from me. Under his breath, he whispers, "You won't believe me, but I really am sorry, Wren."

A sob practically chokes me, sending me to my knees. "You killed her! You killed her and she never knew I was alive," I scream at his back.

He ignores me but I do see him flinch as my words hit, causing him to pause mid-step before he climbs into the SUV and drives away.

"Hmm," Ezequiel mutters, staring at the disappearing vehicle. "I do believe the Reverend meant his words." He turns to look at me and with a wave of his hand, his men have me on my feet. "You will not lower yourself like that again."

"What are you going to do to us?" I question, swiping at my face with hands that tremble.

"Nothing." He pauses. "If I get what I want." Ezequiel gives his men orders in rapid Spanish.

"Silas?" I shout as Ezequiel turns his back.

He slowly turns to face me again, his eyes narrowing into slits. "I am sure you already know the fate of your uncle."

The big man behind me grabs me up in his arms and carries me to a white SUV before I even have time to think about what Ezequiel said. *I already know.* Maria is pushed into the car and then the doors are swiftly locked. Both men, who had taken us from the cell, climb into the front of the car and then toss us a sandwich each and a bottle of water. I glance at them warily. Anything could be inside the water.

"Comer, beber." *Eat, drink.*

Maria rips into the sandwich and starts eating—starved. I'm more reluctant.

"It is good," she says. "Why are you not eating?"

Watching us from the rearview mirror, the driver starts the SUV. He has a permanent scowl on his face, and I don't know whether to risk eating or not. I'm hungry and if they plan on drugging us, they are more likely to put the drugs into the water instead of the food. I actually want to be right as my belly grumbles. Turning the chicken sandwich over in my hands,

I peel the clear packaging away, and take a small bite. Chicken and mayonnaise hit my taste buds and I become hungrier than I thought I was.

"The sandwich is good. I bought it from the store in town. Mrs. Garcia. ¡Sí!" the man who has only spoken Spanish says, gaining a sharp retort from the man beside him, which shuts him up.

Maria whispers, "It is good."

I really don't want to agree to anything, but she is right, it is very good. Instead of voicing that opinion, I turn my attention outside the moving vehicle. I watch the scenery go by, trying to remember my way back to the shack. I'll need to tell Marcel and Rafael when they find me. I know they'll find me. I have to hope.

Hearing Maria gulping, I realize she's drunk the whole bottle of water she was given. She appears refreshed and more awake. No sign of any drugs in her system. I don't know much about drugs, but I'm sure they'd work quickly.

I hesitate with my bottle of water while I twist the cap and continue watching Maria, who asks, "What is wrong?"

Shaking my head, I say, "Nothing."

The water feels really good as it slips down my

throat. Between gulps, I ask, "Where are you taking us?"

"No talking."

"Who are we going to tell?" I persist. "Are we heading into town?"

"Shut up. Long journey," the horrid man snaps.

Hearing the slight noise of an empty bottle tumble, I turn to see Maria slumped in her seat. Blood pounds in my ears as fear washes over me. She's been drugged! *No, she could just be tired.* I shake my head against the fatigue suddenly threatening to overcome me. I can't sleep—I have no idea what these men would do to us.

A wave of sickness crashes over me and I feel dizzy—lightheaded. My hand goes to my stomach and my eyes struggle to focus.

"What did you do?" I whisper, panicked.

"Ponte cómodo, mi hermosa niña." *Get comfortable, my beautiful girl.*

The other man hits his partner in the chest. "¡Imbécil!" *Asshole!*

Cotton balls fill my head as I try and settle back against the seat. It's difficult because my coordination feels off, my arms and legs heavy. Then my eyes close and I can't open them.

45

RAFAEL

My head is buzzing with the amount of coffee I've had since the night before. I'm no good at sitting and waiting. I understand the reasoning, but, even at the best of times, I have a hard time with it. When the girl I love is somewhere close, and could be in trouble, I just want to go and find her. Dad has managed to sit on me for a while, but no more.

Jumping to my feet, Dad and Jeremiah do the same. "I'm going to find her."

Sighing, Dad says, "You don't know what to expect down there, plus you'll be seen."

"I don't give a fuck if I'm seen. They know that we know. I'm not leaving her for another minute. You can either come with me or stay here, but I am going."

I storm into the other room, and locating the weapon Dad removed from me earlier, I check the clip to make sure it's still loaded.

"The team should have arrived by now," I comment as I move toward the back door. "How can we be sure they're not with Ken?"

"They're thirty minutes away, Rafael." Jeremiah checks his phone. "They're splitting into three teams. Here, the church, and town. We have to hold off until they get here. I don't want to screw this up."

"I hear you, but I'm going after Wren. I can't stay here anymore—not when she could need me. Don't ask me to." With that, I take off out of the back door and jump the fence separating our two properties. In the background, I hear Dad and Jeremiah curse before their heavy footsteps are pounding from behind. I don't know whether they're coming with me or trying to stop me. Either way, I don't stop. I don't even stop to think whether or not the Reverend has come back home via the tunnels. I do know he left the church in a fancy black SUV.

Banging into the kitchen, I continue down to the basement. It's just as foul smelling and dark as before. This time, the secret door is standing open, which does cause me to take a moment to catch my breath.

"Stupid," Dad mutters.

"So, this is the entry." Jeremiah moves closer and inspects the area around the doorway. "I don't see any traps."

I should have considered that.

He turns to face me. "We go in together, and you do not run off again. You should know better."

"Please, just help me find Wren." My words are barely a whisper as fear slides down my spine. "What if she's in the cell? We have to check that first, right?"

"If cameras are down here, they'll know we've seen it. In which case, it's probably the last place to put her."

"It's an obvious place to put her." I shake my head. "That's where I'm going first."

"I think he's right," Jeremiah says. "It's difficult to get to. If she screams, there is no one to hear. The same with Silas." He goes into the tunnel and I follow him - Dad takes up the rear.

The tunnels have an empty feel to them as we come up to the crossroads. Glancing at Dad over my shoulder, I meet his frown before he indicates for me to move forward but to take extra care.

My gut tells me there is something wrong. The further we move, the worse the dread. Something isn't right. I don't just mean because I have no clue where Wren is, but because I sense something is about to happen. Dad closes the small distance between us and moves into my side. "I don't like this."

"We'll check and be out of here in ten minutes," Jeremiah whispers back.

The feeling I had is now screaming at me to leave —get out of the tunnel. Up ahead is the room with the cell in—the door wide open. A sound like a small animal scurrying over the ground, followed by the word, "Fuck," in a familiar tone.

"Silas," I loudly hiss.

"Get the fuck out of here, Rafael," is his growled response.

Jeremiah pushes forward and curses. Silas is locked in the cell with no sign of Wren.

It takes me a minute to focus properly on Silas, and when I do, my heart sinks. "Where is she?"

"They took her with another girl. You need to find out exactly what the new head of NCB, Suarez, in Mexico City has. I think he has something that the man who goes by the name Ezequiel wants. The girl is Suarez's daughter, Maria Rosa. They're holding her hostage until he cooperates with them."

Silas continues while Jeremiah tries to pick the lock. "The man Suarez is rumored to be untouchable."

"I've heard that too." The locks click loudly before the door swings open.

Letting out a sigh of relief, Silas steps out. "Thought they'd kill me before they left." He frowns. "I wonder why they didn't?"

"Who the fuck knows. Perhaps you can ask them when we find them," Jeremiah says, turning his attention to the tunnel.

Silas shudders and moves forward. "Let's go, I fucking hate being underground." He adds, "Which way to the church?"

"Left."

"Why do they want Wren?" I ask. "The Reverend is her father. Are they betraying each other?"

"The Reverend isn't in charge." Silas stops and turns. "The main guy is Ezequiel and always has been." He carries on moving, and then we hear a click as we turn toward the church.

"Bomb," Dad shouts. "Run!"

Fuck!

The door into the church is in sight just as a loud rumble rocks through the tunnels. The ground shakes. Earth beneath my feet starts to separate, sinking them as though I'm caught in quicksand. Dad shouts, "Move it," while he grabs my arm, pulling me forward with a speed I didn't know he had—and then a huge explosion ripples through the ground and we're flying through the air. Both Jeremiah and Silas thud against the door in an instant, causing it to slam open. Dad and I land with a hard knock to the ground. My breath leaves my lungs as I struggle to breathe. My body aches and my ears ring. I see Dad's mouth moving but I've no idea what he's saying. I can't hear a word.

Dad and Silas grab my arms and pull me through into the church basement just as the tunnel behind me collapses, sending debris toward us. Moving to my knees, I cough while I try and assess myself. My body feels like I've been hit with a sledgehammer, but I guess the damage from the bomb could have been worse—a lot worse.

I cough as Dad helps me to my feet and looks me over. More dust floating in the air catches me and I hack trying to get it out of my lungs. My hearing luckily has come back at Silas cursing. "No way is anyone going to get into those tunnels now. All that fucking evidence is gone."

"There is the photograph I took of the girls," Dad says. "Has the coast guard picked up the boat yet?"

Jeremiah shakes his head. "Nothing yet. There is a team up at a logging company not far from here. They picked up suspicious comings and goings on the satellite feed when they backtracked." He sighs. "Looks like they've found where the tunnel came out further along from where we found Silas."

Feeling much better, I inhale and slowly exhale—nothing hurts now apart from a few cuts and bruises. The banister up to the ground floor of the church is hanging off. Whoever was in the church at the time, they certainly would have heard the explosion. Unless, of course, they have left, in which case they are long gone and the chance of finding Wren has diminished.

"I'm finding him." Running upstairs, I notice the silence, and then I see *him*.

He sits behind a large wooden desk, a gun in front of him, within reach if he needs it. His eyes remain glued to my face and he looks calm, even resigned. "Where is she?" I ask, controlling my temper.

The Reverend shakes his head. "You won't find her unless they want you to."

"Who the fuck is *they*?" I step forward.

Dad, Jeremiah, and Silas are in the doorway behind me—I see their reflection in the glass cabinet beside the window, over the Reverend's right shoulder.

The Reverend is aware they are there, but he chooses to ignore them. His focus is squarely on me. "I've worked with them for years. Since before your father and the DEA raided the Amarillo compound. *He* knew Wren from when she was a baby. I let *him* see my only weakness when I lied and let Joy believe Wren was dead." He drops his head. "I should have let her leave with her mother."

"Then she'd be dead too," I hiss. "Who is Ezequiel and what does he want with Wren and Maria?"

"He wants his drugs back. NCB took them and have them under lock and key. That's why he has Suarez's daughter. He will kill her if he doesn't get the drugs back. They're worth a lot more than the ones you found here. I'm talking hundreds of millions in US dollars."

He gives a nervous sigh and meets my gaze. "My daughter is worth more than that. She's worth his freedom. His wealth. Unless you find him soon, both girls will be out of the country and never seen again." He turns his back and continues, "He won't kill Wren.

He'll use her to keep me quiet. You see, I know everything. I know his contacts in the DEA and FBI, I know the names of the men in Mexico City, who will do anything for Ezequiel Gutiérrez, on both sides of the law. Maria Suarez is a different matter. He will kill her without remorse whether or not he gets his packages back. He's a psychopath." He turns around and for once I see sorrow on his face. I believe it's real and not for show.

"You chose your friends well," I hiss between my teeth. "But you are wrong about Wren. He will never make her disappear because I *will* find her. You know why? Because I love her. She belongs with me. Not you. Not him. Me!"

Swallowing hard, he holds my gaze while he's thoughtful. "I didn't lie when I said I don't know where they've taken the girls, but I do know he has a boat—not in his name—called *Susanna*. You find that, you'll find Wren."

"I'll make the calls," Jeremiah mutters from behind as I hear his footsteps move further away.

"You killed the only mother I remember. She was a good person and didn't deserve to die. My brother didn't deserve that either. He was a *child*!" I shout the word. "It was a hateful crime, and I'm going to make sure you pay for them both." I pause, fighting the emotion warring inside of me. I want to hit him so badly. "If anything happens to Wren, you'll wish you never heard of me."

"I pay everyday I'm alive, Rafael. No matter what you think of me, I did love Joy and my son. I only wanted him back once I knew where he was. No one was supposed to *die.*" He chokes out and drops his head into his hands on the desk before looking back up at me—his eyes swimming in tears. "The man was obsessed with Wren. He made me sick." He pauses. "When you find Wren, will you tell her I was never going to let Wild have her? I know I scared her, but I needed him to believe it for a short time. That was the last straw with Wild. I killed him so he couldn't take my daughter like he had my wife and son." He swallows. "I burned every image." He holds my gaze as he says this, "No one will ever see them."

I know exactly what he's talking about, and I believe he's telling me the truth.

Dad puts his hand on my arm, and says to the Reverend, "You know you have to go with the agents that have just arrived." He pauses. "Remove the clip from the gun."

The Reverend stares at the weapon as though he'd

forgotten it was there, then he lifts his eyes to me, and whispers, "If I'm not alive, then Ezequiel has no reason not to let Wren go. Tell Wren I love her."

He grabs the gun.

"*NO!*" I jump toward him, my heart racing.

Dad throws himself on top of me and we both go down to the floor with a thud.

The loud noise of a gun being discharged ricochets throughout the small office.

Everything stills.

Moving out from under Dad, I get to my feet, and my stomach rolls. As though in slow motion, I stare at the bloody mess of the Reverend—Lucas Jacobs—while agents dressed in black enter the room and move around him.

Unable to stay, I turn and force one foot in front of the other to get away from the stench of death. My heart pounds as my body fills with fear. Ignoring everyone rushing around, I race outside and collapse on the front steps of the church. The sun has risen fully, and the day is warm and humid. Now though, all I feel is chilled.

Someone sits next to me and I look at him sideways. *Silas.* I swallow behind my fear and say, "The Reverend said they had no reason to keep Wren if he's dead." Tears I'm unable to hide fill my eyes. "He thought they'd release her. I think they have no reason to keep her alive." I drop my face into my raised knees while I try and breathe through the dread now eating away at me.

"He gave us a way of finding her, Rafael. The other girls too." He wraps an arm around my shoulders and squeezes before letting me go. "I promise you I will not give up until I have her."

"We won't give up," I add.

"I have something," Jeremiah announces his presence with those words. "A yacht under the name *Susanna* is currently moored at Bal Harbor Marina in Houston. I have two men staying here until we find them. We need to keep a lid on the Reverend's death. We're leaving in five minutes." He disappears back inside.

Silas adds, "You heard the man." He stands and holds his hand out, pulling me to my feet. "We have surprise on our side, Rafael. We'll find her."

He leaves me to pull myself together.

I stare toward town and whisper, "I'm coming to get you, Wren."

46

WREN

My stomach rolls and I'm not sure whether it's from the drugs they gave me to knock me out, or because I'm on a boat. I've never been able to be on water without getting sick, so I'm going to believe that's the case. The thought of eating the bagels and eggs a man brought Maria and me thirty minutes ago makes me feel worse.

Maria cuddles into my arms, her body shaking with fear. I'm scared too and have no idea where they've brought us. Water is the only thing I am sure of. The cabin door is locked. I know this because I've already tried to open it before screaming for help until my voice went hoarse. My throat hurts now. I should have saved my breath, but I hadn't thought that far ahead. Once I'd started to scream, I hadn't been able to stop.

I no longer have tears to cry. However, my will to get free of these men is stronger than ever. I look down at Maria, unsure of what to do with her. I won't leave her, but she can hardly move. Combined with the drugs they gave us and her own fear, she has become almost paralyzed. The girl is only a few years younger than me, but she appears even younger than that.

Hearing footsteps approaching the door, Maria gasps and I freeze. The footsteps aren't as heavy as those of the man who keeps coming into the room. The key rattles in the lock, and then the door slowly opens and that horrid man, Ezequiel, enters. Gone is the expensive suit I last saw him in, now replaced by slacks, a polo shirt, and a windbreaker. He looks like he's ready to go sailing. He snaps his fingers—I will forever remember that sound—and heavy footsteps move toward us. Maria whimpers.

I keep my eyes on Ezequiel until the men enter into the room carrying two more girls. I blink in total surprise, my veins filling with anger. What right do these men have to kidnap young girls? What right does anyone have to do this?

"You're a bad person," I hiss. "You and the Reverend deserve each other."

Ezequiel laughs. "That is why we have worked well all these years. It is a pity our partnership is going to come to an end. You, my precious Wren, are the only one in this room with a *real* future. *His* silence will keep you alive. I know you think he hates you, but you—" He crouches in front of me and reaches for my hair. I try and move my head, but I have nowhere to move to. "You, my beautiful girl, are his only weakness." He gives an evil smirk. "The other girls will be sold—puff—never to be heard of again."

I frown in surprise. "I don't believe you. He doesn't care about me. He killed my mother and brother. He wouldn't blink if you killed me."

Shut up, Wren!

"You have a lot to learn. I will teach you. You are too pretty to have ended up with Peter Wild, or that *boy*." He stands. "How you are treated will be your choice."

"I will not stay here." I spit on his shoes.

He pauses and then my head slams into the wall behind me as his hand connects with my cheek. Tears spring to my eyes, but I refuse to let them fall. I will not let him see them. My head swims and my cheek feels as though it is on fire. I flinch when he reaches for me again. This time he strokes a finger along my cheek. He pulls it away, and my eyes focus on the blood on the tip of his finger.

"I made you bleed," he says, his voice laced with anger. "Do not make me do that again."

He turns to another man, and says sharply, "Toca a la chica y te mataré." *Touch the girl and I will kill you.*

To me, he tones his voice down. "We are at sea, so do not try and escape. You will drown." With that, he leaves, and his two men follow him out.

Feeling braver than I am, I try and move away from Maria, except she won't let me. Her grip tightens and digs into my skin. I reach up and wrap my hand around Maria's. "I need to check the other girls." My patience is not the best and her grip gets tighter. "You are hurting me, Maria. Let go!"

The girl whimpers and tries to get closer. "Do not be selfish," I snap, feeling guilty. The sharp words work, as she loosens her hold. The moment I feel as though I can move, I do so, albeit stiffly. I crawl on my hands and knees to where they dumped the two girls. Their chests move up and down softly. Probably drugged to sleep like they did Maria and me.

I reach for the dark-haired girl and shake her

gently. "Wake up. You have to wake up." I shake her again as she mumbles. "Please wake up. We need to get out of here." Her eyes snap open and her complexion drains of color. I quickly turn her onto her side as she gets sick, which I think is good, maybe it will get the drugs out of her system quicker. The smell makes my stomach roll in protest.

The girl looks to be okay on her own, so I move to the girl with dark skin and jet-black hair. I don't need to shake her awake because her eyes are focused on my face. "I'm Wren. We need to get out of here."

She pulls herself up. "Where are we?" Her eyes dart around the room and can't settle on any one thing as she pulls her knees up in front of her and, wraps her arms around them. "Oh God! This is what my mom told me would happen," she cries. "She told me never to meet up with anyone I met online."

"Please don't make a noise, otherwise they will come back." I brush the hair back from her forehead. "What's your name?"

"Jessica." She sniffles. "Is Ella okay?" She looks at the other girl, who rolls to her back.

"I'm okay. I think."

"You're both friends?" I ask.

Jessica nods. "Yes. Since kindergarten."

"Can you swim?" The girls nod, along with Maria. "You said we were at sea. I don't know where, or even if there is land nearby. If we can get out of this room and into the water, you all have to swim to land. I don't know what to do if we can't see land though."

Ella looks at me as she drags herself into a sitting position. "What about you?"

"I can't swim," I admit. "But they want me alive and well. I'll be okay for now. You three won't be if you stay here."

"The doors are locked," Maria says.

That is a problem and, as I think about it, I realize the boat isn't moving as though it's out at sea. There is a slight slushing noise, but with how still it appears, the boat has to be moored in a harbor or a small jetty. *He lied because he knows I can't swim.* Then I realize I don't hear the sound of an engine, which solidifies my answer—we are not at sea. Also, the girls have only just been brought into the room. I hadn't given thought to that.

I close my eyes and try to shove my seasickness to the back of my mind and focus on other senses. Sound. Seabirds crying out as they fly overhead. They wouldn't be so far out at sea. Children yelling as they play and splash in the ocean, albeit faintly. They wouldn't keep us on a boat with children having fun. The strongest sensation is the smell of oil. Is this because we are being held close to the engine room? I wish I knew more about boats.

"Listen," I whisper, looking between the three girls. "I don't think we're at sea. I think he said that to scare us into staying where we are." I swallow. "The moment we get the chance, we have to get out of here. We have to."

"I agree with Wren. I'm not staying here for them to do whatever they want with me," Ella says, sounding stronger than before. "Jessica, you'll come too."

"Yes."

We turn to Maria, and I softly say, "You stay with me, okay?"

The girl shakes her head. "My father will give them what they want, then I will go home. I will be safe."

"Don't be stupid." Jessica scoffs. "No matter what, they will not give you back. You've seen them. You will recognize them again. I've seen the movies. They will kill you."

I couldn't have said it better myself, except I think it's made Maria worse than before. The girl moves to the corner we'd been in and silently curls up into herself. I sigh and glance back at the other two girls. "We can't stay."

"I know." Tears come into Jessica's eyes. "I will listen to my mom from now on if I get the chance."

"Me too." Ella wraps her friend in her arms, and they cry.

I wiggle to the side of the door and rest with my back against it, listening for sound. I can hear the faint laughter of children, but nothing else. No footfalls as people move around the boat. I still as I hear a faint sound coming from the other side of the door, as though something metal is scraping against it. It's really soft and I'm not sure whether or not I'm imagining it. Then I see it, a shiny silver key on the floor beside me. Someone has slipped it underneath the door.

Is there someone on the boat who wants to help us?

I quickly retrieve the key and say, "Stand up," with a new urgency in my voice. "Stand up, now," I hiss. "We can't wait."

The girls look baffled, but do as I say, even Maria huddled in the corner. When I have all their eyes on me, I cover my mouth with a finger and show them the key. Eyes widen. Gasps of hope and surprise fill the room, which I quickly hush.

My heart feels like it's about to pound out of my chest, and the fact that I still want to throw up because I'm on water is not helping. I want to be off this boat for more than one reason.

"No matter what happens, we have to stay together and not make a sound. Take your shoes off." I kick mine off and pick them up. After seconds of hesitating the girls do the same. "Our getting off this boat depends on us being quiet. Do you understand? Maria, do you?"

"I'm scared, not stupid."

I smile at her reply, and I'm no longer worried about her letting us down, which had been at the back of my mind.

As quietly as I can, I slip the key into the lock and turn it before gently turning the handle. Fear is eating at me and I hope I'm not doing the wrong thing by trying to get us off this boat. For a brief second, before I pull the door open, I wonder if it's just a sick trap. That Ezequiel is standing there, laughing at our pitiful attempt to escape. I shake the thought from my head.

No sound can be heard other than the birds and

the children playing, so we slowly creep out of the room and along the small hallway until we reach a set of stairs. I don't know anything about big boats as I've only ever been on a small fishing boat. This one, however, is huge and I guess a yacht rather than a boat.

There is still no sound as we move slowly up the stairs to the next level and make our way to the front of the boat. I get a look at the city skyline, but I don't recognize it. It is largely built up and there is nothing to give me a clue as to where we are. Nevertheless, we need to be quick and get off the boat before we're discovered.

As we round the corner, I spot the man Silas had recognized. He's standing close to the exit with his back toward us. I quickly stop and turning, shove the girls back around the side to safety. "Stay here," I whisper.

I don't know what to do. His large form is blocking the platform to the wooden dock. There is no other way off this boat unless the girls jump overboard and swim. I peep around the corner and the man is gone. Doesn't mean he's not close by.

No longer knowing what to, I decide to go for it. I'll make sure they get down the platform first so that if anyone is captured it will be me. He wants me alive, or so he said.

Indicating for the girls to follow, we creep down the side of the boat and I peer around the exit to make sure the coast is clear. It is. "Stay together," I whisper, shoving them forward.

They run down the platform and, not hearing another sound, I follow them. The moment my feet hit the narrow wooden dock that stretches out into the water, incredible pain shoots up my legs—the sun has heated the ground. I quickly stop and slip my shoes on. At least I brought them with me. Ready to run, I turn back to the boat at the last minute and meet the eyes of the man in the suit—Special Agent Ken. Marcel and Rafael's friend. The man points in the opposite direction to which we are about to head, causing me to pause in my step.

He looks off in a different direction, and points again and mouths, "That way."

I don't know whether to trust him or not, but the choice is taken away when a fancy car pulls up at the other end.

"This way," I say to the girls, and we head the way Ken told us to go. I'm confused as to why he is helping and wonder whether he gave us the key.

Halfway down the dock, another pier snakes out with various sized boats lined up tied to the cleats. I used to be the one to tie the nylon rope to the cleat back in Port Michael when I was forced to go fishing with the Reverend.

What we must look like running along, I don't know, but no one stops us, or offers help, or anything. The rich people and their guests just stare. Taking the next right, I finally see land ahead.

Maria whimpers at how close we are, and we all pick up speed and run past the fancy shops at the entrance of the marina.

Stopping to catch our breath, Ella indicates to follow her into the shadow between two gift shops. "We're in Houston."

"How do you know?" I ask. "Are you from here?"

"Nebraska." She points. "Over there, it says, Hilton Houston NASA."

"We need to go to the police," Jessica says. "We need help."

I totally agree, but knowing that Ken is a DEA agent, doesn't fill me with confidence about asking the police for help.

"We have to get further away from here before they realize we are missing." I look around. "Let's walk this way. Maybe they will think we went to the hotel for help."

"Why don't we go inside a shop?" Jessica asks.

"I don't trust them not to call the wrong people," I admit, wishing I knew Marcel's or Rafael's phone numbers to call for help.

Moving out from the shade, we start heading away from the marina, but I can't relax, even being off that boat. I keep looking around us to make sure no one is following.

There are people around, some in hospital scrubs, which makes me think there is a hospital nearby. I soon discover there is when Maria goes down to the pavement.

I don't even know what happened. One moment she was walking with us and the next she dropped like dead weight to the ground. I hover over her, trying to shake her awake. Nothing. No response.

"I'm a nurse, let me see her." One of the people I spotted in the scrubs is now kneeling on the ground opposite me, checking Maria. "She is dehydrated." The woman lifts her head and looks us three over. "What happened to you?"

Ella starts crying, and Jessica says, "Please help us. We've been kidnapped and managed to get off the boat. We need help. Please." She grabs the woman's hands.

"My name is Angela." She pulls a cell phone from her pocket. "My brother is a cop. I'll call him. He'll know what to do—who to contact." She glances back to Maria, who is coming around slowly. "First, we need to get you to the hospital." She dials a number and says a few words, and then she's making another call to whom I presume is her brother. By the time she finishes, an ambulance with no sirens on pulls up beside us.

She smiles. "I asked them to keep the sirens off so that if others are looking for you the noise wouldn't attract attention." I look at her warily, but she smiles. "I promise you are in no danger from me or my brother. I promise."

"Papá," Maria whispers. "I want to talk to him."

"Do you know his number?" Angela asks.

"Sí."

"You call him while we go to the hospital. We are really close to where I work. Clear Lake Hospital." Angela gives Maria her phone, and the girl dials as she's lifted into the ambulance. "¡Papá! La chica me salvó. Por favor, ven a buscarme a Houston." *The girl saved me. Please come for me in Houston.* She pauses. "Sí.

Te quiero, papá." *Yes. I love you, Dad.* Maria passes the phone to Angela, who relays his daughter's condition and where they are taking us.

"My brother will be here soon," Angela says as we arrive a few moments later. "I want you all to stay together, okay? Would anyone else like to make a call?"

Ella and Jessica both nod and decide to call Jessica's mom as she always answers her phone apparently. Angela looks to me. "Don't you have anyone to call?"

I shake my head. "I don't have the number for them." I frown and try to remember. "Are you able to find the number for the DEA office in Corpus Christi? I think Jeremiah might have worked from that office. I'm not really sure and I only know his first name. Or maybe someone knows how I can call Marcel DeLacroix. He lives in Port Michael."

Angela reaches out and rests a hand on my shoulder. "My brother will find him. Please trust us. I can see by the look in your eyes you have been through a lot. I want to help you and your friends, okay? Before my brother gets here, let me examine you and take more details."

I glance around the emergency room before I'm

ushered into an exam area and asked to put on a green paper gown. Angela smiles.

"I will give you some privacy. I'll be on the other side of the curtain with Maria. The other two girls are on the other side of you."

Nodding in acceptance, I woodenly move to the only place to sit - the bed. I don't change, but I do climb onto it and lay my head down. I'm so tired and just want Rafael.

47

RAFAEL

"She's been found." Jeremiah ends his call and turns to look at me in the back of his agency issued SUV. "She's okay, Rafael. She's at Clear Lake Hospital, close to the marina where the yacht is moored."

I blink a few times while trying to take in what he is telling me. "She is really okay?"

"A few bumps, but yes. They looked her over and she's fine. She's asking for you." He turns more in his seat as Dad continues to drive.

Jeremiah had wanted to view the satellite footage of the area as we headed up to Houston, so he had Dad drive. Silas comes awake as Jeremiah talks. He had been worse than the three of us put together after spending most of the night underground.

Jeremiah casts him a glance and says, "Not only do they have Wren, but they have Maria Suarez, and the two girls you saw in the cell. Ella Greenwood and Jessica Dawson. They had been put together on the boat. According to a statement Wren gave to the police, they only got free because Ken James had helped them. He slipped Wren the key to the room and turned the other way when they left." He pauses. "They were about to head in the wrong direction, and he directed them away. I don't know what the hell he is up to, but he saved them."

"Have they arrested Ken?" Silas asks, contemplating something.

"The coast guard is currently trying to box the yacht in as it races toward international waters." He grins. "They'll get them. Security cameras from the marina show men in suits boarding the yacht as the girls ran in the opposite direction. We have no idea whether or not Ezequiel was one of those men."

"This is nearly over. The Reverend is dead, so is Wild. The coast guard will get the others," I say in relief.

"It's not over until everyone is behind bars. Don't tempt fate by saying otherwise." Silas's words are sharp before he relaxes back against the seat. His ease is not fooling me—he's anything but.

"They'll need someone to verify Ezequiel is one of the men on board," Jeremiah continues. "The drugs were found in the computers beneath the church. Interpol NCB has Ezequiel's shipment under tight lock and key in Mexico. No one is getting their hands on that. A lot of precautions have been taken to secure the packages. But we've put a huge hole in the network. My contact in Hidalgo on the Texas/Mexico border said there has been a lot of movement in and around the town in the past few days. McAllen especially. People have been getting worried." Jeremiah smiles. "I'm taking a vacation tomorrow."

"Ha! I'll believe that when I see it." Dad chuckles.

I try to follow Silas and relax now that I know Wren is safe, but I can't because I want to be with her, and the drive is taking too long. Dad catches my eye as he glances through the rearview mirror. He knows me well.

"She's living with us from now on, Dad," I say as I stare out of the window. "The moment I have her in my arms, I'm not letting her go."

"I know, son," he whispers, a smile in his voice. "That's how I felt about your mother. Wren's mom."

He pulls in front of the hospital entrance and Silas immediately exits. "I need to walk."

I frown and watch him walk toward the ocean as Dad grabs my attention by turning in his seat. "No matter what happens, Rafael, it doesn't change the fact that Sarah loved you too. Don't ever forget that."

I close my eyes willing the tears not to fall. The past twenty-four hours have been hell not knowing where Wren was. I haven't slept and I couldn't say what I've eaten. Dad shoved food into my hands, and I ate it. Swallowing hard, I climb out of the car and Dad follows.

The heat hits me in the face while I wait for Dad to finish talking with Jeremiah, who drives off seconds later. I'm impatient to find my girl and see for myself that she really is okay.

The moment we step inside, the smell hits my nose and my stomach rolls with nerves. I glance around nervously while waiting for Dad to get Wren's room number.

He has it and indicates with a nod of his head toward the elevator. "She's on the third floor."

The ride up in the elevator is quiet until we step out onto Wren's floor. The nurses' station is busy with nurses and doctors reading charts, entering information in the computer, and work chatter. A large whiteboard attached to the pale blue wall is filled with rooms and patient information. It's easy to read at a glance.

Next to Wren's room number are the initials: SJJ. I frown, and Dad says, "Sarah Joy Jacobs—clever."

We glance around and it worries me that no one looks our way as we move past and down the hallway to Wren's room. We round the hallway and see three police officers standing in front of doorways. Wren is behind one of them, except there is no one in front of Wren's room. Room 348.

As we approach, the cops place a hand on their weapons and watch us warily. Dad moves in front of me and holds out his hand. "I'm Special Agent Marcel DeLacroix, DEA. This is my son. His girlfriend is in room 348."

"We were told to let you both in when you arrived," the cop opposite Wren's room says.

I move toward her door, but stop when another cop says, "They've just taken her down to radiology. But you can wait in the room if you want."

Disappointment fills me as I shove into the room. I want to tear the place apart and look for her as I rest my hands on the windowsill and look outside. The room has an amazing view of the marina. I close my eyes and concentrate on breathing through my frustration. I just want Wren, dammit.

"Something is wrong," Dad whispers. "Look." He points toward the metal IV stand with a saline bag attached, the wires hanging freely. "It wasn't switched off before it was removed. There is a growing pool of saline on the floor."

I blink a few times and nothing else seems out of the ordinary. "Maybe they forgot." I shrug as tension fills my body, but I know he's right, something is wrong.

"I don't think so. The monitoring wires from the machines have been left dangling on this side, along with the finger clip for checking a patient's pulse. *Fuck!*" Dad yanks the door open, and says in a tight and controlled voice, "Who took Miss Jacobs out of this room?"

I'm close behind Dad and notice the cop's eyes grow with suspicion. "An orderly. He had the correct ID badge. I checked. Officer Zander went down with them?"

"Call him, now!"

"Dad?" I whisper. "Please tell me you don't believe someone has taken her?"

Dad turns and meets my gaze and I know his answer before he opens his mouth. "That room would not have been left that way if a member of the medical staff had taken her down to radiology. I also think the IV would have gone with her."

"Which way did they go and how long ago?" I quickly ask.

"They headed toward the back of the hospital." He points. "They took the surgical elevators. Just before you arrived."

I don't hear what Dad says, as I take off running in the direction pointed out to us. The hallway is darker this way, with much dimmer lighting. My legs eat up the distance and then I'm sliding to a stop in front of the surgical elevator. The numbered lighting on the panel beside the door slowly creeps downward, until it stops on B. I quickly glance at the floor guide on the wall: B is the emergency surgical unit, and the fucking morgue. I jab at the call button and get impatient when the floor number doesn't move.

Maybe the doors have been blocked from closing!

My heart pounds and blood rushes through my ears. Can I actually be lucky enough to follow the elevator to that floor and find Wren. They have a head start on me, but while I'm thinking about what the fuck to do, the elevator lights up on one.

I find myself wondering if she is on B or one. Swearing, I curse myself for wasting time thinking about it, and head for the stairwell. Dad catches up to me as I push through the door. "I think I know which floor they're on. And it has a delivery ramp."

The pounding of our feet echoes throughout the stairwell as we race down it. I don't know whether we should slow down to be quiet or hurry it up before we lose the chance of finding her.

"Have you called Silas? He was outside," I ask Dad.

"I don't have a good signal in here." He huffs, his breathing heavy. It doesn't slow him down, though.

Bursting through the door, I have no idea which way to go. They could be anywhere.

"You go that way." Dad points. "I'll go this way." His worried gaze meets mine. "You have your weapon?"

I nod.

"Be careful, son." He pulls me against him and kisses my forehead, and then he's gone.

Turning, I head to the left and freeze when I turn down another hallway. Silas and Wren are facing a man I haven't seen before. There's a large scar covering part of his face and he's wearing an expensive tailored suit.

Silas curses when he spots me out of the corner of his eye. Wren's eyes light up, but then I see panic well in the beautiful blue depths. "Rafael, go!" she cries.

My legs feel like they've turned into stone pillars and I can't move even if I wanted to, which I don't. I'm not leaving her again. Never again.

"You're here, Wren. I'm staying." I pause and get a better look at the situation. "What the fuck, Silas?"

"This asshole is the one who killed my sister!" Silas waves his gun around, which I'm only noticing now. "Ezequiel Gutiérrez knew the Reverend had found Joy and Roman, so he told Wild to kill them. He was supposed to kill you and your father, Rafael."

He breathes heavily and points the gun at the other man, who I believe is the one Jeremiah is looking for. He too has a gun and it's pointed directly at Silas's head.

"Then I hope you do us all a favor and kill the bastard because none of us will be safe if you don't," I growl as I remove my gun from the back of my jeans.

Silas narrows his eyes slightly and Wren gasps. "Rafael, please don't do this," she begs. "You'll have to live with it for the rest of your life. Please do not kill him."

"You know what I said is true." My hand trembles as I hold my weapon. "He will keep coming after you if he isn't stopped now." I glance at Silas. "He knows that too."

"I have had enough of this. All I want is the girl and you won't ever see me again," Ezequiel says. "Let Wren come to me."

"He's not handing her over to you." I sneer, which turns into disbelief when I notice the look of sorrow on Silas's face. "You can't be serious? That isn't happening. Dad's gone outside to call for backup. This place is going to be swarming with agents and cops soon." *I hope.*

Right at this moment, I'm not sure what the hell is going on because it looks like Silas is ready to hand Wren over to him.

While I'm trying to contemplate my next move, Silas shoves Wren toward me. Ezequiel quickly moves his gun so it's on Wren. Adrenaline pumping through me, I dive for Wren as there are three shots fired.

Silence follows and all I'm aware of is that Wren is under me. Her fingers hold onto my T-shirt as though she's never going to let me go. I must be crushing her, but when I make to move from her, she clings tightly. Assessing the situation, I turn my head and see Ezequiel is on the floor unmoving, so is Silas.

I finally manage to break the tight hold Wren has on me. My eyes quickly search her face and body, looking for proof she's unharmed. "Did you get hit?" I run my free hand up and down her body, she captures it with hers.

"No. I'm fine." She turns her head and sees Silas. "Uncle Silas." She wiggles free and goes to him.

"Rafael," Dad shouts as he comes around the corner. Seeing me safe, he wraps me in a hug while Jeremiah and a SWAT team move forward and check Ezequiel—he's dead.

A medical team drops beside Silas and starts working on him. I tuck my gun into the back of my jeans before reaching for Wren and pulling her into my arms. "I love you," I whisper against her neck. "I fucking love you, Wren." Tears fall from my eyes as I'm full of so much emotion. I don't know how to express to her my relief that I have her in my arms.

Dad squeezes my shoulder, and asks, "What happened down here?"

Pulling myself together, I make sure to keep hold of Wren and explain what happened in the hallway.

Dad mumbles when I finish and, turns his gaze to Wren. "I'm glad you're okay."

"That goes for me too," Jeremiah says, pulling me in for a brief hug. He says to Wren, "Good to see you again."

She nods slightly.

"The coast guard boarded the boat. Ken and three others have been arrested. The DEA has them," Jeremiah adds, and I watch Dad because he used to work with Ken. His betrayal must hurt.

Wren squeezes me and, leaving my arms, hugs my dad. She catches him by surprise, but he soon returns her hug, a delighted blush coating his cheekbones before she's back in my arms.

Swallowing hard, Dad says, "I want you to hear this from me, Wren, so that there is no misunderstanding or worry on your part, okay?"

She nods and I frown wondering if he's about to tell her about the Reverend, but that isn't something where there would be room for misunderstanding.

"From this point forward, you are living with us. That isn't up for negotiation." He smiles. "Are we good?"

"Yes," she says. "The Reverend?"

"We'll talk about him later." Dad moves away to talk to Jeremiah.

I hold Wren's face and gently kiss her sweet lips before resting my forehead against hers. Her eyes search mine and then she asks, "He's dead, isn't he?"

"I'm sorry, Wren."

48

WREN

I HAD REFUSED TO STAY IN THE HOSPITAL AND JUST wanted to be wherever Rafael was, which is Port Michael for the day while they clear the house out.

My nerves tingle with excitement and fear as Rafael pulls the floorboard Silas had told me about away from the wall. Silas had been adamant from his hospital bed that I collect the lockbox and keep it safe. He wants me to see my family history and to know who my mother really was. Rafael is nervous too because he had her as a mother longer than I did at an age where he remembers, while I still do not.

To our surprise it comes away with ease.

"I found something," he murmurs, drawing my gaze.

Dust from crumbling plaster rises up from the hole he's made and covers the slim metal lockbox. He wipes it off with his T-shirt before nervously passing it to my waiting hands.

Silas told me my mom had put the box in here when she was fifteen, like a time capsule. They both added to it over the years. It turns out the house Sarah had left Marcel had once belonged to her parents, and when they'd died, they had left it to Silas and Sarah. Since everyone thought Silas was dead, it became the sole property of Joy Jacobs. The Reverend hadn't known about it at the time, but if he had, he wouldn't have been able to take it from her. Marcel hadn't known about it either, until Sarah had died. What a web we weave.

"Wren," Marcel says my name, and helps me to my feet, "come and sit."

Rafael follows and crouches beside my legs as I place the metal box on the coffee table. The lock is hanging off, so we have no difficulty opening the lid.

The first thing we all see is a piece of folded yellow legal notepaper with my name written in cursive. I frown wondering how that is possible. I swallow the lump of emotion in my throat and carefully remove it from the box. I smooth my fingers over the paper before carefully opening it.

Tears fill my eyes and the paper slips from my fingers, fluttering to the floor beside Rafael. He hesitates and then retrieves it, offering it back to me. I shake my head. "Will you read it?"

His eyes are full of life, pain, and unquenchable warmth as I hold his gaze. He slowly nods and clears his throat. "It's not really a letter, more like scribbled thoughts, I think. Maybe she was in a rush."

```
Can Wren be alive?
How is that possible?
I saw her pale. Unbreathing.
She's always been close to
    my heart.
Hidden inside the locket.
The girl in the garden
    looked like my Wren.
She always had butterflies
    around her.
Like the girl outside of
    'his' house.
I want to speak to her.
To find out her name.
```

    It can't be Wren.
    But what if it is?
    I need to know more.
    It's too dangerous.
    I'm risking everything
        coming back to this house.
    I need to find out if she's my daughter.
    I'll come back another day.
    Bring Marcel with me.
    WREN, please forgive me.
    I love you.

"What's the date at the top?" Marcel asks, his voice broken.

My mind is whirling with this new information, and I don't know how I should feel. I can hear in Marcel's voice that those words cause him pain. I lift my gaze to Rafael and his eyes are red-rimmed. I reach out my hand to Marcel and pull him down next to me, then I take Rafael's arm and urge him to sit down on the opposite side of me. We all need comfort today.

"A week before she died," Rafael whispers, and pauses. "Do you think she was seen and that's how they found out where we lived?" He lifts his hand to the chain around his neck and opens the locket.

"I want to say no, but I really don't know. I think Wild did keep track of her all these years. Maybe for his own game or for the Reverend's. We will never know." Marcel's arm goes around my shoulders and he hugs me. "You know what this means, Wren? It means your mother had discovered you were alive. She planned on finding out the truth, but never got the chance."

Rafael tries to peel the photograph of him, his dad, and brother from the locket, and there, hidden behind is a picture of a man holding a child—Uncle Silas and me. I have pigtails and a toothy grin.

"She kept us *all* close to her heart." Marcel closes his eyes and slowly exhales. "She used to say that everyone she loved was inside the locket. I had no idea how true that was."

Rafael slips the photograph he removed to the opposite side of the locket and closes it. His hands reach up as though to remove it. "It's yours now, Wren."

I shake my head, tears in my gaze. "No. You've kept it close for three years. It's at home right where it is." I kiss his cheek, and say, "Let's see what else is in the box."

Rafael brings it to his lap and slowly goes through the other items in the box, passing them to me and his father. There are baby pictures of me and of me as a small child before the Reverend faked my death. The letters Uncle Silas had told me about—to him and from him. I can't wait to read her thoughts before she knew the Reverend. Then there are newer images. Pictures of Marcel, Rafael, and Roman. There's a larger image, a group photograph of the four of them, with an image of me as a child stuck onto it. Surrounding us all in a red marker is a large heart drawn around us, and to the side it says #myheart.

As the image is passed to Marcel, I pull Rafael to me and hold him while his father holds me. I had no idea I had so many tears to shed but I can't stop them. We are all crying.

More than anything this image says everything. Sarah had loved us all, and she'd even included me in this family image. It means everything to me.

With no more tears to cry, I allow Rafael to wipe my face with a cold washcloth. It's refreshing, although I have no doubt my eyes are red and puffy. He pulls me up to my feet and I catch a glimpse of two photographs remaining in the bottom of the tin. They are both face down and one has faint writing on it. I lift it out and hold it closer. *To Joy. I miss you like crazy. Love from your brother, Silas.* My heart is in my throat reading those words. Turning it over, I catch my breath. It's a photograph of Uncle Silas in his uniform as a US Marine. Silent tears slip down my face, but I smile through them. "We have to make sure Uncle Silas gets this back." I pause and look at the other image of Mom with Uncle Silas. "He looks like a new marine in this one. Mom's a kid."

Marcel studies the photograph. "Sarah would have been eight or nine when that was taken. Silas was ten years older." He moves off into the kitchen and Rafael takes my hand and leads me outside to the front porch for some fresh air.

The wind blows through my hair while my butterflies hover before my eyes. Tiger Lily flutters his wings and I feel him settle on the top of my head. The rest take flight over the fence toward my glasshouse.

"My butterfly girl," Rafael whispers, placing a hand on my back as I watch the color of my butterflies blend together until they're like a moving rainbow. They've always given me peace, now more than ever.

EPILOGUE 1
RAFAEL

"FOUR YEARS." I WHIMPER, MY WORDS CUT OFF AS SHE takes me into her body, rising above me like a goddess. "I forgot what else I was going to say." My hands find her hips and I hold her still because the moment she moves I won't be able to be good.

"Don't say anything right now. Just keep your hands on my hips, your fingers spread wide over my bottom, and your cock long and thick while you watch me ride you."

I practically swallow my tongue as she starts undulating on my cock, her sweet, wet pussy stroking along the hard flesh. I'm buried so deep inside of her that her little clit gets tickled by my pubic hair. While

I'm trying to hold still and let her have her way, she raises her arms and holds her long hair on the top of her head. I groan, pleasure zapping along my dick at the feel of her surrounding me. Her swollen tits sway in my face, her nipples hard, tight buds begging to be touched.

Removing one hand from her, I caress and pinch at her aroused flesh and watch her eyes narrow as soft moans escape her mouth. Lengthening, getting ready to explode, my cock quivers in anticipation. I tickle her baby bump with my fingers and feel the ripples and goosebumps my touch cause. She's extra sensitive all over with the pregnancy, not to mention horny all the time. I sure as hell have no complaints.

"Rafael, touch me," she begs, her hips frantic.

The moment my finger presses against that sensitive spot, her tummy goes rock solid and she's coming so damn hard that she pulls the semen from my body. I sit up and wrap my arms around her hips, holding her down on me while I empty inside her quivering body.

Having her crushed against my chest, her nipples hard bullets, I release one more time before I gasp for breath.

Wren goes limp in my arms, so I cradle her against me, and lie us both down on the bed. I slip from her body and keep her wrapped tightly in the cocoon of my arms. She wiggles closer and wraps a leg over my hip, pulling herself closer still. My dick, once again, rests between her legs and slowly hardens as she rubs all over me. "It's going to fall off if you keep doing that," I comment.

She giggles and slips a hand between us, wrapping her fingers around my erection. "I want to feel you inside me." As she leads me to her entrance, she pushes down and I help her by arching up.

I close my eyes and pray for sanity.

"That's better." She sighs softly. "I'll take a nap now."

My eyes pop open. "A nap? You've got me all excited again, and you want a nap?"

She grins. "I am sleepy, but you feel really, really good inside my body."

I grab her bottom and hold her still. "Are you feeling okay?"

Rolling her eyes, she adds, "I'm five months pregnant. Rafael. You don't need to ask me that every time we have sex."

"I don't want to hurt you."

"You never hurt me." She kisses my chest and nips with her teeth. "I can't help it. You only have to brush past me, and all I want to do is take you down to the floor and get into your jeans."

I grin and laugh. "I don't think Dad would be impressed." I pinch a nipple and feel her pussy contract around me. "Hmm," I mutter and roll her onto her back, pulling her legs up around my hips.

Clenching my teeth, I press forward until there is no gap between us. I rock my hips from side to side, feeling her get wetter and wetter. I dip down and, capturing a large extended nipple with my mouth, suck and pull.

"Oh!" Wren moans, her body contracting around me.

"Come for me, Wren."

Switching nipples, I roll and pinch them, stimulating both—one with my mouth and one with my fingers. Wren tries to wiggle her hips, but mine are holding her pinned to the bed. She reaches up and digs her fingers into my arms, arching upward as she comes. She is so fucking beautiful in the middle of her orgasm. Her body flushes and the tiny noises she makes drives me insane, but with the way her body pulls and sucks on my cock as she comes, I don't have a shot at lasting.

I pull halfway out, thrust home, and come so hard my eyes roll.

EPILOGUE 2
WREN

"Five months pregnant really suits you, Wren," Uncle Silas says as he takes the seat beside me. "Do you have a name yet?"

I turn my face away from the sun and grin like an idiot at my uncle. Both him and Marcel have been asking about whose name we will choose if it turns out we have a boy. They've been asking me since the day I found out I was pregnant.

Actually, it was Marcel who asked us outright if I was pregnant. Rafael and I had been clueless, but excited and happy to realize our love had produced a child. Luckily, this news was discovered right after we'd graduated college—Rafael with a degree in architecture, and me with a degree in English literature. I am finished with school, but Rafael has another couple of years to complete his masters. I'm so proud of him for putting his talent to use. He has plans to build us our own home in ten years' time.

My own plan includes marrying his father off to the nice lady in town who blushes every time he enters her bakery. Her name is Rosemary, and she's about Marcel's age. She would be good for him. I worry that he would one day be lonely when we leave, although I'm not in any rush to move.

"I've lost you?" Uncle Silas questions. "Your mother used to daydream all the time."

I smile and rest my head on his shoulder. "Will you invite Rosemary to the barbecue this weekend? I think she's sweet on Marcel."

He laughs. "You are going to get yourself into trouble, my sweet niece." He chuckles. "I'll invite her."

I kiss his cheek. "Thank you." I pause. "I just need to find someone for you."

He chokes on the swig of Jameson he's just swallowed, and while he's hacking his guts up, I continue, "Don't worry. I've invited Vanessa from your office."

His eyes pop wide and I hold my belly while I laugh. "You should see your face."

"That is not funny, Wren," he growls.

"I think it is. She said she's looking forward to it."

"You're serious?"

"Um, yes."

"I don't date people I work with," he grumbles, but there is a slight smile on his lips.

"As it's a barbecue for your *very* early retirement from the DEA, then it won't be a problem if Vanessa is here, showing off those long legs of hers. I'm aware you've noticed them."

He opens his mouth to say something, but no words are forthcoming.

"What are you up to, dear wife?" Rafael looks between us and lifts me from my seat before settling me down on his lap. "Have you told Silas about Vanessa?"

I roll my eyes. "You knew I would. Besides, Uncle Silas doesn't like surprises."

"Uncle Silas might have to find an excuse to miss his own retirement party," my uncle mumbles.

"I don't believe a word of it. You'll be there because she gets you all hot and bothered. I need a cousin to keep our baby company."

"Holy fuck, Wren!" Uncle Silas splutters and shoves himself up from the chair. Shaking his head, he says, "I think I'll stick close to Marcel." He chuckles as he moves away.

"Do you think his hip gives him a lot of pain still?" Rafael asks.

My eyes focus on Uncle Silas as he moves toward Marcel, a limp in his step. He'd taken two bullets for me—one in his hip, and one in his right shoulder. I think it's always bothered me more than it has him about the way things worked out. Like he said, Ezequiel Gutiérrez is dead and can no longer harm me or anyone else. That had been his objective from the very beginning.

Uncle Silas hadn't only been working for the DEA, he knew all along that Ezequiel Gutiérrez had been responsible for Mom and Roman's deaths. When he'd come into my hospital room and quickly explained his plan of drawing the man out, I had trusted him to keep me safe. I just hadn't expected it to be by taking bullets meant for me. I'd have been dead if he hadn't, though.

"I think the fact that he took his vengeance helps with the physical pain he must feel. He did what he did for us all."

Rafael gently grabs hold of my chin and brings my face around to his.

"You want my attention?" I whisper smoothly.

"I'll always want your attention, but I have news for you, and I want to see your face when I tell you."

I search his gaze.

"The girls will be here for the baby shower."

Throwing my arms around my husband's neck, I squeal in his ear. "Really? You managed to get them all here? For me?"

"Well, you're the only one pregnant that I know of."

"Funny."

"No, what would be funny is if you weren't the only one pregnant."

"Now you're being silly, considering I'm the only female here."

"We need a nap," Rafael comments, sweeping me up into his arms. "Your sweet mouth always makes me hard."

While he carries me through the garden, I think about the girls I met briefly but who understand the nightmares I still have. Both Ella and Jessica have both applied to the DEA while finishing up their criminal psychology degrees. Maria has been in Mexico, under the close eye of her father, but he has finally relented and agreed she can attend school in America next year.

I'm really excited they will be here for mine and Rafael's baby shower. They really are the only friends I have, and trust, other than my close family.

FOUR MONTHS LATER I GIVE BIRTH TO A BEAUTIFUL baby girl. Sarah Louisa DeLacroix. My new butterflies hover at the window. We named her Sarah for my mom, when she'd been at her happiest, and Louisa for Rafael's birth mother.

My life is filled with more love than I ever knew existed, the kind my mother had found with Marcel.

After the Reverend, I never thought I would want to be caught by anyone. Rafael has changed me. He belongs to me now, just like I belong to him.

THE END

DEAR READER

Thank you for reading *Butterflies & Darkness* and for your reviews! It's really appreciated.

Subscribe with your email to be alerted about new releases, sales, and events.
http://lexibuchanan.com

OTHER BOOKS BY AUTHOR

Hawke's Ridge

Maddox (2025)

Den Hollows

One of Six · Two of Six (2025)

Den of Filth (New MC Series 2025)

Reckless Wilder (2026)

Fifth Realm Series (Romantasy)

Quiver of Chaos · Wings & Arrows (2026)

Standalone Romantasy

Persephone Unchained

Tallulah James Mystery

*Dead and a Murder or Two · Dead and the Wedding Crashers ·
Dead and a Deadly Deed · Dead and a Best Friend*

Boston Bay Vikings

*Camden · Bennett · Ethan · Sutton · Carter · Bryson · Ivan · Theo
· Noah · Knox · Jericho · Roman*

Boston Bay Vikings Minor League

Lake · Rhodes · Nikoli · Dario · Madden · Bradford

Single Titles

Butterflies and Darkness · Come Back to Me · Indecent Villain · Lawful · Love Stryker · Tears in the Rain · Whispers of Yesterday

Holiday Season

Holiday Kisses in the Snow · Jingle Bells

Romantic Suspense Series

Twenty Eight Days · The Next Victim (2025)

Blossom Creek

Christmas at Emelia's · A Rake in Blossom Creek · Heatwave in Blossom Creek · Secret Love in Blossom Creek · Mischief in Blossom Creek · Runaway Bride in Blossom Creek · Naughty & Nice in Blossom Creek

Bad Boy Rockers

My Brother's Girl · Past Sins · My Best Friend's Sister · Never Let Go · Saving Jace · Silent Night (Novella)

Kincaid Sisters

Meant to be Mine · You Were Always Mine · Will You be Mine

McKenzie Brothers

Playing with the Boss · A McKenzie Wedding (Novella) · Playing with Fire · Playing with Desire · Playing with Trouble · Playing with their Hearts · A McKenzie Christmas (Novella)

De La Fuente Family (McKenzie Spinoff)

Love in Montana · Love in Purgatory · Love in Bloom · Love in Country · Love in Flame · Love in Game · Love in Education

McKenzie Cousins

(McKenzie Spinoff)

Baby Makes Three · A Business Decision · Secret Kisses · Kissing Cousins · If Only · Princess & the Puck · A Bakers Delight · A Cowboy for Christmas · A Secret Affair · One Christmas · The Pregnant Professor · It Started with a Kiss

Novella's

Educate Me · One Dance · Pure

ABOUT THE AUTHOR

While Lexi is the author of the chick lit series, Tallulah James Mystery, and the sexy wild Alaska series, Hawke's Ridge, she also writes romantasy. This author has over seventy published novels. Based in Ireland, this British author has been writing since 2013.

Follow on social media:

Website: http://lexibuchanan.com
Email: authorlexibuchanan@gmail.com

facebook.com/lexibuchananauthor
x.com/AuthorLexi
instagram.com/authorlexib
bookbub.com/author/lexi-buchanan
amazon.com/Lexi-Buchanan/e/B009SPA94U